DEVIL'S KNOB

RACHEL CALLAGHAN

Cover Design by: Kristina Edstrom

An Imprint for GracePoint Publishing (www.GracePointPublishing.com)

GracePoint Matrix, LLC
624 S. Cascade Ave, Suite 201
Colorado Springs, CO 80903
www.GracePointMatrix.com
Email: Admin@GracePointMatrix.com
SAN # 991-6032

A Library of Congress Control Number has been requested and is pending.

ISBN: (Paperback) 978-1-961347-63-2
eISBN: 978-1-961347-64-9

Books may be purchased for educational, business, or sales promotional use.
For bulk order requests and price schedule contact:
Orders@GracePointPublishing.com
Printed in U.S.A

Table of Contents

Chapter 1

Lark County, West Virginia

SAMMIE RAE SLAMMED her foot on the brake, fishtailing her cruiser as the rickety green truck blew past. Doing eighty on the wrong side of the road, the truck sent an oncoming Subaru skittering across to the shoulder.

The truck swerved abruptly back into her lane and continued on its reckless way. From its driver-side window, above the peeling Goodloe's Towing logo, an arm extended, waving a merry "hi" in cigarette smoke.

The Subaru slid to a stop, silver body shuddering. The driver flung open his door and hopped out. Face persimmon red, hollering incoherently, he pointed at the rapidly disappearing truck. By the plates, he was a tourist from Massachusetts.

"Damn you, Wade!" Sammie Rae yelled into the dusty air. Wade Goodloe, driver of the shabby truck, had forced her hand again. She flipped on her siren and raced off. A half-mile later she was leaning into the truck's window—just for a little discussion—when the Subaru stopped perilously close to her uniformed rear end.

"He ran us off the road!" The woman in the passenger seat leaned out her window and pulled off her sunglasses, screaming at Sammie Rae, "Arrest him right now!"

"Thank you for informing me of the issue, ma'am." Sammie Rae plastered on as pleasant a smile as she could muster. "I got things well in hand."

The woman scowled and slammed her glasses back into place.

Sammie Rae glanced at Wade's head wobbling on his scrawny neck and turned back to the tourists. "Y'all don't want to waste your day with this. It'd mean heading back to Onondaga. Go on now, enjoy the foliage. And if you haven't had breakfast, you and your little ones…" —two children bounced around the backseat, giggling as they gave her the finger—" should stop at The Old Log Cabin just ahead in Devil's Knob. Great ham and grits. The real Appalachian experience."

The woman scowled and turned her head toward the man, who said, "Just do your job, Sheriff."

"Deputy, sir." Sammie Rae pointed to the badge gleaming on her jacket. "Deputy Sammie Rae Wheedle. Sheriff of this county is Mr. Ralph Beebe. Nice car, by the way." A Forester. She'd window-shopped at Hometown Subaru, but no way could she afford a new model. She smiled again and waved them on.

The tourists drove ahead to a dusty turnaround. The man got out again and stood watch, confirming her suspicions—he represented a type all too prevalent in leaf season: entitled, speed-trap-fearing Northerners who thought West Virginians let their own get away with murder—the kind who would follow up to make sure Wade got punished.

"Shee-it, Wade!" Sammie Rae hissed. "Now I got to search your truck and maybe bring you in."

"Can't just fake it, Sammie Rae?"

"I'm up for review, Wade. Some say as I'm not doing my job." She wrenched the truck's door open. "You know the department's a boys' club."

Wade stumbled out of the cab. No surprise; he failed to walk a straight line. He leaned against the truck's front fender and sucked on his lower lip, contemplating the situation. "Well, if you gotta take me in, Sammie Rae..." He shrugged. "Lord knows I need a rest from the little woman. But if you keep me, you gotta deliver to your dad and the others."

Sammie Rae looked at the tourists in an ain't-gonna-take-no-shit way, calling out, "Can't stay in the emergency turnout or you get a ticket." She put her fists on her hips, and the driver slunk back into his seat and drove off.

Wade blew out a high-octane breath. He staggered to the back of his truck, moved the greasy wrenches to one side of the tool kit, and pulled out the box's false bottom.

"Thanks, Wade." At least she didn't have to move his filthy tools. What with a possible review, it was a bad day to come in with hands and uniform blackened.

A glistening pile of Ziplocs filled with white tablets lay in the chest. Sammie Rae asked, "Got a shovel?"

"Course."

"Ralph's gunning for me. Can't have nothin' in my patrol car. You good to dig a little?"

"Long as it's a shallow grave." Wade grinned. His new teeth gleamed in the sun.

"We best get to it."

Wade slammed the shovel's blade into a young tree, leaving a pale scar as a marker. He swayed unsteadily, admiring his handiwork. "You see that good enough or I gotta do the other side too?"

"That's fine."

They went thirty feet into the woods, closer to the mountain that gave Devil's Knob its name. Wade dug a hole behind a tangle of blackberry, dropped the bags in, covering them with a scrim of leaves. Wouldn't fool anyone looking, but who would be out there to see?

"I'll leave my shovel up against this here pine, so's you can brush stuff away without getting mussed. I'll get it when I'm released."

Back at the patrol car, she took out the breathalyzer. "How much did you drink?"

Wade shook his head. "I do decline testing. Charge the maximum. Like I said, I'm glad to go in now I'm caught—me and the wife been having our go-rounds and nights're too cold to sleep in the woods. No reason to ask where I got the shine, neither. I plumb forgot." He scratched his grizzled chin. "Got any weed? They keep me a stretch longer if I have a little on me."

"Sorry. All gone." She wished she'd kept some for him, a little baggy to turn in.

*　　*　　*

A bitter smell hung like smog in the office air. Sammie Rae was the only woman deputy, so sooner or later someone would hint the Mr. Coffee needed cleaning. She'd dodge out as quickly as possible, leaving the pot as it had been, crusted with tarry deposit. No skin off her nose—she had her cup from the Dunkin'.

She pushed past the men hunt-and-pecking on their keyboards and knocked on Ralph Beebe's door. Inside, she stood before the sheriff's oak desk, a relic of the coal baron days. Lightly coated in fear-sweat, she looked down and discovered—to her horror—a bit of her Curvations full-figure bra peeking from between two buttons. The black bra was lacy, recently bought at the Walmart on a secret out-of-jurisdiction trip. The thought of her recurrent misuse of on-duty time made her armpits dampen even more.

Sheriff Beebe's attention was on his computer screen, giving Sammie Rae a moment to tuck her tie into the gap. She leaned her belly against the desk's edge, relieving the low back pain her holstered gun caused.

Her breath came tight. The typing in the reception area kept rhythm with her heart's pounding. She'd feared facing Beebe all morning.

"You read today's news, Sammie Rae?" He leaned closer to his screen and shook his head. "Weird shit going on. People's faces getting eaten."

"What? Faces eaten?" *What stupid crap is he on about now? Focus Sammie Rae!* But it was hard to attend to Sheriff Beebe's words, so unlikely to be true. Not when she dreaded him looking back up.

She couldn't lose this job—good-paying work was hard to come by. Besides, what else could she do? Greet people in a store? Earn minimum wage at a drive-thru? Go from "Get out of the car with your hands up" to "Want fries with that?" A waste of breath—they *always* wanted fries!

"Not paying attention, Deputy Wheedle? I asked a question."

"Nossir, don't turn on the news too often."

"Well, never mind. Just weird shit over by DC, where weird shit belongs." He cleared his throat. "Pray to God it don't come here."

Didn't matter to her if it did. No way he'd let her investigate.

He settled back in his chair. "Point a' this meeting is, I've had complaints saying you're not pulling your weight. Less arrests than the men, less drugs brought in, can't be found from time to time." The unsaid bit was *Girl cops can't keep up.*

"With all due respect, sir..." Her voice trailed off. She'd never thought of him as "sir," but always as Uncle Ralph. When she'd been just old enough to notice, he and her ma had done *it* every Wednesday afternoon in his patrol car. Tucked out of sight behind their chicken coop, that black-and-gold car had bobbed up and down with Ralph's weight. Almost twenty years ago it was, back when he patrolled the country roads, just like Sammie Rae was doing now. She'd considered subtly leveraging that history for job security, but she was crap at subtlety. And she'd considered bullshitting, saying what a huge influence he'd had on her life, but a lot of "uncles" had come after him and Ralph hadn't taken being replaced with good grace. Bringing up his activities with her ma might make him pissed off enough to fire her.

He scowled. "We're being squeezed. Feds say we're over our limit when it comes to addicts, though God knows this area is awash with reasons to be addicted. They don't give a damn about that…"

"I heard Washington's planning to give us a bundle for roads and such…"

Ralph fixed her with a steady glare. "This is about our reputation and dignity, the fact they're threatening to take over our investigation. Treating me like a goddamn hick who can't get nothing done. So, we all gotta step up our game. We know who the dirtbags are."

Sammie Rae hoisted the waistband of her pants with both hands. "How can they take over when it's not our fault? Most stuff's coming up from Mexico—even their pot's better than homegrown."

Ralph shrugged. "They're monitoring arrests, overdoses throughout the state. Meth and heroin. Pills too, prescription or not. The whole shebang. What are you doing to help our drug arrest stats, Sammie Rae?" He cleared his throat. "Who'd you bring in this morning?"

"Wade."

"Wade who?"

Ralph knew exactly "Wade who" but was being official. "Goodloe."

"Been waiting for that sumbitch to get caught with a load. Rumor has it his only real income is dealing. What you find on him?"

It was even more regrettable she'd been out of pot. Wade would have counted as a drug arrest. "Nothing really. Pulled him over for driving drunk. He declined testing." She shrugged.

"As is his legal right." Ralph flicked a pen between his thumb and index finger, tapping it against the scarred desktop. "Shame. But we can't rely on Wade to up our numbers if we can't catch him holding." He paused for a moment. "Could crack down on unlicensed shine, but people'd start going blind from home brew. At least Dolly knows what she's doing— puts out a good product." Ralph tapped his pen a few more times. "Get Wade before the court ASAP then get rid of him. Everybody knows his wife's about to shoot off his nuts for failure to support, but this ain't a marriage-mistake motel." The tapping stopped, replaced by clicking. "Well, get out there. Do your best."

"Any chance filling my request for a K-9?" A dog could be useful on traffic stops. Or if she forgot where stuff was buried.

"Not yet." He turned to a pile of forms and began signing them. The review was over.

After leaving the office, Sammie Rae stopped at the Dunkin' to get a custard-filled and a free drink, ignoring her image in the plate-glass window. She already knew what the side view would show—the uniform, which made men look manly, was a disaster on a woman. Her butt looked enormous.

She asked for her donut in a giant box—the kind that held a dozen without mussing the frosting—even though hers looked mighty lonely inside it.

She sipped her sweet tea before leaving. The Dunkin' was empty except for Howie Angolier, whose back was to her, head rotating side to side on his shoulders—his neck had long ago disappeared into his four-hundred-pound torso. A large coffee sat on his table, along with a strawberry frosted.

Sammie Rae held the box against her chest, walked around him, and said, "Hey, Howie."

His eyes appeared fixed on the front page of the *Washington Post.*

"I say, hey, Howie."

His gaze lifted slow as syrup from the deep pouches above his cheeks. "Hey, Sammie Rae. Sorry, was reading 'bout bodies in DC. Addicts in the park. Pack of loose dogs or something must have been at them. They's all tore up—only bones and some gobbets of flesh left."

Packs of wild dogs roaming DC? Eating addicts? Must have been what Beebe was reading online.

DC was three hundred and fifty miles away. Sammie Rae shook her head to look sad as possible. Didn't pay to get into a discussion with Howie when something stuck in his head. His voice rumbled into an "Mmmm," as he bit into his donut, flecks of rosy-red frosting spraying the table.

"Well, catch you later." She pushed the door open. As she pulled away from the shop, she took out the cream-filled and held it lightly between her teeth.

Soon, she was emptying the hole Wade had dug, putting the baggies into the empty box to keep dirt off her backseat. Shame she hadn't gotten two boxes: one empty and one full of donuts for Wade's waiting customers. And another donut, maple, for herself.

Chapter 2

FUNNY HOW THINGS GO IN CIRCLES, Sammie Rae thought as she turned onto the grass. She glided down to the old henhouse—empty except for the occasional wistful possum or 'coon longing for the coop's chicken-filled glory days. She parked in the spot where Beebe once hid his patrol car, back when her mother was part of the family and her father still worked first shift in the mines. Now, with only him in the house, no one gathered eggs, spread feed, or cleaned out the old straw. Frying chickens came from Martin's Food, beheaded, plucked, and ready for the cast-iron pan, but never tasting like her ma's.

Her car was far off the road, hidden behind the shed and a few young mulberry trees. No one would see the Sheriff Department logo and report her for goofing off. She grabbed two baggies and headed to the tiny house, whose chimney let out a lazy plume of smoke. The heavenly smell of burning hickory made her nostrils tickle.

On the porch, she lifted the screen door slightly to clear the threshold. The jamb looked dry-rotted, but it didn't matter now—it was a glorious fall day and nighttime cold snaps had done in most of the bugs. Come spring, she'd get someone to help her fix it.

"Hey, Pa!" she hollered as a warning. God knows what might happen if someone startled him—he slept with a loaded .22 long, his squirrel gun, about all he could handle now. "Got Wade's delivery for you."

Her father shuffled out of the back bedroom, an old quilt around his shoulders. "Thank the Lord. I been out all night and half yesterday, too. Diarrhea ain't started yet, but I can feel my guts rumbling. Been sitting up, waiting."

Sammie Rae went to the kitchen for water. Turning the cranky faucet was tough for him—his fingers were so swollen they resembled dusky-red bananas. She handed him the glass and one of the OxyContins.

"Need two by now." Irritation scrambled his features into a grimace. "Couldn't get ahead of the pain." He put the tablets onto his tongue. They promptly stuck to the dry surface. "Dammit!" The word was muffled as he spilled half the water on the way to his mouth. He swallowed, sinking into the sagging easy chair. Sammie lifted his feet onto the ottoman.

"Why don't you let me buy a BarcaLounger, maybe a leather one?" Sammie Rae asked. That'd be more comfortable, and, losing the stink of cigarette smoke and long-deceased dog would make visiting more pleasant.

He shook his head. "Ain't worth it. I'll probably die 'fore it's delivered." He was always saying cheerful shit like that, though he was only sixty-two.

"Well, gotta go. I'll stop back later if you need me to. Right now, I'm finishing Wade's deliveries."

Her father's head rested on a stained scrap of tatting, covering a spot where Brylcreem had long ago taken up residence. "A little dab'll do ya" built up over thirty years could be formidable—and not one man in the old family pictures, hair slicked down on either side of a center part, had looked debonair. "Bye, honey," he murmured, sleepy sounding though the pills hadn't kicked in yet.

She almost made it out the door when he asked, "Where's that rascal, Wade, anyways? On another bender?"

"Yes and no. Had to arrest him for drunk driving."

"What? Been driving drunk since he was a snot-nosed teen. No accidents I can remember."

Sammie Rae shrugged. "I need all the arrests I can bring in. Sheriff's scrutinizing me real close."

"Should have scrutinized that bastard myself, years ago." Despite his wry sense of humor, Sammie Rae's pa had been a lot calmer than Ralph back when her mother took off. He'd praised the Lord the "dirty whore"—who he still loved with all his heart—hadn't taken their daughter.

Not wanting to open old wounds any wider, Sammie Rae added, "Beebe said our little drug problem caught the attention of Washington. They're making noise about moving in to help."

"We all know what happens when the government's here to help." He chuckled, coarse and phlegmy.

"Got to do my best to help clean things up, but I'll focus on meth and heroin, leave the pills alone long as I can."

Pa shook his head. "Won't do no good. First, they come for the junk and the meth. Then they come for the prescription stuff. What the hell we fight the Germans for, just to let the government Nazis take away our rights?" He'd been born too late for the Second World War and Vietnam but even his own daddy said he should've enlisted for Iraq, since soldiering—except for momentary bouts of terror—was easier than the mines. All that stooping and shoveling in the underground damp had turned Pa into an old man before his time.

"Yeah, they chew you up and spit you out," he went on. The complaint was as timeworn as his easy chair. "And look what I have to show for it!" He waved his gummed-up hands at the interior of the house. "Shit. Take away my pills." He refused to try heroin, which would have helped more, as his fingers were too gnarled for the syringes and the cooking.

Those hands embarrassed him. A touch of marijuana, maybe. Dolly's home brew for sure.

Dolly's. She'd planned to visit her friend Darla, Dolly's daughter, after the drop-offs. "Gotta go," she said to her father. "Need anything?"

He shrugged and looked off in the distance, beyond the walls of the house, beyond the road and the hills. When she was younger, she'd imagined he was searching for wherever her mother alighted once she'd got the roaming out of her blood. But now she knew it was just the pain making his vision blurry.

*   *   *

Sammie Rae made a few more deliveries—three baggies to elderly black-lung miners and one to Gracie Hopkins. Gracie almost never left the house after eight children—and three failed corrective procedures—left her pissing herself constantly. State welfare only supplied so many adult diapers.

Sammie Rae was too polite to mention the acrid odor in the air. The pink flowers outside, planted in whitewashed tires lining the path to the door, and the panties and sheets fluttering forlornly on the line every time she dropped by, were mute testimony to efforts taken, even now Gracie was a widow.

"Where's Wade?" Gracie asked. "I was gonna ask him to look under the hood of my old Ford." Sammie Rae was half-inclined to think Gracie had a crush on Wade, despite his lazy eye and his sharp-tongued wife. Her husband dying had left her with a hateful mother-in-law and all those kids, and Wade was a kind, easygoing guy.

Gracie laughed the only time that possibility was suggested. "For general company and fixing things, maybe. But no, sweet thing, no interest in a man in *that* way. You wouldn't believe it from all these brats, but Joe was a little 'un, if you know what I mean." She lit another cigarette, took a deep drag. "Bless his heart, I couldn't bear to tell him, but petite as his pecker was, it was like being raped by an elephant. Damn surgical mesh scarred me down so."

Sammie Rae hadn't meant sex—her own ma's legacy and her mee-maw's Christian sayings had left her squeamish. She was careful not to ever again hint at Gracie's love life and sure wasn't going to say anything today. She put the pills on the scrubbed kitchen table.

Gracie rummaged around in her purse. "Got money here somewheres."

"Save it for Wade. I'm drop-off only." Sammie Rae never handled the cash.

Gracie's was the last delivery, so she spent the rest of the day cruising the back roads, hoping to see something—maybe a meth head breaking into an unguarded farmhouse. But things were quiet.

The hours dragged until her shift finally ended. She drove home, stomped up the rickety outside stairs to her apartment, changed into jeans and a stretched-out tee, and headed toward Darla's house. She walked—the exercise might use up the calories from that last donut.

Chapter 3

DARLA WAS RELAXING on the front porch steps with Boozer, the shepherd-collie-pit-God-knows-what mix rescued from a crash that killed its humans. The town beauty, Darla, had a soft spot for the old, the ugly, and the lame. So, when no one claimed him, the dog was adopted into her family, just as Sammie Rae had been.

Dolly, Darla's ma, made sure there were snacks in the fridge and dinner on the table for the girls—she knew Sammie Rae's pa had been weak at regular meals and new clothes for back to school. She'd taken both girls shopping.

"Hey, girl!" Darla called as Sammie Rae walked down the dusty drive. "How's your day been?"

Sammie Rae sat next to her, stretched out a hand to pet the dog's wiry head. "So-so," she said.

"So-so, how so?"

"Had a meeting with the sheriff. Usual bullshit about me being a girl…"

"Which you can scarce help."

"Besides that, Ralph says the Feds're getting serious about coming in-county and taking over drug enforcement."

"Beebe must be shitting himself." Darla lit a cigarette. "You poor thing."

"Enough about me. How's your work going?"

"Slow right now. Needed a break anyway." With a thriving business in accident and crime scene cleanup, Darla could walk into a house where a corpse had rotted for weeks and get right to work. She might have a tender heart, but she also had a steely will and a cast-iron stomach. She was a powerhouse who could single-handedly remove a blood-soaked sofa from a house as soon as the investigators gave her the go-ahead—all this despite her slender frame and feminine appeal. Goggles and surgical masks failed to hide her dark, almond-shaped eyes or the outline of her cheekbones.

Comparing herself to Darla, Sammie Rae felt like a Clydesdale up against a Thoroughbred. But thrown together by fate, world events, and the illicit activities of mothers who refused to toe the line, they'd been best friends since forever.

"The Feds, huh?" Darla narrowed her eyes—a sure sign of mulling over Sammie Rae's problems—inhaled deeply and blew a series of smoke rings.

Sammie Rae stuck her finger into the last ring and broke it. "Oh, Darla, how the living hell am I gonna help Pa? I already carried him to every doctor, hospital, and clinic in a two-hundred-mile radius, but ever since Doc Kaczerowski's license got suspended, the medical community's real stingy with pills." Kaczerowski was put away for his generosity—his very well-compensated generosity—after the overdose deaths of twelve patients. The other local docs, not yet under indictment, weren't willing to risk losing their livelihood, or worse. And sooner or later, they'd have to crack down on Wade, making real OxyContin unaffordable. She didn't want bootleg stuff—who the hell knew what the cartels put in that crap?

Darla leaned back on her elbows, the cigarette dangling from her mouth. Sammie Rae sat up straighter, fighting to stay alert. A full day of worry and the walk in the late-afternoon sun had made her drowsy.

Darla turned toward the house. "Hey, Ma, Sammie Rae's visiting! We could use a little sample out here!"

Dolly lifted the kitchen window's screen and poked her head out. "Hello!" Her accent was heavy, mouth contorted in the effort needed to pronounce the letter *l*, but her welcome was like tea and honey when your throat's sore and you haven't yet noticed it, like someone loving you so much they know what you need before you do. That's how Sammie liked to remember her ma, who'd never been that way. Ever since Sammie and Darla became besties, visiting Dolly's house had been like coming home.

The screen slammed down. A moment later Dolly was on the porch with a Ball jar of clear, pale-amber liquid. "Ginseng shine! Very smooth, very healthy. Best yet." She handed the jar to her daughter and waited for her response. It was easy to see where Darla got her looks—Dolly had the broad forehead, apple cheeks, and pointy chin of a traditional Korean beauty. But where Dolly was short and plump, Darla was tall and long-legged, a gift of her six-foot-two-inch Scots Irish father.

"You need to relax!" Dolly indicated Sammie Rae should take a slug. "Gonna stay for dinner? Not say no!"

"Pa?" said Darla. "Can he drive Sammie Rae home?"

"Oh, don't bother him for my sake. He'll be tired..." Sammie Rae had planned on a diet dinner of salad—but the smell of Dolly's fermented kimchi, which had once disgusted her, was making her mouth water. It would undoubtedly be paired with barbecue, sweet and salty, and savory side dishes.

"No bother!" Dolly exclaimed with a sharp nod before returning to the kitchen. "When I tell him, he drive. But out on long haul!"

When Sammie Rae hesitated, Dolly gave a sharp nod as if things were settled and said, "You stay here tonight." She returned to the kitchen.

Darla took a sip and smiled like a blissed-out saint. "Mmm, this is even better than her regular shine." She passed the jar to Sammie Rae. "Easy now. I don't know how it's gonna hit."

Sammie Rae lifted the jar to her lips, fearing the burn. But it never came. Instead, the liquor felt satiny going down.

"Mom says this stuff is good for you, the ginseng. Never a hangover with it, either." Darla took the jar back and put it down. "But we better have dinner first. Mom's shine can really sneak up on you and she's been known to lie about the no hangover." She sighed. "Surely was a pretty day." The dog licked her cheek. She pushed him away. "Boozer, your breath could knock a vulture off a shit wagon!" The dog settled back on the sun-warmed planks. "Hey, I'm going to a conference next weekend for re-cert. Over by Shepherdstown. Maybe you should come—some good courses on drugs for law enforcement."

Sammie Rae thought for a moment. "I do have that weekend off. Need to visit Mee-Maw down in Mingo County, though."

"Yeah, what you really need," Darla said. "A dose of, 'Lord, I pray you, don't let my grandbaby grow up a floozy like her ma! Keep her from sinnin' with men!'" Darla's imitation was spot-on.

Sammie Rae laughed. Maybe she *would* go to Shepherdstown. She'd never used her continuing education money— sure, those funds were pathetic, and she'd most likely have to pay a good bit herself—but she had no other plans. Anyway, things would be boring without Darla.

"Come on!" Darla nudged her. "Be fun."

"Well, maybe," Sammie Rae said.

"Just hate to leave Lark County, don't you? There's a whole big world out there."

Sammie Rae was used to her nagging—Darla was so much like Dolly. Anyway, the alcohol was making her mellow. She reveled in the view across the neatly cut lawn. What with the flower beds' purple asters, and the late-afternoon sun's angled light, the yard looked nice enough to be a calendar photo. Savory odors drifted from the kitchen; the liquid in the jar was delicious.

Smooth, high-quality moonshine, both traditional corn, and ginseng-flavored Korean brew, had made Dolly popular in the area. That and kimchi, the addictive, fiery radish and cabbage condiment whose added benefit was rendering breathalyzer testing useless—all the officers swore kimchi breath had broken a few units. Pretty soon only hardcore alkies took the shine by itself. Dolly always had some grilled beef *bul kogi* to go with the spicy pickles.

"How about we share a room for the weekend?" Darla said. "Upgrade to the conference facility instead of the Knight's Rest. Special rates for the meeting!"

"You need to go!" Dolly's voice came from inside. She didn't believe in privacy, not from her. "Girl gotta work harder, do more than boys. Show she is better. Go!"

Darla turned to Sammie Rae. "Let's do movie night! Have us a head start on our getaway." She wiggled her eyebrows. "Microwave popcorn."

Movie night always lifted Sammie Rae's mood. "How about *Night of the Living Dead?* DVD still good?" When Darla nodded, Sammie Rae lunged forward, clumsy as the undead. She grabbed Boozer's haunches with both hands. "They're coming to get you, Barbara!"

Boozer yawned and flopped on his side and tried to wriggle Sammie Rae's hands into position to scratch his belly. One leg came up in anticipation.

The door banged. Dolly walked out with her shopping basket and headed to her Jeep. "Out of something," she said. "So…"

"Be good girls!" The two young women yelled at the same time as a cloud of dust rose in Dolly's wake. They settled back to watch the sun drop lower on the horizon.

*   *   *

Twenty minutes later, Darla's father drove up. "What are you two up to?" he asked.

"Pa, you're back!" Darla hopped off the porch, standing on tiptoe to kiss her father's cheek. "Wow, scratchy."

"Long haul from Tucson, hurried home." He smiled at Sammie Rae. "Home to find both my gals here." He looked left and right, shuddering in mock fear. "Where's the little woman what drives me plumb wild?"

Darla rolled her eyes as she always did when her father laid on the hillbilly talk. "Gone shopping. Wasn't sure you were coming home."

"Wanted to surprise her." He rubbed his chin and winked at them. "Now I get a chance to clean up 'fore her royal persnicketyness gets back." He went into the house.

"American man beard too rough!" Darla imitated her mother.

Sammie Rae didn't join in the joke. Every time she saw Darla's mother and father together, it reminded her of her own father's solitude. "Your dad's nuts about your mom."

"Nuts is right. The moment he saw her washing clothes in the Imjin River. No war going on, but he was a casualty, anyway. A casualty of love."

"Seems to be something going 'round," Sammie Rae said. "My pa's one, too, but without the happy ending."

Darla looked down. "Let's go pop that corn and order a pizza. Mom's gonna be too busy to put dinner on."

*   *   *

"What do you think's worse," Darla asked, "being eaten by a zombie or sex with that skinny nerd?" The flickering black-and-white opening scene rolled on the screen.

"With his glasses on?" Sammie Rae grabbed a fistful of popcorn, spilling some on the old leather couch. "I vote zombie."

Boozer shambled toward the pizza smell and the possibility of a crust. Darla rescued the box. "Mom can't see we let him in the house. And turn the sound up a bit—I hear their bedsprings squeaking." She deepened her voice. "Night of the Geriatric Sex Fiends."

"Hush! They're not that old. I think it's sweet." Sammie Rae took in a sudden breath and yelled at the TV, "Run, you idiots! Hole up in the house!"

The screen flickered and the room was silent except for the sound of salt being sucked from fingers.

"Oh, shit!" Darla squirmed closer to Sammie Rae as the young couple tried to pull away from the gas pumps. "Stupid, driving a pickup on fire. Grab the damn torch, head back to the house!"

Sammie Rae said. "If I were him, I'd be all, 'Eat her! I'm off a-runnin'!'"

A moment later, Sammie Rae said, "My favorite line! Sheriff saying, 'They're dead, they're all messed up.' Like, don't be afraid of those flesh-eating things."

"He reminds me of Beebe, but shorter. Butler County, PA, in the '60s is like Lark in the now, and zombies are your Mee-Maw's proof the world needs Jesus to save us from sin."

Darla shot upright. "Ma's heading for the washroom! Up Boozer!" She shooed the dog outside and returned. Just like when they were young, Darla and Sammie Rae clutched each other and squealed at the gore, though it had lost a lot of its horror.

Darla added, "Must've been forty zombies dropping gobs of meat everywhere, off themselves and their dinner. Imagine cleaning up that mess!"

"Well, you could charge a ton." Sammie Rae flipped up the lid of the pizza box to make sure there wasn't a slice still lurking. Boozer had been right. Just crusts.

"Up close, some of them zombies sure look like long-term meth heads, don't they?" Darla said.

"I'm waiting for my favorite part, where little zombie girl sticks a trowel right up in her mom's heart!"

Chapter 4

THE LAST TIME SAMMIE RAE was in a hotel, she had been called about the body of Buzz Thompson, a school friend until he dropped out at fourteen. Just another overdose at the Coalville Inn, a place charging twenty-seven bucks a night for all the bedbugs you could want. Poor Buzz—he must not have been able to afford the Motel 6.

But this conference center was a *real* hotel, classy. The room they shared had two queen beds with quilted, paisley coverlets and a huge flat screen TV, loads of free toiletries in the bathroom, a coffee machine, and a minibar full of goodies.

"You want the bed by the window, Dar?" Sammie Rae wanted the side nearest that bathroom.

"Don't care," Darla said. "Just wanna check out the covers and get to the reception."

"Well, I want one of them fancy-Dan Toblerones and a Coke. Ultra-cold." Sammie Rae lifted the plastic-copper bucket from the credenza. Shook it suggestively but, when Darla didn't respond, she opened the door and went out to the ice machine.

When she returned, Darla called from the bathroom. "I black-lighted—no body fluids on the beds! Taking a quick shower."

Sammie Rae unboxed the candy, broke off a tent-shaped piece and popped it in her mouth. Her mood wasn't as upbeat as during the three-hour trip up I-80. Her heart had soared then, singing along to Dolly's old Patsy Cline and Hank

Williams CDs—Darla's mom was a sucker for classic redneck Americana.

Sammie Rae felt a twinge of intimidation. She sighed, hoping the conference would be a real vacation—one that might provide gems to show up the boys back home or ways to up her drug busts.

She beat out a song on her stomach, a quick burst of Josh Turner's "Long Black Train." The rhythm was muffled by the extra fifteen pounds around her middle, the same fifteen pounds slowing her down during chases—something she really should work on. She broke off another segment of the candy and chewed thoughtfully.

When the shower stopped, Sammie Rae brushed crumbs from the front of the plaid shirt she wore over her tee.

*   *   *

When she and Darla got to the reception, Sammie Rae was glad she'd dressed in her usual jeans and plaid shirt. Just the right outfit for an out-of-uniform rural professional. No one would be impressed if a deputy sheriff dressed like a phony TV detective, working in the rain without her makeup ever smearing, or running through the woods in high heels.

The few women present—not the wifey-types come for a weekend on their husband's expense account—looked to be lawyers or administrators. They wore tailored, big-city suits accessorized with tasteful jewelry. Anything dressy in Sammie Rae's closet would look honky-tonk by comparison.

Most of the men wore day-off clothes—if their day off was spent in church. Respectable button-downs tucked into khakis and ties, knotted loosely. A fair number of male attendees had paunches, their tight waistbands making it obvious they hadn't upgraded their Sunday clothes in a while.

Darla handed Sammie Rae a stack of business cards. "Pick your victims carefully. Only brought a hundred." They split up, heading into the crowd, the men turning their heads to watch Darla go by. At times, from across the room, the movement looked like the wave at a ball game.

Sammie Rae roamed the crowd, slapping the cards against her palm, narrowing her eyes in what she hoped was an intense expression, seeking an in-depth discussion. This was her chance to pick up professional tips by mingling in the crowd—maybe pointers on the illegal drug supply routes, accessing databases, or finding decent—at least adequate—treatment programs for welfare cases. Get something worthwhile to bring back to the office. Something to maybe shut down the complaints that women—especially Sammie Rae—weren't up to the job.

This was also a golden opportunity to sharpen her assessment skills, creating mental profiles based on posture, expression, and snippets of overheard conversations. It was rare for her to be in a crowd of strangers. Back home she knew everyone's quirks.

A slender blonde on the fringe of a group of men twisted her diamond-studded wedding ring round and round, looking over her shoulder, then turning back with a nervous laugh. The man beside her gripped her arm as if he owned her. *That one is easy. She wants to be anywhere but where she is, married to any guy but him. He's a man who's used to getting his way. Maybe a sheriff. Maybe—no, not maybe—abusive.*

Sammie Rae slowly circled and noticed another man in their group, sipping a beer in sullen concentration, staring at the patterned carpet or maybe the shiny snakeskin boots of the wife-holding guy. Sammie Rae eyed him for a moment before noticing the way he glowered at the possessive husband—someone he hated, possibly his boss. His khakis and cheap, checked shirt were from the JCPenney sales catalog. Maybe bought by his mom; no way he was marriage material.

Afraid someone would turn and catch her gawking, she moved from spot to spot, spinning elaborate yarns about the crowd.

It was still afternoon—and it wasn't soda pop in their plastic cups. Some were getting drunker than Cootey Brown, as Mee-Maw Wheedle liked to say. A few were heading back to the bar, unsteady enough to flunk a field-sobriety test.

Raised voices interrupted her thinking—two men involved in a disagreement. She moved closer. One smiled at her in a benign, fatherly way but, after barely a second glance, returned to the argument. Soon he was so worked up, spittle flew from his mouth.

The other man, his back to Sammie Rae, was younger. And like nobody in Lark County. She tilted her head to ponder—kind of fancy, is what you could say.

She stared at the nape of his neck, at the fascinating way his hair was cut shorter and shorter until it faded away into the deep brown skin. It looked like the shoulder of unpaved road after the county crew cut back the weeds. Wasn't a homemade-on-the-porch style like a lot of guys in Lark County. And sure wasn't a ratty ponytail straggling down his back—or worse, all shaved off like the guys who fancied themselves the skinhead answer to competing drug gangs.

His tan leather blazer looked soft as buttery caramel. A well-off, well-dressed guy like him was exotic. There weren't but maybe two hundred Black people in Lark and most of them were poor.

Instead of winding down, their voices grew louder, fingers pointing as if to poke each other in the chest. Wondering what the kerfuffle was about, she stood tapping the toe of her shoe, when the older guy said, "I don't give a good goddamn what the 'experts' say. Most addicts start with marijuana."

"That's outdated gateway crap." The younger man's accent was straight TV-show New York. She stared at his back, which was all she could see without circling around to see his face, giving her curiosity away.

"Most addicts also start with cigarettes and food, not to mention alcohol. But that's not the main point. The main point is profiling, and drug offenses so unfairly enforced and prosecuted…"

"The main thing is people dying," the older man said.

"Nobody ever died from weed! You want to focus attention on killer drugs, try opiates and the execs who get away with pushing them."

Sammie Rae began to worry they'd catch her eavesdropping, though they were paying her no never mind. Personally, she'd rather deal with a pothead than a roaring drunk.

She headed to the cash bar. She'd no sooner put her beer money down when someone said, "Hey, Lark County!"

She turned—the guy with the interesting haircut and expensive clothes was pointing at her ID and smiling at her, but the smile didn't seem quite honest. Before, when he was arguing with the other guy, he'd had his back to her, so when had he noticed her or seen the badge saying where she was from? And why wasn't he wearing one?

"Al Lansing." He held out his hand and she reached to shake it. His handshake was strong but his skin smooth and warm. "I noticed you standing near me."

"That's okay. You were busy." She wondered if she'd missed a clue as to why he'd want to talk with her. "Sammie Rae Wheedle, Lark County Sheriff's Department."

"The whole department?" His grin made her feel about twelve years old. Especially since he was good-looking, with dark eyes full of smug humor. An arrogant, high-bridged nose and russet undertones to his skin possibly indicated some Cherokee ancestry. Yup, good-looking, despite a few deep acne scars on his cheeks. He had a face she would easily remember.

She scrambled to regain her composure. "Of course not, just a deputy. And are you 'Officer Lansing' or 'Agent Lansing?'"

"Just call me Al, Deputy Wheedle."

"From New York?"

"Thanks, but how did you know?" Lansing asked. Before she could think of an answer, he laughed and said, "Just kidding. The accent of course! Originally, but now based out of DC. Bet you don't see many people like me in Lark County." He raised one eyebrow and stared into Sammie Rae's eyes.

"No, not many city slickers." She smiled her best "aw shucks, butter wouldn't melt in her mouth" smile. It was obvious what he really meant.

"I'm so disappointed," Lansing said. "Was hoping to find out if I'd pass for a local." He didn't look sorry. "Well, anyway, first time in West Virginia—I drove in this morning. Really pretty."

Martinsburg was right on the border with Maryland. He couldn't have seen much more than the center's parking lot. "You should see the rest. Most beautiful place on Earth. God's country. 'Course, nothing like what it used to be before the open mining took down half the mountaintops. But still, the redbud and white wild cherry in the spring…" She wished she could describe the dogwood once glorifying every hillside before the plague decimated their beauty.

"Well, I plan on seeing a lot more. Now, if you'll excuse me, there's someone I have to say hi to." He strolled toward a group chatting across the room.

Flattery always made Sammie Rae wary, even if just about the beauty of her state. What did he want from her? Was he playing her for a fool?

She had him pegged as a federal agent. They'd say anything to get what they wanted. She watched as he flowed into the new conversation like a trout into a slipstream. Really was damn slick.

*   *   *

The next morning, Darla and Sammie Rae headed to the conference hall to check out the day's talks. Only a few attendees were moving about. Flanking the doors to the meeting rooms, two tables of overweight, middle-aged ladies were registering late arrivals.

"Should we give them cards?" Sammie Rae asked, meaning the men scowling and shifting from foot to foot, irritated by the slow process.

Darla shook her head. "Look like a bunch of hungover pissants. Let's wait for a break. Maybe everyone'll be in a better mood. Coffee first."

A tray of pastries sat next to coffee dispensers, carafes of cream, and bowls of sweetener packets. "Breakfast first," Sammie Rae said.

A few attendees were standing about, munching on the gummy Danish, and drinking Starbucks. "No cards—definitely not decision-makers," Darla murmured.

They took their food to the meeting room, where Addiction Causation and Treatment in Impoverished and Marginalized Communities, A Dialogue was scheduled.

The stage was set with two chairs. The speakers, both physicians, came through a side door and climbed three stairs to their seats. Sammie Rae stopped picking the raisins from her bran muffin and lifted her head—the doctor on the right was the most stunning man she'd ever seen. His cheekbones created sculptured hollows above an angular jawline, and his mouth was as shapely as the angel's on some coal baron's grave. Not the avenging kind of angel, but the sorrowful kind. The kind of angel who had a mouth made for kissing. She'd seen one in a cemetery when she was twelve and thought, *That's the difference between the man buried here and my daddy—one'll be kissing that angel for eternity and the other forever pining for someone he never could keep ahold of.*

"Kissing the angel" was Sammie Rae's name for what she did alone at night while the house was quiet and the woods dark with the silent flight of owls hunting mice. Things that made her blush with shame. Things not even Darla knew. Now here, right in front of a whole heap of people, was her angel made flesh.

The moderator introduced the two men, though Sammie Rae only heard the name and credentials of the stunner: Thaddeus Overton, MD, graduate of Harvard Medical School, specializing in the epidemiology of addiction in poor and underserved communities. The bio-blurb read, *Dr. Overton spent the past four years with the World Health Organization in Haiti, a country where 80 percent of the population live on less than a dollar a day. Forgoing the relative comfort and safety of the cities, he has taken advanced medical care, addiction treatment, and nutritional support to the underserved and remote towns and villages.*

Sammie Rae's heart took a dip when the room darkened for a slideshow—background for the talk—featuring Caribbean misery with a few inner-city America shots.

He doesn't just look like an angel, she thought. *He is one.*

The glow from the screen further obscured Sammie Rae's view of Thaddeus Overton as he spoke.

"While medical care is still insufficient in the cities of Port-au-Prince and Carrefour, it is most difficult to access in the rural areas." His laser pointer indicated spots in the center of the country. "This is especially true in the isolated valleys in the Massif de la Selle. But though the government and NGOs find it difficult to provide care, addiction manages to find its way into the most remote areas." The next slide was an aerial view of a verdant paradise, the one following showed a collection of tumbledown shacks with emaciated women and children. "The beauty of the land hides the living condition of its inhabitants, who live in desperation, facing crushing poverty and poor sanitation. These areas are dangerous for outsiders. There are many locals hostile to, and resisting of, change. Many still believe in witchcraft, seeking medical care from practitioners of voodoo."

The audience sat upright at the mention of voodoo—at last, something interesting!

He cleared his throat. "We attempted to incorporate and honor their traditions."

The slideshow ended. The lights came back on. He asked if anyone had questions.

A local reporter, a pretty woman of the type often seen sizing up the hogs at the county fair, took the audience mic and attempted to find out more about him. The girl's cooing voice made Sammie Rae want to slap the smile off her face.

The bland, professional expression on his face left for a fleeting moment and then he said that the information would be limited to his work. Sammie Rae smiled. He'd done the slapping for her. *As if he could read my mind.*

As the discussion was winding down, Darla whispered in Sammie Rae's ear, "Don't think your interest in the *topic* passed me by. The line of drool down your shirt gave you away."

"That's just nasty!" Sammie Rae squealed. Her loud-pitched noise caused Dr. Overton to fix his gaze on her. Her cheeks quickly burned, and a knowing smirk was Darla's response.

In the next session, Drug Routes Through Appalachia, the seats filled slowly, perhaps because people stopped to scavenge remaining bits of the free breakfast. Sammie Rae sat at the side of the aisle for easy escape.

Someone slipped into the seat behind her—the smoky, spicy scent of a man's aftershave wafted to her nose. He bent forward enough for his breath to fan hot on her neck, tapped her right shoulder, said, "Good morning, Sammie Rae."

She turned. Al Lansing was smiling at her like a fence lizard in the warm spring sun. "We never got to finish talking, though I sure intended to." He'd made it sound as if their conversation had ended on her account.

She turned back to the slides, ignoring him. The story of her people, her state, was too important.

County by county, the statistics on the opiate crisis rolled on. Somehow, when coal moved out, drugs moved in and, despite so many families living firmly below the poverty line, people found the money for addiction. And addiction led to deaths.

Sammie Rae sighed. She'd seen it herself so often, families who couldn't afford to bury their loved ones when they overdosed. Everything had to go toward raising orphans left behind.

But despite the lecture's importance, her right foot kept tapping nervously. Lansing's scent, his breath behind her, wove their way into her consciousness. Sammie Rae struggled to concentrate on the screen, on the map of her state, carved up by drug gangs operating out of big cities like Detroit. *First the mining companies and now the gangs, everyone raping West Virginia.*

She tried taking notes, but all she managed to write down were the gang names—Seven Mile Bloods, Cash Out Crips, and Hustle Boys—and doodles of her father, sitting on his chair, squirrel gun across his lap. And a few of Beebe snorting like a bull, smoke coming from his nostrils at the thought of Washington taking over his investigation.

Worst of all, the prickly breath on her skin was making her think of sex—a squirmy, tightening, damp-panties sensation. Mee-Maw had warned her about that, told her what to do— she made sure to keep her bottom firmly set on the padded-vinyl seat of her chair, lest she give the wrong impression. Kissing the angel. Or was it the devil?

At last, when she couldn't stand it anymore, she turned around and asked, "FBI or DEA?"

"DEA."

Drug Enforcement Agency? Wants to see more of the state? She could practically feel the steam coming from her ears. *Shee-it! He cozied up to me on purpose!* It seemed Beebe wasn't being paranoid. The Feds were indeed coming to Lark County.

Several of the other attendees made angry shushing sounds. Lansing laughed.

Embarrassed, Sammie Rae returned her attention to the speaker's slides. Graphs showed trends in West Virginia drug trafficking over the past few years. *Interesting!* But the ghost of Lansing's exhalations stirred the hairs at the nape of her neck.

When the lights came on, she slid her seat back and stood. Before she took a step, Al Lansing tapped her arm and said, "I look forward to you showing me Lark County!"

"Be delighted." Sammie Rae said as she pushed her way out of the room, squeezing by jocular men whose bellies made it difficult.

Darla was waiting in the hall, smoking. She waved Sammie Rae over, arched one eyebrow and said, "So, Dr. Thaddeus Overton."

"Who?"

"You damn well know who, Sammie Rae Wheedle. Thaddeus Overton—the name bodice-ripper hero enough for you? Reminds me of the books your mom ordered from the bookmobile when it rolled into town."

Sammie Rae was astonished. "You remember that about my mom?"

"Hell, yeah. I remember everything about her—main reason nobody much gossiped about my mom, weird foreigner that she was. Got to start her business without nobody noticing—they were so into your mama's drama. But hush up and quit interrupting. He's even more gorgeous up close, but so skinny! I don't think he's been eating right. Not in a coon's age."

"You got the hots for him?"

"Don't have the hots for nobody, 'less they can help my business." She took a deep drag. "And he can't. He nearly choked when I asked if they needed a cleanup company in Haiti."

Sammie Rae laughed.

"Knew that was dumb—from the slides he showed, the whole country looks like a crime scene. But dumb as it was, it was the only way I could think to meet him. Then I said, 'Just kidding,' and he smiled. Told him I worked close with the Lark County Sheriff's Department and my best friend was a deputy and here with me."

"You didn't!" Sammie Rae felt another warm flush rise to her cheeks.

"And how West Virginia is kind of like rural America's Haiti—poor as shit, cut off from the world, and polluted too—but White. Full of addicts, heroin, speed, pills. He seemed real interested in seeing our area and in meeting you, Deputy Sammie Rae Wheedle, so I gave him my card." Darla smiled. "I only talked to him for you."

"What's that mean?"

Darla ignored her question. "Maybe I'm plum crazy, but standing next to him, I gotta whiff of turpentine, like you get in an old meth house. Nothing fresh, mind you, and judge not and all..."

"Maybe it's his clothes, from being around addicts, having them breathing on him? That's what he did there, right? Treat them? And you know how hard it is to get the smell of meth outta anything. Oh, shit!" Sammie Rae saw Al Lansing making his way toward them. And so, she dismissed—in fact, barely heard—Darla adding, "And the faintest smell of decomp..."

Chapter 5

For the rest of Saturday and into Sunday morning, Sammie Rae glanced up whenever anyone entered a room. She scanned the crowd milling about the refreshments, but the DEA agent had disappeared. Meanwhile, she kept notes, much better ones than with Al Lansing's hot breath on her neck.

Out in the reception area at midmorning snack break—more Danish, now slightly stale—there was a new announcement on the board. Dr. Overton was about to give a more in-depth presentation on care delivery in the rural areas of the third world.

Darla sauntered over. "Here's your chance to get up close and personal." She hooked her arm in Sammie Rae's, dragged her into the room, and attempted to seat them in the first row.

Sammie Rae pulled to a halt. "Uh, uh! It's too hard to see up close. Let's sit in the middle."

Darla clicked her tongue. "Okay, but you're gonna ask him a question afterward."

"What if I don't have anything to ask?"

Darla scrunched her brow in concentration. "He said Haiti was the home of voodoo. You could ask more about that."

"Very funny but no." Sammie Rae plopped down into a seat.

The small room filled up quickly. "Way more females in this room than registered at the conference," Sammie Rae whispered, looking around. "Think I see the hotel front-desk girls." She pointed toward the dais. "Geez Louise! Look, down front, the old ladies from the sign-in table!"

"Apparently, they're fascinated with Haiti, Land of Enchantment." Darla snickered and slouched back with her arms crossed.

Sammie Rae shook her head. "That's some American state's motto."

Dr. Overton entered and walked to the roll-down screen. His tie was gone, and, with his gray suit, he wore a pale turquoise shirt. The color was like the Caribbean in a travel poster, gently lapping an island's sandy shore. The color enhanced… what Sammie Rae couldn't help but notice… the deep green of his eyes, which glittered out to her seat in the small room, as if he was looking straight at her. He stepped under the lights and smiled at his audience. The chatter ceased with a deep, collective sigh.

Sammie Rae didn't think he looked thin. More elegant and wiry. Refined, English-y. Like a hero on the cover of one of her mother's Barbara Cartland novels.

He gave an introductory statement followed by, "Wow, hello all! Great to see so many interested in addiction treatment for the poor, especially the rural poor." A few nervous titters sounded as the lights dimmed.

The slides started with the NGO he worked for in Port-au-Prince and moved, as he had, further and further from the city clinics. In the rural areas, his clinic functioned as a traveling treatment center for basic care. He clicked on a slide of HIV-infected children in a small village and said, "Almost two out of every hundred people are positive. Many of the isolated areas lack access to medical attention, yet heroin and meth reach them. Seems the suppliers have a better network than the NGOs."

"Jeez," Sammie Rae said. "Some of the kids up in the hills here are puny, but those kids beat anything I've seen when it comes to skinny!"

"And he takes care of them." Darla popped a purple Jolly Rancher into her mouth. She tucked the lozenge in her cheek and lifted the right side of her lip. Singing "Devil in Disguise" under her breath, she did a passable imitation of The King.

Sammie Rae turned and stared. The one thing she'd never told Darla about was her secret angel. Or the solitary pleasure it brought her alone in her room, trying not to let the bedsprings squeak. That ecstasy she'd felt while rocking on a lump of hand-stitched quilt was so wrong. For sure, she'd never divulged this secret to her grandmother down in Mingo County, though Mee-Maw was real big on pressing you to confess sins.

The thought of that stern, judgmental presence brought the odor of lavender to her nostrils. With it came the memory of the old lady pushing her into a straight-backed wooden pew, whispering, whispering, *The Devil is real, child. You need to know him, need to pick him out whether he be a slithering snake on the ground or the most beautiful thing you ever seen. Only one thing he can teach you—how to be cast out of everything good.*

The lights came on. The talk was over.

"I've got a few questions for you to ask." Darla clicked the candy against her front teeth, which were rimmed in purple. But when Sammie Rae rose, Overton was already surrounded by women and sidling toward the exit.

"Don't worry," Darla said to her as the doctor escaped before Sammie Rae could approach him. "They're no match for Lark County's finest!"

*   *   *

When Sammie Rae headed to their room at the end of the conference, Darla sat with her feet up on the desk, keying into her laptop. She greeted Sammie Rae with, "Hey, I heard some interesting shit." She held up an index finger, paused, keyed a bit more, and said, "They been finding body parts around DC. How people like me basically cracked cases with stuff the lab techs left behind. Like one chunk of victim up in the crotch of a tree. Turns out they were all meth heads."

"Huh. Deals gone bad or some vigilante taking out tweakers?"

Darla shrugged. "Nobody knows. Especially since they were gnawed on. Didn't know DC had so many wild animals. And now there's two west of DC. Ooo!" Darla rose and came toward Sammie Rae, hands extended like claws. "I'm coming to eat your face!"

Sammie Rae waved her away. "Quit the *Living Dead* shit."

Darla sat back at her laptop. "Anyway, it's a grade A mystery."

"Mystery?" Sammie Rae said. "Back home, the rumors would be flying about The White Thing."

"Didn't you tell me about… what did they call them? Zombie murders?" As usual, Darla was only half-listening. "Huh." She swung her laptop around and pointed at the screen. "I'm thinking of buying a spectrometer. For IDing lots of shit, but mostly fentanyl powder."

Sammie Rae got up and rifled through the minibar, grabbing the last Toblerone. She snapped off one of the cute little chocolate hills and sighed.

Darla clicked the keys, blowing a lock of hair out of her eyes. "Damn it! The sites don't give prices unless you email. I been saving up. Want to know if it's near enough." She sucked on her lower lip a moment without turning around. "Don't be eating a whole bunch of fattening crap, Sammie Rae."

"I'm addicted. As that guy Overton said, 'Sometimes addiction is the only escape people have.'" Sammie Rae held up the triangular yellow box. "And please call it *expensive fattening crap.*"

"Whatever. Chuck me a chunk." Darla caught the piece Sammie Rae tossed to her. "Maybe I could buy one and you guys could rent it from me…"

Sammie Rae shrugged. "You'd have to make it right cheap for our budget." She sat on the bed and flopped backwards to stare at the ceiling and tried to make her next comment nonchalant. "I met a guy named Lansing, a federal agent. Black. Curious, haven't seen him around today. Far as I can tell, he blowed out of here."

Darla leaned forward, intent on the laptop screen.

Sammie Rae continued, "Probably back to DC, because of those zombie murders."

"Huh. Could he be the one I saw you talking to at the bar? The first day?" Darla keyed a few strokes, without looking at Sammie Rae. There was a moment of silence before she said, "I kind of found him… let's just say, interesting."

"You?" Sammie Rae pushed herself upright. Darla's tone had left little doubt what *interesting* meant. "You're never interested in anybody. Not like that."

Darla glared at her. "Focused on my business doesn't mean dead from the waist down. Sometimes be nice to share my outsider status. When I'm ready."

"Well, we're ready to get out of here," Sammie Rae said. "So put your shoes on Darla Lou, don't you know you *are* in the city?"

Darla laughed. "Okay, okay, I get the picture. We're leaving!"

They tossed their belongings into their suitcases. It was time to return to Lark County. On the road home, Darla sang and whistled to her mama's favorite mixed CD. Sammie Rae sat deep in thought.

Chapter 6

IT TOOK SHERIFF BEEBE two days to notice the hints Sammie Rae dropped, hints aimed at impressing him with her dedication—giving up her weekend for the conference, going the extra mile. But, when she ran into him in the parking lot, his response wasn't what she expected. "If you think the department's payin' for that conference, you can forget it. Rule is put in requests a month ahead…"

Put in requests a month ahead, and then wait for them to be turned down. Unlike the requests you grant the boys, even at the last minute? But, as Dolly said, "Life is simpler when you plow 'round the stumps."

"No sir," was all Sammie Rae said. "Paid for it myself."

Sheriff Beebe leaned back against the hood of his patrol car, a stance that must have been seductively macho to Sammie Rae's mother more than a decade ago when he was, indeed, a fine figure of a man. But now the way he stood emphasized his flaccid belly and the sag of his shoulders. Like her daddy, Ralph was getting old.

He picked something in his teeth. "So, you're saying the conference convinced you I was right? 'Bout the Feds sending agents?"

"Uh, no, sir! Uh, yes, sir! I mean, you were right. Met one there much as said so."

"Well," Beebe crossed his right shoe over his shin and tapped the sole with his club. A clod of dirt fell off, breaking into dusty bits. "Tell me when you spot one on our turf. Meanwhile, pull your weight. Arrest a local junkie or two."

"Yessir." She turned smartly on her heel and headed back into the office.

"Hey, Wheedle," one of the male deputies called as she passed on her way to the breakroom. "D'ja learn anything sitting on your butt while we were here working?"

"Shut your trap, Charlie!" Ray Ben said—her only sort-of-friend in the department. "Don't listen to him, Sammie Rae. What he says don't mean diddly-squat in the long run."

"Why not give a summary of the talks? We could use some updates," Charlie said. "If you understood them, that is."

Sammie Rae had never liked Charlie's looks—overgrown kindergarten bully, snub nose making his long upper lip chimp-like. "That might be a good idea," she said, anger tightening her jaw. "Got some notes. Maybe I can write them up and Ray Ben can read 'em to you."

"Okay, all of you, out on the road!" Sheriff Beebe stood inside the door separating the intake desk from the waiting area with its cracked plastic chairs. In response to his command, the deputies stood, buckling on gun belts and clapping hats on their heads. Sammie Rae turned from the entry to the breakroom, where her leftovers sat in a small plastic tub, awaiting lunchtime, and grabbed her gear. "Except you, Wheedle. Desk and dispatch duty today. Ray Ben'll be your backup, 'case there's trouble. Meanwhile, Ray Ben, get your damn reports done." Beebe went into his office and shut the door.

Charlie tossed his car keys in the air and caught them with a snap. "Desk duty, huh? More like spend the day convincing him you deserve your job." He winked and laughed.

"Just like her mama did!" one of the others said.

"What job was that?" Charlie yelled.

"Use your imagination!"

"But 'least her mama was one hot piece!" another said. "That's what my uncle Lee said."

At the mention of her mother, Sammie Rae's fists tightened around the jacket she was holding. She took a step forward, then stopped. A retort, no matter how clever, made matters worse—she'd learned that over the years.

Laughing, they pushed past each other, heading outside. She watched until she could no longer see their taillights through the side window.

When they were gone, Ray Ben turned to her. "Never you mind, Sammie Rae, just the way they are." Breathing through his mouth—he sure needed those tonsils out—he added. "Like to go for a beer later?"

"Don't think so, Ray Ben," she replied, feeling a flush of guilt rise in her chest. "But thank you, kindly. Meeting up with Darla." He never learned, never quit—been asking her out since ninth grade—just turned and shuffled back to his desk, lumbering like the bear Old Man Tittleson used to keep in his roadside zoo.

Sammie Rae took out a thumb drive. Making sure Ray Ben was hard at work hunting and pecking his way through his neglected stack of arrests and calls, Sammie Rae searched for all the drug arrests during the past five years. She eliminated those incarcerated—though some were probably dealing from inside—and the deceased. And Wade Goodloe. Those still roaming free had their info loaded onto the thumb drive. After a moment, she went back and downloaded Wade's record. Someone might figure out what she copied and, should her activities become known, leaving him out would look suspicious. She slipped the thumb drive into her pocket to take home to her battered old Dell laptop, hoping it still worked.

The reception buzzer interrupted her paperwork. In the waiting area, a woman was bending over three small children. Sammie Rae called, "Yes," into the small aperture in the bullet-proof glass and the woman straightened—Annie Napier, Gracie Hopkin's oldest, just a few months older than Sammie Rae. She sported a split lip and a bleeding cut on her cheek.

"Oh, Christ on a cracker," Sammie Rae said. "I thought you was gonna leave him!"

"Sorry, Sammie Rae." Annie looked contrite. "But he came begging and pleading and swearin' he'd never hit me again. And you know I love him." Annie had been the only girl at their high school to rival Darla in beauty, a cheerleader with a blonde ponytail and forget-me-not blue eyes, one of which was now swollen shut.

"You promised me you wouldn't go back. Promised for the sake of the kids."

Annie began to cry. Sammie Rae's chest tightened. Tears leaking from that battered eye had to hurt. "That's why I'm here, Sammie Rae." She wiped her nose with the back of her wrist and pushed the biggest kid forward, her seven-year-old. "See Denver?"

Denver sported a brand-new cast made of hot pink fiberglass. He held it up for Sammie Rae's inspection. "Doctor made it!" he said. "My arm's broke."

"Your daddy do that to you?" Sammie Rae asked. Denver nodded. "Annie, did it get reported in the hospital? Social worker make a file?"

Annie flushed as Denver announced, "Maw tole them I fell off my bike into a fence post."

"While I was gone, little idiot here picked out pink for the cast. What you think Jesse's going to say about a girly color like that?"

Annie had begun dating Jesse at fourteen, been together ever since. The odds were, Annie would never stay away from him, just as he'd never stay away from crystal or heroin. But Sammie Rae still had to do her job. She buzzed the door. "Come on in. I'll take a statement."

Annie waffled for a minute, then the littlest kid wailed, throwing her dolly on the floor. That seemed to decide something in Annie's mind. "I got to get Allison here her supper." She lifted the girl into her arms. "Come on, kids. Spam and soup beans on the stove."

"You don't deserve this, Annie."

"What you want me to do? Move in with my maw and her passel of young'uns?" Annie turned to go.

"I still got to call Social and make a report…" Sammie called after them, knowing it would do no good if little Denver was convinced to lie. She decided to move Jesse up her list for arrest. Thinking of Denver and Allison and whatever the hell the third kid's name was, it was tempting to add Annie along with her husband. Shame, they'd been the dream couple once, the pair everyone envied, sparkling like lightning bugs on a warm spring night.

"Hey, Sammie Rae!" Ray Ben called, holding up the phone. "Beebe wants you out on patrol, soon as Charlie gets in."

"Why?"

"Beats the heck outta me. Odds are Charlie gave another fine upstanding citizen the shits and a complaint was lodged. He should be back in about a quarter-hour." Ray Ben trudged back to his desk. He was the slowest typist of all of them— the joke was, despite his name, he couldn't see straight. His mother had heard ads for Ray Ban glasses and said how they stood for elegance and class. Sadly, she'd got the name wrong.

Charlie returned, whistling. "You're up, superstar," he said to Sammie Rae. She felt her pocket, where the thumb drive was safely stored. Maybe she'd drop in on Jesse Napier. Just let him know she'd be around.

Chapter 7

HER PERSONAL CELL RANG out Journey's "Don't Stop Believin'." Sammie Rae pulled over to the side of Upper Muddy Road on the way to the Dunkin'. Traffic was scanty.

"Guess what?" Darla's voice yelled from the phone.

"What?"

"Remember that doctor at the conference? The gorg one you were all squirmy over?"

Sammie Rae gasped in protest.

"You dast not deny it now—was written all over your face," Darla shouted into the phone—she must be somewhere noisy. "Well, he seems to be interested in a certain little bit of law enforcement fluff! So, I gave him my card and, what do you know, he called!"

"And that shows he's into me? How?"

"He's coming to look at local property…"

"Property in Lark County? Sure he's not an addict? Why the hell else come here?"

"He asked could we maybe show him around. We, not me, so there!" The call was ended before Sammie Rae had a chance to protest.

When was he coming? And why should I care? She'd be a damn fool to think someone like him, educated, traveled—not to mention movie-star stunning—would be interested in a pudgy, dishwater-blonde, twenty-six-year-old, high-school-almost-didn't graduate from rural West Virginia. She headed back into town, speeding up as she passed the donut shop.

Sammie Rae dropped in at Darla's after her shift, but Darla wasn't home. "Come, come," Dolly yelled from the kitchen as Sammie Rae stepped up on the porch. "I have *mandu!* Just made! *Gogi* and *yachae!*" After almost three decades in the States, Dolly still called her food by Korean names and ended almost every sentence with wild enthusiasm.

Sammie Rae loved Dolly's dumplings. The *gogi* were her favorite, pork savory with ginger, garlic, and scallions. "I'll just have one or two," she said. Thank goodness she'd forgone the Dunkin'.

"What you mean, only one or two? That not like my girl! Come in! I bring the plates. Lemonade too."

Sammie Rae sat at the old, enameled table in the hot and fragrant kitchen. Dolly loaded two plates, six dumplings each, dipping sauce, a bowl of rice, and kimchi. "Don't worry, plenty more!" Plopping into a chair with an "oof!" she patted her cheek. "Too fat—my face getting round like moon." Her chopsticks plunged a dumpling into the sauce and then her mouth.

Only one. Two at most, Sammie Rae vowed, though the smell of the dumplings was intoxicating. "Where's Darla?"

Dolly shrugged. "Working. Girl is busier than cat burying poop."

Sammie Rae laughed. That was an expression also favored by Mee-Maw.

"She be here soon. Cleaning drug place full of needles and dirty stuff. She say shake and bake, too." Dolly's face creased with concern. "But what is going on with you, second daughter?"

Sammie Rae looked down as she chewed and swallowed—if she looked into Dolly's sharp little black eyes, she risked tearing up with the childhood memories of this kitchen. Thank God Darla had befriended her and brought her here. Sammie Rae's father had been gone all day working, sometimes drawing a night shift. And her mother...she tucked that thought away. "I'm okay."

"Trouble at work for you, Darla said. It keep going on, Beebe get cut off." She drew her finger across her throat. "No more shine."

"It's not just the sheriff, Dolly. It's the guys, the other deputies."

"Don't you worry! Just keep being better than them." Dolly chewed on a spicy pickled cabbage leaf, leaned forward, and stage-whispered, "What I hear 'bout this guy coming? Handsome guy? Doctor, too?" She chuckled. "Every Korean mama want her kid to be doctor or marry one."

Darla walked in, sweaty and grimy. "Hey, Sammie Rae! Mom nagging you about getting married?" She wiped a lock of hair from her forehead. "Better you than me." When Dolly got up to hug her, she said, "Let me shower first. I stink! And God knows what shit's on me!"

"Potty mouth." Dolly shook her head when Darla left for the bathroom. "So pretty, so not like lady. You are polite, make a man happy. Who will marry her?"

They ate in silence, all their dumplings savored, until Darla returned in her robe, hair wrapped in a white towel. "I'm famished!"

Dolly delivered a loaded plate for her. "Worked hard today?"

Darla nodded and picked up her chopsticks.

Sammie Rae leaned toward Darla and dropped her voice. "So, when's he coming?"

Dolly's head shot up. "Who? Doctor?"

Darla ignored her mother and grinned at Sammie Rae in a knowing way. "You mean Thaddeus? In two weeks."

"Did you find out why here of all places? Don't we have a rep as the most backassward, hillbilly state in the US of A?"

"You'll have to ask him. All he said was, he wants a real private, out-of-the-way place. Maybe it reminds him of…" A car horn honked outside. "Customer, Ma!"

"No need to yell! I hear!" Dolly hustled out to the shed where she stored her jars of liquor. The kitchen door banged shut.

"The old Henderson place." Darla tapped her chin as she did when torn between thoughtfulness and sarcasm.

"What?"

Darla snickered. "Don't be coy. For Doctor Overton. Out of the way, quiet, lots of land, rambling house with stone walls still in pretty good shape, cheap…"

"Cheap because no one wants to go there. Remember how Dolly spooked us saying she'd seen a ghost there? Made us stay away because it was dangerous?"

"Sammie Rae, we were like twelve then. She was working her Korean-mama juju to keep us close to home, handing us a pile of crap with our after-school snacks. After all the scary shit you've seen, surely you can't buy into that."

"I don't know, lots of monsters around here."

"Ha, ha, so not funny. There's no real monsters."

"Yeah, so, if monsters aren't real, why do people all over the world believe in them?"

"People need monsters," Darla said. "If they don't have them they create them, to explain why things go wrong. Maybe people need things that're for sure evil, horrible for no reason, to excuse what real people do. Don't you feel better after watching zombies die in the movies? Want to know why, ask the doctor."

"Right. That'll impress him with our sophisticated ways."

Darla made a face. "Back to business. This has nothing to do with the Henderson place. It's just an old house. It doesn't hide a monster."

"It's isolated and if he's maybe sickly…"

"He'd be the best person to decide, what with being a doctor and all. I'll get a list of places and we'll show him around. Half the real estate agents 'round here are divorcées hungry for a new man. No sense taking chances with him being gobbled up."

Sammie Rae narrowed her eyes, changing the subject. "Did you tell Dolly I was having trouble at work?"

Darla winked. "Takes pressure off me. And she's worried about you."

"It's fucking relentless, Dar. They're on my case all the time. The other guys. Beebe. If I don't keep my job…"

"You gotta. People depend on you. Your pa and Gracie and all."

"How can I prove myself? Make even a little dent in the number of addicts? We arrest them and they're back out in a flash." With the tip of her chopstick, Sammie Rae traced a soy-sauce pattern on her plate. "The big dealers are slick and out-gun us." She sucked in her stomach and put her hand into her pocket. "Speaking of flash…" She plunked the flash drive on the table.

Darla picked it up and examined the paper label. "SRHL, huh? Sammie Rae's Hit List?"

"I didn't think anyone would figure that out."

Darla went to the refrigerator, pulled out a quart bottle of orange soda and stood drinking from it. When she finished, she returned to the table. "Who's on it?"

Sammie Rae reeled off some names. "All small fry, including that wife-beating jerk Jesse Napier."

"So, what you plan to do with it? If you can't get the big dealers, you got to lower the numbers of penny-ante sellers and customers, right?"

"No idea. Not yet."

Dolly slammed the screen door behind her. Two hectic red spots highlighted her cheeks.

Darla turned to her. "What's happened, Ma? Trouble with the sale? Remember, we got Sammie Rae here."

"No customer. Was Flossie Carter." She faced away from them.

"Ma? Are you crying? What's the matter with Flossie?"

"Not Flossie. Her boy. Went to Ohio, look for work. But no work for him"

"And?" Sammie Rae asked. Flossie Carter was one of the first women in Lark County to accept Dolly as a neighbor, someone to greet in town, almost a friend.

"He used that fake heroin…" Dolly paused to wipe her nose.

"The shit that gives you Parkinson's?" Sammie Rae asked.

She nodded. "They sending him home for Flossie to take care of, all stiff like old man." She went back out onto the porch—Dolly never cried in front of anyone.

Sammie Rae sighed. "Maybe if there were good treatment programs here. Or at least a supply of decent drugs to keep him going."

"Hell, if there were jobs here, he would have stayed." Darla spat out a dried pepper bit.

"New meaning of dying to work."

"Well," Darla added, "He's ruined now—no coming back from that."

Chapter 8

THE SPORTS CAR WENT PAST Sammie Rae so fast, the blast of air whipped loose strands of hair across her face. She turned on the siren and set off in pursuit. A Porsche insignia mounted on the rear was clearly visible, but the license plate was all gaumy with mud—another violation. No way that fancy, low-slung car had traveled the rough dirt roads—and it hadn't rained in a week. The mud was deliberate.

Watching the Porsche hold the road, Sammie Rae sighed with envy, as she struggled to make the turns. Then, to her surprise, the sports car slowed at a crossroads and she was able to pull ahead and block it. She got out of her car and walked to the driver's window.

"Morning, Deputy," the driver said, his voice mellow, slightly rumbling, masculine. Familiar—Al Lansing, easy to recognize despite his sunglasses, his grown-out hair, and the beginning of a beard and mustache.

She bent to look further into the car. "License and registration," she said.

"Got it right here. Don't you remember me from the conference a few weeks back?" With a huge grin, he reached out with the requested documents. "You gonna give a fellow officer a ticket?"

"Do you know how fast you were going?"

"Yep." He opened the door and stepped out into the dappled shade of a sugar maple still red with autumn color. "Real, *real* fast. This car is too much fun to drive."

"And it's another violation to have obscured plates. As a fellow officer, you know the rules, so why not follow them?"

"Good point!"

His cheerfulness grated. "Please get back in your vehicle."

"Would you like to give it a spin?"

Sammie Rae glowered without responding. He chuckled and slid back into the leather seat.

She considered calling in the traffic-stop information to the Sheriff's Office. But hesitated and pondered the situation. Wouldn't it be more to her advantage to defer and bring Beebe the information of his arrival in person? Perhaps even with a hint of the government's plans? Risky—what if Lansing went straight to the office and said he ran into her?

Sammie Rae leaned into the sports car again. "Agent Lansing…"

"Told you to call me Al."

"I'd be glad to escort you to meet Sheriff Beebe."

"To tell the truth, Sammie Rae, this week I'm on vacation. Just tooling around, checking out the 'hood, so I'd rather not meet the heat until I have to." He smiled broadly again. Sammie Rae had heard of crocodile tears, not crocodile smiles, but this grin looked dangerous, reptilian. And, somehow, alluring.

"Well then, welcome to Lark County."

"Thank you. But help me out—I'm getting hungry and hate fast food. Where's good to eat?" He cocked his head with another smile. "And could I buy some company treating you to a meal? Would be great to meet some locals, get the lay of the land."

Lay of the land? Was he mocking her—and all of Lark County—by a take on "aw, shucks?" Still, it seemed best to keep him on her side, or at least get a head's up on his investigation, if only to keep her father's—and all the others'—supply line safe. Maybe she could feed Beebe information a little at a time. "Sure thing. I'll get you to your lodgings. Then we can meet back up at dinnertime. But it's gotta be Dutch treat."

"I get it—keep things professional. No worries there."

She felt a slight pang of senseless rejection. She patted the side of the car. "Drive at the speed limit and get those plates cleaned off."

He nodded, started his engine, and turned on the CD player. The pounding beat drove a flock of whitethroats from the bushes. She felt a flash of anger, as if they were *her* birds.

Back on the road with Lansing's car behind her, Sammie Rae called Darla. "Hey, remember that guy at the conference? The Black DEA guy? The one you found 'interesting'?"

"Yeah? What about him?"

"Just stopped him for speeding on 81. Not giving him a ticket—professional courtesy—but he wants to meet the locals. You're a local, right?"

Darla was silent.

"Maybe you and me and the interesting guy should all meet up. Bet he's come to work our neck of the woods for the DEA. Come here making moves on me, 'cause I'm supposed to be too young and dumb to play the game. He wants info up front, and I'm the rube who's supposed to give it to him."

Darla hummed a bit of "Young, Dumb, and in Love."

Sammie Rae *tsk*ed to stop her. "Lord knows, I don't want him—or any of them—to come, but no way to keep them out. With the damn dealers down from Detroit and up from Mexico, better armed than we are, we're losing ground."

"So, where do I come in?" Darla said.

"Help find out what he's really up to. Game plan and all."

Darla went silent again.

"Come on, you know I can't do it without you! And, besides the fact you love me, could mean work for you cleaning up any federal cases here. There's bound to be some. A friendly connection to give you a leg up on the bigger companies."

"Dammit, Sammie Rae!" Interested in Lansing or not, Darla couldn't resist the chance of getting business. "Okay, I'll meet with y'all. Where?"

"How 'bout the Wandrin' Minstrel for burgers and beer?"

"Yeah, he'll sure 'preciate the hokey name and the crowd there. Why not the Big Hog Bar to see how quick the first bottle's broken over the Black revenuer's head?"

"Revenuer? There's a term last used by my grandpappy!"

"Tradition! Gets everyone all riled up."

Sammie Rae hugged herself with glee. Darla was already playing along, even if she wouldn't admit it. "If all the bars are out, then the buffet over by Onondaga."

"Oh, yeah, Nelson's Buffet's sure to impress a fancy-Dan genl'mun from the big city!" Darla was snorting with laughter.

"You talk straight-up hillbilly, Dar, he'll think we're a'funnin' him. Which I hope we'll be doing."

"Well," Darla said, "we need to plan this out, being as it's war. I think it's time for bringing in the plot of your mama's trashy novels—seduce and abandon. Give him a taste and leave him hungry! I'm gonna vamp it up!"

"You are so kind to me," Sammie Rae's voice was slopping over with sarcasm. But her mother's beloved books always had a beautiful heroine, a tall, handsome hero to fall for—and they always ended with hot sex followed by lasting romance.

Perhaps her mother had found that romance, far away from coal dust, mud, and Sammie Rae's father.

*   *   *

Sammie Rae left Lansing at the Travelodge in Comfort, with instructions on how to get to the buffet, and went home to change from her dusty uniform. As she walked in the door, her cell rang. Darla.

"Mom followed me around until I told her what was up. I could just hear it in her voice, Sammie Rae, she was so happy; she grinned like a possum shitting peach pits. A single man—he is single, isn't he?"

"I think so. Leastwise he kind of acts like he is—flirty in a sneaky way." He'd certainly breathed right into her ear at the conference.

"Sneaky flirty could be cheating flirty."

"Well, we'll just have to find out, won't we?"

*　　*　　*

Sammie Rae knew most everyone in the county—knew what they knew, what they did, and exactly how indiscreet they could be. Going to dinner at six, after the early bird special hour but before the steam table got crusty, would cut down on the locals and leave mostly tourists, mostly from the great buffer states of the Midwest.

She and Lansing for sure would run into Howie, who spent the hours from four to eight eating with slow and majestic dignity—especially if it was smothered chicken night. But Howie was no problem—he never initiated conversations, choosing instead to concentrate on his plate and the long walk back and forth from the buffet. For most country folk, eating out was a rare and special occasion. And Beebe? He wouldn't touch the buffet with a ten-foot pole—swore people's germs were in the food, despite the sneeze guard.

Liddie Nelson stood behind the cash register. She greeted her pa's customers, charming pixie face framed by close-cut russet hair. With those looks and welcoming innocence, her presence helped keep the atmosphere family friendly. "Hey," she said when Sammie Rae walked in with Lansing—the surprise on her face was barely noticeable. "Just sit anywhere at all."

"Cute kid," Lansing said.

"I used to babysit her," Sammie Rae said, followed quickly by, "She's only sixteen." And then she bit her tongue, afraid she'd offended him. She didn't mean to imply his interest in the girl was inappropriate—just that Liddie's parents were very protective. Any attention by a strange man could lead to the girl losing her job. She needed it. Her father believed kids who didn't work shouldn't be handed an allowance.

Following Sammie Rae, Lansing seemed oblivious to the stares directed at them, but she was used to easygoing friend-liness from locals, friendliness with a side of mind your own business. That was the custom of the hills, so the silence from the tables was as unsettling as the looks. The well-dressed Lansing was out of place, especially accompanying the local Sammie Rae. The one good thing was that none of the locals would rat her out to Beebe. Informing the law was against their ethics.

They went to the steam table and toted their loaded plates to their seats. Lansing had snared two huge breaded fried pork chops, mac 'n' cheese, field peas, and green beans with bacon. How could he eat like that and still be slim?

He sat with a big sigh, sliced a chunk of meat, and chewed thoughtfully. When his mouth was empty, he said, "For buffet, this is some fine eating." He chuckled.

Sammie Rae felt her cheeks flush—there had been the faint hope he'd feel so big city and superior, he'd be a little bit off-balance. "Thought you'd like some down-home cooking."

"Grew up with my granny. Her mother went to Paris in the '20s with Josephine Baker. Came back and made her daughter into the Black Julia Child. It was straight fancy French at home. My mother didn't cook. Not a thing but crack."

Was he trying to gain her sympathy? Show her he was no stranger to the damage addiction did? And who the hell was Josephine Baker?

"Of course, my mom was out of the picture almost all my early years." He dug into the macaroni. "Are the desserts good? Sign says sweet potato pie."

Before Sammie Rae could reply, Darla walked in, wearing skinny indigo jeans shredded at the knees with a low-cut, red knit, draped-neck top. Her hair was down and shiny-clean, a mantle of inky silk over her shoulders. She looked good—almost too good. She'd *made an effort*. She'd never done that before. In high school, she'd sailed along like no one would dare judge her, or, as the bitchy girls said, *like her shit didn't stink.*

This night, Darla was a fresh breeze stirring the atmosphere in the steamy restaurant. "This here's Darla," Sammie Rae said, "She was with me at the conference."

Darla gave her most charming smile and offered her hand. Lansing stood and reached across the table to her. The hem of his jacket dragged in the gravy. He didn't notice, so Sammie Rae said not a word beyond, "Darla, this is Agent Lansing."

The "Call me Al" came quicker than ever.

"I certainly will, Al." Darla voice was a throaty purr. She slid into her seat with the grace of a pageant girl, and asked, "What brings you to our neck of the woods?"

"Right now, I'm on vacation."

Oh, bulldookie, thought Sammie Rae. "Agent Lansing's from DC. He's with the DEA."

"Very impressive!" Darla looked at Sammie Rae's plate. "My, that chicken looks good!" She smiled at Lansing. "I don't get to eat out much. Too busy with work…"

She didn't get a chance to describe her work, as Lansing pushed his chair back and said, "Can I get you anything, Miss Darla?"

"Well, maybe a bite of spaghetti… and if they have ham. Oh, tater tots… and those green beans. And corn."

After Lansing headed to the steam table, Sammie Rae said to Darla, "You can't be too dainty to tote your own plate while ordering like a Mountaineers linebacker!"

"You hush up!" Darla took a bite of Lansing's untouched chicken leg and said, with her mouth full, "Mom's fried chicken is better." She put the chicken back on the plate, bitten side down. "Look, now we know he's a gentleman. And I got my dinner paid for. We'll just make contact and leave him hungry—and we won't be hungry at all."

Lansing returned with everything Darla requested. He picked up the chicken leg, looked surprised, but didn't say a word about the missing chunk. His gaze fixed on Darla, he ignored both his fork and Sammie Rae.

Sammie Rae went for seconds. She looked back at their table—Lansing was leaning forward, talking, almost like he was conspiring with Darla, but she stayed upright. She was eating quickly, as if wanting to keep her mouth full so she didn't have to speak. When Sammie Rae returned to the table, Darla's plate was empty.

"Oh, goodness," Darla exclaimed, wiping her lips with dainty grace, "look at the time! My mama's expectin' me home to help with dinner!" *More bull.* Dolly never let anyone help with her cooking and that had always suited Darla fine. She hated anything domestic.

"Dinner?" Lansing's eyebrows raised as he glanced at Darla's plate.

"Sammie Rae, will you give me a ride home?" Darla asked. "My pa dropped me off."

"I'm not done eating! Not to mention, this is a business meeting."

"We'll have plenty time later," Lansing said to Sammie Rae. He put down the roll he was eating and said to Darla, "Be glad to drive you."

"You should see his car—it's right sweet." Sammie Rae said with what she hoped was a suggestive smile.

"Yeah, it's out front next to the giant pickup…" Lansing said.

Sammie Rae broke in with, "Howie's Ford Raptor."

Darla flicked her head, her tell for annoyance. "If your ride's that low-to-the-ground hard-top convertible in cherry red, Sammie Rae's wrong—it's not sweet, it's downright sexy! I'll take a ride some other time. Right soon!" She handed him a business card. "Number's the only one I use. Come on, Sammie Rae, Ma wants to see you, too."

Though Lansing kept his eyes on Darla, looking like a moonstruck calf, Sammie Rae led the way to the steam table, got a take-home container of macaroni and a few other soft foods her father could eat. They waved as they left the restaurant. Both Lansing and Howie waved back.

*　　*　　*

A little way down the road, Darla turned to Sammie Rae. "Y'know what he asked me while you were up getting more? He asked if my being part Cherokee was a problem for me.

Nerve of him, assuming shit! I was so mad, I coulda knocked him into next week!"

"You tell him it made you mad?"

"Course not! You still need your info. And besides, his damn car *is* sexy. I want a ride." They'd arrived at Darla's house. "Comin' in?"

Sammie Rae shook her head. "Got to visit my pa. Haven't been over there for four-five days and he needs this food...I'll drive you back to get your car in the morning." She waved as she drove off and opened the windows wide—might have just been her imagination, but the scent of desire was stinking up her car.

*　　*　　*

"Hallo?" Sammie Rae called, walking up to the porch.

Her pa's muffled voice replied, indistinct, but calm, "In here." She went through the empty parlor and the kitchen and into the bedroom he'd once shared with her mama.

Her father sat on the bed, quilt bundled up in his lap. He lifted his left hand in greeting and said, "Hey there, honey. Good to see you. Fetch me a glass a' soda pop from the kitchen."

"You hurting too much to get up today?" Sammie Rae asked.

"Naw, I just been busy."

Something in the dark corner behind the crooked old chifforobe made an indistinct groaning noise. Sammie Rae took a step toward it, but her father said, "Careful there, Sammie Rae, that snake might bite."

Sammie Rae stopped in her tracks. "A snake? Snakes don't moan."

He smiled and unwound the quilt in his lap, revealing his .22, the muzzle's end poking out of the cloth. "Do when I wing 'em."

Whatever it was rustled on the floor just out of sight and groaned again. Sammie Rae peered around the cumbersome piece of furniture. A man lay crumpled on the floor, his head up against the one-by-four serving as baseboard. There was a small, dark puddle spreading under his torn pants—he was dripping blood from both legs. "Goddamn ole man," he yelled. It was Eben Robertson, a meth head she'd arrested twice. By the look of him, he'd been using heavily—so thin his eyes bulged; it seemed his skull was trying to climb out through their sockets, and his skin was scabby like Wade's rusty old truck.

"Jesus, Eben!" Sammie Rae said at the sight of his face. The leg situation looked painful but not serious.

Her father chuckled. "Don't he look like those walkin' dead things in the picture shows, the ones you and Darla used to love?" He tried snapping his fingers but gave up quickly. "Zombies!"

"Did you call for help, Pa?"

"Phone don't work."

"You didn't forget to pay the bill, again?" She took out her cellphone and called the emergency line, requesting the ambulance.

He snorted in response.

Sammie Rae turned toward the kitchen, where the cord of the old phone dangled, useless as tits on a boar hog.

"Put your gun down," she said to her father. "EMTs will be here soon. Tell me what happened."

"Was here on the bed, just restin' when I heard a noise, so I opened one eye and saw him sidlin' into this room. Thought he might be after my pills and I can understand that, but when

I saw he was looking through your ma's jewelry chest, I dropped him like a bad habit." He patted the .22. "Told you it was a good idea, keeping my squirrel gun handy."

Sammie Rae wanted to say the jewelry wasn't worth shooting someone over—nothing of real value and her mother wasn't coming back for anything left behind. But she was overcome by sudden love for his toughness, his determination to stand his ground, so instead she said, "You'll have to give a statement…"

"Just did. All there is to it."

Sammie Rae walked over to the man on the floor. "What you got to say, Eben?"

"Feels like shit! Like I been sucked through a knothole! Goddamn ole man could of killed me!"

Her father chuckled. "Eben, you done knowed me since you was little. Ever notice me miss what I aim at?" He looked at Sammie Rae. "Go head and search him. Odds are he's got something on him to count as a drug bust. You don't have to say I bagged him for you."

"I'm a' kill you one day, you old bastard!" Eben writhed on the floor, rattling the mirror on the chifforobe, foamy spittle streaked with blood on his lips. He must have bitten his tongue with the few teeth he had left.

"Lookee," her father said, "that there was once a baby in his mama's arms. Now he ain't even human."

Sammie Rae wondered if she should put a blanket over Eben's legs or offer him a glass of water. He wasn't hurt bad, but it would be a nice gesture.

The ambulance crew arrived, banging the screen door. "Back here!" Sammie Rae yelled.

They brought their equipment to the door of the tiny bedroom, said, "Hey" to Sammie Rae, "Wassup, Mr. Wheedle?"

to her father, and "Fer Christ's sake, you again?" to Eben as they loaded him onto the stretcher they'd left in the hallway.

Sammie Rae waved goodbye from the front porch and called the office, suggesting that, since the shooter was her father, someone else take over the case. The return suggestion was, since it was only Eben and he wasn't dead, and, since everyone knew Sammie Rae's father was housebound, the shooting was self-defense. And the odds were, attempted burglary would see Eben released with probation. He'd be laid up for a while, anyhow, so why bother filing charges?

"Now you take me," her father said, dragging his quilt and using the .22 as a walking stick, "I kin barely get into any trouble, no matter how many pills I take. And heroin and that new shit, fentanyl? They just curl up in a ball, high as a kite and mellow, if'n they don't die." He settled into his easy chair in the living room and motioned for her to join him. "'Course, they rob a bit, but if they get loaded, they're no trouble a'tall. Meth, now, meth is the real problem."

Sammie Rae couldn't help but laugh. Nodding his head—despite the grizzled cheeks—with his mouth pursed with self-righteous certainty, he was a dead ringer for one of her conference's speakers. "How you get so smart, Pa?"

"One thing, honey, you gotta learn about what's important to you." He picked up his old remote and aimed it at the TV. "Yup, meth. Turns the bastards crazy. Makes 'em not people anymore. Makes 'em dead inside where not even the good Lord can reach."

Sammie Rae went to the kitchen to heat the food she'd brought her dad, loading the mac 'n' cheese into a battered pot and lighting the burner. She hoped there was enough propane in the tank to get it all warmed up—he'd refused to let her get him a microwave, saying, "They're too dang dangerous with a pacemaker!"

Her father didn't have a pacemaker. As far as Sammie Rae could tell, there was nothing wrong with his heart, nothing physical. It was broken though, broken from missing his wife.

Chapter 9

SAMMIE RAE AND DARLA sat in the little picnic table tasting area set up next to Dolly's storage shed. To accommodate her customers, especially the ladies, Dolly had baskets of petunias and pansies hanging from the shed's eaves and a bug zapper on a pole next to the table. The zapper went *bzzzt!* periodically as a fly flew into it.

The warm sun and the ginseng liquor cut the autumn chill rising from under the wild rhododendrons a few feet away. Broad-winged hawks flew overhead, announcing themselves with cries that made Sammie Rae nostalgic for her childhood. It was the fall migration—another sign time was passing. "Remember your dad used to take us to watch them every year?" she asked Darla.

"Yeah." Darla tossed her chin up toward the sky. "These ones are awful late. Think it's global warming?"

"Don't know. Got more important things to worry about." A tanager shot by—a flash of red Sammie Rae hoped would escape the hawks. "Have you heard from Lansing yet?"

Al Lansing had all but disappeared after the buffet dinner. For the past three days, he'd left the motel early in the morning and stayed away until late, once overnight. Sammie Rae's network of spies, headed by Wade and staffed by everyone on his delivery route, reported that the DEA agent was meeting up with state troopers across the county line.

"He'll call," said Darla. "Just another arrogant bastard tactic. Be patient."

"Patient? He's been attracting attention all over the county, but sneaky-like." Sammie Rae couldn't keep the agitation from her voice. "Beebe had us all stand at attention like it was the first day of school. Said one of us had to've noticed a flashy Black guy sticking his nose into everything."

"He knows he's DEA?"

Sammie Rae gave a tight little laugh. "Nope! Beebe thinks anybody with a slick car must be a dealer. Wants us to find out everything about him, 'whoever he is.' Hoping for a big takedown."

"Aw, how cute! The Beebe couldn't investigate his way out a paper bag. What a sad-sack, lonely guy." Darla knocked back another shot.

"The thing is, Dar, he is lonely. Not like my pa, but he's a victim of the same…" She couldn't bring herself to say the words locked in her heart. To refer to her missing mother as a whore, even though she was one. "Just like Pa, he was in love."

"Couldn't help hisself." Darla's speech was on the edge of slurred.

"Even so, I feel bad. The sheriff's job is on the line for sure. Maybe mine being on the line is just a case of shit rolling downhill. I feel guilty, like I'm conspiring against him."

"Hell, no, you soft-hearted idiot!" Darla pushed the liquor toward Sammie Rae. "Take another snort—good for what ails you—and let it go. He was a cheating bastard, taking up with a married woman. And it wasn't your fault your mom dumped him. He's gotta know that." She slapped her palm on the table. "But anyway, it's not bad the feds are coming. I worry you'll go up against those boys from Detroit and get killed."

Sammie Rae chewed on a hangnail and spit the tiny shred out before speaking again. "I should own up, tell Beebe Lansing's no criminal. But as soon as he finds out, he'll put me on desk duty, and he'll assign one of the boys to liaise with the DEA." She buried her face in her hands. "Shit."

"Don't tell him. Not yet." Darla squinted one eye and held her right thumb and index finger apart a quarter inch. "Al Lansing's this close to flopping on the line like a little brown trout. Give me time to reel him in."

"Better hurry before Lansing gets wise to what goes on around these parts—I got no idea who supplies Wade. Always been safer for everyone that way. If he gets picked up, how will I get enough for my pa and the others?"

"Darlin,' you do have a big heart. Squishy-soft maybe, but big as Cheat Mountain. We just got to figure out a game plan." Darla thought for a moment, then tapped the side of her nose in a caricature of a wise, movie drunk. She leaned across the table. "You 'member in school how, if we were going to flunk history, we made sure to do real good in math so we'd not get in much trouble?"

Sammie Rae nodded.

"And isn't it true the really dangerous users, the real pains in the ass, are the speed-freaks?"

Sammie Rae nodded again.

"So, we'll do the same thing now as high school. You're gonna flunk Oxy, but you'll do real good at something bad." Darla knocked back another shot. "'Stead of math, it'll be meth!" She giggled and a little dribble of shine dropped on her shirt.

A customer pulled up in a battered pickup so old it had a split windshield. A small man slid out, stooped, gnome-like and aged before his time, sheltered under a filthy felt hat—Tossy Daniels, a recluse from the deep woods. Tossy had once run his own still, until he bowed to Dolly's superior product. Sammie Rae had always been curious about him but trips out of his holler were few and far between.

"You know, he served in Korea like my pa, but during the war there," Darla said. "Only time out of the county. Brought a bride home, too, but after she spent a year with nobody willing to talk to her, she took off. He moved back to the cabin he was born in and stayed away from most everybody. Blamed them, I guess." She stood. "We need to clear out and leave them be. Let's go in the house."

Sammie Rae swung her legs from her car and followed Darla. They passed Dolly as she came from the kitchen, wiping her hands on her apron.

"Speaking of shy and lonely guys…or maybe I should just say solitary…" Darla said, once they were seated at the table. "We're house-hunting Saturday with that doctor guy. He'll be driving in around ten."

"I'm working."

"No, you're not. You already said you're off. Asked me to go to the Walmart."

Sammie Rae felt the blush rising to her cheeks and turned toward the window. Outside, Dolly sat at the picnic table across from Daniels, who drank directly from a pint jar. Neither were speaking, but the old man seemed relaxed. Sammie Rae didn't feel much like talking anymore either, not even to Darla. She'd dreamed of the cemetery angel during the night, wings folded around her, mouth against her lips, the taste of cold marble like iron or blood. And was awakened by waves of desire spreading from her belly to her throat.

"They're not saying nothing," Sammie Rae said, pointing discreetly at Dolly and Daniels.

"Yeah. Always have done. He drinks, she doesn't; but when she comes in from one of his visits, she's never hungry. It's like she got filled up with him just being around."

"You don't mean…" Sammie Rae was horrified. The fastidious Dolly and that filthy recluse? Dolly cheating while her husband was away hauling livestock in his semi?

Darla snorted a brief laugh. "Fuck, no! But it's like she's one of them hungry ghosts she used to scare us with…"

"I remember! Dolly's bedtime stories!"

"A bunch of Buddhist shit hiding under her church-lady clothes. She sits there and sucks like a vampire on his memory of Soo-Min, his runaway bride—like it hangs in the air between them, no words needed, missing that woman, someone Ma never met. I think Ma's lonely no matter how well she's fit in here. Got no real friends. No good reminding her Soo-Min left before my father went over, or that Soo-Min had to be dumber than a box of rocks to go back when Korea was shit-poor. She probably starved or died of some awful disease. All Ma cares about is, had Soo-Min stayed, she would've had an *eonni*, a big sister, here."

They both jumped as a phone rang. Darla glanced at her screen, her mouth open in an *O* of surprise. Sammie Rae detected a hint of something else—she was pleased. The screen read *Al Lansing*. Darla answered, walking out of the kitchen.

"I can't believe I did that!" Darla said, when she returned.

"Well?" Sammie Rae said. "What can't you believe?"

"Invited him to dinner. He said he wanted to meet my family. What the hell?"

"Did you set him straight? Or does he still think he'll get pemmican and acorn-meal fry bread?"

"Yup, just because I look funny and live in the woods. Figured it would help you if he's off his game." She stopped and giggled. "Maybe he'll bring wampum for the hostess."

Sammie Rae said, "It'll be great, when he comes—can't wait for Dolly to look him over. No one, and I mean no one, is better at sizing up a stranger."

"You're right. Never knew her to be fooled."

"Just tell her to hide the shine."

Darla laughed. "Ha! She knows to a microgram what's legal. I told her he was DEA, and her antennas went up, trying to tune to the channel that tells what'd bring more pleasure: selling shine from under the nose of a government agent or getting her wayward daughter married off."

"I'd give my eyeteeth to watch her!"

"What the hell you talking about? You damn straight will be there! You're part of the family, Sammie Rae Wheedle."

"I'll just sit back and listen to her worm info out of him while he's trying to make time with you."

"You thinking I'll be squirming, right?"

"What about your pa?" Darla's father had been known to glower at boys who dared to look his daughter's way.

"It's the start of deer season next week. Another reason to put it off. He'll be gone like a bat outta hell—you know how he loves to shoot anything that moves, long as he can barbecue it. Anyway, Ma wouldn't want him to see her manipulating another man. That'd rattle his bones."

Chapter 10

"HEY, WHEEDLE!" Sheriff Beebe yelled from his office. "Get off your duff and out to the Cudbert place. Sims's damn goats are eating up Miz Cudbert's prize chrysanthemums."

Sammie Rae considered protesting but only for a moment. It would do no good.

"I'll go for you, Sammie Rae," Ray Ben said. "Last time you went up against Sims's billy you were out of work for two weeks."

A chorus of snickers arose. But Ray Ben was serious, and he was right. The goat had knocked Sammie Rae onto a rock and bunged-up her right knee. It was nice of him to offer, but she didn't want to encourage him thinking she'd ever be sweet on him. And she certainly didn't want to encourage the other deputies to make more fun of him than they already did. What was said about her didn't sting so much anymore. Not since the conference in Shepherdstown. "That's all right, Ray Ben. I can handle it."

"You sure?"

"Ooo, ooo, someone's a'crushin' on our Sammie Rae," Charlie crowed, wiggling his hips as he walked around Ray Ben.

"Leave him alone," Sammie Rae said.

"Aww, don't get your panties in a wad!" Charlie rocked back in his chair.

*　　*　　*

Adelaide Cudbert was sitting in her aged 4Runner, pulling at her curly gray hair, and periodically yelling, "Get the fuck away from my prize flowers, you damn varmints!"

The goats were making quick work of her chrysanthemums along with the anemones in the next bed. It was a near marvel how smart those animals were—the poisonous foxglove and bell flowers stood proud and unmolested.

"Do something!" Adelaide Cudbert screamed. Her glasses were fogged with tears.

Sammie Rae sighed and muttered, "Yes'm."

She got out of the patrol car and, stepping cautiously, approached the herd. The does didn't raise their heads, but the billy's eyes flashed a malignant golden amber. He ducked his head up and down in warning. Sammie Rae was ready this time, her gun in her hand. As the buck began to march toward her, she yelled, "Looks like you remember me, you son of a bitch!"

"Sammie Rae, you watch your words!" Adelaide Cudbert had been Sammie Rae's third grade teacher. Out of respect, Sammie Rae didn't remind her she, herself, had just cussed.

Sammie Rae walked slowly toward the goat, maneuvering to keep him on the other side of the garden's planter, an old claw-foot tub filled with sunflowers. She was pretty sure the billy wouldn't risk ramming into the cast-iron sides.

The goat moved, too, craftily skirting the tub at an angle, attempting to throw her off guard. He was getting close enough to lower his head and make a run at her. Meanwhile, Adelaide was moaning as the does busily ate, churning her flowers into cud.

As soon as his head began to drop, and his right front hoof pawed the ground, Sammie Rae aimed her gun at the ground a few feet in front of him and fired. He slid onto his haunches and shook his head, looking like a doddering old man. Sammie Rae was aware this was an illusion. The king of the herd was wily, dangerous, and experienced in goat-to-human combat. "I don't want to shoot you, you old bastard. You're too tough to be good eating."

The goat's eyes darkened with evil anger. Sammie Rae shot again, into the ground to the right of him and then to the left. The billy jumped and raced backward, running out of the garden, down the drive and out of sight. His harem followed, their stained butts lifting with each leap. She let out a deep breath and holstered her gun.

Adelaide Cudbert opened the door of her vehicle and slid out. Her chartreuse housedress, ornamented with purple felt pansies, rode up above her hose and she forced the skirt down over her ample hips. "Well, Sammie Rae, that makes up for the time you ruined my poor dear husband's dinner."

"When was that?" Sammie Rae had only a vague recollection of the deceased Mr. Cudbert—a man of mammoth size, looming in a doorway.

"Had to be third grade, doesn't it?" Mrs. Cudbert squinted with the effort of remembering "But I was kidding!" She walked over, her arms wide open for a hug, and broke into a cascade of chuckles as her belly banged into the holster on Sammie Rae's belt.

"We were so happy to have you over for the night! The Lord never saw fit to bless us with children. You were so adorable, just the cutest little thing! And so much fun—just yakked on and on."

Sammie Rae thought hard. The taste of roast beef and green beans came to her. And something sweet—strawberry ice cream? Though her mouth watered, no association, no place, no company came with the remembered deliciousness.

"You and your daddy hear from your mama yet?" Mrs. Cudbert asked, though everyone in town knew it had been almost eight years.

Sammie Rae replied, "No, ma'am." A memory sprang into her head, a blurred memory of waiting after school, her jacket and sneakers soaking wet, crying. Familiar fear closing around her lungs. Something must have happened to her ma—had to be the reason she was alone in the rain. All the other kids had left. Crying and wishing she'd gone with Darla. And then an umbrella and a talcum-powdery arm leading to a warm car and a warmer place loaded with little ceramic cats. But no recollection of bringing a fork to her mouth.

"I'll call Tom Sims and tell him to round them up. Keep them penned in with a higher fence. Or else, next time, that goat'll be dog meat. You just call if you have any more trouble." She returned to her car, started the engine, and pulled out of the drive.

Her favorite road back to town led through a narrow valley full of saplings and thick deep green, ferny underbrush. It climbed upward again to a view of the town's outskirts. Sammie Rae's home on the main road was easy to see—the rickety wooden steps up to her apartment, the hair stylist beneath, Dotty's Do's, was easy to make out, its plateglass window gleaming in the sun.

She stopped the car and got out to admire the scenery on this extraordinarily fine day. Cars and people moved below her, bigger than ants—more like scuttling roly-polies. And West Virginians, like those bugs, were likely to curl up and wish outsiders would just go away.

Jesse Napier's house was set off from the town by a copse of tulip trees. Unlike most of the other outlying homes, no smoke lifted from the chimney. Sammie Rae recalled her promise to check in on Annie and the kids. As she climbed into the car again, she added *and make sure that damn Jesse lays in a store of firewood.* Winter was coming.

Usually, Annie's front yard, a mess of weeds, trash, and bare dirt—so different from her mother Gracie's carefully tended tire flowerpots—was occupied by her kids. Allison, the littlest, was almost always seated on a filthy blanket, crying, with Denver looking after her while the middle child cradled her dolly and rooted in the dirt with a stick. Today, the yard was abandoned except for a rusted swing set and a tricycle missing a rear wheel. Jesse's pickup was gone. The place was silent except for the sound of leaves scuttling across the ground with every gust of wind.

She parked on the road, walked to the front door, and knocked. Denver opened the door. He held Allison with his casted arm. The baby's diaper sagged and dripped wet onto the floor.

"Denver, where's your mama?" she asked.

"She's sleeping in the back. Pa tole us not to leave this here room." He turned back to the TV, which was showing a soap opera, the sound at top volume. Sammie Rae went to the remote, but Denver added, "Tole us not to turn the sound down, neither."

No one could sleep with that racket going on. Sammie Rae walked through to the tiny kitchen, which was filthy—tin cans standing open with spoons in them, a large sticky spill on the floor, pots and pans in the sink, flies buzzing. Past the doors to the bathroom and the kids' room was Annie's bedroom. She knocked but there was no answer. Had Annie and Jesse gone off, leaving the kids alone? Or was Annie holed up inside, hiding from yet another beating?

She put her hand on her weapon and pushed on the door. It creaked as it swung inward. Annie Napier lay face up on the bed. Her eyes and mouth were open, flies crawling in and out and landing on spattered drops of blood. The long blonde hair she'd been so proud of was matted and deep purple bruises bloomed on her neck. The dresser was knocked over, the bedclothes dragged onto the floor. Annie had put up a fight at last.

Sammie Rae slapped her palm over her mouth. She leaned over, hand on the bedpost, retching and retching until she was bringing up bile and spots swam before her eyes. She'd never been sick at a crime scene before, but this was different—this was her fault. She'd let things go too long. If only she'd stopped in sooner and put the fear of the law into Jesse. For sure he had no fear of God.

Searching the rest of the house, the two other bedrooms, one just a tacked-on shack, was fruitless. That goddamn bastard was nowhere to be found. She turned to leave, planning on hunting him to ground, but the baby's wail reminded her of what needed to be done. She sighed and wiped her lips on her sleeve. Jesse Napier had just moved to the top of her hit list.

*   *   *

Bad news traveled faster than good in Lark County, and this news had traveled with lightning speed. By the time Sammie Rae arrived at Gracie's house with social services and the Napier kids—cleaned up by the emergency caseworker— Jesse's mother, Wanda, was there.

Sammie Rae sighed when she saw Wanda's banged-up old Lincoln. Hopefully, the two grandmothers, enemies for decades, would come together in the face of this tragedy, if only for the little ones.

The sooner she handled the situation the better for the kids, and so, hat in hand, leaving the kids in the car sucking on the lollypops the caseworker had brought, Sammie Rae entered Gracie's house.

"Hello?" she called. "It's Sammie Rae."

Gracie rushed to hug her. "Oh, Sammie Rae, whatever are we going to do without our Annie?" She stood on tiptoe to look over Sammie Rae's shoulder. "Where are my grand-babies?"

"They're safe, out in the car."

"How will we make do?" Gracie sobbed. Poor Gracie, a widow with four of her eight kids still at home. Adding Annie's three would make for a very crowded house. Sammie shot a glance at Wanda Napier.

"Don't you worry none, Gracie. Them kids'er Jesse's, too." Wanda said. "He loves them."

Gracie turned her head. "Jesse? Don't you be talking about him! If he loves those kids why'd he do this to their ma?"

"Gracie," Sammie Rae said, the words almost sticking in her throat. "We can't say yet, not for sure. We don't know Jesse did this."

"Where is he, then?" Gracie demanded.

Sammie Rae didn't answer. Time enough for the fault lines of Lark County to widen, for Gracie and Wanda to be at each other's throat—though the purple marks on Annie's neck had undoubtedly been made by her husband.

Wanda wasn't ready to quit. Jesse was her only, her spoiled child. Had been ever since way before kindergarten, where he threw fits to get his way. "Right, you can't say he's to blame."

"Can't say he beat the tar outta her almost every day?" Gracie pushed away from Sammie Rae. "Wasn't that enough for him?"

"He would never have really hurt her," Wanda Napier said. "He loved the heck outta his family, her and them kids!

Then some damned fool stuck their nose in and talked her into leaving him!"

Sammie Rae interrupted. "Gracie, the kids have been waiting in the car for a while. They must be hungry and tired. Should I take them to social services for the night?"

Both women spoke at once, Gracie saying, "Oh them poor babies! Bring them on in," and Wanda saying, "I'm their mee-maw, too, and my house is better for them!"

Sammie Rae backed toward the door, feeling as if the two could turn on her at any moment. Let the caseworker do the negotiations. Not everything was police work.

*   *   *

Back at Jesse and Annie's house, the coroner had Annie's body on a stretcher, covered by a gray plastic body bag. The bag was zippered up over her face—they were about to load her into their van and head to the morgue. The crime scene investigators for the county were swarming throughout the house.

"'Bout time you came back," Charlie said when Sammie Rae pulled up. He waggled a beefy hand covered in a nitrile glove. "Sheriff wants to talk to you."

Sammie Rae sighed and pulled on shoe covers. Inside the house, Beebe was standing alone, sucking on a lollypop—one of the kids must have dropped it, hopefully still wrapped. "So, Wheedle, you just happened to stop by here and discovered the body?"

"Well, sir," she said, "I was doing a welfare check. Annie came by the office a little while ago…" Sammie Rae tried to sound firm and assured. "The oldest kid had a broken arm, and I was pretty sure Jesse was why. Thought he was beating the crap out of Annie, too, since he'd done it in the past."

"And you didn't tell her to leave him? Get the kids away?"

"Sir, she'd already had little Denver saying he fell off his bike. Social services declined further investigation."

"Sure this couldn't have been better handled by a more experienced deputy? Seems like Jesse could've been good for our dealer arrest stats. Lot of fentanyl and meth in this house—you might have found that out by just coming here unannounced."

Beebe turned as one of the crime lab crew walked up and said, "Done here, Sheriff."

The burning anger under Sammie Rae's breastbone choked back any response she might have given. It mingled with the acid guilt welling up. Would Annie still be alive if Sammie Rae had kept her mouth shut, if she'd opted for intimidating Jesse instead of urging his wife to leave? And would that have been possible? Her experience was, little could be done to change the direction of a meth addict's rage.

As the lab crew hauled their cases of evidence and equipment to the van, Beebe said, without looking at Sammie Rae, "We best get your pretty friend out here to clean things up. Drug residue in the cupboards, blood splatter all around. Gracie'll be wanting the kids' things after a while, and she don't need to see that shit." He tossed the lollypop stick onto the ground. "You get any notion where Jesse went, be sure and tell me. Don't take nothing upon yourself." He paused to search his eyetooth with his tongue, giving Sammie Rae time to compose herself before he went on with, "Already set up roadblocks everywhere, notified the surrounding counties, but he got a good head start. The real search starts tomorrow. Plan to wear your walking shoes."

"Yessir," Sammie Rae said. "If you want, I'll call Darla right now."

"Good. Then run on back to the office and file your report." Beebe got in his SUV and pulled out.

Her phone rang just as she was about to dial Darla. "Sammie Rae?" It was Ray Ben. "You okay? I know they set out to give you a hard time."

"I'm fine, Ray Ben," she said, though nothing felt fine at all.

"They just jealous you found the body."

Jealous? Yeah. But it was nice to have a sympathizer in the department, even if it was only Ray Ben. His heart was in the right place, always. Anyone else would have said, "They set out to give you shit." He was sweet. Dumb as a stone, though.

Chapter 11

EARLY SATURDAY MORNING, Sammie Rae and Darla walked to the meadow behind the garden shed, planning to relax and talk out of Dolly's hearing. Sammie Rae stepped gingerly, her legs and feet hurting from three days in the woods searching for Jesse Napier, whose pickup had been found abandoned near the old mine. The sun wasn't high enough to burn off the dew, and the tattered badminton net sparkled with droplets like a spider web after a rain shower.

"We can't find hide nor hair of that lowlife rat bastard." She kicked a rock ahead of her. "Dammit, Darla. It's my fault. I should've showed up at the house every day I was near, just to let him know the law was looking over his shoulder."

"What good would it have done? He beat her up time and time again and she stayed with him. Classic, right? Asshole waits 'til the little woman's leaving and *BAM!* he kills her. And nothing's ever his fault—if you asked him now, say, 'Jesse, why'd ya do it?', he'd blame it on Annie. Or on meth. Say being crazy high was what put him over the top in his war against the world, as represented by his wife."

Sammie Rae kicked the rock into the bushes and turned to speak but Darla barely paused for a breath. "Everybody should've minded their own business. Maybe Jesse would have died from an overdose or in a deal gone wrong—Annie would still be alive." She picked up a racket that had laid in the grass for years, found another and handed it over to Sammie Rae.

"Back when we were in school," Sammie Rae began, "Jesse was such a star. Always thought he'd be one to make it out of here. He was so good-looking, too."

"Handsome is as handsome does." Darla searched the ground, moving the grass about with her racket.

"He's a big camper and hunter. Maybe he's holed up out there, somewhere."

Darla shrugged. "He'll turn up. Gotta remember, shit floats. Hey, look!" She held a shuttlecock up and batted it to Sammie Rae.

Without thinking, Sammie Rae snapped the shuttlecock back over the net. It wobbled as it traveled the air—too many of the feathers were missing from the discolored plastic. It had served its purpose during their pre-teen years, taking their minds off worries and helping pass time.

Darla missed a shot when the racket slipped from her hand. She licked her fingers, shiny from the breakfast sandwich she'd wolfed down at the Dunkin'.

"Go wash those hands for Chrissakes!"

"Wow," Darla grinned. "Like you think I need another mother."

"Sorry." Sammie Rae dropped her racket back in the grass by the shed. "Hey, maybe your hands are sweaty 'cause you're jittery about Lansing. I never saw you like that over a man!"

Darla rubbed her fingers on her sweatshirt. "Speaking of Lansing, does he know about Jesse and Annie? They told me at the lab there was enough fentanyl stashed to choke a whole herd of horses."

Sammie Rae shrugged. "Don't know; haven't spoke to him."

"You're right, he does throw me off my game—a bit. Lansing's for sure not ordinary. He's cunning, a hunk with them dark, pantherish looks."

Sammie Rae hadn't noticed anything remotely cunning or pantherish at the buffet. In fact, once he met Darla, he'd looked like a steer stunned in the slaughterhouse. Still, she upped the ante. "Sexy?"

"Got me sweatin' like a whore in church!" Darla laughed again but her high cheekbones flushed with color. "But it's not just looks, you know—it's the way he acts. Just imagine I took a big ol' chunk outta Charlie's chicken leg! He would'a just given me one a' his 'patented sex looks' and taken a bigger bite around the missing piece to establish his male dominance. But Lansing didn't say a word. Didn't play the game."

"Peeved you when he had the nerve to assume you were Cherokee, right?"

"Wouldn't be a man if he weren't halfway testoster-tarded." Darla said. "Anyway, ain't a game if he holds all the pieces. He's gotta give me some—on purpose or not."

"Your ma'll set him straight."

"You don't know the half of it." Darla looked up at the sun. "Time to get ready. Take your ass home and put on the dress we bought to wow the doctor. Leave your hair down—it'll make you look like an angel."

*   *   *

Darla's face puckered into a scowl when Sammie Rae walked into the Dunkin' Donut. "What in tarnation?"

"I just couldn't wear it. Felt not like me, like I was on *RuPaul's Drag Race*." Sammie Rae tugged her flannel shirt down over her jeans. At least she'd ironed it after it came out of the laundromat dryer.

"I love that show," Darla said. "But you gotta bait the hook to catch a fish."

"I'm not my ma," Sammie Rae said.

Darla laughed. "Your ma's hook stayed baited all the time." She stood and walked to the counter. "I'm getting a coffee. You want something?"

"Nope." The butterflies in Sammie Rae's stomach took up too much room to let even a well-chewed donut hole down her throat.

Darla returned to the table with her cup and raised it in a toast to the plateglass window. "Think he's here."

A glistening black SUV—with the word *DISCOVERY* above its front grill—pulled into one of the parking spots. "What's a 'Discovery?'" Sammie Rae asked.

Darla shrugged. "Dunno but seems both our guys drive some fly cars."

"Fly? Do people even say that anymore?" Sammie Rae said, then fell silent as the car door opened and Dr. Thaddeus Overton got out. His shirt was so white it shone in the daylight, rivaling the sun's reflection in his hair, but despite the glow surrounding him, he radiated weariness, the living embodiment of her cemetery angel. Despite the landscape, so familiar to her, he stood in such sharp focus that he seemed timeless, like looking at old View-Master slides. And Darla was right, obviously he could use a feed.

"Dr. Overton," Darla called as he pushed the door open and stepped into the Dunkin'. It was only a few steps until he was at their table. "This is Deputy Sammie Rae Wheedle, of the Lark County Sheriff's Department. From the conference."

His brow crinkled and then smoothed. As his lips moved, time slowed for Sammie Rae, and the "Yes, of course I re-member" came out like the adults' voices on *A Charlie Brown Christmas*: Wha-wha-Wha-wha-Wha!

"Why do you want to move to Lark County?" Sammie Rae blurted out as soon as he sat, and immediately regretted the question.

"Why not here?" Darla was indignant. "We got natural beauty. Good barbecue…"

"I'm looking for a quiet place to settle, at least for a while." He shrugged. "Maybe even forever. A really quiet, out-of-the-way—even isolated—country place."

"Well," Sammie Rae said, "if you want out-of-the-way, we got lots to show you. Best get a move on." She moved toward the door, pushing away the thought *hiding out.*

Darla coughed into her hand. "Like a coffee to go?" she asked Overton. "Something to eat?"

He smiled at Darla and shook his head, saying, "Very hospitable, but no. I just ate."

Dammit! Sammie Rae Wheedle, you should have been the one thinking of his comfort! She held the door for them, and they stepped out into the bright autumn day.

"Let's take my car," Sammie Rae said.

They started toward it, but Darla stopped at the sight of the battered, filthy blue compact. She pointed across the parking lot. "My pickup's over there."

"Why don't we take mine?" Overton said.

"But we wanted to show you the countryside." Sammie Rae said. "And the roads are kind of rough."

"You drive then," Overton held out the remote key to his car, which glistened in the sunlight, as did everything else about him. "It's a Land Rover. Can go anywhere."

"Yes! Drive, Sammie Rae. Dr. Overton can sit up front with you. Suicide seat's the best view."

"Always is!" Overton laughed and headed to the passenger side. Darla hopped in the back.

In the car, Sammie Rae discretely inhaled, checking for the turpentine odor Darla had described. But all she smelled was a rich, island scent as if he'd just arrived from a tropical paradise. It wasn't Old Spice, the only men's cologne she knew.

*   *   *

Overton was gracious but found the houses they previewed unacceptable. Some were too close to town, some on busy roads, some too small, and some, mostly the pseudo mountain chalets were, to Sammie Rae's surprise, too done up. "The renovations are not what I want," he said, "but it would be a waste to rip them out and start over."

Darla nodded. "Want to put your mark on the house you buy."

Sammie Rae peered down the road before pulling out of the last house on their list, a mountain-lodge lookalike she'd thought monstrously expensive at almost three-hundred-thousand dollars. "All that's left is the Henderson place. Been deserted for years and comes with over four-hundred acres. Not sure what they want for it. If you want privacy…well, no one goes out there."

"A lot of land." Overton lifted one eyebrow.

"You can get someone to farm it, if you don't want to take care of it yourself," Darla said. "But they might want a bunch for that big a spread."

"Don't worry about the cost. Let's go see it."

They sped along the main road. Sammie Rae was surprised at how well the Land Rover handled—and when they started down the overgrown and rutted dirt road leading to the Henderson place, she was in awe. The damn fancy ride could climb over anything.

As they rounded a bend, the gray fieldstone house loomed at the road's edge, its facade half-hidden by a tangle of vines. The building was grimmer and the location more desolate than Sammie Rae remembered. The ancient forest seemed to be closing in.

"The house was a stagecoach stop when it was built. They just pulled up and unloaded for the night on the way west," Darla said, leaning her elbows between the front seat head-rests, her warm breath on Sammie Rae's cheek. "But the railway got built, and then the highway bypassed this part of the county; ended any reason to come this way."

If he didn't like this house, he might not choose Lark County. The rest of West Virginia had plenty of places for sale and most of it could be had for a song. He might have said cost didn't matter, but no house hunter really meant that. Wasn't natural to not like a bargain. She added to Darla's sales pitch. "The county stopped maintaining the road, cutting down even on ramblers out for a Sunday drive. Peters out just beyond the property."

"It really is isolated," Overton said.

"People used to say it was haunted," Darla said.

"Just Darla's mom, to scare us from coming here," Sammie Rae said.

"Besides," added Darla. "You got a ton of acreage for a yard. It's gorgeous land. Gives plenty of privacy." The two of them sounded like an overeager tag team.

"Plenty of woods, too. Some nice arable bottom land…" Sammie Rae indicated those attributes by pointing the directions in which they lay. Describing the property was easy—it took her attention from his perfect profile, from the curve of his lips, from his eyes, whose deep green made her unsteady. Like she was in a rowboat on Summersville Lake.

"Sure neither of you get a commission on this?" Overton said. He got out to stare at the house. The roof was sagging in on one side and kids had long ago stoned the glass from most of the windows. But the thick walls looked solid.

They made their way to the front door. Muscadine rambled over the front, the vines alive with birds finishing off the last of the year's fruit. Sammie Rae pulled down some of the overgrowth to clear the way to the entrance. A flock of brown sparrows whirred into the sky.

"Wow," Overton said, running his hand over the huge front door. It was solid white oak, the marks of hand hewing making the surface richly textured. The latch and hinges were old and rusted and sported irregular hammer marks. He pushed with both hands and the door creaked open.

The downstairs was spacious; a massive stone fireplace was centered on the wide-plank pine floors. Part of the second story was missing—only the joists indicating its place. The roof above was open to the sky. A tree had sprouted and grown thirty feet toward the sun. "Butternut. Squirrel must've been in here, saving for the winter," Sammie Rae said.

Overton looked at the crown of the tree and the open sky above. "That squirrel's long gone."

"Structure looks basically sound, and the slate roof is still here," Sammie Rae said, pointing to the pile of mostly unbroken tiles on the floor. A distressing note of desperation had crept into her voice.

Darla took over. "The walls show old-timey skill in the way they're fit together. Would cost a fortune to bring in all that stone today. And you can't find big trees like two hundred years ago. None of the joists look rotted. Should be able to fix it all up, no problem."

"Yeah, no problem," Sammie Rae echoed.

Overton turned his eyes on her. She saw amusement in their depths. "Is that so?"

Her heart sank. "Guess it's too big a project."

"On the contrary," he said. "I'm going to make an offer."

When he turned away, Darla poked her and smiled, as if one of them had won the lottery.

They walked from the building. Outside, the sun was low on the horizon and autumn chill filled the air. A harsh wind blew down from the hills. "Brrr," Sammie Rae said. Her heart still soared with his words, even as she thought, *Stay calm, might be nothing in it for you.* "Should we stop in town and get some supper?"

Overton looked at his watch and frowned.

Her heart faltered in its flight. "Sorry, were you heading back to DC tonight?" From behind them, Darla cleared her throat as if to assure Sammie Rae she was still there.

He shook his head. "I scheduled an entire weekend to look at houses. Thanks to your help, the search is over sooner than expected, and now I can hole up in the motel, get a bit of rest. Hopefully, Monday morning the purchase will be wrapped up for my trip back. Do you have any suggestions for an agent I can use?"

Sammie Rae sighed and let Darla jump in. "They'll be so glad to get rid of this place, they'd probably meet you at midnight at a crossroads. We can call as soon as we're back in town. Guy's name is Donner."

"Like in Donner Party?"

Sammie Rae nodded. Darla laughed.

He stifled a yawn. "Sounds great, Deputy Wheedle. Might I take a rain check on that meal until tomorrow night? If you're free, of course. I'll need a general contractor, if I can pick your brain."

Chapter 12

"WAKE UP," THE VOICE on her phone said. Sounded like Charlie but she wasn't sure. "Time to get on the road. Head down Chap Road toward Van, then take Pond Fork toward Bob White. You'll see a roadblock set up and we'll be waiting there."

"What's going on?" Sammie Rae could barely speak as her mouth was sticky with sleep. The clock read 4:30 a.m.

"Just get going." It was Charlie. No one else sounded so smug.

She peed, struggled into her uniform, popped a few mints—stolen from the office stock of Walmart candy—in lieu of brushing her teeth, and went to her car. She drove with care because early dawn was the time of roaming wildlife. Hitting a deer would really be a crappy way to start the day as well as put a dent in the patrol car.

Her brights pierced the gloom until she saw the barricade ahead. She pulled to the side and got out.

Sheriff Beebe was standing next to a pickup with deer-stunning spotlights set high on the cab. A man in hunter's camouflage stood next to it. He looked shaken, his face sickly pale under the bright lights, shuffling side to side in the scuttling leaves, as if desperate to leave. Charlie was leaning against the patrol car closest to her and drinking from a coffee thermos. In the dim light, his bulk was surrounded by a halo of mist. Sammie Rae walked up to him. "You guys called me out for a deer jacker?"

Charlie took another sip. "Uh, uh, nope. Not *for* the hunter, for what the hunter *found*. You'll see."

Sheriff Beebe stepped away from the camouflage-wearing man. "Well, congratulations," Beebe said. "You got us the month's big case and now you'll handle it. Get your flashlight and follow Charlie into the woods."

The overgrown bushes made for slow going, even though trampled down—the path the others had used was clear but narrow. From the deep groove and the animal prints—mostly whitetail—it was an ancient game trail. The flashlight swung in Charlie's hand as he pushed low hanging branches aside and let them flick back at her.

"Ow! Fuck you, Charlie," she exclaimed as a leafless twig whipped across her left cheek.

He chuckled in response.

Wiping her hand on her face to check for blood, she missed him stopping and so bumped into his back. "Didn't know you cared," he said.

"Think you're funny, huh?" She moved to step around him, but he took her arm and said, "Don't think you wanna be first, Sammie Rae."

He shone his flashlight on a ring of stones with burnt wood inside it. "Seems like we found where Jesse was camping. And look—here he is." He moved the beam of light, revealing a body on the ground beneath the leafless saplings. The body lay prone, the clothes and flesh beneath in tatters. It resembled an animal carcass abandoned after the best meat had been taken.

"How do you know that's Jesse?" Sammie Rae whispered. The glow from their flashlights created a halo about the little clearing where the body lay—possibly on its back from the torn cloth it still wore. The halo dissipated as it spread, creepier than the total dark would be. Sammie Rae had the sense of being watched and yet unable to see if anything was there waiting for her.

The back of the head was turned to them, at a slight angle, with scraps of bloody scalp hanging from the skull. The cheekbone glistened white, damply reflecting her beam.

"Go on," Charlie said. "Walk around the other side. Just don't touch anything."

She shot him a look, annoyed he was talking to her like a rookie, and stepped with care, making sure to not step on pooled blood or other evidence. She looked down. The eye on the right was missing, but the nose seemed undisturbed as did the left side of his face.

"I think it might be Jesse…" her voice trailed off.

"Oh, kee-rist!" Charlie exclaimed and stepped carelessly over the corpse. He took a large stick from the ground and lifted the head a few inches off the forest floor. With the intact side of the face showing, there was no doubt it was Jesse. "Satisfied?" Charlie asked. "Okay, then, let's tape the area off."

The rising mist and eerie predawn gloom made the yellow tape glow as they stretched it from tree to tree. "Thank God, we're finally done," Charlie said. "I'm freezing. Could use coffee and some ham and grits. Eggs over easy." He took a few steps toward the road. Sammie Rae followed until he turned and said, "Whoa, where you think you're going?"

"You're not the only one who's cold and hungry," Sammie Rae said.

"Your crime, your scene. This mess is all part of Annie Napier's death, so stay and protect it—Sheriff's orders. Much more munching by the wildlife and there won't be any Jesse left—already ate out most of his organs." He turned around again and moved away, saying, "Crime lab techs on the way."

"How soon?" Sammie called after his rapidly disappearing back. The last view of Charlie's shoulders showed him shrugging.

"This is shit!" Sammie Rae said and kicked the ground. Now he was gone, she could vent her frustration without them complaining about her acting like a girl.

There was a fallen tree no more than three feet from the body. The trunk wasn't huge, but it was high enough off the ground to provide a dry seat—though uncomfortable with her knees bent almost to her chest. Sitting on it gave her a clear view of Jesse's remaining features and, seemingly, a clear view of her for his solitary bright blue eye, which was open, shining-wet from the humidity in the air. Perhaps it was just that he hadn't been dead long enough for it to dry out.

The morning mist was heavy, or it had started to drizzle—Sammie Rae wasn't sure. She hunched forward, pulling her collar up around her neck. "So, Jess," she said to the eye, "was it worth it? Is meth really so wonderful you had to ruin your life and kill Annie and leave your kids orphans? Not to mention ruining your looks."

Jesse didn't answer, though a hawk moth, attracted by the beam of light, fluttered above his face, its shadow giving the uncanny effect of flickering movement. She moved the light, aiming up at the tree limbs glistening in what had rapidly become a light rain. Drops on the ground stirred the leaves. It would be impossible to hear anything stealthy creeping up on her. She whipped the flashlight around behind, just to check. Nothing there.

She took a deep, loud breath, glad no one was there to see her unease, then shone the light back on Jesse's face. Sure looked chewed on. But what had done it and so fast? He wasn't even bloated yet. Beyond his body, she saw his tent lay sagged-in and his campfire, though cold, had no leaves on it yet. Wild dogs? Coyotes? Or a bear—they eat dead things, but they rarely kill unless threatened. It was the wrong season for a sow bear protecting her cubs and Jesse would never have stumbled unaware on a foraging bear. He was an experienced woodsman, like most in Lark County. Even with a speedball high, lessons learned as a kid would have kicked in—he'd have hung any provisions too high up for any critter but raccoons.

Maybe it was the Mothman. He could've pounced on Jesse from above. She shivered. *Maybe it was the same thing killing those folks outside of DC, just moved west to wilder country. Maybe Darla and I shouldn't have watched* Night of the Living Dead *again.*

Shame she wasn't a smoker. A cigarette would give her restless fingers something to do. Her restless and cold fingers—she'd left her gloves back in the cruiser. She slipped her hands into her pants' pockets and felt her flash drive. "Hey, Jesse," she whispered. "Did you know I have a dirtbag druggie hit list and you made it to the top? A local celebrity."

Jesse didn't answer.

"I gotta thank you, though, Jess. You saved me from being the one to deprive those sweet little kids of their daddy."

Without any movement, his eye seemed to focus on her. She heard his voice. *Yeah, Sammie Rae, thank me. But, if only you'd stopped by, my kids wouldn't be orphans.*

She jerked back, almost sliding off her seat. "Shit, Jesse, can't be you!" He didn't reply.

Crashing in the bushes, loud enough to be a bear returning to the feast, interrupted her discussion with the dead. She stood, teetering for a moment, and drew her weapon.

"Fuck!" a gruff female voice yelled. "Damn slippery leaves!"

"Damn Beebe wouldn't wait for morning." That was a man speaking. "Not like the corpse was gonna get up and walk away." The technicians had arrived, carrying equipment through the still dim forest.

"Over here," Sammie Rae called, holstering her gun.

They arrived in the clearing. The head tech, Sue Ann, easy to recognize—she was the brick-shaped figure in a mud-colored anorak. "Hey, Sammie Rae," the woman said. "You out here alone? Must be freezing your butt off while those assholes have a coffee klatch in their nice, warm cars. Donuts, too. I would have brought you one if they'd have told me about you. Weather turning nasty."

"That's okay, Sue Ann," Sammie Rae said, though a donut and coffee would have been nice. Then again, if she was meeting up with Overton in the evening and hopefully many times after, she should stay away from donuts. Coffee though— she'd need lots to stay alert.

The last of the crew stumbled in with equipment, and techs settled into their work. In the low canopy of the trees, birds began to awaken with a chorus of chirps and tweets.

"Okay if I go off a ways? Do a bit of private business? I been out here almost two hours," Sammie Rae said.

"Can't have been more than an hour," Sue Ann replied. "But sure always seems longer when you're alone with a stiff. Go on and take a leak." She didn't wait for a reply but bent over to take a close-up of Jesse's head.

Sammie Rae moved down the trail to a secluded spot behind a thick wild azalea, glad it was one of the evergreens.

The area beside the trail was disturbed as if something had moved through there desperately, carelessly. She made sure to empty her bladder far to the side, squatting in a mossy spot after checking for poison ivy. Thank goodness she'd grabbed some tissues from the box in her car.

She pulled her pants up and zippered them. The disturbance on either side was odd. Moving a little further down the trail, she spotted a footprint as if someone had slid. It was too smeared to be identified by size or pattern on the sole. Had Jesse been running from something?

Going back uphill was harder, what with the trail increasingly slick with mud, but she made it back without falling and told Sue Ann what she'd found. With a nod, Sue Ann directed one of the men to check. He looked annoyed—it had begun to rain in earnest and the chance of finding usable evidence in the mud was negligible. The other two were bagging Jesse's body, preparing it for transport to the county morgue.

Sammie Rae stood around, miserable in the now driving rain until they were ready to go. She helped carry the stretcher over the uneven ground, her boots squelching with every step. On the way, Sue Ann turned and said, "It's just a game the boys play, Sammie Rae. Don't let them get to you."

Back at the road, only the crime lab van and two patrol cars remained, her own still and dark, the other with exhaust steaming white from the tailpipe. Ray Ben emerged from that car as soon as they exited the woods onto the grassy verge, where the county had cut down the weeds.

"Here, I'll help," Ray Ben called, rushing to relieve Sammie Rae of the stretcher. Once everything was stored in the van and the crew were on their way, he opened the passenger door of his car and motioned her inside. "Engine's been running and it's warm already, but I can crank the heat up if you need. Meanwhile, I'll go and get yours heated up. I didn't touch the coffee or the breakfast my ma packed 'fore I left home."

Sammie Rae slid into the warm seat and opened the lunch box. Ray Ben's mom had made two sandwiches of fried egg with slabs of home-cured ham on her own molasses bread. Sammie Rae took a bite of one and sighed, her eyes closed with pleasure. A mistake. Imprinted on the underside of her lids was Jesse Napier's half face, his bright blue eye wondering why she hadn't continued their discussion. She thought of Annie, of the flies sucking at the moisture of her face. She lost her appetite. She put the sandwich down. Back in high school she would have given anything for Jesse to have spoken to her, but now she'd give anything for him to go away.

Ray Ben returned and got in the driver's seat. He looked down at the open lunch box. "Weren't the sandwich to your liking?" he asked. "I didn't have her put no mustard or ketchup on."

"It was great, Ray Ben," she said. "Think I'm just too wore out to eat."

"Think you're warmed up enough to drive home safe?"

Sammie Rae nodded, wishing for the first time she had more to offer him. She ran to her car, where the heat was high enough to put her to sleep. She cracked the window for fresh air and turned toward home.

Ray Ben followed her the whole way, peeling off as she entered her driveway. She no longer had the energy to feel bad—once inside, she drank a small tumbler of Dolly's best to ensure dreamless sleep and collapsed onto her bed.

Chapter 13

THE PHONE WOKE HER again, but now it was 4:30 in the afternoon. Darla's voice was chipper. "Hey, Sue Ann called and told me Jesse was found. What was left of him, that is. Sounds like he'll never hurt nobody again."

Sammie Rae moaned and rubbed her face, annoyed she hadn't called before falling asleep. Sue Ann looked for any excuse to call Darla—she'd crushed on her for decades. "Yeah, he was a real mess. It was a horrible night, but I don't want to bore you and repeat the story."

"Sue Ann made it sound like Jesse was ready for the gas-pump barbecue in *Living Dead*. Not to say he didn't deserve it."

Zombies ripping chunks from the young couple, slurping down their intestines like a string of sausages, was movie horror, but Jesse was real life. Sammie Rae yawned. "I should stay home tonight and Google those killings by DC. If I can make a link, I'll get points with Beebe."

"Oh, no fuckin' way you're bailing!" Darla said. "I don't care how pissy your mood. Enough of that—don't want to dwell on the negative before your date. Need help getting ready?"

"Stop it—he just wants help with the Henderson place. I have no idea how exactly, but it's no date."

"Nonsense. It's your job to turn it into a date. Look cute. Flirt. Nothing obvious 'cause he's too classy for country-slut stuff." Darla made a humming noise that meant she was thinking. "I'm coming over. Bringing some tops for you to try on. Low key—he's not a player; he's a noble serve-the-poor do-gooder."

"Then why don't I put on some old rags and go roll in a mud puddle?" Sammie Rae snapped. "Maybe aiming for charity will get me a real date!"

She should have known Darla would find that funny. Ignoring the peals of laughter, Sammie Rae flopped back down on the mattress. Darla would be there soon enough and there was no reason to get up. She had her own key.

*   *   *

When Sammie Rae left her house, she wore a silk blouse of Dolly's, stored away for twenty-five years. Nothing of Darla's had fit. It may have been old, but when she moved, its rich, iridescent green invited a closer look—a faint peacock-feathers pattern molded over her curves. She looked in the mirror over her old dresser and was pleased. The color complemented her blonde hair, and her complexion looked rosy instead of chapped. The fit nipped in toward her waist. She could pass for "curvy."

She almost walked past her car, unused to its color without the protective coating of road dust. It sparkled in the setting sun. Inside, every fast-food wrapper had disappeared, along with the unwanted mail and old magazines. The interior smelled fresh, and without a tacky cardboard fir tree hanging from the rearview mirror. Darla had cleaned up.

She waited for ten minutes, pacing in the buffet's parking lot. At last, Overton's Land Rover pulled in and he stepped out, looking refreshed and rested. And, with better color in his face, he was even more devastatingly handsome, kind of like Robert Redford back a gazillion years ago in *The Way We Were*. Except Overton's cheekbones could slice cheese and the angle of his jaw was every bit as sharp. But all his beauty made Sammie Rae nervous. Next to him, she felt as plain as a house sparrow, despite her shiny silk blouse. Since the rain had stopped, she'd left her coat unbuttoned, hoping the slide of silk across her bosom was alluring, rather than cheap.

Oh, well, there was no backing out now. "You look relaxed, like Lark County's already been good for you." Sammie Rae tossed him her best Taylor Swift hair flip and ignored her stomach muscles protest at being sucked in.

"It's very peaceful." He turned toward the restaurant.

Her belly relaxed a bit. "Most of the places to eat around here are fast food. You can't really sit and talk. This here buffet has lots of choices and the food's good. Not as good as what you can get in Washington, of course, but not bad for these parts."

"As long as I get to talk with you, the food doesn't matter." With a little laugh, he said, "You'd be surprised at what I've eaten."

With a fixed pageant-girl smile—which hopefully didn't look demented—Sammie Rae walked toward the entrance with him. She berated herself silently—how could she have been so stupid as to accuse him of food snobbery? The slides he'd presented, showing the area of Haiti where he'd worked, were full of mobs of starving people. He sure hadn't been eating prime steak and twice-baked potatoes every night— thin as he was, probably not even baked beans and Spam!

He held the door open for her. They were greeted by little red-haired Liddie Nelson, on duty again as hostess. She greeted them with, "Busy tonight, but we got room for you."

Sammie Rae scanned the tables, pointing to one as far from people she knew as possible. They draped their coats on the chair backs, and he pulled out her seat. "It's self-serve," she said, nodding toward the steam table. Maybe he'd he been away from civilization too long.

"Let's just sit for a moment, first," he said.

She slipped into her chair. He sat across from her and leaned forward, his blue-green eyes level with hers. Her heart jumped and her mouth went dry. *As long as I get to talk with you,* reverberated in her mind as she bided for time by taking a sip of water. He was so beautiful, a do-gooder, an angel!

Hopefully, the buffet included the smothered chicken and ribs. He deserved the best.

"Let me tell you why I wanted us to meet." He leaned further across the table as if about to tell her something private, something between them.

A fleeting thought urging caution was easy to quash. All it took was one look at his face. A few bits from her mother's romance books glowed in her mind—with her name in place of the heroine's: *His hand was clean and cool and dry, and her heart pounded harder as she looked into his remote, gray eyes. "Hello, Sammie Rae Wheedle," her worst nightmare said. "Welcome to Temptation."* Though his eyes were blue-green, and they were still in Lark County, if he was Temptation, she wanted to walk right in.

"Why?" she said.

"Well, I'm a stranger here and I'll need to have the Henderson place completely renovated."

Sammie Rae's heart jumped again, but this time it was only to make a suicidal leap down to her stomach. The conversation had taken a turn from intimate.

"I don't know anything about construction."

"Maybe so, but you do know the people around here. You can tell me who's reliable, quick, and honest. I can't be here to oversee—not for a little while."

"Oh," she said, leaning back in her chair. "You want me to find you a contractor."

"And help with the permits and all—you must have a lot of contacts in the county offices."

"Some."

"I'll come for a long weekend twice a month or so, but I need to be in DC area to wrap up some business. Would be wonderful if you'd be my contact person. I don't mean overseeing. If there's no competent contractor here, I'll bring one in from the city."

Sammie Rae's eyes skittered away from his gaze, lest he see disappointment in them. "We got to get our plates loaded," she said, pushing back from the table. "The good stuff goes fast." She waited for him to follow, but he didn't. To keep from turning back and looking foolish, she continued to the loaded buffet.

There were ribs, but disappointment and the previous night made her queasy at the thought of gnawing meat off bones. Hard to pull off dainty with ribs, anyway. She took an iceberg wedge and drizzled on a little ranch dressing, but, without anything else, her plate was sad, almost as depressing as she felt. She added a baked potato with some crumbled bacon and a smallish piece of chicken fried steak with sausage gravy and a cathead biscuit. When she returned to her seat, he was leaning forward, his arms on the table, holding his elbows in his hands.

She sliced into the steak, but its coating of glistening stopped her from putting it in her mouth. How could she have been such a fool? Thinking he was interested in romance? A man like him, a doctor, movie-star handsome?

He shifted in his seat as if he found her concentration on her plate disconcerting. "I'll be glad to pay you as a consultant."

That felt much worse. She stuffed a piece of meat into her mouth and immediately wished she'd chosen the undressed end of the lettuce instead. A capper to the evening would be puking on Dolly's silk blouse.

"Don't need to pay me," she said, as soon as she was able to cheek what was in her mouth. "I'll find you what you need."

"Oh, good! I hoped so—was looking forward to spending time with you. A lot of time." He leaned across again. "If I'm going to be living here, I need a guide. Someone to tell me about life in Lark County."

She swallowed, an unfeminine gulp. "There's not much to say. Kind of quiet around here—people left when the coal companies started going belly-up. Left or moved in with family. Lot of empty houses and nobody to buy them. Beautiful country but a lot ruined what with mountain topping, run-off polluting streams, mudslides. A bunch of broken-down people who used to work in the mines. It's pretty boring most of the time, but I guess that would be just what you want, right?" She could just hear Darla saying, *Great sell job, Sammie Rae! Sounds like friggin' paradise!*

He scratched the hair above his right temple. "Boring? Can't be boring for you, being the only female deputy."

Sammie Rae shrugged, pride tickling her insides. He'd said *female deputy* without making it seem faintly like a joke. "I did just handle a homicide and a suspicious death. Both drug related."

Did he stiffen a bit at that?

"Sad story. Maybe not as poor as the people you saw in Haiti, but just as hopeless—just two of so many deaths here. A couple, their kids left orphans." She hesitated. "Aren't you eating?"

"I'm more interested in conversation, in what you have to say."

Get him talking about himself, Sammie Rae! Use what little you know about him! "Why don't people leave Haiti?"

"Many would if they could, but it's not as simple as driving across the state line. No one's opening their arms and welcoming Haitian refugees."

She traced a circle in her gravy with a hunk of her biscuit. Strange. The more she told him, the less he appeared as the sum of beautiful parts and more as a whole. "Well, here it's having no skills but mining and small farming. No education. Ties to the land going back hundreds of years. Ways that don't fit in with the rest of the country, like neighbors knowing each other and relying on each other. Superstition and fear and insecurity mixed with pride in being independent. Some do leave and find work; others leave and just get further into drugs. And I guess drugs become their community, their replacement for what's lost."

"Drugs are their community—very true. Drop a junkie off anywhere and in fifteen minutes they've found where to buy. You were born here, right?" he asked. "So, your roots in the community must be deep—family and friends."

She'd never talked about herself with anyone who didn't already know her and her history. How to tell him about her runaway mother, her father and his pills? How to say her main support, her loving family, was someone else's?

"Does it all wear on you, seeing people you care about getting hurt?" he asked.

"Of course," Sammie Rae said. "But it's complicated, least when it comes to pills. So many folks were chewed up and spat out from the mines and the crap health care here. They're hurting and they need relief." Again, Darla's voice popped into her head: *Let him get a word in edgewise! Men like to talk about themselves. Find a way to make it about him!* "Besides narcotics, we got big problems with meth, cocaine, and crack. Haiti's got bad problems, too, right? I bet that got to be tough on you, even if you were a doctor and a stranger."

He looked slightly amused, and she felt herself flush as if she was playing checkers with a champion and made an obvious amateur move.

When he spoke, his words seemed aimed at easing the conversation for her. "Haiti not only has problems, but drug smuggling through the island brings a lot of drugs here, so the issue is relevant to you. Of course, the local Haitians don't make out like bandits—they're only working for the *real* bandits. Haiti has miles of unguarded coastline, a largely inexperienced police force, ill-educated and superstitious rural areas, tons of corruption, and a population with better things to worry about—from their point of view—than helping prevent American addiction." He gave a chuckle. "Things like getting enough to eat and some future for their kids. A huge area hasn't recovered from the 2010 earthquake. And unlike the poor parts of the US, Haiti's not surrounded by a wealthy nation helping control drug traffic."

"Not sure how well our government's been helping us." She stopped herself before mentioning Al Lansing, not wanting his shadow—or Beebe's—hanging over their dinner. "But you managed to do good there. How did you handle all the problems?" He was silent for a second, so she added, "Anything you say might help me 'round these parts."

He gave a little snort. "Your friend called this area 'America's Haiti.' Not even close but I get the picture. How did I handle things? Took me a while but I realized we needed to offer something immediate, something focused. Having a basic but reliable health clinic built trust. Folks came in for vaccinations and urgent care. When it came to addiction, we focused on speed, meth, and crack. Cocaine's too expensive for most Haitians."

"Same here, I think, though I never asked a meth head, 'Hey, you too low-down for something New York-y, like coke?'" The grease atop the chicken-fry was congealing so she took a bite of the biscuit to bridge the silence. *Don't do all the talking, Sammie Rae! Guys like to think they're interesting.* She wanted to tell the voice in her head to shut the hell up. But she'd never heard Darla pander to a man—to her the problem was always *their* egos. "Are you going back?"

Thaddeus shook his head. "It got to me after a while, especially when I started to make friends—real friends—with the locals and witness their struggles. I don't want to call it hopeless. Just say I was ineffective, and then... Well, enough of the past—now I want to be where I can do some good. I'm going to build a treatment facility here, out at the Henderson place. Already have some grants in place and a good bit of family money to use."

In Sammie Rae's mind a sky-writing plane buzzed, trailing the letters *STAYING HERE!* to blaze against a bright blue sky. She took an extra-big bite and choked. Damn biscuit was dry. A few sips of water and she was able to say, "Well, this is out of the way, like your clinics in Haiti and poor, maybe not as poor but pretty hopeless. And all you want from me is to help with the building issues?"

The full force of his looks was turned on her as his eyes, ocean deep, met hers. She wanted to trace down his forehead and the slight bump on the bridge of his nose to those sculpted lips. What had gotten into her?

"Being in government and with deep ties to the community, I figure you could help with referrals. Local support streamlined things on the island, so it should work well here. I want you to work with me. Hand in hand as it were." He reached across the table and took her hand in his, his grip firm, the skin smooth, but it felt familiar, as if the tendons and bones were known to her. "But what I want from you is to tell me everything about Lark County."

Chapter 14

"**DEPUTY WHEEDLE, I HEARD** you were out to Nelson's Buffet last night, is that right?" Sheriff Beebe asked, rolling his new chair from side to side. Charlie stood to the side of the desk.

"Yessir, I was." Sammie Rae wondered who the hell had told him but wasn't stupid enough to ask.

"So, while Charlie here was filing his report, you were on a date."

Think fast, Sammie Rae! She bit down on the inside of her lower lip—just the hidden wet, fleshy part—to divert her anxiety with pain. "Uh, no sir, it wasn't a date."

"Looked like one, from what I heard. The gentleman you were entertaining was real attention gathering. Seems our little Sammie Rae was out with a movie star. Maybe wants more than she can get around here."

The wheels in Sammie Rae's head were spinning. Someone had ratted her out. Most men might notice another man's attractiveness, but they'd never mention it. So, it was most likely a woman. Either a woman or Bobby Jessup—she'd always been suspicious of his manliness. She wished she knew, but as the saying went, "Wish in one hand, shit in the other, and see which one fills up faster."

Didn't matter who, though, what mattered was how she spun this. "Sir…"

"Don't 'sir' me too much, Sammie Rae."

"Yes," swallowing another *sir*. "Understood. Well, I apologize. After being in the rain for so long, just soaking wet, I went home and crashed. Slept for hours. Then I dragged myself out of bed—couldn't pass up the opportunity that guy represented—an opportunity to turn things around here."

"What the hell you mean, Sammie Rae?" Charlie looked puffed-up like he wanted his words to come out swinging.

Beebe turned red and pounced on Charlie like a panther on a cottontail. "Did I ask you for your input? Did I give you permission to ask questions?"

"N-n-no, sir."

"Told you all not to 'sir' me!" Beebe roared. "Get the hell out of here."

Charlie ran for the door without protest.

Beebe took some loud breaths through his nose. "Gettin' too big for his britches. He ain't sheriff, least not yet." He tapped his pen against his teeth, *clack, clack, clack*. "So, what do you mean?"

Sammie Rae said, "I went to the conference last month to get tips for us. Tips on how to handle the shifting profile of drug enforcement." She quashed a smile, not wanting to appear pleased with her own fancy words. "Remember? The conference I paid for myself? That's where I met the *doctor* I ate with last night. He ran clinics for addicts in rural Haiti and wants to move back stateside."

"Haiti, isn't that one of the big transit hubs for drug smuggling?"

"Haiti and Jamaica in the Caribbean. Least I think so." Sammie Rae could've bit her tongue off. She wanted to look more knowledgeable since the conference, but Beebe liked to be the smart one. Information had to be fed to him craftily, as if he were supplying it. Especially the everybody-knows-that kind of stuff.

"Haiti, the voodoo place?" he said. "Raisin' the dead with black magic? Every movie about New Orleans has Creoles and killing animals and chicken bones."

"Think so, sir, but being fair, snake-handling's still legal in this state."

Beebe shot her a look, making her clam up fast. "So, about the doctor? The one who kept you from filing your report on your very first murder case?"

"Absolutely right, sir. At the conference when I heard he treated addiction, I thought, just what Sheriff Beebe wants for our community—an alternative to locking them up only to have the judge let them out. Something real good for reelection. That's what I wanted to bring back to you."

Beebe fell silent. He began to clean under his nails with the point of his Swiss army knife. After a moment, Sammie Rae continued, "I convinced him to look at Lark County and left him to mull it over. Last night, he decided to rebuild the old Henderson place and locate a treatment center here. For sure, our involvement would show the federal government that Lark County takes treatment and enforcement seriously. Not to mention the voters." Before Sheriff Beebe could answer, Sammie Rae added, "And imagine the good local publicity if he'd open a small clinic in town for general ills? We've been short of docs for a while." She paused for a breath. "So, I need to work on him, you know, to keep the ball rolling. I can see how it sort of seemed like flirting."

Beebe pursed his lips like he was getting ready to call a flock of ducks in for the kill. "Well, I didn't think of you as a flirter, anyway. You say you were working? Well good for you. I was just worried—you know, about you becoming like your mother."

How fucking dare he? Sammie Rae willed herself to remain motionless, though she felt like she'd been slapped.

"Go on ahead." Beebe continued, "Go file that report."

As she turned and stepped toward the door, he said, "You losing weight, Sammie Rae?"

*　　　*　　　*

"Know what was weird, Dar?" Sammie Rae said, leaning against the counter in Dolly's kitchen. "I told Overton about my problems with Beebe and the need to cut down on the number of addicts roaming around…"

Darla was sitting on the tiled counter. She drummed her heels against the cabinet below. "Be careful—remember you barely know him. Believe me, lot of guys can't be trusted."

Sammie Rae rubbed her shoe on the floor, on a stain from a long-ago food fight, blackberry jam flicked from a spoon versus peanut butter rubbed into hair, continuing until they were both exhausted. All Dolly'd said was, "Okay, girls, when all done, get out Pine-Sol." And then she'd started baking up some cookies.

Who was there for her but Darla and Dolly? Even her pa was so wrapped up in misery, half the time he forgot his own kid existed—unless his pills didn't show up and then he called on her. Maybe if she could convince Thaddeus Overton to go into general practice, even part-time, she might be dropping off pills every month. Legally, no risk of the supply being cut off. She'd be a hero in her own home.

"Hey, I'm still here," Darla said, pushing her foot into Sammie Rae's waist. "So, what was weird? You telling the doctor about your work?"

"No," Sammie Rae said. "What's weird is Beebe was dressing me down about my late reports on Annie and Jess, and I told him about Overton, since someone told him they seen us at the buffet, but he never asked a thing about Lansing.

Made me wonder if he figured something out, if someone told about Lansing and me meeting up."

"Maybe he forgot because Al was only around a little while. But he's back now. Coming to dinner tonight."

"Tonight?"

Darla nodded. "Waiting until now to tell you, to make sure you'd come."

"Huh." Something was going on. "You're worried about something."

"Oh, Sammie Rae, I know it's sudden, but think I really like Al. And Mom can be so overbearing. She's liable to scare the bejesus out of him."

"Why would she do that when her dearest wish is to marry you off?"

"Well," Darla said, "if only that was all there was to it. But hell's bells, we're jumping the gun here, right? Who knows exactly what Al Lansing's game is, what he wants."

"I can guess what he wants, Darla. Just don't forget to find out what he's planning on doing here for the government."

Dolly interrupted their talk, coming in with loaded shopping bags of fresh produce. She put them on the table and rushed to give Sammie Rae a sweaty hug. "Good you are here! But why you not wearing a nice dress? Same old plaid shirt and jeans—he think you not interested in men!"

"I just don't want to get in anybody's way." Sammie Rae squinted in a broad wink and shifted her eyes to Darla. "He may not be a doctor like you hoped, but he's got a good job and a sports car!"

"Sports car? What kind sports car?"

"Porsche."

"Expensive! How much he earn?" Dolly emptied her bags.

"Don't know, but I'm sure you'll find out." Sammie Rae looked around for any telltale jars. "You put away all the shine, right? He is a federal agent."

"Don't worry! Only left out ginseng drink. Government man too stupid to know Korean shine! Now…" she dropped into a whisper, "if you not interested, make sure my daughter look good! Go on, go to her room."

*   *   *

Sammie Rae left Darla applying mascara and returned to the kitchen. All the clattering and chopping she'd heard had really paid off—there were more *banchan* on the table than ever, little dishes of pickled cabbage of course, but also radish kimchi, Korean sweetened potato salad, those tiny baby fish Sammie Rae would never try, and a dozen more. Dolly had set up a tabletop grill with fine mesh to hold thin slices of barbecued beef and chicken. A huge savory pancake was on the stove.

Dolly was at the sink, cutting sweet red peppers into thin slices. "One more *banchan*! Sweet vinegar pickles with sesame taste. Just waiting for this Al Lansing to come, then put meat on grill." She tossed the peppers in a bowl and put them on the table with the rest. "Darla?"

"Pretty as an aspen in the fall, Dolly."

"How your daddy? He like to come for dinner?" Dolly asked this every now and then, though Sammie Rae never said yes. "Darla's daddy on way to Michigan. We need a man in the house."

Sammie Rae laughed at her father representing the men of Lark County. "I offered to tote him here in the patrol car, but he won't leave home now. Not for nothing."

Darla made her appearance. She wore a simple sheath, shell pink, down which her inky hair cascaded. She looked lovely, more spring than fall. "Dinner looks great, Ma." She took plates and laid them on the table.

The slam of a car door made Dolly jump. She pointed to the table. "Think enough?"

"I'll see who it is." Sammie Rae stepped out onto the porch. The scarlet Porsche gleamed in the early evening light. Al Lansing was bending over the passenger door. He took his jacket from the backseat and slipped it on.

"Hey, Deputy! I'm here to meet some locals," he said. "Maybe have some good old possum stew."

Sammie Rae pushed down her outsized smile. Exaggerating her dialect, hoping her reply was just borderline indiscreet, she said, "Shucks, any ol' Appalachian mama just might make you some sweet possum meat! Come on, Dolly's dying to meet you…"

"Dolly? Like Parton?" He didn't wait for an answer. "You know, I'm part Cherokee, myself. In fact, my nickname growing up was Red. Can't wait to meet Darla's family."

"Uh huh, and they're waiting to meet you." Sammie Rae turned and led the way back to the house.

Sammie Rae opened the door, and they entered the kitchen. Dolly turned around, almost dropping her cooking chopsticks and Lansing paused mid-stride.

"Dolly," Sammie Rae said, "I'm pleased as punch to introduce you to Mr. Al Lansing. He's in for a treat—real home-made, delicious Korean food."

Lansing recovered quickly, saying, "Call me Al." He held his hand out to shake Dolly's hand.

Instead of responding, she grabbed a dishtowel and wiped her hands, taking a step back, saying, "Hands greasy."

At her delay, Lansing's face froze as if he had seen something Sammie Rae hadn't. She looked from one to the other, sure of his discomfort but uncertain why Dolly wasn't being her usual welcoming self.

Darla seemed oblivious to Dolly glowering at the stove as they took their seats. Too oblivious.

"Well, this is a treat," Lansing said. "Much more than I expected." He'd lost his cocky attitude—his elegant slouch was now a dejected slump.

Standing at the stove, Dolly cut the *panjeon* in silence. The air around her seemed to have congealed, like her blood curd soup.

Darla handed Lansing a small bowl of rice and placed a pile of beef *bulgogi* on the grill, saying, "Will only take a minute to cook."

Sammie Rae stayed quiet—Dolly's temper had never been turned on her and she never wanted it to be. Any joke about Native American food had died in her throat.

An awkward silence filled the kitchen. The only sound was the sizzling from the charcoal grill as the thin-sliced meat browned.

"Smells incredible," Lansing said.

As she placed a generous serving of browned beef on his plate, Darla said, "Add whatever you like from the little dishes." She pointed at the *banchan*. "The red stuff there's pickled radish and that's cabbage. But careful, it's all spicy."

"I'm used to barbecue," he said, smiling at Darla, "full of hot sauce." He picked up one of the tiny translucent fish from a *banchan* dish and gazed at its clouded eye. No one said a thing as he replaced it in the dish and took a bite of the browned beef and chewed. "Mmm…"

Sammie Rae risked a bit of humor. "Not quite possum stew?"

He gave her a wry grin, but to her surprise, Darla came to his defense. "My mom made possum *bulgogi* once. Didn't you, Ma? Got the carcass off Franny Hallowell's kid for a large jar of her mid-range."

"Mid-range?" Lansing asked.

Dolly slid the pancake's plate onto the table. "How you come to meet my girls?"

"Well, ma'am, it was at the professional conference a few weeks ago. They did such a good sell job on this area that I came for a visit. On my way into town, the deputy here *arrested* me. Apparently, for driving while Black."

Sammie Rae froze, her cheeks burning. Dolly moved back to the stove, shuffling in her house slippers.

"Aren't you sitting with us, ma'am?" Lansing asked.

"Dirty pans," Dolly said, taking the *panjeon* skillet to the sink.

Darla served a slice of the pancake to Al Lansing but didn't take any for herself. "Come eat, Ma," she said. Her voice had a hard edge.

"Not hungry." Dolly was clattering the pots and running water.

Lansing took a bite of the *panjeon* and put a large chunk of radish kimchi in his mouth with it. His eyes grew wide, and he began to cough. Usually, when someone claimed to love hot food, and couldn't handle the heat in her mom's cooking, Darla found it funny. Now she leaped from the table and got a glass of milk. "Thank goodness, my dad likes cereal," she said. "Milk's the best thing for chili burn."

Dolly watched her daughter without helping. At last, she spoke up. "Darla, I want talk to your friend. You take Sammie Rae, go get best *myeongsul*, for family only."

"No, Ma," Darla said. "Staying right here."

Sammie Rae's jaw muscles tightened. Darla had complained of her mother's interfering and domineering ways, but always behind Dolly's back, never openly confronting her.

Dolly turned slowly, her small round body seeming to glow with malice. She moved slow as a horror movie fiend. Lansing shrank back when she took two steps toward him. "You say our Sammie Rae stop you 'cause she racist? Not honest police?"

"No, ma'am," he said, shaking his head. "I was just making a joke."

"Some things you don't make joke. Spoiled American man looking to hear 'poor baby.' You know what it like to be taken from home and put in camp? Watch children starve? You never go hungry." She banged the rice pot in the sink. "You think you know suffering."

Lansing pushed back from the table, his hands lifted a bit, palms facing Dolly as if she was something he could stop. He looked at Darla.

"Mom!" Darla said.

Her mother didn't turn around. Instead, she said, "Slaves one hundred fifty years ago! My *halmeoni* was slave. All her family still slaves."

"Maybe I better leave." Lansing's face paled. He stood slowly and stepped from the table.

"I'll walk you out," Darla opened the door to the porch and led him out.

Without them, the kitchen was silent. Sammie Rae stirred a bit of beef into her rice just to seem busy. Dolly stood by the window and looked out.

After a moment, Darla came back. "I got to go for a walk and get some air," she said to Sammie Rae. "Come with me." It wasn't a request. Before following, Sammie Rae took a last bite and gave a last look at Dolly, who flung her head as if to say, *Go.*

The evening had become chilly. Darla walked fast, so fast Sammie Rae scurried to keep up. She didn't know what to say.

Finally, Darla stopped, clenched her fists. "Arrrrrgh!" she growled up at the stars.

"All your mom did was defend me," Sammie Rae said.

"Don't be stupid," Darla said. "She's upset I brought a Black guy home."

"Your mom's not like that." But Dolly had stepped back from Lansing when he held out his hand, her face contorted— it assumed an expression Sammie Rae had never seen before— shock and surprise at the sight of a man she'd previously been eager to meet. Sammie Rae couldn't think of another reason to explain her behavior.

"Oh, yeah? She's always going on about the Watts riots and looting the Korean stores—which was years before I was born, so what does it have to do with me?"

Sammie Rae waited, trying to figure out what to do. If only the evening was going smoothly—Dolly beaming at them as they stuffed their faces with *kalbi* and *dolsot bibimbap,* Darla staring into Lansing's eyes, and Sammie Rae watching him melt. Melt, become pliable, molded into becoming her DEA informant. Informant and maybe more. A present, gift-wrapped, to make her Beebe-proof. The chance of that was fading away like morning dew in the sun. "But if you knew, why didn't you warn her?"

"Hell's bells, Sammie Rae, if she'd had a head's up, she might have refused to let me bring him home. And she might have made sure my pa was home—imagine that! My only chance was surprise—besides, I figured she wouldn't be a total butthole. Especially not with you here."

"So that's why you wanted me to come?"

Darla sucked her cheeks in. "No, you're family."

Sammie Rae pulled a wild rose hip and chewed on the sour ball. "Your mom cooked her heart out."

"So?" Darla demanded. She put her fists on her hips. "Whose side are you on?"

"I'm not picking sides, Darla. You know I love both of you." Sammie Rae backed away. "But I will talk to her." She headed back to the house.

Dolly was packing the food into plastic containers. "Darla not coming in?"

"She will soon. Sad to see you two upset at each other."

"That man think sun come up just to hear him crow."

Sammie Rae slid back into her seat. "You worked so hard on this dinner."

"First time I see my daughter excited by a man." Dolly said and then laughed.

"What's so funny?" Sammie Rae asked.

"I was afraid she never have husband, never make me mee-maw."

"Why?"

"Sammie Rae, for smart girl, sometimes you not smart. Darla's pa and me both thought Darla was funny. You know what that mean. We thought she love you."

"We do love each other. Have since we were little."

Dolly gave her a cut the crap look. "You know. Like she *in love* with you, like those two ladies over in Tennessee by border, who make cheese for rich people. Darla never had time for anybody but you."

Sammie Rae thought back over their friendship. Darla had never done anything to justify that worry. "Well, then, you should be glad she likes Al Lansing. He's got a good job, a fancy car, and he's sure not a girl!"

Dolly sat down and folded her hands together. "Darla didn't have easy time being half-and-half—not fish, not fowl, not American, not Korean. How 'bout a kid half-half Korean and half *gum eun sa ram?*"

That was a term Sammie Rae had never heard but the meaning wasn't hard to figure out.

Darla slammed the screen door behind her. She looked at Sammie Rae and said, "I was listening at the window." She turned to her mother. "If I had a kid like that, Ma, I'd move away from here."

Dolly's face lost its color. "Move away? You think Pa and me did wrong, should have move away from here?"

Darla's expression softened. "I don't want to, Ma. I want to stay here with you and Pa and Sammie Rae. But I'm not you—you don't care what people think. And I'm not Sammie Rae—she wants to be family to everyone around here. But me? I'm tired of being the one who's different. I want someone who'll be different with me."

Dolly stood. "Let me go get best *myeongsul,*" she said, and headed to her shed.

"See?" Sammie Rae whispered.

"See what? See I love her, and she loves me? Doesn't change the truth. I'm an outsider, she made me that way, and now I get to choose another outsider if I want."

Chapter 15

AT HER DESK THE NEXT MORNING, Sammie Rae's brain slammed against her skull with the same ringing sound as Dolly banging the jar of *myeongsul* on the table—before she poured them each a generous amount. And then another.

"Hey, Girl Cop!" It was Charlie, who seemed able to sniff out her hangovers. "Got another missing person case. Missing persons, actually. You and me, Sweet Stuff."

"Cut the shit," Sammie Rae replied. "You know my name."

"Okay then, Wheedle, saddle up!" Charlie smiled, tossing his keys in the air as he headed to the office door.

"Where we going?"

"The Nelsons'."

Charlie clammed up, but just a mile down the road he said, "Went to the buffet the other night. Liddie Nelson was working her cute little tail off. Said you came in the other night with some guy, looked like a celeb—she was all twinkle-eyed over him."

"You jealous?"

"Anyway," Charlie said, "now she's missing."

"Liddie? How long?"

"That's what we're going to find out."

It was sleeting, an early winter storm. Surprising Sammie Rae, Charlie took the curves with care. "Tomorrow morning, everything could be covered in clear ice," he said. "Then we'll have a whole day of shit what with folks sliding everywhere. Crashes, broken hips, faceplants."

Why was he being pleasant and chatty? Had he decided to bury the hatchet—and not in her neck? Was his good behavior on Beebe's orders?

Charlie turned in at the Nelsons' custom-built two-story log house. The freshly painted porch spanned the entire length and showed signs it was ready for the change of seasons. The porch swing was missing its cushion, two chairs were covered with white duck fabric, and wood was stacked with precision on the left side of the house. The Nelson house had always made Sammie Rae embarrassed by the home she'd grown up in.

"So," Charlie said, "Liddie's boyfriend's missing too."

"Drew McCall?"

"Very same. Hopefully, they just went off together."

"Hope for the best, I guess."

Charlie sniffed loudly and opened his door. "Rumor has it, McCall's been shooting black tar. Moved up from snorting powder. The Nelsons are just sticking their heads in the sand letting their sixteen-year-old go out with a no-good over twenty."

"Not like you can tell a teenager what to do."

Charlie's tongue explored the space next to his lower molars. "Heard you were a little angel, though, when you were a girl. Surprising."

"Oh, shut up!" Sammie Rae snapped.

They walked to the house and Sammie Rae knocked on the door. Melva Nelson answered, her eyes swollen from crying. "Sammie Rae! Thank goodness you're here!" she said. "Come in." She noticed Charlie standing behind Sammie Rae. "You, too, Deputy Burnham."

Charlie lowered his eyebrows and, when Melva turned away, shot Sammie Rae a resentful look. She stuck her tongue out at him. They followed Melva down the wood-paneled hall, walls covered with photos of the Nelsons' wedding and then of her girls from birth to high school. In the kitchen, Liddie's father, Kenny, sat at the Formica table, his hands folded in front of him. The kitchen was cold, and though it was morning, there was no evidence breakfast had been cooked.

"Hey, Mr. Nelson," Sammie Rae said. She and Charlie stood beside the table.

Charlie took off his gloves and tossed them on the wooden tabletop. The Nelsons jumped at the sound.

"How long's she been gone?" Charlie asked.

"Last time we heard from her was yesterday morning. She was going on an errand for me—to get some Hostess powdered donuts." Melva Nelson choked back a sob and then gave in to it.

Kenny Nelson's face had a strange expression—pride with a faint apologetic cast. "Melva's in the family way again, after all these years. Gets these cravings."

"Congratulations are in order, then," Charlie said to him and turned to Melva Nelson, with a nod holding a hint of understanding. "So, you've both been around. You know what the kids here are up to."

"Yep," Kenny said. "But our Liddie's a good girl. A real good girl."

"I know," Sammie Rae said. "See her by your buffet working hard all the time. Sweet kid."

"Pretty as a picture," Charlie added.

"Well, thank you," Kenny said. "Problem is, lately she's been hanging around with the McCall boy. He's a worthless piece of crap."

Melva turned on him, fast and unexpected. "I told you not to say anything about him to her, and, if they ran away together, it's your fault for making your feelings oh, so plain!"

"Have you checked with the McCalls?" Charlie asked, holding up his right hand like a traffic cop stopping an accident from happening.

Kenny snorted. "Their kid's been running loose since he was in preschool. Bet they can't remember the last time they seen him. But yeah, we rang and rang, and no answer."

"Chances are they'll come back when they run out of money. Hasn't even been forty-eight hours." Charlie moved as if they were finished.

"Any reason to think she didn't leave of her own accord?" Sammie Rae asked.

"Not if Drew's involved. She was always running out the door to hang around his neck," Kenny said.

"Any reason to think drinking or drugs are involved?" Sammie Rae asked.

Melva shook her head. "Not Liddie." Her husband looked away.

"What was Liddie wearing when she left?" Sammie Rae asked. "Did she take anything with her?"

"She went upstairs to change, but I didn't see her go. Ollie was home. We can ask her." Melva rose and led them into the living room where Liddie's fourteen-year-old sister Ollie sat on a ruffled chintz couch, her face hidden in a wad of tissues. She was sobbing in great, shoulder-shaking gulps.

Her mother sat next to her. "Now you hush, Olivia. We're all worried about Liddie." She stroked her daughter's arm. "They'll find her, but they need to ask a lot of questions before heading out. You can't be much help if you're crying so bad you can't even talk."

Charlie remained standing, but Sammie Rae took one of the side chairs, pulling it closer to the glass-topped coffee table. She looked into Ollie's hazel eyes. "Do you know where Liddie went?"

The girl's gaze skittered away from Sammie Rae's. "No." The answer came too fast.

"What was she wearing when you saw her last?"

"Jeans…"

"The ones with the cuts under her behind?" Melva interjected.

Ollie's face grew darker, sullen. "Yeah, the ones you hate. And her red jacket." She drew her knees up and bent forward with her arms around them, as if trying to make herself too small to be noticed.

"Uh, maybe I could talk to Ollie alone," Sammie Rae said.

Melva Nelson shook her head. "I want to stay."

"Be more helpful if you didn't." Sammie Rae turned to Charlie. "Could you go with Liddie's mom and dad to look in her room? See if anything might give us an idea where she went."

Charlie hesitated for a moment, then his eyes darted to the hostile fourteen-year-old on the couch and his mouth twitched slightly. "Good idea. Mr. and Mrs. Nelson, how about you both take me to your daughter's room."

Kenny Nelson turned to go but Melva hesitated until her husband pulled her toward the stairs. As soon as they were alone, Sammie Rae turned to Ollie. "What do you know about Liddie that you're not telling your ma and pa?"

"Nothing," the girl answered, keeping her eyes on the toes of her stockinged feet. Her socks had a repeating pattern of kittens, making her seem even younger.

"Nothing about nothing or nothing about drugs?"

Ollie looked up. Her neck seemed fragile enough to snap with the sudden movement.

"Look," Sammie Rae said. "I haven't told your parents what I heard about her and Drew, but Liddie could be in serious trouble. How long are you going wait to make sure she's safe?" She waited but Ollie was silent except for sniffling, her ponytailed head bobbing up and down with each sniff. "Bet you got an idea where she'd be found. Come on, I know you since you were little—you always keep each other's secrets."

Ollie picked at the end of one sock, enlarging a hole until her big toe's nail protruded—it was painted candy pink. "Is that Liddie's nail polish?" Sammie Rae asked.

"No, she bought it for me." Ollie's sobs deepened.

"Liddie's sixteen now, right? Driving? Takes you places, makes sure nothing bad happens?"

Ollie nodded, wiping her nose with the sleeve of her corduroy shirt. "You think something could've happened to her?"

"Could be. All's I know is, I wish I'd had a big sis like her. If I'd had, I'd done anything for her." Something dropped on a rug upstairs—the sound made Sammie Rae turn her head. "Think they're coming down soon."

"She should've been home by now."

Sammie Rae leaned both her hands on the coffee table. "That's why we're worried, Ollie. She sure should be home. I know Liddie does drugs and I know she'd never bring drugs into the house. So, where do they go? You want to tell me or want me to tell your parents?"

The Nelsons and Charlie were talking in the upstairs hall as their cushioned footsteps padded on the carpet. "Ollie?" Sammie Rae tapped the table with both hands.

The girl's speech was rushed. "They go to the old mine. The one out near Cazy where the guy fell through the crack and died. They sealed up the entrance, but kids broke out enough bricks to climb in. I went once for a party. They got sleeping bags and other stuff stored there."

As the others came down the stairs, Sammie Rae stood and patted Ollie's hair. Then she straightened and said to Charlie, "Let's go."

"Where are you going?" Kenny asked. He turned to his daughter. "What did you tell them?"

"Just some general stuff about where teens go," Sammie Rae said, giving Ollie a brief smile. "Places to check out."

"We'll call soon as we know something," Charlie called over his shoulder. They left Kenny and Melva standing on the front porch, Ollie between them.

*   *   *

There was a steady downpour by the time they reached the old mine. Drew McCall's pickup was nowhere to be seen. "Yesterday was fine," Charlie said. "Not a drop of rain. If they're here, they must've walked from town."

"Or one of Drew's friends dropped them off and left."

They skidded through the mud to the bricked-up entrance. Enough of the wall had been broken out that it was possible to squeeze through the opening.

"Shit," Charlie said, turning on his flashlight. "One thing you can't do is keep boys away from a risky hole." He aimed the flashlight at his face and winked. The effect was ghoulish.

"Think you're funny, do you, Charlie?" Sammie Rae asked. His joke hadn't stopped her rising anxiety. The image of Liddie Nelson, russet hair pulled out by the roots, face half-eaten, swam in her mind like something rising in a fetid pool.

Sammie Rae huddled next to Charlie, rain running down her neck—the inside of her uniform jacket was soaked. He pulled out a few more loose bricks, leaned into the hole, and panned the beam inside. "Can't see a damn thing. You sure the kid told you the right mine?"

Sammie Rae pulled out her own flashlight and climbed inside. The stench of trapped smoke, cigarette and pot, lingered in the dank air.

"See anything?" Charlie called.

"No, but I'm going in further."

"Wait for me." He climbed in and stood next to her for a moment as he tried to brush the mortar dust from his pants, but the rain had turned it to muck. Together they moved a little deeper into the mine. The floor became drier as they went, littered with discarded McDonald's wrappers, Hardee's shake cups, pizza boxes, and tattered porno magazines. Sammie Rae tripped on a Subway sandwich, hardened into rock and surrounded by chicken bones. It was like a school diorama of a Neanderthal cave. Her nostrils stung in the cold mist.

The support beams creaked and moaned above them, and little clots of dirt dropped in the floor to join the other dust. But in that dust were many footprints, most made by waffle-print sneakers. Sammie Rae aimed her flashlight down the shaft. A mound of grayish cloth lay against the left wall. As she walked closer, aiming her light, the gray color changed to a mottled pattern. "Liddie?" she called. "Drew?"

There was no answer. She stepped slowly. When she reached the mound, she touched it gently. Beneath the cloth of what seemed to be a camouflage sleeping bag was a solid mass. She pushed a little harder and an arm flopped out onto the floor. It was unmistakably male, with a lurid tattoo of the devil. A flash of relief washed over her. It vanished when she raised the edge of the bag. Liddie Nelson lay cradled in Drew McCall's other arm. Sammie Rae cupped her hand against Liddie's cold cheek.

"Look peaceful, don't they? Not at all like Jesse Napier." Standing over the bodies, Charlie took out a cigarette.

"Put it back," Sammie Rae said. "You never know what gases are in a mine."

He looked at the cigarette longingly but put it away. "Heroin lets you go out easy, not raving like meth."

Sammie Rae turned Liddie's head. The cheek that had been on the boy's chest was intact, but blotchy, traced with purple spiderwebbed veins.

"Liver mortis—she's been dead a while. But at least nothing's gnawed on her. Or just not yet. With all this garbage, there's sure to be rats." Charlie bent over the sleeping bag. "Look, he's still got the belt around his arm. No mystery how these two bought the farm—must've been a gentleman and said, 'Ladies first.'" He lifted Liddie's arm. "Huh. She's only got two tracks. A beginner. Here, help me roll 'em over so I can find the works."

"Call it in, first. Have the crime guys come out, do things right." She checked her phone. "No reception. Let's go outside and try."

"Why wait? Might take them hours for crap like this—two more OD'd stiffs like all the ones piling up in the morgue. They'll just haul the bodies in. Meanwhile we can bag up the small stuff."

He was right. Overdoses with no sign of violence were low priority, even two kids like Liddie and Drew. All she and Charlie could do was gather up what they found. At her silence, Charlie said, "Cheer the fuck up, Wheedle. Maybe with the mines going again, people back to work, the 'sad daddy—family's better-off without me' suicides will drop off and your overdose pals will be priority one." His snicker turned into a dusty cough.

"Real nice," Sammie Rae said. "You're not coming with me when I tell the Nelsons." She didn't want Charlie talking to Liddie's parents or to Ollie. She doubted the Nelsons would want it, either.

Charlie backed up a few steps. "Hell, if you're not gonna help, I'll just roll him over myself." He grunted as he lifted the side of Drew's body slightly off the ground. The syringe, needle still attached, slid down across Liddie's flat belly. "Told ya." He dropped the body back with a soft thud. "Go get some bags from the trunk."

"You go," Sammie Rae said. "I had enough time in the rain with Jesse."

He looked at her for a long second and said, "Be right back."

Sammie Rae waited in the dank chill. Funny, her father had always refused to let his family set foot in the mine he worked, even to see what it was like. "Too dangerous," he said—yet here she was, looking at two dead kids, as the mine continued its soft grumbling, slowly filling with earth.

Charlie returned, raising small puffs of dust, obscuring the footprints that hadn't already been lost. But then again, the floor of the mine was crisscrossed with prints from boots and sneakers of all kinds. There would be scant chance any would be useful.

"Shame we won't need cleanup here," Charlie said. "Wouldn't mind if your friend Darla came while I was waiting." He pulled on a pair of latex gloves and opened a biohazard bag before crouching to retrieve the syringe. "Is she seeing anyone?"

"Who's asking?"

"Very funny. I'm serious." He stood and wrote the date, time, and location on the bag with a marker. "Wanna look in the pockets? I'll move her off him." He tossed another pair of gloves to Sammie Rae, then lifted Liddie's body so Drew's jacket and front pants could be reached. "Wallet's probably in back. But really, I always liked her—Darla."

"That why you'd always go '*Ching-chong, ching-chong*' when she walked by?" Sammie Rae put on the gloves and reached into Drew's pockets. She found a few joints, poorly rolled, keys, and about seventy cents in change. She dumped them into a bag and reached underneath the boy's slim hips, patted for a wallet and found none.

"'Cause I was scared shitless of her, that's why. 'Cause I didn't want nobody to laugh at me even though she freaked them out, too. She was so fuckin' *fierce*—freaked out everyone but you."

Sammie Rae wondered if this divulgence was excuse-making crap, but this wasn't the time to call him on it if it was. She swung her flashlight to shine the beam on Charlie's face when he called Darla fierce. His eyes were opaque and his lips shiny with saliva.

"Check the girl out before you get up."

She reached into Liddie's pockets and found nothing, searched the sleeping bag for a purse, without success.

"So, she with anyone? Day or so ago, I heard she was out with some fancy Blood. She going to the dark side?"

"I really couldn't—wouldn't say." No way she'd give the satisfaction of a reply. Instead, she stood, dusted down her pants, and walked off, tossing over her shoulder, "I'm going to inform Liddie's ma and pa and the McCalls, if I find them. Right after I call the office. Tape's in the trunk, right? Don't want anyone else bumbling in here." Her voice echoed off the rock walls as she moved. "See you later."

*   *   *

Sammie Rae stopped the car behind a screen of perny holly on the road above the Nelsons' house and took several deep breaths. No matter how often she faced a family with the news of a death, she was overcome with the feeling of being buried deep—far deeper than a grave—where the air was sour and ruined.

As soon as she could breathe normally, she pulled into the Nelson driveway, got out and walked toward the porch. The door flew open, and Kenny stepped out with Melva holding onto his arm. He looked at Sammie Rae's face and his expression clouded. "You found them, didn't you?" he asked.

Sammie Rae moistened her lips with the tip of her tongue and tasted the dust of the mine. "Let's go inside."

"Just tell us!" Melva said, her voice rising into a wail. Kenny turned and folded her against his chest, in the same position Drew McCall had cradled Liddie.

The careful words Sammie Rae had thought to use left her mind. They went to the living room where Ollie still sat on the couch.

"I'm so sorry," Sammie Rae said. "We found her, but it was too late."

"She's gone?" Melva asked, her voice choked. Sammie Rae took her hand as Kenny squeezed his wife more tightly— a good thing as her legs gave out and she collapsed. He slid her into the easy chair and knelt beside her.

Ollie rose from her seat, her hands fluttering like the wings of injured birds. "Were they in the mine?"

"They? Was Drew McCall there, too? He dead?" Kenny Nelson stood. His face darkened and he bent toward his daughter. "Ollie, you knew where they went?" He turned back to glare at Sammie Rae. "Did that little shit Drew do it to her? I'm going to break his fucking neck."

"Drew's gone, too. Ollie couldn't have known," Sammie Rae replied. Wasn't true, but they'd just have to deal with that another time. "Like I said, she just gave us some ideas where to look. Places kids hang out."

With nowhere for his anger to go, Kenny Nelson slumped onto the arm of his wife's chair. Melva took soft gulps of air after each sob. "How?" she asked, as mucus ran from her nose to mix with her tears. "How did our baby die?"

"I can't speculate on that," Sammie Rae answered.

Melva and Kenny stared as if she was betraying their trust. "What now?" Kenny asked. "Can we see her?"

Sammie Rae reached into her breast pocket and drew out the county coroner's card. "Call the number and they'll tell you when it's okay. And, of course, you can call the sheriff's office any time. Or me. You know my number."

Sammie Rae left the house, looking back over her shoulder at the door, wishing she was seeing signs of life, someone at a window waving goodbye, or the sound of a teenager streaming the latest music. But the windows stayed empty, eyes looking inward.

It was time to hunt down Drew McCall's family. She drove to Anthony's Bar and Pool Hall to look for his cousin, Casey, who'd recently returned from college in Pennsylvania.

All the single guys spent evenings at the pool hall, what with beer and plenty of easy girls hanging around. The music was loud, MC5, celebrating Fred Smith. The three tables were in use, the clatter of the balls breaking the music's beat. Sammie Rae wished they were playing country—it was easier to talk about death with country backing you up.

"Hey, Sammie Rae," someone shouted, but others looked up from their cues with annoyance. Understandable—she was in uniform and most of them had been arrested at one time or another. She wended her way through the room, avoiding the puddles curdling on the floor. The air stank of cigarettes, beer, and pot.

The dark corners were lit only by neon signs advertising drink. The pool tables were lit by the grimy plastic lights—

beneath them, the players seemed like sun-deprived creatures abandoned in the mines.

Casey McCall was nowhere to be seen, but his best friend Patrick leaned casually against one of the tables, his heavily tattooed arms folded, making time with a slender young woman in too-short denim cutoffs and expensive cowboy boots. Probably a slumming tourist attempting to fit in and be country cool.

"You seen Casey?" Sammie Rae asked, ignoring the girl sizing up her uniform with an amused sneer, the right side of her upper lip curled as if channeling Elvis.

"He just went in the john. But gender's no barrier to the law, is it?" Pat said. "Just follow him in." The girl laughed.

Sammie Rae headed toward the toilets, planning on waiting in the fetid air, but Casey came out before she reached the door. He'd cleaned up nicely, his once scraggly brown hair cut short, a spotless, pressed shirt tucked into his jeans, new muscles widening his shoulders. "Casey, I gotta talk with you," she said.

"Oh, yeah?" he asked.

"Two things. First, how can I reach Drew's parents?"

"Why?" Casey asked. "Not like they were loved by the *constabulary*." He laughed. "They didn't move for good. They're just up in Pittsburgh with my mom and dad. His mom's all eaten-up by cancer and his dad never was good at taking care of anything. This about Drew? He in trouble again?"

It would have been proper to inform the McCalls first, tell them about their son, but there was really no secret to keep, not in Lark County. "Drew's dead, Casey. I need to tell his parents."

"Dead, huh?" He sighed. "Not surprised. We used to be real close, used to play together all the time until he got into drugs. He OD'd?"

"Yeah." She bit her tongue; upset she'd told him. Added, "Looks like it."

He pulled out his cell phone. "Want me to call? My mom and pa are crazy about my aunt—always have been. Mom'll break it to her best anyone can. His dad could give less of a shit. Anyway, might be better coming from me."

"No, nice of you to offer, but I've got to tell them. Just give me the number. I'll call from the station." Sammie Rae wanted to tell Drew's mother he'd taken Liddie Nelson with him. They'd hear all about the deaths sooner or later, but the news shouldn't come piecemeal. Besides, she didn't want it circling back on the wires that Liddie had OD'd. Not until she could confirm it, obvious as it seemed.

Casey transferred the number. "You said there were two things you wanted to tell me. What's the other?"

Good thing it was dark and the blush she felt wouldn't be obvious. "I've heard real good things about the construction company you started. People say you're getting things done right." It wasn't people so much as Darla—she'd seen his repairs of fire damage. "On time, too."

Casey pulled his shoulders back slightly. "Well, that's a real friggin' change of topic!"

Sammie Rae felt her cheeks grow hotter—her words did seem inappropriate for the situation. "Sorry! I guess we can talk later."

"Nah, that's okay. It's not like there's a ton of building going on around here lately. Would have stayed in Pittsburgh but I couldn't deal with my grifter uncle. He was taking my parents for everything he could, using my dying aunt to do it." He stopped to look off into the distance, far beyond the walls of the pool hall. "Once my aunt dies, Pa'll make sure his ass is gone. But I appreciate you passing on the compliments about my work."

"You tied up with projects at present?"

Casey cocked his head, the better to see her. "Hope this means you got something for me." He hitched his pants up further, his thumbs in the belt loops.

"Someone's buying the old Henderson place and needs it renovated. I don't have all the details yet. Owner's gonna bring an architect and a structural engineer out from Washington to draw up plans."

Casey whistled. "Doing anything to make that old wreck usable would be a big project. Hell," he gave a little, tight laugh. "Drew and me were responsible for a good percent of the damage, back when we were teens. Who knew it might pay off one day? All's I'd have to do is get a crew together."

"Can you do that?" Stupid question—men would line up for the work.

He nodded. "And just for you, I'll make sure they're all crackerjack. Any idea of the budget?"

"I've been told enough for whatever needs to be done."

Casey's eyes widened with apparent delight. "Wow, great. I'm ready to go whenever the work can start." Sammie Rae moved to leave but he grabbed her sleeve. "Who's this fixing up the Henderson place? Nobody around here has the money for something like that." She gave him a hard look and he dropped her arm. "No offense, but is it the flashy dude who went to dinner with you and Darla or the mysterious movie star who was at the buffet with you?"

"For Chrissakes! Doesn't anyone around here mind their own business?"

He let out a roaring laugh, turning the heads of everyone in the pool hall. "Hell, no! You would know better than anyone, Sammie Rae!"

Chapter 16

AT THE RESTAURANT UP IN Apalachee County, Lansing leaned forward, risking a spill on the cracked linoleum—the rickety plastic chairs belonged in a backyard, not at a dining table. He wiped the grease from his lips with a napkin and dropped it on the bare wooden table. "Ahh, this is the best soul food I've had in years. Good as you can get in DC." He put his arm around Darla, seated next to him, and rubbed her back. "Wow, babe, who would have thought there'd be such good catfish here in Crackerville?"

Darla shot him another Dolly-like glance, the oh-no-you-didn't kind of look. His loaded fork shook slightly as he lifted juicy collard greens to his mouth. A lump of ham slipped off the tines, landing on his neatly pressed shirt. "Damn!" He jumped from his seat.

Just as Dolly had taught them, Darla and Sammie Rae dipped their napkins in their water glasses. But Lansing stepped back as if they'd threatened him with acid.

"That won't get out the grease," he said. "Got some Tide to Go in the car. Be back in a minute." He headed out to the Porsche, parked just outside the fly-specked plateglass window. The car was being admired by scruffy young boys, who Sammie Rae worried were leaving fingerprints on the glossy surface.

"Amazing," Sammie Rae said when the door closed behind him, "Tide to Go? More a little housewife than your ma! Who the hell wears a white shirt to eat at a place like this?"

Darla grinned. "A dude with a Porsche, that's who! Trying to impress us he can be both casual and country. Cute, huh?"

"Cute? What does Dolly say?"

"Don't know how much she knows, or if she's just waiting for it to blow over."

No way Dolly failed to see something was up, as Darla was wearing her man-bait low-cut top again. With a new necklace, a decent-sized diamond—or nice cubic zirconia. She blushed deep into her cleavage and squeezed her shoulders together at Sammie Rae's appraising stare. The stone twinkled in the fluorescent ceiling light.

"Oh, yeah! Did he arrive with that? Payment in advance?" Sammie Rae couldn't resist saying. Closing one eye in an elaborate wink, she mouthed, "*Babe*."

"Oh, hush up," Darla said without a trace of anger.

"Love at first fuck?" Sammie Rae rhythmically tapped the table with her spoon. "Tell me, tell me!"

Seen through the front window, Lansing was furiously wiping at his white shirt.

"Kiss and tell? What kind of girl you think I am?" Darla said, indignant. She turned toward the window before going on. "Maybe it's sudden, but I feel like I met someone…" She paused and looked at Sammie Rae. Her eyes seemed to click into focus. "…finally met a *man* who comes from the same planet I do. But listen—I told him about you and the shit you take at work. He knows what it's like to be treated like an outsider. He wants to help."

Sammie Rae's gullet spasmed with an upsurge of acid. "You didn't tell him about me and pa and Wade, did you?"

"Of course not. I only said things were complicated, like in any poor, rotten, drugged-out place. Said the boys were out to get you fired just because you're a girl. Anyway, he's super interested in Jesse's death. I said you were one of the first on the scene. He thinks Jesse's linked to the ripped-up meth heads by DC."

"DEA handles drug smuggling, maybe selling, but murders? You think he's gathering stuff to use against us, like another death to add to the stats?" Sammie Rae shook her head. A chill ran up her spine, and the musty odor of the mine filled her nostrils. But Drew and Liddie wouldn't come up in the conversation, not if she could help it. *Specialize! Be good at meth!* "Shh! He's coming back."

Lansing collapsed into his chair. "Think I got it all out."

"Praise the Lord." Darla smiled.

The ghost of a grease spot was still visible on his shirt, ringed by a water mark. "Looks great!" She looked up from the spot to his face, fearing he'd react badly to Darla's sarcasm. But when he looked at Darla, his eyes were shining, so dark in his strong-featured face, and his expression was ninety-proof adoration.

If only Thad Overton's face changed like that—the sculpted, graceful curve of the lips—just at the sight of her!

Darla nudged Lansing. "Go ahead, ask about the mangled corpse."

Sammie Rae hated the memory of the living Jesse, but describing him as a mangled corpse? For Chrissakes, they'd grown up with him! Could it be Darla was so into Lansing that her loyalty was shifting from Lark County? *Dammit, another thing to worry about.* "What do you want to know?" she asked, taking a forkful of food.

"You were on the scene shortly after the body was discovered, right?" His dark eyes had a searching look.

"Yep." Sammie Rae waited for him to ask more.

"The body was pretty chewed up, right? Looked like animals got to it?"

"It was."

"Huh. Same with the ones around DC. You knew about them, right?"

Sammie Rae nodded.

He twisted his fork in his hand. "Mostly a meth addict?'

"Jesse was a low-level dealer and a frequent user—as often as he could get his hands on something. Anything. No secret—everyone around here knows."

"Meth addict and general all-round abusive, wife-beating scumbag," Darla chipped in. When Sammie Rae shot her a look, she added, "Well, it's the truth. Can I taste your mac 'n' cheese?"

"Get your own." Sammie Rae took a sip of her drink since her mouth was suddenly dry. If Beebe heard she supplied the feds with information—without running it by him—she'd be out on her ass.

"Aww, don't sulk," Darla said, "Al won't say he got anything from you, will you, honey?"

Sammie Rae looked up to the heavens and mouthed, *Honey.* Darla wrinkled her nose and shook her head slightly.

"I won't. Believe me, I'm on your side. The government's done a shit job. Doesn't know how to stop people from wanting drugs. Can't seem to separate *want* from *need.* All they can do is bust traffickers and people poor enough to commit crimes to get their drugs. It isn't fair."

Who said life was fair? He was puffing out a lot of hot air, sending platitudes to Sammie Rae's ears. Being manipulated pissed her off. "Why are you so interested in Jesse?"

The waitress came by and asked if they wanted dessert—peach cobbler or Coca-Cola cake. Lansing looked up, smiled, and looked at Sammie Rae and Darla. When neither wanted any, he said, "We'll be heading out soon. Just the check."

As soon as the waitress left, he turned back to Sammie Rae, "This isn't the right time or place to be discussing this.

How about we take a little nature walk as soon as you're free? You can show me the country like you promised."

She shifted uneasily in her chair. Each time with him was a risk—what if she was seen with him but didn't report it at work? "First let me introduce you to Sheriff Beebe."

He held up his hand. "No problem."

The check came and Lansing paid. They walked out together, Lansing and Darla arm in arm. When they reached the Porsche, the children scattered except for one, a blond boy of about ten with rough-cut hair and the oversized feet of someone on the brink of a growth spurt. His tee was an obvious hand-me-down, handed down prematurely. The kid ran his hand from the headlight to the passenger-side door as if stroking a pet. "Nice car," he said.

Sammie Rae looked down the street at her blue compact, which was still recovering from Darla's wash and had only accumulated a few streaks of bird droppings.

"Would you like to sit in the driver's seat?" Darla asked the boy. She turned to Al Lansing. "Is it okay?" Her voice was Dolly's when someone tried to say no to food.

Distress crossed Lansing's face, but he quickly rearranged his features to bland friendliness. "Do I need to open the door, or can you just hop over the side like in the movies?"

Could Darla really force Lansing to let this dirty little rug rat in his flashy ride? The boy looked at Lansing from under sulky eyelids. He said, "Thought it was the pretty lady's. Not sure my ma and pa would want me gettin' in your car."

Lansing shrugged. "Don't want you to get in trouble with your parents. Let's forget it."

"Yeah, let's forget it, you nasty little runt," Sammie Rae said.

Darla took a step forward, her necklace flashing in the setting sun. "Nobody's gonna tell on you to your parents. Just imagine telling your friends—I saw how all a' them looked at it." She smiled at him. "I'll stay right here and make sure everything's okay."

The kid hesitated, looked down the block. Darla held her hand out to Sammie Rae and said, "Give me your badge." Her eyes told Sammie Rae she wanted immediate cooperation.

Sammie Rae fished the badge from her pocket and handed it to Darla, who crouched down to the kid's level. "This here lady is a deputy down in Lark. She's got a lot of friends around here in law enforcement and anybody gives you any guff, she'll be on him like a fly on shit. Get on in. Sit on those leather seats. Mess with the steering wheel. Go ahead, be double-oh-seven."

The boy looked from Darla to Sammie Rae and then back again, avoiding Al's eyes. Then his mouth opened in a grin. "Sure thing!" He grabbed the top of the car's door and scrambled up the side, his sneakers leaving muddy smears. Lansing tensed but didn't move.

The boy slid into the driver's seat and turned the wheel, seeming to shed years and attitude as he leaned forward and made *vroom, vroom* noises.

Sammie Rae whispered in Darla's ear. "You just flexing your muscles?"

"Want to give you the chance to talk with Al," was whispered back.

Sammie Rae straightened and said, "Know what?" to Lansing. Curiosity was gnawing at her, fighting with distrust. "I don't have to be back for any reason, why don't we lean up against that there closed laundromat and chat? No one around to listen in and Darla's keeping an eye on the car."

With a smug smile, Darla looked from Sammie Rae to Lansing and back again. "Yeah, good idea." Using the shiny car, she'd manipulated them into being conspirators, if not friends. "I'll stay right here and make sure there's no monkey business." She dropped her voice. "The glove box is locked, right?"

"Sure." Lansing's jaw muscles bulged; his teeth tightly clenched. Letting the boy sit in the car was Darla's idea, but Lansing had caved and now it was too late.

"You two'll have time to talk, get to know each other." She gave Lansing a peck on the cheek, and, reluctantly, he crossed the sidewalk with Sammie Rae.

"So, Jesse's death?" Sammie Rae leaned against the laundromat's wall.

"Two reasons I'm interested. One is that the cases around DC haven't been solved. Is this a copycat or has the killer moved? Second is more personal—one of the Washington victims was someone I knew since I was a kid. Face was half-eaten, and the rest of the body wasn't in the best of shape. Was this Jesse in the same condition?"

"Was your friend, was he…" Sammie Rae paused to consider her words. "…or she, a relative?"

"He. Someone I spent my summer vacations with, in Louisiana—my grandmother saw a small town as the antidote for a kid faced with big-city crime, drugs, and being disrespectful. Gran didn't want me to turn out junkie like my mom. At sixteen my friend fell in with a girl, whose mother fancied herself a *mambo*…"

"Mambo? Some old dance?"

Lansing laughed. "Not a dance—a voodoo healer. My friend got real into it. Took it away with him, all the way back to New York. The people he hung with had ties to Florida and Haiti. They started dealing with a *bokor*, a Haitian sorcerer, and voodoo drugs. But meth was more profitable and easier to come by, so they dropped the religious pretext. And for my friend, the adage was true: if you sell meth, you get into meth."

Haiti? Voodoo? Jesse's murder in Lark County, coming from Washington, DC? Overton's face flashed in her mind. "We got a saying in these parts, 'If you wallow with pigs, expect to get dirty.'"

Darla opened the car door. The kid hopped out and ran off.

"My friend was the first death—a tabloid called it 'voodoo murder,' claiming a Haitian drug zombie ate his body. We quashed that, saying the rag was racist, calling it voodoo just because he was Black. Told the editor we were wise to his own coke habit." He looked down the block at the disappearing boy. "Any chance there's a pattern, it would sure be helpful to have the autopsy report for Napier."

Darla walked over. "Done talking? I've had enough car-guarding for the day."

"We haven't gotten to Jesse yet," Sammie Rae said. She turned to Lansing. "I don't have the report from the medical examiner. Believe it or not, we got one of them around here, though they've been backed up for a year. But before I share anything official with you, I got to introduce you to Sheriff Beebe. Maybe just to save my ass."

"Okay," Lansing said as he walked to the car, opened the trunk, pulled out a small bucket with cleaning rags and spray bottles, and began furiously wiping down the leather seats.

Sunk deep in thought, Sammie Rae remained leaning against the laundromat, gazing in at the soap powder dispensing machine. *Overton was in Haiti recently. Could something have followed him here? What has he been up to?*

She wasn't ready to share her concerns with a federal agent.

"Wake up!" Darla nudged her. "Look at him over there, cleaning like a madman!" She pressed close to speak to Sammie Rae quietly. "Just got a call about a minor housefire. Owner needs me—soot and water after the fire department.

Anyway, if I stay gone too late, I'll just get shit from my ma. She's been sniffing on me when I get home. Last night I asked if she was trying to replace Boozer. Carry me back?"

"'Course, though it'll be a big step down from riding in that!" Sammie Rae nodded at the Porsche. Its side was apparently being sterilized.

"Hey, Honey," Darla called. "It's cool with Sammie Rae to give me a ride home."

He lifted his head. "Was looking forward to tonight, but I got to be in Frederick in the morning, anyway. I'll call you, same time as usual unless I get hung up."

Sammie Rae and Darla waved goodbye and walked a few car lengths to the battered blue compact. The door creaked when Sammie Rae opened it. "Not as bad to ride in as before you cleaned it," she said. "I added this," and tapped the new air freshener, which spun like a green pinwheel.

Darla turned on the radio to her ma's favorite country station. She didn't say a word, her mind obviously on Al Lansing. Sammie Rae waited until they were about halfway home, when, bursting with unspoken thoughts, she said, "Nice of him to let that kid in his car."

"Not his car," Darla answered. "Seized property. But yeah, nice." She lapsed back into silence.

"Really into him, huh? Thinking of leaving and moving away?" The wintery, leafless trees always made Sammie Rae nostalgic. Right now, she was nostalgic for the time before Haiti and voodoo zombies and handsome men. "But you love your ma."

Darla scratched her head. "Yeah. I do love her. And I miss talking to her. Been giving me the silent treatment."

Sammie Rae laughed. "Silent? Dolly? No way!" She turned silent as a semi roared by, encroaching on their side of the road. She longed to go after the truck, be the deputy, face them down with a lecture and a ticket. "You'll have to find a way to worm yourself back into her good graces. Want me to come over and mediate?"

"Maybe."

"Good, 'cause I can't live here without you." The thought nauseated her.

"Might have to," Darla said.

"That serious already?" In Sammie Rae's mind, though abrupt relationships were almost as common as abrupt break-ups, they were often more violent.

"Hmm, could be. But relax. I know you're staying put— your pa's here and your dreamboat's sailing into town. But you're my best friend. My sister. I never want to go nowhere you ain't." Darla turned the radio down. "And I don't wanna go where my business ain't." She dropped the accent and Sammie Rae knew that meant she was too troubled to keep up the joke. "Hell, don't want to start over in a place with big competition, don't want to be dependent on a man—but right now, I do want to be with him."

"Well, when you're sure, better start looking at places between here and DC. We'll just put a lot of miles on our cars." That was only part of the problem. "You think your ma'll ever accept him?"

"She'll just have to." Darla said glumly. "Maybe you'll convince her of that."

It'll go over like a turd in a punch bowl. Sammie Rae decided to change the subject. "I'm curious, when your ma was ragging on Lansing, what did she mean? That her *hal*-something was a slave."

"*Halmeoni.* Means grandma."

"Really seemed to be something that stuck in her craw."

Darla heaved a huge sigh. "God, I hate all that old stuff. Bubbles up like tar on a summer day, turning everything into sticky, smelly shit. But okay, here goes. Ma's grandma, who I never met, was a comfort woman."

"What's that?"

"My ma will kill me if she found out I told anyone," Darla said. "She's embarrassed about it. Doesn't know I know—my dad told me years ago and swore me to secrecy."

"Come on," Sammie Rae said. "It's me you're talking to!"

"Okay, here goes." Darla held her hand up in the air, moving it down notch by notch as she went through her story. "My great-grandma, Mom's grandma, was fourteen when the Japanese forced her into being a sex slave for their soldiers. When she returned after the war, she had my grandma with her, a half-Japanese baby. The village shunned her for being the enemy's whore and having a mixed-breed bastard." Darla paused to uncap a bottle of water and take a sip. "Her mother was dead by then, but her father and brothers demanded she abandon the baby to die. When she wouldn't, he sold her as a slave to another family. The Korean War gave her the opportunity to escape. She found a husband, a night soil collector. You know what that is?"

Sammie Rae shook her head. The word *whore* stopped her dead—that's what the kids whispered in the schoolyard about her ma, what her pa said and, sometimes, when she felt really betrayed, what she thought herself. Her eyes were fixed on the road.

"There was no indoor plumbing, just like most of Lark County back then. They used pots at night—he collected what those pots held."

"Some places around here still do the same, but nobody collects the shit. What the hell for?"

"Fertilizer. Anyway, shit-smell aside, turns out Great-Grandma was the lucky one of the family. That shit collector took her to his village, which, after that war, was just south enough to be on the good side of the DMZ. The rest of her family was stuck in the Communist paradise of North Korea. But wasn't all like paradise—her husband beat her, and every time he did, he called her a whore."

"Did he adopt your grandma?" Sammie Rae said.

"Take the little bastard as his? Hell, no."

"And that baby's baby was Dolly!"

Darla nodded. "And though she was only a quarter Japanese soldier and a quarter comfort woman, she was lucky an American soldier was too dumb to understand the shame."

Someone sped around them, passing on a curve in a no-passing zone and honking.

"Poor Dolly," Sammie Rae said. "Explains a lot."

"You think so?" Darla asked after slugging down more water. The talking seemed to have made her throat dry. "Does that explain why I'm supposed to have all that shit affect my life? What the hell did I have to do with her history? The little girl my mom used to be is long gone. She's a happy wife with a husband who never gave a crap about her grandma's past."

What good would protesting do, saying Dolly adored her daughter and only wanted to protect her? Or saying Dolly was lonely and missed having a big family? Darla was unwilling to pay heed to Dolly's pain. One look at Darla's face, set in anger, convinced Sammie Rae to keep her big mouth shut.

Chapter 17

"**WHAT I OWE THIS HERE** visit to, Sammie Rae?" her father said as she walked down the drive. He pointed his chin toward the road. "Left your car."

"Well, Pa, the last time I drove all the way down the tailpipe got knocked off." Sammie Rae stepped onto the porch. "Wish you'd let Beau Conlon grade the hell out of the drive."

"And I wish you'd bought a pickup like I tole you, 'stead of your little piece of crap. Coulda got you a good used one from my friend Merc."

"Don't start that again—this was what I could afford. And I can't be driving a vehicle with the VINs filed down." She paused to look him over. "Why you sitting out here all wrapped in your blanket?"

He rocked her mother's old porch rocker a few more times. "Didn't you notice it's colder than a well-digger's ass? Winter coming on."

She sighed. "Why ain't you sitting inside by the fire, then? I laid in plenty of wood."

"And I do thank you. You're a good daughter. Now if you'd only get my old truck running, I'd be mighty grateful."

"Come on, you know you're in no shape to drive." She settled into the other rocker. "Stiff as an old board, crippled in the hands, not to mention popping Oxys like they was candy."

He moved his mouth as if working on an all-day sucker.

"You're mad," she said. "You always do that when you're mad."

He moved his jaws faster, glaring off into the distance. A spot of red appeared at the top edge of the blanket wrapped around his hunched shoulders. The spot grew larger and a drop rolled down the cloth.

"What the blazing hell?" Sammie Rae jumped up and grabbed the blanket's edge. He tried to stop her, but his hands didn't open in time. She pulled gently at first, then yanked the cloth away from his neck. An oozing line of blood ran from his chin to his earlobe.

"Mind your own business, Sammie Rae Wheedle." He put his hand up to cover the wound. "Just a shallow nothing."

"No, you're hurt!" How did an old man living alone with so little contact with people, so little of value, get into so much trouble? "What happened?"

He *humphed* and looked away.

"I better dress it right." She went to the kitchen drawer where she'd stockpiled gauze and paper tape to fix up his bumps and skin tears.

When she returned, he said, "Feels a little swollen. Maybe you should get that mountain tobacco stuff."

"Arnica, Pa. The cream I got you."

"That's what that hippie shit is? Well, I'll be."

She fetched the cream and dressed his neck, batting his hands away. "Now tell me how you got this and no bullshit. Doesn't look like a cut—kind of wide and shallow like a bullet grazed you." She put her fists on her knees and leaned forward to stare into his eyes. "You're going to tell me what the hell went on."

"First get me my pills."

"No. Once you have them, you won't give a crap. Tell me first."

"Okay, okay. I'm a-telling you now. The truth, I swear! Hazie Jacobs called me this morning."

"Hazie?" Sammie Rae didn't know of any women friends of her pa's. Not to be calling him on the phone.

"Don't interrupt. She rang me up, said there was some suspicious activity goin' on at the old Quonset hut her husband bought years ago. As I recollect, he got a real good deal, but you know the Jacobs men, they let everything go to shit. The hut's solid but it's rusty as heck…"

"Pa, how the living hell did you get shot?"

Her father chuckled. "Went over by Hazie's place…"

"How'd you get there? Somebody pick you up?"

"Nope. Would've been safer if I'd've had a working car, but someone didn't see fit to make sure I had one." He paused for effect, his expression smarmy, two degrees above sly. "You know that riding mower you bought me when you got hired on at the county? Still works if you put a little gas in it." He waggled a finger at her. "Somebody forgot I always keep a can."

Driving the mile, probably pulling slowly to the side to trade insults with irate drivers—no wonder he and Wade got along so good. It had been years since her pa had touched that mower.

"Yep, fired up my ride, wrapped my blanket around me for being warm and to keep my rifle outta sight, got to Hazie's. She drove from there to the hut in question and then we went on foot. Good thing she still had her husband's walker—couldn't bring mine on the mower and the cane wouldn't do much good on rough ground."

"The gunshot?" She was losing patience. A riding mower on the state road and probably high as a kite on extra OxyContin to bear the jolting. A lunatic, elderly knight in armor riding to save a scrawny elderly widowed damsel in distress. Last she'd seen Hazie, the woman resembled a plucked pullet, all saggy, pimply skin over tiny bones.

"Near the Quonset, I see guys loading plastic bags onto a truck. Bunch a' guys but not from around here—two of 'em was black as night and the other light-skinned, maybe Mexican." His voice sped up, excited to relive the incident. "Then they see me and fire off one shot. Wings me. Hazie screams and turns out her son, that no-good Johnny Lee, is with them and he yells out, 'Hold on! It's just my ma and the old loony from up the road.' Peeve me no end. I'm not old, not yet! Good thing he stopped them 'cause I got my aim on one a' them by then. Self-defense all the way."

Her pa was getting too enamored with self-defense as an excuse for foolishness.

"Then you hightail out of there like two gimped-up snails?" Was he demented? She pictured him trying to escape gunshots, taking a wincing step, moving the walker, the ground uneven and littered with sticks and slippery leaves. "Besides, maybe you're not old yet, but I'd sure as shit like you to be old one day."

"Well, they gave up on taking potshots at us. Maybe they saw I was armed. I'm still a good enough shot to bag one or two before they stopped me. Then three a' them hopped in the cab and took off, leaving Johnny Lee to close up."

"Lucky you didn't get killed." Shit, now she'd have to get Darla to help haul the mower away. "I'm heading there to look things over and report to the sheriff."

"No, you ain't, Sammie Rae. That's Hazie's son you're talking about, worthless piece of crap though he is. I owe her too much for you to get him arrested. He gets hauled off to prison, who's gonna support her? I barely got a pot to piss in."

Owe her? What did he owe her? She looked straight into his eyes and he colored like the maples before their leaves dropped. Oh, my *God!* He might be endlessly pining for her mother, but sometime or other, the sneaky old bastard and Hazie'd been warming each other's bones.

"Okay, Pa. None of my business, though I ought to report your wound. All gunshots get reported."

"Hunting accident. Guy never saw me, and you wasn't there." He smiled briefly before worry reclaimed his features. "Promise not to? Don't make me lie to Beebe—always went the other way."

She blew out a big breath and promised. She checked his wound and went back to her car. As soon as her father's place was out of sight, she headed to Hazie's.

*   *   *

The Quonset hut wasn't hard to find, though Hazie's late husband had placed it down a dip in the land behind some oaks. A narrow trace, wide enough for a panel truck, wove between the trunks. It was as rutted and rocky as her pa's drive. She pulled to the shoulder and got out, wishing she had her holster on, feeling she was loony as her old man.

Sure enough, in the soft dirt were the four round marks of a walker, with shuffling footprints between them and more shuffling footprints, but smaller, off to the side. Hazie. Some of these tracks had been erased by tire marks but she didn't need to follow them. The old folk would have gone up the trace until they had to venture into the much more uneven ground between the trees. Didn't matter—where would this lead but to the hut? It was on Hazie's land and her house was an eighth of a mile down the road.

Continuing along, she froze at the crack of a stick breaking and the irregular sound of a poorly tuned engine. *Shit again!*

She hadn't told anyone where she was going, not even her pa, who'd be higher than buzzards looking for a corpse by now.

She stepped off the trace and hid behind a loblolly pine, hoping it wasn't too puny to hide her. A pickup, black with rusted fenders, drove by, bouncing in and out of the ruts and puddles. Johnny Lee was driving. Sammie Rae heaved a sigh of relief as the vehicle continued toward the road. She started moving again.

Another thirty feet and she remembered her car was parked on the road by the entrance to the trace. What an idiot she'd been. And the trees on either side were bare, not an evergreen in sight. She began to run.

The Quonset hut was just yards away when Johnny Lee pulled alongside her. "So, it's you, Sammie Rae," he said. "Saw your car and turned back to see what the hell a sheriff's deputy's doing on my land."

She stopped running and bent over to gasp. *Think fast and talk faster!* She looked him in the eye. "I'm off-duty, Johnny Lee. Not in uniform. Looking for my pa. He was going to help your ma check on something up in here. He didn't come back home, and now I'm scared shitless." She let air out of her lungs as loudly as she could. "He's a wreck and your mom's not much better. I feared one a' them might've taken a fall."

Johnny Lee threw the pickup into park. It shuddered and died. He got out, walked to the rusty hut, picked up the huge lock and dropped it back. It clanged against the metal door. "Well, now," he said. "He's not in there—seems like it's locked up nice and tight."

"Your ma don't have the combination, does she?" Sammie Rae asked. "She couldn't never have gotten in, right?"

Johnny Lee ran his hand across the skin of his shaved head. He seemed perplexed. "It's got a key," he said. "She ain't got one. Can't get in that way neither."

"You seen your mom?" Sammie Rae asked. "If she's out with my lunatic pa, she might be in danger."

"I'm going home to check on her," Johnny said. "You head back and see if your pa's at his place by now."

Relief flooded Sammie Rae, washing out from her lungs. But he was watching her instead of leaving. "Give me a ride back to my car, Johnny Lee. I'm wore out."

"I was gonna clean up the hut, but okay."

Sammie Rae would have loved to say, "Go ahead," or "Need a helping hand?" but kept on acting desperate about her father. She'd come back later—no matter what she found she'd keep her promise to Pa. She wouldn't report what he'd told her.

Chapter 18

"HEY, THERE!" THADDEUS Overton's voice said when Sammie Rae answered her phone. She was waiting in line at the Dunkin'. "Sorry I missed your call. I was tied up."

Sammie Rae pictured Overton tied to the posts of a woman's bed, the bed of a hot-as-hell voodoo queen. The thought made her chuckle nervously. She'd already worried about Lansing coming in to meet Beebe, and about Darla. And now she was twisting in the wind pondering what Overton's "tied up" meant.

"You called me," he reminded her.

"Yessir. I got a contractor lined up."

"Well, hello to you, too." His voice had an amused edge. "A contractor! Great! What's his name?"

"Casey McCall. Young but has a great reputation. Darla recommends him."

"Young and eager? Fine with me. Ask if he has time to meet with the structural engineer and the architect. Maybe take them out to the site. You and Darla, too. You could take them to the buffet. They'd get a kick out of it."

She waited for him to mention coming himself. Her wait was interrupted by Gracie's daughter. "Nine dollars, ninety-nine cents, please, Deputy Wheedle." Gracie had raised all her kids to be polite. Kimberly held out the box of donuts.

"Just a minute," Sammie Rae said into the phone and tucked it between her cheek and shoulder. She pulled out her wallet. "I'm getting donuts for the office," she said loudly.

"Nice of you," Overton replied. His voice was more distant now. "Hope to be there in a week or so—I have some things I need to deal with first. For the move."

Fumbling with her wallet, she dropped the phone. When she retrieved it, he was gone.

Kimberly handed Sammie Rae the receipt. "I know Ma thanked you, but I want to thank you myself, all you done for Annie and the kids. Come by and visit soon."

Sammie Rae nodded and left. She put the donuts and a bag of coffee in the patrol car's trunk, got in and buckled up. Then worry hit her. What did he mean by things to deal with? A relationship he had to end? Worse, one he was thinking of taking to the next level? She went back in the Dunkin'. "Forgot the paper," she said to Kimberly, putting some change on the counter.

"TWO MORE MUTILATED BODIES," the headline screamed. One in Fairfax County, Virginia, the other in Culpepper. Both hard by DC, neither reported by name or description of victim. She tossed the paper into the trash can by the door, got into her car, and pulled out. The details would be on the internet, anyway.

When she opened the door to the inner office, the cry, "Donuts!" rang out from the boys. Sammie Rae cradled the box, defending it from predation. "For the sheriff and a guest."

As she walked by Beebe's private office, the door swung open. "Wheedle," Beebe called.

"Yessir?" She stuck her head inside.

He was looking unusually crisp, his shave so close and his hair so glossy that he must have stopped by the barber for an early morning visit. His voice rumbled from his chest, deep and impressive. "Today, Wheedle?"

"Yep," she replied. "I brought refreshments." She looked around. His desk was neater than she'd ever seen it. "Can I leave them here for safekeeping? You know, so y'all get first pick."

Beebe nodded. She placed the box on the desk with care—to avoid powdered sugar spilling—and went to make a big pot of fresh ground coffee. It would be torture for the others to smell as it brewed, but they wouldn't get any until the sheriff said so.

She was measuring water when the noisy office stilled. Sammie Rae looked out the window. Al Lansing's car had just pulled up. He got out and headed to the door, dressed for work in a meticulously tailored suit.

When she turned around, her colleagues had popped up like a bunch of gophers, their eyes wide, several whistling in appreciation, like when Darla came by.

"Who the hell is that dude?" Charlie asked.

"I'm sure the boss will tell you later." Sammie Rae went to the door to greet Lansing. Up close, his suit looked as if it cost nearly as much as his car. Slick and stylish, but also intimidating—perhaps the cut of the jacket made his shoulders appear so wide. He was dark, mysterious, like the new Superfly. Like a major drug lord, or so she hoped. And then, surprise! His usual cool melted away as he grinned like he was greeting a long-lost friend. "Why Sammie Rae Wheedle! So great to see you again." He turned to the general office. "Morning, gentlemen." And back to Sammie Rae with, "Now where is this sheriff you've been bragging on?"

She walked Lansing to Beebe's office door. The sheriff sat at his desk, facing them, looking official. And nervous—the beefy fingers of his left hand pulled at his shirt collar as if it strangled him. He jumped up.

"You must be Sheriff Beebe." Lansing walked toward Beebe. "Albert Lansing, Special Operations, DEA." He placed his badge and identification on the desk. At the same time, he reached out to shake the sheriff's hand.

"Agent Lansing, pleased to meet you." Beebe bent forward with his arm extended. His gaze slid down to his desk and then up to Sammie Rae. "Deputy Wheedle, get plates for the donuts. And coffee. You do like donuts, don't you Agent Lansing?"

"Who doesn't?" Lansing sat in one of the chairs opposite the sheriff. "A great culinary tradition."

"Good, good. We're known for our hospitality here," Beebe responded, jovial. Too jovial. "Welcome to Lark County, Agent Lansing."

Sammie Rae left for the break room. When she returned, the men were chatting amicably. At least Beebe was—Lansing was mostly smiling, nodding, and saying, "You're so right," to the sheriff.

"You know," Beebe replied, nodding like a bobblehead, "we here are proud of our history. Why, the great state of West Virginia was created by breaking away from Old Dominion. We fought for the Union." He cleared his throat and looked up at Sammie Rae. "Thank you," he said as she put the tray down. He frowned. "Just how did you meet Agent Lansing, Deputy Wheedle?"

"Please, call me Al," Lansing said.

Sammie Rae felt her mouth open in an unflattering *O* as she tried to calculate what to say.

Lansing continued with, "I met a woman at the conference. A real wow of a woman."

Beebe interrupted with a wave of his hand. "You can go now, Deputy Wheedle."

Lansing laughed. "Not that kind of story. Deputy Wheedle's important to this. Anyway, about the woman…"

"Tall, kinda exotic-looking?" Beebe's face held the ghost of a smile.

Lansing nodded with a widening grin. "Must be the one. Name of Darla. She introduced me to your deputy here. Since I was coming to run the show for the Agency, I asked about local law enforcement. To figure out who I could work with."

Sammie Rae was afraid to move—by the size of his grin, Lansing was having too good a time. Was he overdoing it because he thought Beebe was an idiot? She and Darla had joked about the sheriff—maybe Darla had repeated their comments to Al. She shivered at the thought of her boss realizing her treason. He wasn't stupid.

Beebe inclined his head, looked Sammie Rae in the eye, and lifted his arm again as if he was going to dismiss her. At the last moment, he dropped his hand to the donut box, opened it, and said to Lansing, "First pick to you."

"Don't mind if I do." Lansing selected a plain cruller. Beebe took a bulging strawberry jelly dusted with powdered sugar.

"To make a long story short," Lansing went on, "your deputy here convinced me you were the man." He emphasized "the."

"The man?" Beebe's face was warily neutral. "What did she say?"

"Wasn't so simple." Lansing paused for a bite. "She didn't up and tell me a single thing, didn't do a hard sell. No, it was her demeanor and professionalism, her questions and comments in the lectures that impressed me. She wasn't diverted from seeking new techniques for use back here. I positioned myself behind her, listening closely and watching what notes she took…"

Sammie Rae winced, remembering her doodles and focus on the free food at the conference.

"…she impressed me with her dedication. Not only that, she referenced you when asking questions, so obviously she was working under a man who wanted his staff knowledgeable. Any leader who inspires such respect and loyalty, is the man we need. I approached her." He sipped his coffee and looked at Sammie Rae, still standing as the heat of a blush rose from her collar. "Just to get to you. And, in case you're wondering, her friendship with Miss Darla was a perk I appreciate, but not the deciding factor."

He gave Beebe a broad wink, a smarmy man-to-man wink, and said, "Maybe Deputy Wheedle could leave us to talk. Brew some more of this delicious coffee." He gazed into his cup and said, "A little stronger, maybe."

Beebe's eyes slid up Sammie Rae's uniform from waist to collar, but before he reached her face, he said, "Shut the door behind you."

*   *   *

The latch clicked behind her as she walked into the general office.

"So, who the blazes is that?" Charlie asked. "P. Diddy?"

"Think he goes by just Diddy now," Ray Ben said.

A chorus rose in the room. "Shut the hell up, Ray Ben!"

Sammie Rae pirouetted on the toes of her work Oxfords. She smiled at Charlie. "Nope," she said, thinking, *Darla's boyfriend*—but she'd wait to drop that on him. She went to brew more coffee. Stronger, blacker coffee.

The pot was still dripping when Beebe opened the door. He was grinning like a fool—no, as her pa would say, "Grinning like a damn fool." He shook hands with Al Lansing again and said, "Deputy Wheedle, would you please take our guest out for some Mexican? Show him we got more around here than fast food."

*   *   *

The Porsche, top up, followed her patrol car toward The Hacienda. After a mile, he sped up, pulled in front, stopped, and walked toward her. Before she could unbuckle to meet him, he opened her passenger door and slid inside. "Don't have time for lunch," he said.

"What did you say to the sheriff?" she asked.

Lansing chuckled. "I made him my local contact, my tell-no-one super-secret unofficial agent. Said I'd even get my FBI buddies in touch with him on the down-low, as needed. FBI made him cream his shorts." He laughed again. "I was almost offended. But he'll settle for me. Deal is, he'll give us information—through you as my contact, just to make sure it stays hush-hush, meeting out of the office with Darla as an excuse—and I'll let him in on what's up with our investigation."

"Really?"

Lansing blew out a breath with a loud, fluttering noise. "No fucking way. But he'll never know it."

"Wow." Sammie Rae said.

"Yeah, think your job is secure. Now, if you'd just get the file on Jesse Napier, including the autopsy. Everything known about him, especially his contacts. Beebe will have a copy ready for me."

"Sure thing," Sammie Rae said, "I really appreciate all you've done."

"Hey, no problem." Then Lansing's demeanor grew less confident, his posture slacker, as if his bones had softened.

"Anything you can do to help me with Darla's mom, I'd be grateful."

"Be glad to try." Sammie Rae had never seen anyone change Dolly's mind. "But about the Napier case. There was this thing, when I got to Jesse's body. Half his face gone—the side he was lying on was intact. Didn't even know who he was at first, not 'til I saw the left side. He was just lying there peaceful-like, no sign of a struggle. I moved off down a game trail, behind some bushes, and saw marks, like he was running from something or someone. It was too dark and raining too hard for anything to be clear."

"Could have been running from anything—people, a dog pack, wild animals. But why is this happening all the way out here when the others were clustered near DC?" Lansing looked off at the barren trees. "Every time, a good bit of the face was gone. Still waiting on the DNA to ID them."

"I didn't see fresh animal tracks. But would the attacks be so consistent?" Sammie Rae asked. "Guess if you're defending yourself with your right arm, a dog or coyote pack could bring you down with your left side up. I didn't see clean cuts like with a knife or clear bite marks, but the edges did seem kind of gnawed. Could have been after death, though."

"Same as the others, consistent—brought to mind the Miami zombie from back in 2012." Lansing opened his door. "Call me soon as you have the postmortem." He got out before Sammie Rae could say, "I don't have your number." As he pulled away, she said to herself, "But Darla does." She drove on to The Hacienda and ordered takeout enough for two, getting a receipt for reimbursement. It would be safe to take the rest of the day off.

Chapter 19

"**MEXICAN GRUB, YOU SAY?**" Sammie Rae's pa cast a cold eye on the meat, rice, and beans in the take-out container. He held up the tortilla. "Ain't they got no real bread?"

Sammie Rae rolled some of the fajita mix and rice in her tortilla and took a bite. Her father could fuss all he wanted—free food was free food, and this was damn good. When she got tired of his grousing, she left, sure that when she returned to clean up, everything would be gone. Except maybe the meat. Tough to chew when half your teeth were missing.

She drove to Darla's house. Darla's truck was gone but Dolly's SUV was in front. Sammie Rae parked next to it. As soon as she slammed her car door, Dolly was on the porch.

"Thought you may be Darla," Dolly said. "But come give me hug, Other Daughter."

Sammie Rae was glad to do so, sinking into Dolly's warm roundness.

"Come in, eat something!" Dolly put her hand on the small of Sammie Rae's back and pushed her toward the kitchen.

"I just ate and I'm still working, so no shine," Sammie Rae said. "But I wanted to know if I can use Darla's internet. Mine's so slow and keeps crapping out."

"She not here but I love to have company. Connection in her room—I will bring my mending in."

Sammie Rae headed down the hall to Darla's room, where the laptop sat gleaming on the desk. She used Darla's personal

"

account password to log on, searched for "Miami zombie 2012," and found a Wikipedia entry under "Miami cannibal."

The perpetrator ate the face of a homeless man after an altercation, and nothing had been found to explain his actions. At first, they blamed it on bath salts, a cheap, speed-like street drug. It wasn't found in the man's system. She bookmarked the link and returned to reading. One line caught her attention—it said the cannibal's car was draped with a Haitian flag. "Oh, shit," she whispered.

Dolly came in the room with a basket of clothes and Sammie Rae closed the page.

"Darla always do that when I come in room." Dolly's brow lowered. "You girls look at porn?"

Sammie Rae forced a laugh. "Of course not. I was looking at some crime stuff and didn't want to upset you." A silly comment—Dolly could handle anything, as long as her family was okay.

"You hungry?"

Sammie Rae shook her head. "Dolly, you believe in zombies or vampires?"

Dolly furrowed her brows. "Why you ask?"

"Jesse Napier. We still don't know what attacked him. But whatever it was, it really ripped him up in a strange way. Not like any animal kill I've seen."

"Lot of things we don't know for sure." Dolly was silent for a moment, pondering. "In Korea, had *kumiho*, fox spirit. Often look like very beautiful girl but take away *hanbok*, horror underneath. I maybe see one time on moonlit night, eating a corpse." She shrugged. "But maybe just starving woman. Dogs can always tell a fox spirit, attack them even if they look like people. Everywhere in world, people know creatures that change body and kill."

Scarcely reassuring. Sammie Rae turned back to the computer. She pulled the thumb drive from her pocket and plugged it into the port, bringing up her hit list. At the top was Jesse Napier's name. She put a line through it just as her phone rang. It was her pa. "Sammie Rae," he whispered into the phone. "Johnny Lee just called me on Hazie's phone. Come quick."

Johnny Lee was the second name on her list.

*   *   *

It was so cold, Sammie Rae wasn't surprised the porch was unoccupied. She left the engine on and ran to the house, calling for Pa.

"Right here," he yelled, sounding frightened, not his usual irritable—or his usual high—self.

In the bedroom, Pa was sitting in her mother's boudoir chair, wrapped in his blanket, as usual, sparse, gray hair sticking straight-up. His .22 was replaced by a shotgun. "What the hell, Pa? What's all the fuss about?"

"Johnny Lee called. Think you oughta call him back."

"Where's your squirrel gun? I never saw this gun before." She lifted her chin toward the shotgun.

"You did, but not in years. I'm anticipatin' something close and personal."

"That gun's recoil'd knock you into last Tuesday." She wasn't going to get any more out of him, so she went to the kitchen's new phone and hit redial. The other end rang and rang until finally Johnny Lee answered.

"Sammie Rae Wheedle here," she said. "You called my pa."

"Yeah. Can you meet me?"

"Come to my pa's. You got him all riled up."

He hesitated a moment. "No, they don't know who he is yet."

"Who? The guys he saw at your place?"

"He told you?" Another hesitation. "You report it yet?"

"Pa told me not to. Said you all were threatened…"

Johnny Lee cut her off. "Ma's missing. Her bedroom's all messed up. Found her cell on the floor and got your pa's number off it. Meet me but keep the old man safe home. I'll be by Stilton's Creek on the west side, just off the road." He hung up.

"Pa?" she called, heading for the front door.

"He want you to go, go!" Her pa yelled back. "Find Hazie. I'll hold down the fort."

"No fool like an old fool," Sammie Rae muttered as she jerked the car door open. She gunned the motor and raced to meet Johnny Lee.

*   *   *

Johnny Lee was pacing the creek's bank, but he'd taken the time to throw a camouflage tarp over his pickup.

"You running away from something?" As she picked her way through deadfall and piles of rotting leaves, twigs snapped, breaking the wood's stillness. A woodpecker started up drilling—the sound made her jittery.

"I would be running but for my ma going missing." Johnny Lee looked like hell. His face was drawn. Under his right eye, a muscle jerked. "She's been taken for sure."

"You know who's responsible, right? Let's go back to her place, so's I can look around and then call it in. We'll find her."

"Sammie Rae, they're real bad people—bunch of psychos. They'll get a lot worse if they know I brung the law in." He pulled out a pouch of Red Man and put a wad in his cheek. He chewed for a moment and it seemed to calm him. "Ma's all I got."

Sammie Rae dug the toe of her shoe into a mound of mushrooms poking up through the leaves. "They know where my pa lives?"

"Not 'less they make Ma tell them." Johnny Lee laughed with a short snort. "She's a tough old biddy, though. Raised me alone."

Didn't quite raise you right. "Who are they, Johnny Lee? What were they loading on the truck my pa saw? What was in your shed?"

"I think you know what," he said. "As for them, most come outta Miami. What was in my hut was small potatoes, so they weren't none of the big guys. Call themselves the Bon Tons. Some kind of Haiti bullshit."

Her heart pounded fast, faster than the woodpecker's *rat-a-tat-tat.* "Well, we best get going. You wanna follow?"

Johnny Lee shook his head. "They'll be looking for my truck. Looking for me. Safer if I ride with you."

They walked quickly back to her patrol car and got in. She started the engine and turned to Johnny Lee. "How much did you steal?"

"Didn't steal none!"

She backed out, her hind wheels spinning in the mud for a moment. "Then why are they after you, despite you giving them a hidey hole?"

"Ma tole them to get off our property."

"They're after you but took your ma instead 'cause she told them to scoot? You want me to believe it's not 'cause you stole off them?" Sammie Rae bet the Haitians couldn't find Johnny Lee and thought taking his mother would flush him out. She turned down the road, headed to the house Hazie shared with Johnny Lee.

Johnny Lee had gone red in the face. "Maybe a little," he muttered, the tough attitude gone.

"Hell's bells, they know my pa was with her when she saw them."

"Like I said, they're bad guys. Real bad."

They pulled into Hazie's place, an ancient log cabin, clapboarded over. They got out of the car and Johnny Lee looked around, the muscle under his eye jumping. She held her hand on her pistol until she stepped onto the porch, then she pulled it from her holster. "Hello?" she called as she walked into the house.

Johnny Lee came in behind her, yelling, "Hey?"

There was no answer. The only sound was the loud ticking of the mantlepiece clock. They moved through the house, the pine floors creaking underfoot.

"Nobody here," Sammie Rae said, dropping her pistol arm to her side.

"Find my ma, Sammie Rae. Make sure she's safe. But don't get the sheriff involved or the bastards'll kill me and her for sure."

"You know where they might have her? Know what direction they took? Any idea at all?"

He shook his head.

"How the hell do you think I'll find her if I can't get help?" *Johnny Lee, number two on my hit list. Number one was a bully, now deceased, second one a moron and a coward.* "You know of anybody around here involved with this Bon Ton gang?"

"Nobody I know of."

She had to ask. "Any strangers you could identify? Someone who stands out, like a stranger, a White guy? Blond?" She swallowed hard. "Real good-looking?"

Johnny Lee side-glanced her like she was crazy. "No Whites at all. But all's I knew were the ones who came here to load and unload. Couldn't tell you if they was good-lookers— was Haitians. How you judge them? All look alike to me."

"I'm going to head out and look for her. You coming?"

"I'll stay here for if Ma returns. Got a spot to hide where they'll never find me, but I'll be keeping watch. Remember, no sheriff!"

"I said okay," Sammie Rae said as she left. She got into her car and drove back up to the road heading to her pa's to make sure he was fine.

*　　　*　　　*

Sammie Rae called Wade Goodloe, arranging a meet at his garage. She also called Lansing—her promise had only covered the sheriff—then went into her father's house. "It's me!" she called. Pa was exactly where she left him, still wrapped in his blanket, still holding the shotgun.

"You find Hazie?" he asked.

"No. Going out looking now. You got any idea where she might be? Say if she left on her own?"

He looked at the window. "Hazie ain't left her land in ten years. Johnny Lee does all the shopping."

"I'm going then. Call if there's trouble."

He patted the shotgun. "Just you watch out for yourself. Anyone comes near here, they'll buy themselves a five-gallon bucket of whoopass."

Sammie Rae left the bedroom, shaking her head. Before she got out the front door, Pa shuffled up behind her, using his shotgun as a cane. "Want it on record, should your mama come back, Hazie and me was just having fun. Nothing can't be stopped in a heartbeat."

"Chrissakes, Pa, none of my business," Sammie Rae yelled, running to her car.

*　　　*　　　*

Sammie Rae sped toward Wade's garage. The road to the south side of town was empty until she came up behind a slow-moving flatbed loaded with chickens. She was passing when the truck's horn sounded. It swerved into her lane and the driver slammed on his brakes. Several crates bounced from the flatbed. White feathers flew in the air. Sammie Rae jerked her car back to the right and then the left. Her car skidded, anti-lock brakes failing, front end tapping the truck's bed.

Her car went up on two wheels, threatening to roll. She gasped, jerked the wheel again, pumped her brakes. The car hit the crates and swerved more toward the drop-off on the road's right side. Seemed like forever before she managed to pull onto the shoulder, still moving. The truck's door swung open and a man with a long gray beard slid out of the cab onto the shoulder, right in the path of her car.

"Oh, no, no, no!" she yelled, waving to get him out of the way.

He jumped back just in time as her car slowed, bushes grabbing at its wheels. Sammie Rae got out, leaned over, and tried to catch her breath.

"Damned bunch of goats on the road and now I'm gonna have to pay for those chickens," the driver said as he reappeared, scratching his chin as he inspected the front of her car and the rear of the truck.

Up the road, the hind end of a goat was disappearing into the undergrowth. Knees wobbling, she walked to her front grill. Chicken blood, embedded with feathers, decorated the paint and chrome. She saw the bumper had taken the hit well.

"Truck's fine." The driver rubbed his shaggy gray beard. "Okay if I get the rest a' these chickens back on their way?"

"Just stay out of the way and let me pull out. I'm on a call."

The truck driver nodded. He turned and took a step, startling an injured hen which, flapping and squawking, achieved enough flight to slam into Sammie Rae, smearing her with feathers, sticky with blood. "Shit!" she yelled. "Shit, shit, shit!"

Giving the truck driver the stink eye to prevent him laughing, she got back in her car, reversed, and was back on the road to meet Wade.

He was waiting for her outside, wiping his hands on a filthy cloth. He scowled when he saw her car but staggered toward her. Drunk again. He leaned into her window and greeted her with a boozy exhalation. "Wussup, Sammie Rae?" When a feather floated up and landed on his nose, he wiped it away without comment.

"Need your help, Wade, and need it now. Hazie Jacobs's missing and Johnny Lee thinks she was taken."

Wade let his rag slip to the ground. "Hazie? Your pa's squeeze?"

Did everyone know her father's sex life? "Yuh, Hazie Jacobs. Could be in real danger. I need you to get to everybody, find out if anyone knows anything."

"Shit!" Wade stamped his foot. "It's them fuckin' Haitians, isn't it? I told that idiot Johnny Lee, 'Don't have nothing to do with them.' Was them, right? Hack you with a machete soon as look at you."

"You have any involvement, Wade?"

He shook his head. "I'm too penny-ante and they're too dangerous. Just was aware what they was up to, moving goods, working with some local idiots. That was okay with me—them Haitians distract attention."

"Johnny Lee said there were four guys, but one was maybe Mexican. Called themselves Bon Ton or some such."

Wade shook his head. "Haitians don't work with Mexicans. Maybe just a mixed kinda guy." His eyes cleared suddenly, focused on her face. "I'll get on the horn and see what I can dope out."

Chapter 20

Sammie Rae drove the back roads, heading for the turn-around to meet Lansing. All the while, she scanned the woods for Hazie.

Lansing was leaning against the signpost when she arrived. As she hopped out of the car and walked toward him, his eyes focused on her, the corners of his mouth twitching in a barely controlled grin. She straightened her shoulders and hooked her thumbs in her belt, striding with professional purpose, only to have him crack up when she got close. "Were you out ticketing ducks?"

"Very funny. You going to help find the old lady or not?"

He shot her a look. "Testy, huh? I'm here because you asked me, not to get shit from you. Why not call for reinforcements from your colleagues up here in Apalachee County? Don't they work with you Lark guys?"

"Promised I wouldn't involve the sheriff." Sammie Rae explained the threats made to Johnny Lee, Hazie, and most importantly, her father.

"So, you called me. Clever."

"If the creeps are who Johnny Lee says they are, we'd need help, anyway."

"Haitians, you said."

"The Bon Tons."

"The Bon Tons? Haitian?" He squinted in surprise. "No, can't be Bon Tons. Must be Ton Tons. A group we've been watching." He pulled out a cell phone and, his back to Sammie

Rae, made a brief call. He turned to her, and said, "Come on. We're taking my car."

The top was up but Lansing's car was drafty—the stench of someone's pig farm hit Sammie Rae in the face as they flew down the road, so low to the tarmac they seemed to be doubling the number on the speedometer.

"Does *Ton Ton* mean anything?" Sammie Rae asked.

Lansing grinned. "Another touchdown for American education!" He shook his head. "Later—we're almost there." He stopped at the turnoff for a dirt road. "I'm gonna let you out here while I go bullshit them. You go through the woods to your right. Go straight east and you'll wind up at the back of the house—only house around. Lay low, see what you can see."

Sammie Rae touched her door handle. "Why don't we go together and confront them?"

"I said, bullshit them, not confront them. Look at me— pure gangster. Look at you in your uniform. Think you could pass?"

Sammie Rae opened the door and got out. But before she could leave, Lansing said, "Don't worry, my guys'll watch out for you the whole time."

"What?"

"Don't be too flattered. A surveillance team's been on them for a while—that's how I know about this place." He drove down the road, going slow to accommodate his ride.

Sammie Rae stared after him until he was nothing but a dust cloud, then dodged into the brush. She slipped between the aspens and across the rough ground, clambering over fallen tree trunks. But as quiet as she went, the birds noticed, falling silent and ceasing their search for food. Any alert hunter would know something big, something worrisome, was afoot.

Loud crashing through a tangle of kudzu-smothered saplings made her stop and duck behind a huge oak. Her pulse pounded in her ears. She held her breath, picturing gunmen with semiautomatics checking the perimeter of the building whose dirt-colored corner was just visible ahead.

The crashing grew louder. Between the vine-shrouded trees dashed something gray, smaller than a man, smaller than a deer. A wolf? But this creature wasn't quite wolf-like. The animal disappeared behind a wild rhododendron.

She looked up to see if the oak was climbable, should the creature return, but the tree had no low branches. A man's voice rang out, cursing in pidgin French. The gray animal reappeared, came a few steps closer, and was followed by several others, some brown, some white with brown markings. The Sims's goat herd, gone feral, more than thirty miles from home.

The billy stopped, lifted his nose, and smelled the air. He glared at Sammie Rae as if recognizing an old enemy, his strange eyes' rectangular pupils rotating to lock in on her body. He lowered his head and began to paw the ground.

The voice sounded again, loud. *"Kabrit!"* and then *"Tasso!"*

A shot hit the ground near the ewes. The ram lifted his head again and raced back to his herd, which took off, headed away from Sammie Rae. They were followed by the sounds of the hunter crashing through the bushes.

The goats moving through the woods would obscure any noise she'd make, so Sammie Rae left the shelter of the oak and crept closer to the building. She dodged behind an abandoned ATV and then an old freezer.

A moment later, she'd reached the back of the small, ramshackle house. Nothing moved in the overgrown, junk-filled backyard, nothing near the stairs leading up to the back door, which stood ajar.

From the front came the sound of a car door slamming and then Al Lansing's voice, speaking English. "Where's Wilke?"

A man's voice answered. The reply wasn't clear but obviously they knew Lansing and he knew them. Sammie Rae crept closer to the back steps. A third voice spoke from the front, but the words were so accented they were incomprehensible. Al's voice rose; he sounded angry as he said, "Get Jameson out here!"

A door creaked loudly. A different voice spoke, higher pitched but still unmistakably male. "We get you the product," this man said, his accent thick. "Small delay, just small delay! No problem."

"Not what I'm here about, fuckwit. Which one of you assholes gave the Lark sheriff info? Why'd he drag me in?" Lansing again.

Sammie Rae smiled. He'd covered his visit to help her.

"Happens again, our deal's off." Still Lansing's voice. "Let you get your prison wallets reamed for drugs."

Sammie Rae reached the stairs. Two of them sagged, nearly rotted through. She leaned forward until her left hand rested on the sturdy top step and bent horizontal. With her other hand, she eased the door open further. From the low position, she looked across a worn and filthy kitchen floor. At the table, sitting entirely naked, was Hazie Jacobs. From Sammie Rae's vantage point looking straight-up to crotch level, the sight was doubly shocking.

Sammie Rae crept up the stairs, worried the men would return to the kitchen. There wasn't much time to waste. "Psst, Hazie! Hazie Jacobs," she said.

"That you, Sammie Rae?" Hazie crossed her arms over her pancaked bosom, one arm so low it almost covered her groin. Her voice whistled; the words slurred. "Whach y'all doin' here?"

"Came to get you. So come on over here."

"Cain't!"

"They hurt you, Hazie?" Sammie Rae stood, ready to go into the room.

"Nah, just took my clothes and left me naked as a jaybird. Don't even have my teeth."

"Get your ass over here!" Sammie Rae hissed. "We gotta get going."

Shaking like a wind-beaten reed, Hazie slid off the chair and looked around. "Damn heathens ain't even got a tablecloth." She inched toward the back door, her bare feet shuffling on the old wood floor. As soon as she no longer held onto the table, she collapsed on the floor.

Sammie Rae leaned in further and gripped Hazie's right arm. The greasy floor made the going tough, but she helped Hazie crawl to the stairs. Thankfully, no splinters made her yelp. Outside on the dirt, Hazie stood swaying.

"Come on, quiet-like," Sammie Rae whispered. "'Fore they see you're gone."

Hazie scudded her feet rapid as a little windup toy but gained less than a yard. "Ain't got my shoes."

"Jesus." Sammie Rae turned and bent her knees. "Quick! Grab hold of me and I'll carry you."

Hazie flung her arms around Sammie Rae's neck and Sammie Rae hoisted the old woman onto her back, lifting the scrawny naked legs over her hips. She took off, moving as fast as she could through the uneven, trash-laden yard, skirting a mound of bald tires and a rusted bicycle, until she reached the woods. Her breath roared in her ears, ragged and harsh, but she was able to keep going. The old lady couldn't weigh more than eighty pounds.

A few more feet and Hazie was sliding down Sammie Rae's body. "Cain't hang on—too cold."

Sammie Rae straightened to let Hazie land on her feet. She took off her uniform jacket, pulled it over Hazie's shoulders, and buttoned the top button so it would stay on the old lady.

"Don't even cover my privates, Sammie Rae," Hazie complained, clambering back onto Sammie Rae.

A short distance further, Sammie Rae froze—the hunter had returned, singing in French with a surprisingly beautiful voice. She knelt behind a downed tree—its dead leaves provided cover and the stump a temporary rest for Hazie's behind. The man passed, the carcass of a female goat slung over his shoulder, its brown and white head bobbing with each step. Sammie Rae moved again as his voice faded away.

Hazie was also panting, her toothless exhalation dampening the hair at Sammie Rae's nape. They were nearing the road but Sammie Rae wasn't sure she'd get going again if they stopped.

She was forced to rest for a moment, leaning her forehead against a tree trunk to stay upright. Hazie's weight was causing back spasms. A memory echoed: *Don't you dare quit on nothing, Sammie Rae! I didn't ruin my figure to pump out a loser!*

She forced herself upright and moved on, lifting Hazie higher on her back. A moment later, the old woman had slid again, down toward Sammie Rae's belt. She grunted into her ear, "Dammit, Sammie Rae! Your dadgum pistol's getting fresh with me!"

They reached the dirt drive at the country road. Al Lansing's car was waiting. "Get in," he said, looking back toward the house.

Sammie Rae let the old woman slide down. Her own arms and shoulders felt as if she'd been beaten for hours. Hazie looked up at her and said, "Chrissakes, you look like you been rode hard and put up wet." She turned to Lansing and scowled.

Sammie Rae also scowled at him sitting in the car. "I can't lift her again."

He jumped out, opened the passenger door, and grabbed Hazie, who looked too shocked to comment. He set her behind the front seats. Sammie Rae in front beside Al, they took off down the road.

"Put up wet?" he asked, leaning toward Sammie Rae so she could hear him over the engine.

All she said was, "More like shot at and missed, shit at and hit," and shivered as a draft through the leaky ragtop hit her sweaty chest.

"Carried her the whole way?"

"Piggyback. She's pretty scrawny." As Lansing took a tight turn, she was flung against the door. She regretted not wearing her seatbelt. "I had to do training with a fifty-five-pound pack before they'd hire me."

Hazie was slumped down, snoring, her toothless mouth wide open. A flash of sympathy shot through Sammie Rae— the old lady looked worn out.

"You're pretty incredible," Lansing said, shifting his gaze to Sammie Rae, but just for a moment. He reached over and patted her hand.

She looked down, comforted by the warmth of his skin, off-balance with the fascinating contrast between the skin of their hands, but also annoyed at his condescension.

"We don't want her talking to her son, have him talk to the Ton Tons and blow everything. Especially if they snatched him and put his feet to the fire. Doubt he'd survive the ordeal." He turned onto a small, unpaved road.

A gasp from the backseat—Hazie was up. She yelled, "Where you taking me? Who the Sam Hill is he?" She hit Lansing on the back of his head and screamed, "Help! Help!"

Lansing yelled, "Hey! Get her to stop!"

But Hazie wasn't done. She shivered violently and said, "Hot tea, Sammie Rae Wheedle! Get me some right now!" Her expression grew cagey. "You didn't tell that idiot Beebe, did you? Those bastards'll kill me and Johnny Lee and your pa for good measure. Beebe can't keep his big yap shut." Her voice trailed off into muttering, with nothing Sammie Rae could understand.

"Jesus," Lansing swore. "Does she ever shut up? We did the Ton Tons a real favor hauling her ass away. Bet they couldn't wait to get rid of her." He accelerated on a straight stretch. "Speaking of getting rid of her, where am I letting her off?"

"Shit." Sammie Rae hadn't done enough thinking. Hazie couldn't go home and Pa's house wasn't safe. Her own apartment was up a flight of rickety stairs—she'd have to stay home full-time and watch over the two of them if she brought them there. "Can't think of nowhere safe but we got to get her warm and calmed down." She arched her back to pull her cell phone from her pants pocket. "But not back to her house, or to my pa's."

Wade answered her call. "Sammie Rae, you find Hazie?"

"Got her with me, Wade. Need a safe place to stash her, somewhere not linked to me or Johnny Lee. Place for her to cool her heels."

The sound of teeth being thoughtfully sucked filled the pause. Then Wade said, "Got someone up near Tinkersville, name of Mamie Cousins. She'll take care of Hazie for sure and ain't no one would suspect she'd would be there." He gave her an address and rough directions.

Sammie Rae didn't need—and didn't want—to ask why someone would be obliged to Wade. None of her business. She'd never been in Tinkersville, a little town in Apalachee near Boyerstown, and didn't know anyone there. She'd learned about it in school, though—it was one of the old Black communities of West Virginia that were fading away. Lansing might not stir as much comment there.

She tapped him on the shoulder and told where they needed to go. He looked at her and said, "You're cold, too." He pulled over, brakes squealing, and shrugged out of his jacket. He handed it to her and took off again.

She couldn't get the jacket on, not at the speed they were going on the twisting road, and so laid it against her chest. It covered her from knee to neck and was still warm with his body heat. She looked up at him, then, remembering the reported interaction of her gun with Hazie's privates, discreetly wiped the grip with the jacket's hem. Lansing didn't notice.

Chapter 21

THEY PULLED UP AT A TIDY house that, despite its modest size, was white-columned like a mansion. A heavy Black woman in a shiny emerald dress and pink scuffies stood under the portico. Sammie Rae and Lansing got out of the car.

The woman said, "You the sheriff?" A look of doubt crossed her face. "Ain't in a patrol car."

Sammie Rae said, "Yes, ma'am. I am a deputy sheriff."

"Who's that?" She pointed at Al Lansing, scowled, then held up her hand. "Never mind. Don't want to know. Wade said she can't walk, so he can carry her inside. If he's a gentleman. Lord knows, my knees won't lift nothing." She stopped at the threshold, said, "I'm Mamie Cousins, by the way. This here my house," and went inside.

Lansing looked up to the top of the portico. "Hmm, a mini-plantation Black-owned house." He shook his head and went toward the car's backseat.

"Don't you touch me!" Hazie screeched.

He looked at her calmly, folding his arms across his chest. "Want me to take you home to your son? Lot of guys want to talk to you two."

Hazie looked away and then seemed to give up. She held up her arms like a weary toddler and was lifted from the car with one smooth movement.

Mamie Cousins led them into her parlor, a room that was a riot of flower patterns, the rug as emerald as her dress, with repeating cabbage roses every foot. The walls were pastel stripes overlaid with printed nosegays, and the upholstered furniture was chintz. The effect was dizzying.

Mamie Cousins pointed to a fainting couch and said, "Just a moment." She spread a big towel on the seat. "Set the old lady down there."

"Old? No older'n you!" Hazie said.

Mamie Cousins ignored her. "Gonna make tea, warm her up. Cover her." She pointed to an afghan lying on the arm of a chair. "Come with me, missy."

Sammie Rae tucked the cover around Hazie and followed Mamie into the kitchen.

"You tell Wade Goodloe he owes me, now." Mamie took a cozy from a large teapot and turned on an electric kettle. "And who's that dealer you brought into my house?"

"Don't you worry none about him. He's okay. We sure do appreciate your help."

They returned to the parlor with the honey-sweetened tea. Mamie Cousins pointed at Hazie, who was dozing again, and said, "Got to get her something to wear."

"Don't think I want to be here for this," Lansing said, heaving himself from the armchair with a grunt. He headed for the door. Sammie Rae paused to take back her jacket and followed him outside.

"Did you really have men in the woods?" Sammie Rae asked. "Watching out for me?"

He laughed. "You'll never know."

Mrs. Cousins came outside, her green dress reflecting the sun. "Got her into something she liked. A tote of whiskey shut her up, if only for a minute." Her wig sat slightly askew as if she'd been in a struggle. "You could've helped me." She looked at Lansing. "Not you—the little sheriff girl."

"Sorry, ma'am." Sammie Rae followed Mamie Cousins into the house. There was Hazie, back on the fainting couch, but leaning over. She was dressed in sapphire blue, a dress so big on her it wrapped around twice. It was secured by the kind of kitchen string used to keep a roasting chicken's drumsticks together.

"Sammie Rae!" Hazie cried, her voice slurred. "Your pa with you?"

"Of course not, Hazie. Just us two who brought you here." Sammie Rae pointed at Lansing. "Pa and Johnny Lee are real worried about you. They'll want to know you're safe."

"Up to you, I'd still be naked and froze dead as a doornail. Now pay her and take me on home to my boy." Hazie tried to push herself upright but failed.

"Pay me?" Mrs. Cousins said, jamming her fists into where her waist should be. "You don't be paying people for good deeds."

"'Course not," Sammie Rae said. She tapped her temple, attempting to excuse the rudeness.

Hazie noticed. "I ain't batty, Sammie Rae. You do that again and I'll snatch you bald-headed!" Something dripped onto the floor under her.

Sammie Rae lifted Hazie with one arm, exposing a wet spot on the chair's towel-covered seat. "I'll pay to get your dress cleaned," she said to Mamie Cousins.

Mrs. Cousins shook her head "Let her keep it. But I'll get a bucket and scrub brush for you." She headed toward the back of the house.

"I'm surprised at you, Hazie." Sammie Rae hissed. "That lady is sure gracious to you. Why you acting so mean?"

"Didn't you notice? That lady black as those Haiti people were. Could be one of 'em."

"She even made you tea," Sammie Rae said. "I never knew you to be against the Black people around here!"

"You never knew me to be snatched up by a gang of foreign hoodooers. Even lost me my good teeth."

They lapsed into silence, which Sammie Rae hoped would last. But Hazie didn't do silence well. "How'd you find me? Bet it was that Wade Goodloe."

Mamie Cousins returned with a battered galvanized bucket. "I'm gonna need some help, since I'm keeping her a while. Pay my granddaughter five dollars an hour for chores."

"Ain't stayin' here." Hazie's mouth pursed. She looked to the side, the sly look returning to her face as she muttered, "Don't never have to pay my Johnny Lee for chores. Loves his ma, he do."

Mamie Cousins plopped herself into an armchair and gave Hazie the evil eye. "I don't want you here anymore'n you want to be here."

Hazie crinkled her nose, which might have been cute forty years ago, but now made her look like a hound on a trail.

Mrs. Cousins squinted in return, muttering something about white trash.

"Y'all need to get along," Sammie Rae said. She turned to Mamie Cousins. "I appreciate your hospitality. Hazie's not like you think, never has been. Just the stress of the past while getting to her."

She turned to Hazie. "You'll be safe. Wade fixed it up."

At the mention of Wade, Hazie relaxed. "That Wade sure comes in handy at fixing things up. Things not working right. Just ask your pa 'bout his little blue pills." She winked at Sammie Rae.

Sammie Rae knelt to clean the carpet. "I don't want to hear about it." Any information about Hazie and her father was worse coming from her.

"We all get old, but we still have our wants. By the by, Sammie Rae, you ain't getting no younger."

Sammie Rae shook her head. Her pa sure had a thing for mean women.

*   *   *

"Who's this Wade?" Lansing asked. His driving was leisurely now.

"Just some local color." No way was Sammie Rae going to out Wade's connection to her pa and all the others. Anyway, Wade was penny-ante. "You were gonna tell me about the Ton Tons."

"*Was I?* Okay, Haitians bring in meth, heroin, and lately, lots of fentanyl. Been monitoring them for a while."

"Come on, Al. Something I don't know, like who you're really after. You've been watching them but haven't gone after them. Or are you just doping out the network, locating the labs, storage, etcetera?"

"Very good." His smile was just visible in profile. "A real possibility that's what we're up to."

"Condescending bastard," Sammie Rae said. Even to her ears, that for sure didn't sound joking.

Lansing looked surprised.

"What?" she said. "Didn't think I'd know the word *condescending*? Or was it *bastard*? Either I'm your colleague or I'm not."

His face softened. "Of course, you're a colleague. But Haiti's a backwater to most Americans, an unfixable mess. Everyone forgets ordinary people live there, struggling to make a living. The Tonton—one word, the origin for the name of this band of losers—were a paramilitary group— thugs, really—who preyed on the ordinary people. The Tonton worked for a miserable son of a bitch called Duvalier.

Papa Doc Duvalier, president of Haiti from his election in 1957 to when Hell finally called him home in '71."

"Why did he have a gang of thugs?"

"To stifle any political opposition or threat to him. His soldiers ran amok, committing crimes so horrible, the people nicknamed them the *Tonton Macoute*. Burned people alive. Hacked them up with machetes. Raped as a means of control." He turned his gaze to her with an abrupt movement, his eyes glittering. "They were thought to be monsters because real humans could never behave like that."

Sammie Rae was flustered. She blurted out, "People really believed in voodoo and boogeymen?"

"Not like the White folks around here don't have their little quirks—handling snakes and talking about seeing the devil deep in the hollers."

"Not most and don't say *hollers*. You're putting people down for being poor." The sun was setting full on her face, the last rays warmer than at midday. "So, Tonton Macoute, a 'boogeyman'?"

"Haitian for *Uncle Gunnysack*, the boogeyman used by parents to keep kids in line. A monster who grabbed children and took them home in a burlap sack. Ate them. This bunch of turds we're investigating want to inspire the fear the Tonton did back in Haiti."

He kept his hand on the gearshift.

She put her cold hands into her jacket pockets. If only she'd searched for Tonton when she looked up the Miami zombie. "The guy in Miami was on drugs, right? Real zombies don't exist."

"Well, in another Florida case, an FSU student walking home from a restaurant killed a couple in their garage. Was eating the man's face when the police arrived. They thought he was on flakka at first, but he was supposedly just nuts—a psychotic break. I still wonder if it was really something they didn't know to test for, if there aren't more designer drugs we haven't discovered yet."

Shit. She'd have to go back to Darla's house and use her laptop to find out what the heck flakka was.

"And some say germs turning cows and deer into mindless zombies could—and even have with mad cow—infect people. People in Haiti say voodoo mambos turn people into zombie slaves. Damned if I know what's true."

"Watch out!" Sammie Rae yelled. Lansing braked just in time as the goat herd, down one member, shot out from the bushes and crossed the road.

"Phew, close call!" Lansing said.

The billy was last in line. He paused, gave Sammie Rae a long, thoughtful look across the hood of the low-slung car. She shivered.

Lansing asked, "Are you cold or does the thought of real zombies scare you?"

"Tell me, do outsiders, like Americans, ever get involved?"

"Are you asking if White people get mixed up in voodoo?" Lansing asked. "If you mean with the gangs—of course, from smuggling to buying the drugs. But you knew that, Deputy Sammie Rae Wheedle. And even Marie Laveau, the Voodoo Queen of New Orleans, married two White guys. So, who the hell knows? You got someone in mind around here? Someone we don't know about?"

No way she was going to tell him, but ever since he put his warm hand over hers in the car, she couldn't remember if Thaddeus Overton's hand had been warm or cold.

They pulled to a stop at her car. "Here you go," Lansing said, leaning across to open her door.

Sammie Rae unbuckled her seat belt—suddenly so warm she couldn't wait to get out in the open air.

"Wait a moment," he said, taking hold of her arm. "I want to tell you something."

She hesitated.

"Just wanted to say you really wowed me. Risking yourself for that old woman, carrying her out the whole way, knowing how to handle her. You're really a strong young lady."

The blush of pride heated her cheeks, mingled with the flush of disloyalty. *I'm not strong—Darla can single-handedly lift a couch and drag it out of a house!* But Sammie Rae was too flustered to continue the discussion. "Thanks," she said. "Gotta go check on my pa."

*   *   *

"Where in God's name is Hazie?" her pa asked.

"Safe place, Pa." She walked past him into the kitchen. "You eat today?"

"Yeah. Had me some beans out of that there can and a slice of bread. Now tell me where she is."

"Better you don't know. We'll have to get you somewhere safe, too."

"Ain't lettin' no one and nothing drive me out of my home. You can just forget it." He shifted in his seat and winced, pulling at the crotch of his pants, baggy what with all the weight he'd been losing.

"Come with me?"

"I said no." He wriggled and shifted his pants crotch again. "Dammit!" he yipped, high-pitched like a hound whose ears had been yanked.

"What's the matter?"

"Aw, Wade got me some Mexican Viagra real cheap. Half the time it's worthless shit. But this time it's the real deal, and Hazie's gone."

188

"For Chrissakes, Pa!" Sammie Rae fled the room, slamming the front door behind her. She got in the car and sped away.

Seemed like she was always running out on her pa once he got talking.

*　　*　　*

As soon as she walked into the office to hand over the patrol car keys, Ray Ben said, "Sammie Rae, sheriff wants you."

"Wheedle!" Beebe called from his office.

"Yessir?" she said, going to the door.

"Another body, chewed on just like Jesse Napier—Johnny Lee Jacobs."

Sammie Rae gasped. "Johnny Lee's dead?"

Beebe nodded—his hands tented in front of his mouth like a church steeple. "He's dead and his ma's missing. Funny thing is… this one's also linked to you."

"How's that, sir?" Had someone seen her go to Johnny Lee's storage?

"Odd coincidence with the Napier case, what with you being the one to find Jesse's wife dead and Jesse ending up being something's dinner. And now, rumor has it, your father was fooling around with the deceased's mother, Hazie Jacobs." Beebe sat back in his chair as if he'd scored a point and could afford to relax. As if he'd found an excuse to make her pa guilty of something.

Sammie Rae felt the air leave her lungs, cutting off her breath—like Hazie was still hanging around her neck, choking her. Did Beebe know she and Al Lansing had rescued the old woman? It was a few seconds until she was able to speak again. "Sorry, sir, I don't understand."

"Isn't your father Hazie Jacobs's boyfriend?"

He had no questions about her actions. She nearly giggled with relief and at the thought of Pa being called a boyfriend, as if he were someone's high school dreamboat. "Pa hasn't left his house in forever. How could he have been fooling around with Mrs. Jacobs? And no way he has anything to do with her son being found dead."

"Huh, hasn't left his house? Heard tell he drove his riding mower all the way down the county road to her place. Hazie been making him frisky again. Everyone in Lark knows they were canoodling."

Everyone but Sammie Rae.

"I want him talked to about Johnny Lee. Mrs. Jacobs, too, being as she's missing," Beebe said.

"I'll do that, sir," Sammie Rae said.

His expression dripped with scorn. "You know you can't interview your own pa. I'm sending Charlie out. He's the sharpest investigator I got."

Sammie Rae laughed. Charlie, sharp?

"I might understand you laughing, viewing Johnny Lee as no big loss—most of us would agree with you—but you don't seem broken-up about your pa's girlfriend going missing." He narrowed his eyes as he looked at her.

Only one thing to do. "Sorry, sir. For sure, I'm concerned, but I just found out about her and my pa. Need time to get used to that."

Beebe dropped his eyes to his laptop, a tell that she should move on.

Sammie Rae swallowed, relieved the moment had passed. She said, "That Lansing guy said the DEA and the FBI are mighty interested in Jesse's death, being as it was just like the ones outside DC. But one death here didn't trigger a big reaction. Johnny Lee—if he's a victim of the same killer—

could be of real interest. He did meth like the others, and with two addicts dying here the same way as the Washington murders, seems like we got a pattern, like the killer or killers have crossed state lines. Makes it federal crime. Less likely to be animals, too." She paused for breath.

Beebe rocked in his chair, chewing on his lower lip. "Right, right. Nobody outside this office knows 'bout Johnny Lee. We could work this up without a swarm of feds crawling all over Lark County. Keep it quiet and could be us solving it, not them."

"Sir, maybe should we tell some bunk to Agent Lansing? Throw them off the track? That would keep it under your control. Shame for them to come in now when we might just have a local copycat."

Sheriff Beebe sat up straight and nodded. "Maybe we need to keep Hazie from talking, assuming she's still alive."

"I could see what info Lansing has, beyond the media stuff, about the murders near DC. And what, if anything, they plan to do now they know about Jesse's murder."

Beebe smiled one of his cat-got-the-cream smiles. "Let's see what can be worked out. I'll send Charlie to talk with your pa while you look for Hazie. Oh, and follow up with the M.E. about Johnny Lee."

Chapter 22

SAMMIE RAE DROVE TO DARLA'S house to beg off their scheduled weekly watching of *The Walking Dead*. As she pulled down the drive, Dolly was heading toward the still, her plump little arms swinging with determination. She didn't look over at Sammie Rae's car.

The house was strangely odorless; nothing savory bubbling on the stove. "Hello?" Sammie Rae called.

"Hey, where you been?" Darla's voice answered. "I'm in my room, all ready for some blood and gore."

Sammie Rae dropped her rear onto the end of the bed. Darla was reclining against pillows—and one stuffed tiger, her turquoise-nailed hands waving in the air. "Been giving myself a mani," she said. "Come on. Those little hooves of yours could use help. Your hands, too." Darla blew on her fingertips. "I broke a nail today, lifting sixty-year-old linoleum scorched in a fire. Hired two temps to help and they were both worthless."

"Sorry, Dar, got no time. A new murder. This time it's Johnny Lee Jacobs. The Beebe put me on it 'cause it's so like Jesse's."

Darla put her hands up to her face in shock, her new polish kept safe. "My God! Eaten-up face?"

Sammie Rae nodded. "Another zombie murder."

"Nobody deserves to go out like that." Darla put her hands down. "And at least Beebe's doing right by you. He knows you're his best."

"Thanks to Al Lansing lying his head off." She touched the pocket with her cell phone, thinking of calling him to tell of Johnny Lee's death, but decided to wait until she was alone and had a bit more to say.

Darla waved her hand again. "He told me about it. Man's slicker than snot on a doorknob, but he thinks you're great. Seems you're gonna work together some."

There was something vague in her demeanor, even at the mention of Lansing. A tickle of memory in Sammie Rae's brain puzzled her—when had Darla been like this before? "Yeah, we are," Sammie Rae said. "It's all hush-hush, though."

"As if you need to say."

"Speaking of work, I need a favor. The Henderson place… I promised to be local contact for Overton's consultants, since he's in DC. The structural engineer and architect are coming tomorrow to look the place over, but what with Johnny Lee's death… You have time to take them to dinner?"

"The doctor's paying?"

Sammie Rae nodded.

Darla shrugged. "Sure."

"Great. You're better at decor and shit. Mind if I use your laptop for a sec?"

"Sure, too busy for a manicure but time to use my computer." Darla laughed. "When's your cheap ass gonna pay for a decent internet connection? Go ahead. I'll just lie here and listen to some tunes." She put her ear buds in with two careful fingers and lay back against the pillows.

Sammie Rae went to the desk and hurriedly searched for information about Haiti, the Tonton, zombies, and new street drugs. She wasn't going to risk looking ignorant again.

And, at last, she ginned up the courage for a search under "Thaddeus Overton, MD." There were photos and stories about Overton speaking and accepting awards, but nothing personal—no website, no Facebook, no Twitter, no images of him with a woman. It was like he didn't exist.

*   *   *

At Hazie's house, drag marks led from the hatch of a root cellar underneath the house, all the way to the Quonset hut where Johnny Lee's body was found. She shuddered at the possibility he'd been conscious while being dragged, since no care had been taken to make the trip painless. Blood, bits of clothing, and shreds of Johnny Lee clung to tree trunks and rocks. There was no substantial pool of blood until the end of the trail. What was left of Johnny Lee had been taken away by the lab, but the ground remained saturated with gore.

"How'd he get found, Ray Ben?" Sammie Rae asked.

"His mutts been tied up by the house for days with no food nor water. Set up a ruckus, howling all night—kept the Sims from sleeping. Thought it was maybe their missing goats tormenting the dogs."

"That billy's a real mean mother," Sammie Rae said.

Ray Ben nodded. "We drove out, heard the dogs from the road. So, we went down to the house and was obvious the poor dogs'd been alone for a while. No Hazie, no Johnny Lee. Poked around 'til we found him. No sign of Hazie though."

The lock on the hut was dangling by its shank. Sammie Rae opened the door and was pelted in the face by a filthy cord and an odor that could strip the paint from a barn. She pulled the cord and a fly-specked lightbulb came on. The only thing inside was a pile of human feces.

"Shit!" Ray Ben said, stepping to her left. If Charlie was with her, his comment would be a joke. Ray Ben's specialty was stating the obvious. "So, what you think, Sammie Rae?"

"I think you're right, Ray Ben. That is a big load of shit."

"No, I mean you think it's animals what killed him or people?"

"You hunt, don't you, Ray Ben? Look for spoor?"

He nodded.

"That look like the shit of any animal you ever tracked?"

Ray Ben stood scratching his head. "Sue Ann from the crime lab told me they'd left a present for us out here. Think this was what they meant?"

Sammie Rae rolled her eyes and started walking back to the house. "Know what, let's go look in that root cellar."

"We looked in there. Hard to find the hatch as Johnny Lee'd plastered grass and twigs on it with manure, you know, to camouflage. Yard's such a mess anyway. Surprised whoever or whatever killed him found where he was. All we found down the cellar was some weird voodoo stuff and a whole lot of canned food. He also had a little weed and a tiny bag of crystal. No weapons. Sue Ann took photos but didn't take nothin' out but the drugs and a knife."

"Weed, speed, and feed, huh? Johnny Lee knew something was going bad. Shame he didn't take precautions for his ma."

Ray Ben stumbled on a rock, caught himself holding onto a sapling's branch. "I went to school with him, you know. We both repeated third together. Guess he was as dumb as me but 'least I tried."

"A lot dumber'n you, Ray Ben. You're a deputy now and he's…" Sammie Rae lapsed into silence as she went along the path. Ray Ben followed her without interrupting her thoughts. When they reached the house, she said, "You know, if I wanted to flush a rat from a trap, I'd set fire to it. You see any sign they had arson on their minds?"

"We went to the dogs and then into the house and didn't see nothing, so we followed the drag trail to Johnny Lee." He held out his right hand and extended his index finger. "That's right, found the body." He unfolded his middle finger from his palm. "Called the lab and animal control for them poor dogs…" He went to his ring finger. "Followed the drag back to the house and found the root cellar…" His little finger. "Looked around the front of the house and the opposite side to where the root cellar was. And the back."

"Stay here a sec," Sammie Rae wanted to be alone to view the voodoo stuff. She put on her latex gloves, turned on her flashlight and went down into the cellar. Clothes, paper, and cans were scattered about, food—looked like Hormel chili—spilled on a mattress lying on the floor. A chair was knocked over on its side. A small table was backed up against a wall, on which hung an upside-down cross. Atop the table was a chicken, wings pinioned on either side of the body, head hanging off the edge. Its throat was slit, congealed blood running down the beak. Beneath the head was a basin to catch the blood.

After the chicken blood she'd just had on her, it felt like a personal message—not from God, or at least the God she knew. She shone the flashlight on the rough cross above the chicken.

The cross was really two pieces of scrap wood, painted black. The lettering on it was also rough, like that of a child or an adult unused to writing. She pulled the cross from the wall and righted it. It read HE IS COME! BEWARE THE WHITE BOKOR!

Though Sue Ann's crew had taken photos, she turned on her phone's flash and took one of the cross and a few more around the room before climbing out of the cellar.

"See, I told you was something weird." Ray Ben stepped back from the hatch. "And the chicken had a human skull on its breast. Sue Ann took that away. Was a old one, though, dried out and stained from dirt, like someone robbed a grave."

"Uh huh," Sammie Rae muttered, pondering the display she'd seen. Something just didn't seem right. It was unlike the voodoo shrines she'd seen online. No candles, no reference to the gods. Too stagey. Too set up for effect. For convincing the yokels. Not something she would mention to anyone—for fear of being laughed at—but it lacked *power*.

The only thing that made her feel weird was the inscription on the cross. What did it mean? She picked up a piece of pipe from a pile of rusting metal and began to move the weeds around, working from that side of the house around the back and then to the other side. Hidden beneath the dried-out vegetation, flush up against the faded clapboard siding of the house, was a full gasoline can.

"Well," Ray Ben said, "Sure looks like they did plan to smoke him out."

"But no fire started," Sammie Rae added. "Seems they were lucky enough to find the trapdoor and surprise him." She photographed the can where it lay and picked it up to bring back to the lab. "Okay, let's go."

They started back to their patrol car. Sammie Rae carried the can in and put it in a large-sized evidence bag in the trunk.

Ray Ben drove back to the office—she didn't mind, though she'd driven them out. She wanted time to think. When they pulled into the lot, Sammie Rae opened the door but, before she could step out, he said, "Wait one sec. Somethin' I gotta tell you."

"Yeah?" Sammie Rae asked, anxious to see if Sheriff Beebe had heard anything more about Hazie's disappearance—and her involvement in it.

"I been savin' my money, Sammie Rae. Got enough for a down payment on a double-wide." He hesitated for a deep breath and to wipe his sweaty forehead with a tissue. Opened his mouth to say more.

"That's nice, Ray Ben," she said, quick as she could. She slipped from her seat and headed into the building. "Okay if you take the can to the lab?"

He nodded. She left before he could unlatch his seatbelt.

Inside, she walked straight to the door of Beebe's office and knocked.

"Yes," came from within.

"We're back, sir." She opened the door.

Charlie was seated across the desk from the sheriff. He said, "Been waitin' on you, Sammie Rae."

For once, Beebe didn't shut him up. Instead, he looked at Sammie Rae as if she should be careful about what she said. She wasn't sure exactly what to be careful of.

"Waiting on me, Charlie?"

"Yeah. Went all the way out to that shack your daddy calls a house and he refused to let me in. Said he'd shoot my balls off if I didn't leave. He's crazy as a loon."

Beebe tapped the desktop with his pen, waiting like a cat for a mouse.

"Could've hauled him in for threatening an officer of the law…"

"But you didn't have a warrant," Sammie Rae said. "Did you?"

"No, we don't," Charlie said, his face Boyardee red. "And that old bastard knew all about needing that."

Beebe sat up straighter. "No cause and no right to be calling Deputy Wheedle's daddy an old bastard. I suggest you take your ass on out of here with the rest of the men hunting for Miz Jacobs."

Charlie stood, knocking into the desk and scattering a pile of forms. All Beebe did was rub the bridge of his nose between his thumb and index finger and sigh deeply. Charlie left, clapping his hat on his head and slamming the door behind him.

"What did you find out at Johnny Lee and Hazie's?" Beebe asked. "I heard there was some weird shit… Sue Ann mentioned a shrine of some sort in the cellar where Johnny Lee was hiding."

"I saw the cellar, sir. And it was weird, sort of voodoo-like, but not like anything I saw on the internet."

Beebe raised one eyebrow. "How come you looked at voodoo stuff online before going to Jacobs'?"

Sammie Rae's brain froze for a second. *Because I was just riding around with Lansing, creeping up on the Haitian gang hiding Hazie* wasn't a good answer. Because of what she'd seen in the root cellar? BEWARE THE WHITE BOKOR.

A bokor was a zombie master, but every bokor she'd read about was female. The logical answer was that Johnny Lee's killers were trying to throw the law off their own scent and onto someone else.

"Is there some kind of link you already made here?"

Her brain unfroze, sped up cycling through the possibilities of what to say. *Overton worked in Haiti and would know about voodoo, but why bring him into it? Overton is a stranger in Lark County, and strangers staying are rare enough to seem suspicious. He said he'd be in Washington all week. If that's true, he wasn't in Lark Country at the time of Johnny Lee's death.* Thad Overton might be her cemetery angel come to life, but in the back of her mind was Mee-Maw Wheedle's voice, echoing up from Mingo County. *The Devil comes as everything you ever wished for.*

"I'm waiting, Deputy Wheedle." Beebe glared at her.

Sammie Rae blurted out the best she could come up with. "What with Haitian gangs running drugs though the state, thought it was a good idea to look into their culture. Hard to look up Haiti and not run smack into voodoo and zombies."

"Bet that's true."

"Yessir, but my research suggests that shrine thing at the Jacobs's was just not right."

Beebe rose from his seat. "Good thing I got a voodoo expert on the case, then. Come on, I'm going out to your pa's place and you're coming with me to make sure he welcomes us in."

Sammie Rae laughed. "You think that's a guarantee?"

Chapter 23

BEEBE DROVE, HIS GLOVED hands tight on the wheel. They passed the courthouse and the Lark Heritage and Arts. Down a narrow back street, Sammie Rae could see the jewelry and gift shop and the Southern Baptist Church. She felt a flush of pride—her state was maybe not as historic as the Old Dominion, but pretty, nonetheless. Home.

Once out of the town, mobile homes perched above the river, threatening to fall in and rot like the nearly submerged carcasses of abandoned vehicles below the bank. This wasn't the way straight to her pa's.

"Taking the scenic route, sir?" Sammie Rae asked.

"Just to clear the air, I feel the need for a little relaxing drive. Been years since I drove out to your ma's place."

Her shoulder blades pulled toward each other. "All due respect, it's been years since it's been my ma's place."

"That's right," he said. "You was just a cute little blonde tyke back then." He lifted one hand from the wheel and patted her left knee.

Her back stiffened even more.

"Always thought I'd be your pappy, one day." His voice was so mournful, so wistful, it was almost worse than if he'd been making a pass.

They arrived at her father's. He was sitting in one of the porch rockers, holding his .22. "Off my property, Ralph," was how he greeted them.

"Now, Pa," Sammie Rae started.

"You stay out of this," Pa said. "This is between me and that pot-bellied, low-down, sorry hump dog next to you."

"Now, no call for that, Samuel. We used to be friends."

"Friends don't steal each other's woman. You knew I loved her."

"I loved her too, more than you. I got nobody now. You're with Hazie."

Her father lifted the gun. "None of your damn business."

Beebe's hand went to his holster.

"Enough!" Sammie Rae yelled, stepping between her father and Beebe. "Remember Hazie's missing and that's what we came about!"

Her father looked straight into her eyes with so guileless an expression, she knew he was going to lie. The sheriff would get nothing out of him, nothing that would put her under suspicion.

Beebe tried, anyway. "Report has it that you went to visit Hazie. Rode your damn mower on the county road, for which I really should cite you."

"Didn't catch me in the act, unlike…"

"Back to Hazie," Sammie Rae said. It occurred to her that a snort of Dolly's ginseng would make the conversation flow more smoothly. "Why don't we step inside? Cold out here and in there I stocked a little refreshment. You didn't finish it off, did you, Pa?"

"No. You hid it too damn well." Her father rose, stumbled, and was caught by Beebe before he fell. He jerked his arm away and opened the screen door.

Inside, her father collapsed into his chair and Ralph settled into the sofa, looking around in a way that worried Sammie Rae—his gaze softened, became nostalgic. If Pa noticed, it could only provoke him.

She poured them hefty portions of the *myeongsul*. Ralph held his glass up to the light.

"Tonic for my rheumatiz," her father said.

"Looks good," Beebe said. "Down the hatch." He drank it all at once, coughing as the fumes hit his windpipe. He held out his glass for more.

Her father did the same, saying, "Got no idea where Hazie is."

Another shot and they both eased into their seats.

"Tell you the whole story," her pa said. "I did go over to her place on the mower." He recounted what he'd seen, the trip through the woods with Hazie, Johnny Lee with the Haitian men at the Quonset hut.

Mid-story, Sammie Rae rose to look for crackers in the kitchen. The room was filthy, the sink loaded with dishes, the counters held moldering bits of ham sandwiches and stains of mustard and mayonnaise. With one ear cocked to follow the tone of their voices, the clink of the jar against their glasses, she cleaned. It might be the only time she had to do so.

When she returned to the room, the jar of *myeongsul* was nearly empty. The two men were blubbering, wiping tears from their eyes.

"We was such good friends, Ralph," her father said. "What happened?"

"Led astray by a Jezebel," Beebe sobbed. He straightened, swaying slightly in his seat. "Why, you know what, Sam Wheedle? We were taken advantage of. Seduced and abandoned! We're the victims here!"

They both started sniveling, and Beebe said, "Lord, I sure do miss that woman."

Pa wailed, "Not as much as me!"

They leaned forward over the rickety coffee table and poured more.

Sammie Rae was going to have to drive Ralph Beebe back to town.

*   *   *

Beebe had to sober up before returning to the office, so Sammie Rae let him—and her pa—sleep off the shine. She'd give them two hours and then wake them with strong cups of the stale Folgers coffee in the cupboard. Hopefully, their livers would do the rest. Meanwhile she sat on the porch, glad to be out in the crisp early-November air.

She pulled her phone from her pants pocket. "Hey, it's me," she said when Lansing answered. "Hazie Jacobs's son Johnny Lee…"

"Was found ripped apart just like the others," Lansing said.

How the blazing hell did he know? The question was on her lips, but she stopped in time to avoid looking foolish. He wasn't going to tell who the government's informers were. "Beebe wants our department to investigate the murder. See if it ties into Jesse Napier's—if we have our own killers here or if they're related to the deaths around DC."

"And who in your office is going to be involved?" His voice was skeptical.

"Me, as long as…"

"As long as Beebe gets the glory?"

She laughed. "I was going to say, as long as I report back to him."

"We can work that out. But if you come across anything— and I do mean *anything*—that even begins to encroach on our investigation of the Ton Tons, you keep it to yourself until you run it by me. That clear?"

"Yessir," Sammie Rae said.

"*Yes, Al* is all I want. I'm not your boss. Say, 'Yes, Al.'"

"Yes, Al." She smiled at the thought of being treating as a colleague, maybe even a friend. She told him about the chicken in the root cellar and the feces in the Quonset hut.

"Sounds like they're sending messages: fear them if you're an idiot ripping them off and shit on you if you come looking for them. Not unusual. I'll take it as a message to me as well as to you, until proven otherwise."

"That's simple enough." Sammie Rae was glad she hadn't divulged her online searches. Thank goodness she'd stopped before she'd mentioned what was on the cross. Or any possible link to Overton.

"And now there's a favor I want," Lansing said. "We're looking for any information to help the government against the pharmaceutical companies and the medical professionals supplying opiates. Anything against addiction for profit. Cases have been built against a good number of providers—docs and nurses as well as pharmacists—but we only just started going after the corporates. We need to get deep into local scenes to begin working our way up the chain. Build the foundation for each case. I immediately thought of you."

Sammie Rae held her breath. What she'd long feared was coming true: Pa, Gracie, all her friends were in danger of losing their pills, the very things that made their lives livable. Not to mention Wade, who'd go to prison for dealing. Wade and his customers would never turn her in for the few times she'd done deliveries, but she had to protect them. She glanced over her shoulder, though her father and the sheriff were out of sight in the dark house. "Guess I could help."

"What would you say about going undercover? Pretending to be a corrupt cop?"

She swallowed hard to suppress the nervous guffaw she felt welling up. "Uh huh, think I could do that."

"Great. I'll be in touch soon and get you all we got on the zombies of DC. That should give you credence with the sheriff." He ended the call. She wished she was still out riding with him.

She returned to the living room where Pa slept with a long piercing note at the end of each snore—it sounded like a stuttering siren. And on the battered sofa, Beebe exhaled through his nose with the deep rumbling of a coal train running over rough track.

She checked the time and decided they could sleep while she finished tidying the kitchen and doing a load of Pa's clothes in the back porch's decrepit washer. Caught a glimpse of herself in her ma's old chifforobe mirror: *Sammie Rae Wheedle, double agent and housemaid.*

The men were sheepish when they awoke. She chalked that up to exposing their soft underbelly of emotion. But no matter how heartfelt their emotions, neither of them mentioned that Sammie Rae had been abandoned. After all, when her ma skedaddled, they were adult men, and she was just a kid. A flash of anger at them, especially Pa, burned in her. He'd let her take over the chores of a housewife, cooking and cleaning and listening to his moaning about being lonely, saying she was all he had.

Thank the Lord she'd had more than him—she'd had Darla and Dolly.

Yawning, the men barely looked at each other, choosing instead to stare at the filthy rag rug. Sammie Rae cleared her throat. "This mean it's all over and the two of you can be civil to each other?"

"Guess so," Beebe murmured.

"Tell you what," Pa said, "I'll get another quart of Dolly's best someday soon and we'll swap stories. This daughter of mine'll drop you off home afterwards."

"Or I could lie on this couch right here," Beebe said. "Not like I got anyone waiting for me at home. But what about Hazie?"

"Cross that bridge when we come to it, one way or the other. Time heals all wounds." Pa did his best to look saintly.

Ask us if we found her, Pa! Sammie Rae knew the sheriff might wonder why he didn't seem more concerned.

And then her pa said, "I do my best not to worry, 'cause worry never did bring no woman back home to me." He looked adoringly at Sammie Rae, who was careful not to roll her eyes. "I know my little girl will tell me everything when y'all find Hazie. Meanwhile, you and she'll do your best to bring her back safe and sound."

On the way back to town, Beebe, who was still drunk far as Sammie Rae could see, said, "I know that man inside and out. I done him wrong, and it caused us to fall out. How could I ever imagine he was guilty of hurting a woman?"

She dropped him at his house, saying she'd pick him up in the morning.

*　　*　　*

Early the next day, Sammie Rae was in the Dunkin' getting coffee and eyeing the donuts. There was a fresh batch of Boston cream and the fragrance in the store made her head spin. But she'd been so good lately—her pants were finally a bit loose—it was a shame to give in to temptation. A tray of strawberry jelly came out, glistening from the oil and dusted with a generous amount of powdered sugar. She caved, reaching for an extra dollar.

"Not so fast!" a deep, gruff voice behind her said, clapping a hand on her shoulder.

Sammie Rae wheeled around, ready to block a blow. Darla stood there, laughing. "Fooled you," she said.

"Dag nab it, Darla! You almost made me soil my britches," Sammie Rae said.

"Hate to see you break your winning streak. You look like you're down at least five pounds."

"Seven, by the pharmacy scale. You come looking for me?"

Darla nodded and smiled. They'd reached the front of the line. "Strawberry jelly and two coffees," she ordered, holding out four dollars. "Keep the change."

They took seats at a table near the window. As soon as they were settled, Darla tore off a quarter of the donut, squeezing a generous amount of jelly on the piece, and handed the rest to Sammie Rae.

"How'd it go with Overton's contractors last night?" Sammie Rae asked.

"Was like a bunch of British royals dropped in at the Nelsons' buffet—fuckin' dumbstruck by our trailer-trash excess—twice fried and double-wide. Hard to keep the architect and engineer guy talking, 'cause they kept looking towards the steam table and exclaiming, 'They're bringing out something new!' Ate like prize-winning hogs."

"The Nelsons do put out a nice spread."

"Only one wasn't stuffing himself with sausage gravy on breaded meat was your doctor. Can't risk ruining those looks."

"Overton was there?" Sammie Rae said. "Wasn't supposed to be."

"Yup, there he was in all his glory." Darla sat back in her chair, her donut and coffee forgotten. "Said he'd been camping at the Henderson place for three or four days, just to see how quiet it was at night. He was a little put off you weren't at dinner, but then we got talking about what the place needs."

Sammie Rae's heart pounded. She took a gulp of coffee and choked, emotions warring inside her. Overton had been in Lark County when Johnny Lee was killed. At his new property, no one around to see his comings and goings. He hadn't told her of his changed plans—maybe he thought Darla wouldn't mention them. Sammie Rae checked the time. "Got a minute before work. So, was he really upset I didn't show?"

"I made excuses for you and the consultants seemed happy enough with me." Darla said.

Of course, they were. All the men breakfasting in the Dunkin', some who'd known Darla since she was tiny, were giving her looks, what with her wearing tight jeans and a deep U-neck tee.

Darla went on. "Thad thought I gave them good information…"

Thad?

Darla lifted her coffee, sipped, and grimaced. "Bitter." She put the cup down. "Guess my work does give me a bit a' insight into local building practices and pitfalls. We all talked for two hours about the project and then got into more personal stuff, but by then the two DC guys were back at the motel."

Sammie Rae had roaring in her ears. Her eyelids felt tight when she blinked. "You sat at the buffet talking after the others left?"

"Hell, no, I'd had enough fry-smell and Nelsons' was shutting down, so we went for a ride in his Land Rover. God, that thing's comfortable! My legs are too long for Al's little ride. And I brought Boozer as a chaperone—you know dogs don't ride in Porsches. But I thought if we're going to work with Thad, the more we know the better. He was sure talking."

"And what did he tell you?" Sammie Rae's heart thudded against her breastbone. Overton was supposed to be in Washington, taking care of some mysterious business. Had he lied on purpose? Or had he, expecting to see her at dinner, planned to bring her up to date?

"Just a sec." Darla got up to complain about the coffee. Sammie Rae's phone rang—the morgue asking when she was coming up to Boyerstown. The deputy chief medical examiner in the case would only be around until midmorning.

That was okay—Sammie Rae suddenly had a strong desire to check on Johnny Lee's autopsy, to be on the move, hear Al tell her she was professional. "Tell me later," she called to Darla, who was back at the counter. "Don't leave out a single thing."

She cheeked the wooden coffee stirrer and went to her car. As she left the Dunkin' parking lot, thoughts buzzed in her head like a swarm of wasps. She was tender all over, like she'd been stung. How had Thad and Darla ended the night? In bed together? Worry was gnawing at her brain, but jealousy was like a vise around her heart.

Sammie Rae chewed on the slender bit of wood, flipping it over and over with her tongue. She couldn't blame Overton if something had happened. Men always reacted to Darla. In high school, everyone had been sure she'd be snatched right up, destined to marry and have a bunch of kids. But Darla had done no such thing. She'd never shown interest in anything but success in business, her family, and being a loyal friend to Sammie Rae since kindergarten.

Odds were, nothing happened between Darla and Overton. Not yet. There was no proof he was part of the zombie deaths, just coincidences. But she should warn Darla to be cautious, especially in finding out why he quit Haiti. And she'd ask Al to help her find a link, any link between Overton and the Ton Tons.

Chapter 24

FACING JOHNNY LEE'S BODY was harder than viewing Jesse Napier's. Jesse had been cruel and abusive. He'd deserved to die, though she'd never admit that to anyone but Darla. Johnny Lee was a different story. Far as Sammie Rae knew, he'd never hurt anyone. All he was guilty of was being stupid, a poor idiot with no marketable skills. He could have gone down the mines, if there'd been any jobs, but who the hell would have trusted him with the open pits' heavy equipment?

Sammie Rae was escorted into the huge autopsy room by the morgue attendant, who checked his clipboard to make sure the right corpse was pulled. "Really backed up with cases now. Getting lots a' business," he said before he left to bring Johnny Lee. "Mostly routine overdoses but I'll hand you this, the Jacobs and Napier boys made life right interesting."

He left to access the coolers, returning quickly with a sheet-shrouded body on a stretcher. "The doc'll join you in a minute."

"Can't you…?"

He pursed his undersized red mouth and shook his head, "Last time I opened my piehole to one of Lark's deputies, I saw myself quoted in the Coal Valley News. I need this job."

Sammie Rae leaned toward the sheeted lump—all that was left of Johnny Lee Jacobs—but the attendant snapped, "Hands off the deceased."

A few minutes later, the medical examiner arrived—Dr. Pinkney, a plump, good-natured bald guy she'd met before in court. He'd worn an ill-fitting suit then but now he was in scrubs, covered with a stained rubberized apron. "I could have just emailed a report to you, Deputy Wheedle. Mailed the official copy. Saved you a trip."

"Sheriff Beebe wanted me to clap my eyes on Jacobs since I was there when Napier was found," Sammie Rae said. "And to tell the truth, I was curious if they looked the same."

"I can tell you they surely do. Get ready." He took latex gloves from a box on a shelf behind the stretcher and nodded to the attendant, who folded the sheet down from the body's head. "Dammit!" the M.E. said. A ragged piece of hairy flesh hung over the face, and he flipped it back on top of the skull. "Make sure it goes back in place after we open the calvarium," he said to the attendant. "That was the scalp, or what's left of it. Brain was normal, by the way."

Sammie Rae nodded and said, "Structurally normal, maybe."

Pinkney gave a short snort of laughter and stepped back so she could look more closely. He echoed the assistant with, "Don't touch."

"Don't worry."

The damage to Johnny Lee's face was strikingly similar to Jesse's—the right side was missing, not clean wounds but roughly gouged out. The eye was gone, loose tissue like insulated wires hanging useless. His nose flopped over, unsupported by cartilage, and bone appeared in patchy areas on the cheek. His lips were pulled over on the left into a bizarre half-smile as if embarrassed that most of his mouth was missing.

She walked slowly around the stretcher to his left side. That eye was intact. Sammie Rae couldn't help but bend slightly to look deep into its pupil. *Johnny Lee, you dumbass…*

"You say something?" Dr. Pinkney asked.

She shook her head, silently vowing to keep her thoughts to herself. Anyway, unlike Jesse's reminder of her interference in his life, it seemed Johnny Lee had no last words for her.

"It's been a couple days, so the globe of the eye is shrunken. Lid's come down a bit." He took a slender instrument from a tray and poked at the edges of the gaping flesh near the middle of Johnny Lee's face. "You can see there are no long, straight incisions nor are there clear bite marks. The flesh is mangled. There are, however, here and there…" He poked his instrument into a hole near the top of Johnny Lee's neck. "…puncture wounds which could be from canine teeth—possibly of an animal. But…" He probed the hole a bit more.

"But," Sammie Rae said, "if there's a mark from a fang, where are the marks from the rest of the teeth?"

"Those marks—if they were ever there—might be missing because of the large tissue loss or the bite not being deep enough for the other teeth to engage—just think about a dog bite. However, disagreeing with my colleagues, I don't think an animal made this puncture. We sent swabs for DNA from this and from different areas of the large wound. Hopefully will tell if there's animal saliva."

"That what killed him? Having his face ripped off?"

Dr. Pinkney pulled his probe from the wound and tapped it against his left hand. "You know I can't say until everything's back from the labs. I will definitely state he was alive when he suffered the facial trauma. May have died from shock. He has a lot of fresh injection sites and a good bit of meth in his blood, so he had to have used within three days or so of being killed.

"The deceased also had been restrained—see the ligature marks on his wrists? And some interesting things in his stomach—a drug we haven't yet identified and a quantity of human flesh."

"What?" Sammie Rae jumped and stumbled, stopping her fall by leaning both hands on the stretcher. She got her balance back and wiped her palms on her pants, though she hadn't touched the corpse. *Johnny Lee turned zombie and then victim?* "He ate himself? Can't believe it."

"Seems possible he was fed someone, though that's a fine distinction." Pickney shrugged. "Preliminary tests indicate the ingested material is possibly bits of Jesse Napier's missing heart, but we need DNA corroboration."

"It's been more than a week since Jesse died, and Johnny Lee just got himself killed."

"Very good. No, he couldn't have ingested the flesh that long ago and still have it in his stomach. And it wasn't raw but seared on the outside. Under the surface, we could see it had been frozen. Mr. Napier seems to have been Mr. Jacobs's last meal. Did he cook much?"

"Jeez," Sammie Rae said, "that's too horrible." She shook her hands—they still didn't seem to be clean. "Just please make sure nothing leaks to the press. Imagine if his mother hears about this."

"Do my best, but we have a pretty large staff here and something like that might get out." Dr. Pickney pointed at the puncture wound again. "Apologies—diverted by your question about how he died. I wasn't quite done with this. The edges of it are so sharp, I think it was made with an instrument. Never seen an animal tooth with a true right angle."

*   *   *

Sammie Rae drove slowly; her distracted thoughts made it risky to go anything close to the speed limit. The images in her mind were too brutal: Johnny Lee, gnawed up and with bits of Jesse in his stomach. He didn't die of meth—few people

did. Meth mostly just ate away at people, not as fast as what-
or whoever was committing these murders. Meth took bits
away, slow, losing teeth to meth mouth, gouges in the skin
from clawing away with the itching. Most of the overdoses
were opiates, at least in Lark County. OxyContin, fentanyl,
heroin. Though if heroin was pure and you didn't overdose, it
didn't seem to hurt you.

Since she was in Boyerstown, she drove to Mamie
Cousins's to see how she was doing with Hazie in the house.
It couldn't be easy but not as hard as it'd be once Hazie heard
about Johnny Lee. Not that Sammie Rae would tell her anywhere near everything.

The gravel on the circular drive crunched under her wheels
so loudly it was surprising no one appeared under the portico.
Sammie Rae got out of her patrol car and pounded on the door
with the big lion's head knocker. It took a moment before the
door squeaked open and Mamie Cousins's face peeked out.
"Oh, it's you," she said, showing nothing but her head, wig
missing, hair in curls held down with bobby pins.

"Yes, ma'am," Sammie Rae replied. "It's me."

Mrs. Cousins swiveled her head to either side, scanning
her yard. "At least that do look like a sheriff's car, not some
drug dealer's flash ride. By yourself?"

Sammie Rae nodded.

"Well, come on in, then." She opened the door wider. Her
polyester kimono hung open; beneath it, she wore only a bra
and a stretched-out girdle. On her feet were the pink scuffies.

Sammie Rae stepped into the house and followed Mrs.
Cousins to the back. There, in the kitchen, at a small breakfast
table, were Hazie Jacobs, Wade Goodloe, and her pa, all but
the last missing items of clothing. "What the hell are you doing
here?" she asked.

"And hello to you, too," Pa replied. He held fanned-out cards and had a pile of coins in front of him. "'Case you're wondering, Wade here brung me. Toted some of Hazie's stuff from her house."

"No trouble at all," Wade said. "Had to make a delivery to Mamie, anyway."

"Was tired of wearing somebody else's clothes," Hazie said. "Don't fit."

"'Cause you're scrawny," Mamie Cousins said. "Gotta fatten you up."

"Wait!" Sammie Rae said. "You had Wade go to Hazie's place?" She turned to Wade. "Anyone follow you?"

Her father interrupted. "Needed some personal items so I went with. Hazie didn't want Wade handlin' her delicates."

Sammie Rae groaned. "Shut up Pa, this is important. Did anyone see you there? Anybody come 'round here?" She pushed a mixed pile of garments from a chair set against the wall and sank onto it, her hand over her eyes.

"Want us to deal you in?" Mamie Cousins asked. "Or would you like some refreshments? I made corn bread this morning and just made the coffee."

"Not playing strip poker with you all, especially Pa."

"'Cause he cheat, honey? We all know that. Why you think he got the most clothes on? It's why we stopped bidding money."

"Speaking of cheatin'," Wade said to Mamie, "puttin' that there robe on is cheatin' too."

Sammie Rae rose, her eyes rolling in disgust, and left for the parlor to call Al Lansing. When he didn't answer, she collapsed into an easy chair, trying her best to ignore the garish carpet and the overheated room. Not to mention the stupidity of her father, Wade, and Hazie, which made her vision swarm with black spots.

Hazie came into the living room. "Don't be mad at your pa. He just trying to help me. Any news about my boy?"

Shit! With the shock of seeing her father in the kitchen, of the danger he and Wade had put Hazie and Mrs. Cousins— not to mention themselves—in, Sammie Rae had put all thoughts of Johnny Lee's corpse out of her mind. She'd planned on breaking the news of his demise to his mother in private. Gently, of course and withholding the details.

Pa followed Hazie into the room, Wade and Mamie Cousins trailing him. Her father looked hard into Sammie Rae's face and put his arm around Hazie. He said, "Go on, girl, tell the woman."

"Hazie, I'm sorry. Johnny Lee's gone."

Hazie Jacobs's mouth opened as if she was going to scream, but nothing came out. Instead, she wobbled, eyelids fluttering, and slumped down. Sammie Rae's pa could only support her weight for a fraction of a second, before they crumpled to the floor. Wade bent to help and was pulled down with them. Sammie Rae was too late to stop the fall.

"Oh, my!" Mamie Cousins said, looking down at the heap of bodies as Sammie Rae reached them and helped them up. "Wade, honey, are you all right?"

Wade nodded and stood. Sammie Rae helped Hazie and her father to the fainting couch. Mrs. Cousins stepped behind the couch to pat Hazie's back. "I know what it's like to bury a child," she said.

"Apologize I had to give you such sorry news," Sammie Rae said.

"How'd he die?" Hazie asked, wiping her eyes with the back of her hand.

"Overdose." The lie slipped easily across Sammie Rae's lips.

"That's good, that's good," her pa said, hugging Hazie. "Means he went soft-like."

Hazie began to sob. "He's been all I had since his pappy passed." She turned to Sammie Rae's pa. "Least now I got you."

Pa didn't respond. Hazie, looking down at her lap, said, "When can I see him? Don't have the money for a fancy funeral, but I want to send him off good as I can."

"You best not, Hazie," Sammie Rae said. "I identified him for you." She was interrupted by her phone. "Just a sec," she said. "Gotta take this call."

"Al," she said into the phone as she stepped out onto the porch. "Hold on a minute." She went to the patrol car and got in for privacy. "I got a lot to tell, and maybe more to ask. But most important, my idiot father is here at Mamie Cousins's. Wade Goodloe's here, too. I'm not leaving until they're safe."

"What are they doing?" Lansing asked.

"Playing strip poker. Aside from the visual of all those saggy wrinkles, it's peaceful for now. But after Hazie's son, Johnny Lee, I've got a bad case of the heebie-jeebies. Like I'm a target just sitting in the car, but I didn't want them to hear me call."

"Thanks for trusting me with the information. Give it an hour or so and I'll call when I've got people posted, okay? And leave the car where it is—maybe it's a deterrent."

"Okay." Sammie Rae hadn't seen any of Lansing's people when she rescued Hazie. Either they were real good or they didn't exist. She had no choice but to trust him, though. No way could she watch over her pa and Hazie by herself.

"Let's grab a late dinner tonight after things are in place. Time for you to be seen with me and time for you to tell me about your father, Wade, and anything else I should know."

A thrill rippled through her. This was big time law enforcement, but she'd have to be cautious. She looked around her and left the car, heading back into the house.

Her pa was standing in the doorway. "Won't ask who you was talking to. You've got your secrets, I got mine." He took a step onto the porch—he was walking better, barely putting any weight on his cane. "You don't want Hazie to view him. Chewed up, was he?"

"Leave off, Pa. No need for Hazie to know and whatever I tell you will go straight to her, I bet."

Like a judge with a gavel, he pounded the cane against the cement of the porch. "Got a pretty big mouth on you, missy. Just 'cause you're a sheriff, you think I can't protect my women-folk? Took care of you after your ma lit out!"

No use arguing or saying she remembered things different—wouldn't change things a bit. "Sorry, Pa. I know you can. Just don't corner nothing meaner than you." Using one of her granny's sayings on him was dangerous. He'd been nursed on that teat since birth and knew all the comebacks. She softened it with, "You're a damn fine shot. But where's your gun? Back at the house?"

"Tarnation! Left it inside." He turned and left the portico. No one was in the living room, so she followed him into the kitchen. They were all seated at the table, silent as the dead. Hazie was staring down at her hands, like a small, punished child.

Sammie Rae's mind screamed, *Pa, sit down beside her!* As if he read her thoughts, he did, taking Hazie's hand and saying, "There, there."

A voice muttered in her head, one she hadn't heard in years. Her mother's. *Why the hell you want him to be nice to that old biddy? I liked him waiting on me, no matter how long I was gone.* The voice grew sly. *Wasn't that what he always told you?*

"Shut up," Sammie Rae whispered. "I'm sick and tired of hating you." Someone touched her back, right at her spine, sending a shiver down to her tailbone. She turned. It was Mamie Cousins. "Don't be too hard on him."

"What do you mean?"

"Follow me back to the parlor, honey." Mamie's scuffies slapped the floor as she turned and walked out of the kitchen. Sammie Rae obeyed. It seemed like her entire time in this house was following crazy old people from one room to another.

Mrs. Cousins sat on the fainting couch and patted the seat next to her. "You thought you was whispering low, but I heared you. He's not all bad."

"Mrs. Cousins, ma'am, with all due respect, I have no idea what you're talking about."

"Back in there," Mamie said, "I heared you. You was whispering you were sick and tired of him."

"I didn't mean..." Sammie Rae began.

"Hush now. Your pa is your pa. He's a good man—been real nice to Hazie through all this. Him and that Wade." When she mentioned Wade, Mamie put her hand up to her bobby pinned head and said, "I do hear Mrs. Goodloe is not very nice to her husband."

"Well, Wade does often drink to excess. A wife gets tired of that, I think."

Mamie sniffed loudly. "Mr. Cousins drank too much from time to time. An understanding woman knows to forgive, yes, she does. Life is hard." She stood and pushed her feet more firmly into her slippers. "Excuse me, honey, but I got to go make myself presentable, go upstairs, and put a fresh wig on." She went up the stairs, leaving Sammie Rae on the couch.

It was quiet in the parlor, the voices in the kitchen muted. Almost unbearable fatigue worked its way through her body. How long had it been since she slept? She longed to nap; her eyes grew heavy, but every time she shut them, she saw the ravaged faces of Jesse Napier and Johnny Lee. Instead of sleep, she drowsed, jerking upright when she slipped into a dream.

Her phone sounded. She answered, "Hello?" No one there—it wasn't a call, but a text. No one texted her on her personal phone. If she didn't answer, they called back until she did.

Can you meet earlier? In an hour, soul food restaurant like before. Security in place at Cousins. Al.

She answered, Will be there.

Meeting early meant she could eat and drive back to Lark County. But that still left an hour to kill. *Kill* wasn't a good word. She groaned, stretched, and stood.

Back in the kitchen, the card game had resumed, no longer for items of clothing. All the money was now on Hazie's side of the table. *So sweet! Pa's cheating again.*

Sammie Rae's lips pulled down the corners of her mouth, which was trying hard to spread into a smile. She kept them pressed tight, though, since his attempts to make the bereaved mother feel better could only fail. Hazie's face was wet with tears—her wrinkles like a river delta.

"Deal me in," Sammie Rae said, dragging over the chair by the wall.

Chapter 25

AL LANSING WAS ALREADY seated when Sammie Rae arrived at the restaurant. "I ordered smothered oxtails for both of us. Tonight's special. Love them—my grandmother made them for me when I was little. One of the few country things she cooked up in New York, never served them to her friends. Ah, they were delicious."

Sammie Rae hated oxtails. She'd seen too many cattle, standing in the fields, crapping down their tails, to think of eating the dish. It was presuming to order for her, like they were a couple, and she almost said something rude in return. He'd made that tough to do by revealing more of his past— tamping down her anger, as did the sight of his face softening at the memory. "That's fine," she said.

"Great. Seems they were in danger of selling out," Lansing said.

"You want a drink?" the waitress—pretty and young, skin a glowing amber color with a dusting of freckles across the bridge of her nose—asked Sammie Rae. She seemed put-out at serving her. "Sure got a nice car, sugar," she cooed, setting a glass of cola next to Lansing's napkin.

Lansing didn't respond to the comment, but Sammie Rae smiled at the girl and said, "I'll have what my boyfriend's having." The waitress wheeled about and stalked off.

Lansing widened his eyes. Cute amusement crinkles formed around them, and Sammie Rae asked, "Your plans change?"

He looked down and fiddled with his napkin, refolding the paper into a small square. "I was supposed to meet up with Darla, since she was working pretty close, but she didn't finish what she wanted to."

"Oh, yeah, she told me. An office worker committed suicide. Body found by the Apalachee sheriff. Darla said her desk was piled with work to be done over the weekend."

"Any news on our murders?" Lansing asked. "I've got nothing new. Nothing here or around DC."

She shook her head. "Nothing clear, only suspicions. More like I'm a pond skater in a murky swamp, moving on trust the Lord will guide me…"

"Pond skater?"

"Bug that walks atop the water."

"Oh," he said, "Jesus bugs."

Was he playing her by showing he could be country, too, making another comment like the oxtail one? By accepting the charade they were on a date?

"Anyway, my hunches…" She told him about her visit to the morgue but before she could mention her thumb drive with names—the coincidence of two on the list now victims— the waitress brought their food.

The girl set a plate gently in front of Al Lansing, oxtails in a brown gravy mingling with the potato salad's mayonnaise. Greens steaming in a little cup. Sammie Rae's serving nearly slid off the plate when it was dropped onto the table.

Sammie Rae poked the oxtails with her fork, moving them around. She said, "Were you gonna eat here with Dar?" and put a forkful of potato salad into her mouth.

Lansing didn't answer her question—he was eating the oxtails as if he'd been starved. "Mmm, these are just like I remember."

"You sure do seem to enjoy those." Sammie Rae held her plate toward his. "Have some of mine."

He paused to take a breath. "You don't want them?"

"Oh, Mrs. Cousins insisted I have some cake." She patted her belly. Wasn't the first lie Sammie Rae had told him and it sure wouldn't be the last. She pushed most of the meat onto his plate and sat back. Idly fiddling with her potato salad, she was free to observe Al. His movements were neat—his fine long fingers making the fork almost dance, his full, plush lips closed over extra-white teeth, the strong muscles in his slightly acne-scarred jaw working the bones. There seemed to be a lot of marrow to suck.

Watching him, her chest felt confined in her shirt. She looked down, mortified—the funny tingling sensations made her nipples protrude, pushing against the cloth. Her old bra was too washed-out to hold them in. She should have worn the nice, padded cup Curvations one.

Her pants also felt tight, but not in the waist like usual. It was her inseam—as if the part of her high up between her legs was swollen.

Concentrate! This meetup wasn't social, it was work, exchanging information about drugs and deaths. For Sammie Rae, it was also about supplying what her people needed to deal with pain, despite what the government did. And there was no way he was attracted to her, not when he'd been seeing Darla. She dragged her mind back to what was important.

Lansing was still dealing with the oxtails. He paused for one moment, looking in her eyes—his own brown, flecked with green and gold. "You don't know how much I appreciate chowing down with gusto in the company of a woman! In DC and New York, the women like dressy places with teeny, mysterious bits on the plate. Who the hell thought of wasting time with quail eggs?"

"They taste different from chicken eggs?"

"Nope. Just smaller." He lifted another bone. "You and Darla are so different from those women." Looking over the bone in his hands, he said, "In a good way."

The compliment was nice, but the mention of Darla cooled her down, made her deflate as if shot with a poisoned arrow, poisoned with guilt. Her granny's voice in her head, *What you get for them dirty thoughts, gal!* Sammie Rae adjusted her trousers, like her pa had, but more discreetly, by sliding her rear back in the seat.

She shouldn't have those thoughts about Darla's man. But was she still with Al? "Have you spent time with Darla lately?" she asked.

He dropped the bone. With a voice cold as a pond in January, he said, "We're not here to talk about Darla." Then he picked another piece from his plate and continued eating.

Wow! Is he wondering about Darla and another man, same as I am?

That damned conference! Things were different before they'd gone, back when they were being pampered in Dolly's kitchen. Back when there were no men involved. She silently vowed that, soon as dinner ended, she was heading to Dolly's house to straighten things out with Darla. She couldn't lose her, and she seemed so far away the last time they'd spoke.

If she lost Darla, she'd lose Dolly as well.

Lansing wiped his fingers on the napkin, sighed and leaned back in his chair, his plate empty. He tucked his shirt further into the waist of his pants—his belly was so trim it seemed a show-off move—and said, "Ahh, that was great. And now we can talk." He took a toothpick from its little paper sheath. "Tell me about Wade Goodloe and his distribution network."

Sammie Rae froze.

"Look, I know what's been up with you and Wade, but I just want to hear about it from you. What do you have to say for yourself?"

"Who's been talking to you?" Sammie Rae instantly regretted the question.

He laughed. "You know I'm not going to answer that now, or maybe ever. Don't worry, we haven't been watching you. Just dribs and drabs of info from here and there."

That was worse than if they had been watching her. Someone gave them information. Now all of Lark County— and half of Apalachee—was potentially untrustworthy.

"Relax. What I learned makes me even more glad to have you on my side. You're ethical, even when skirting the law. You never took a penny for yourself and never personally took any of the drugs." He leaned forward to look closely at her. "Your eyes, they're a really beautiful blue. An honest blue."

Darla's boyfriend shouldn't be talking to her the way he was. And she shouldn't be responding like she was. "Someone like my father, after working like a…" Sammie Rae hesitated, swallowing hard, realizing her voice was getting higher, almost shrill. "…like a slave all his life, has no reason to hope, no reason to live when he's in pain. But those young meth addicts have given up when they have no right to. They haven't even tried living. Why not focus on them?"

She was prepared for anger, but Lansing became calmer. "You really want to protect your people, don't you? And everybody in Lark County is your people. To keep people alive and prevent overdoses—like the two young kids you found in the old mine, we got to get this under control. Trust me, I hate tweakers as much as you, but what's killing the most people are opiates." He cleared his throat. "Tell me, who supplies Wade and who does he supply?"

"Don't know and if I did, wouldn't say. I'm not throwing Wade under the bus." She mashed several chunks of potato into bits with her fork.

"You wouldn't be. What if Wade and his local clients are offered immunity?"

"Yeah, well, identifying his suppliers—or even looking into them—could get Wade dead as a doornail. And other people, too, nothing but poor, broke-down people, for fear they been the ones who told."

The waitress returned and picked up Lansing's empty plate. "Glad you liked it, sweetie," she said, her back to Sammie Rae. "We got cobbler for dessert. Like some?"

"Got ice cream?" Lansing asked.

Sammie Rae pushed her own plate to the side—sending gravy slopping onto the table—and said, more loudly than she planned, "We're done."

"Just the check, please." Lansing again appeared amused by Sammie Rae's outburst.

The girl grabbed the plate and left in a huff.

"By the way..." Lansing leaned toward her. "I've started the process of making you official, an investigator. Wouldn't be within the framework of any ongoing regional task force. You'd be undercover. Nothing to make you noticed in the community. With a big bump in salary and health care benefits."

Sammie Rae tried not to show her surprise. The offer was great. It would change her life. And it meant she was valued as a professional, something even more exciting.

But what would working closely with him mean? Betraying Darla? Sammie Rae stood. "I gotta go."

"Well." He smiled again. "I'll call you. We're not done, not by a long shot. And you wouldn't, shouldn't, give up being Lark's best. The county needs you."

*   *   *

In the twilight, houses and fields were indistinct, blurring as Sammie Rae sped toward Lark County. As fast as the car was going, her heart went faster, as if trying to flee the confusion she felt, even *it* left her behind.

A few miles over the county line, there was an abandoned barn. Charlie had shown it to her, bragging, "When I want to catch forty winks or eat my lunch in peace—or…," with a wink, "…meet up with someone's wife, I just pull the car in through the open door."

The headlights picked out the overgrown path to the barn, the weeds not high enough to do anything but snag on the wheel wells. Around the far side, out of sight from the road, the barn doors were open, listing like eyelids on a drunk.

Sammie Rae backed into the barn, raising a cloud of dust. Leaving quickly would be no problem.

Al Lansing had admired her eyes, the one feature she was proud of. She wasn't tall or slender, her blonde hair was limp and looked washed-out, but her eyes really were a fine, late-afternoon sky blue. Just like her mama's. Remembering his deep gaze, the tight feeling lingered between her legs, as if her privates were squeezing entirely without her consent. The tightness grew more powerful.

Her private parts—Darla would laugh, saying, *What's the matter, Sammie Rae? Granny Mingo won't let you say pussy?* And then she'd grow serious and say, *You're not your mother. Words won't make you like her!*

Sammie Rae reclined her seat, closed her eyes, and tried to picture Thad Overton. She saw the elegance of his face, his high cheekbones, the perfect cupid's bow of his lips. She moaned, realizing she couldn't picture his eyes. He refused to come alive, remained a hazy figure wavering like golden smoke until the man she was imagining transformed.

Her belly contracted like it had been punched. The muscle tightened, with the rhythmic ones in her vagina—her *pussy*—lifted her hips off the seat. She released the belt cutting into her waist and slid her hand down the front of her pants. In a moment she was twelve again, back in her bedroom, in her little, white-painted iron bed. Listening to Pa pace the floor in the other room, staring at the ceiling, feeling the little buds of her breasts, almost too tender to be touched, sliding her hand down under the panties she wore to sleep, until she reached the little nub of flesh, already standing at attention, and began to rub. Gently at first, then, as her breathing quickened and her heart beat a rhythm faster and faster, she pressed with more force. The cemetery angel pressed against her, his perfect face, his grace, his salvation, all hers. She was climbing his robes, holding onto his arms, as the marble warmed into flesh. Struggling upward until she saw his face as it transformed, the soaring cheekbones softening, darkening, the carved bow of the lips growing thicker, more plush, sensual, no longer inspiring the secret play of a little girl, but the lust of an adult woman. What she was doing was wrong now, no excuses, wrong but so, so arousing.

She slid her hand down further until one finger slid inside her, the heel of her hand pressing against the front of her, where sensations spiraled into her belly, down to her knees, and up to her heart.

She was going fast, getting somewhere, somewhere she shouldn't go, but like a runaway train, she couldn't stop.

Thud! Sammie Rae gasped. Her eyes flew open and her arm jerked, pulling her hand free. Something or someone had hit the windshield.

The glass had a splat of blood beneath the rearview mirror. She shot upright, unholstered her revolver, opened the door, and stepped out. On the barn floor, a bat fluttered, squeaking. Dazed and short of breath, she stood for a moment and then a warning clicked in—bat out in the daytime, acting weird. Rabid!?!

Sammie Rae jumped back into the car and started the engine. Turned on the windshield washer and drove out onto the road, her vision blurred by the wipers' smear.

*　　*　　*

The moon was no more than a sliver. In its dim light, the woods brooded, the leafless branches reached down like sharp fingers. Sammie Rae sat in the car for a moment, unnerved by the clammy chill of the night air.

With most of the house dark, the glow from the kitchen window shone bright and welcoming. Her breathing eased. She was back home, at Dolly's house, at Darla's home. Sammie Rae climbed from the car and shivered like a dog shaking off swamp water.

"Where you been, Other Daughter?" Dolly greeted her when she entered the kitchen. "Would have made pork *mandu*, I knew you were coming."

Sammie Rae unzipped her jacket. "If you have time for tea, I'll sit with you. I missed being here. Work kept me going some, busier..."

"...than a cat buryin' poop." Dolly winked—it was her favorite saying.

"Otherwise, I'd never stay away, especially not if you make *mandu*."

Dolly seemed satisfied with that answer. "Then I make tomorrow." She went to the range and put the kettle on.

"So, did Darla get the office in Apalachee cleaned?"

"First time you ask 'bout Darla's work." Dolly squinted at Sammie Rae. "If you mean, did she keep date with Black man, no."

"Because?"

"Because mother always right." Dolly's expression bordered on smug. Elbows planted on the table, crossed hands kneading her upper arms.

The kettle whistled, interrupting their talk—Sammie Rae ignored the sound. No one made tea but Dolly, not in her kitchen.

After a moment, Dolly stood and turned off the flame. She brought the full pot and two little cups to the table. "That man is big show off with fancy suits and red sports car." A few minutes later, she lifted the teapot's lid. "Oh, ready." She poured for herself and Sammie Rae.

Sammie Rae gazed down into her cup and said, her voice so small it surprised her, "He's not a bad guy."

Dolly checked the clock and winked. "Second thought, have time to make *mandu* for you. Ordered gyoza wrappers from Amazon." She went to the refrigerator and pulled out a package of ground pork and began frying it with garlic and ginger, filling the kitchen with a heavenly scent. "Don't tell Darla's father about wrappers. He think I make everything from scratch."

Sammie Rae sat back, content to watch her cook. Dolly seemed so happy that Darla had stood up Lansing. Was the Darla-Lansing romance over?

Chapter 26

BY THE TIME SHE LEFT Dolly's house, Sammie Rae was so full, her belly might burst open. "Jesus, like Jesse Napier's corpse," she said to herself. The thought brought up the image of Johnny Lee's full belly. At that, an acrid bubble of garlicky pork and chili paste came up into her mouth.

"And now I'm going to bed," she said, looking over her shoulder to back out of the drive. She longed to stretch out at home.

But she didn't. Instead of heading into town, she was surprised—yet somehow not surprised—to find she'd turned the wheels in the opposite direction, toward the old Henderson place. She had some questions for Dr. Overton, questions that would either set her mind at ease or take things in a whole new direction.

Beware the white bokor is come. Shouldn't go alone. Should tell Al Lansing where I'm going and why.

The fear of seeming like a fool stopped her at the turnoff. The air inside the car turned stuffy. With the windows down, the dark crowded closer, though the sound of crickets was cheery, magical this late in the season.

She had nothing but suspicions and a comment written in a staged scene. *Come on,* Darla would say, *thinking that makes you seem dumber than a box of rocks. You're a frickin' cop, Sammie Rae! You can't accuse someone of being a murderer—especially not a murdering zombie—without real-world evidence.*

She shifted into drive again and started down the dirt path to the Henderson place. She'd ask some general questions, mentally justifying the late hour arrival as investigational technique. A way to catch him off guard.

Perhaps laying eyes on him would erase the image she'd had in that stupid bat-infested barn. The image of Overton beginning to change into Lansing. The man Darla had dropped like a sack of potatoes.

The wind moaned soft and low, moving the bushes like ghostly hands. It was hunting season, but the road was crowded with deer, standing motionless on the verge, staring as she went by. They should have been wary but instead seemed dazed, mindless, their eyes glistening dully as if her headlights stunned them. Or as if something in the deep woods frightened them more than any human could. She arched her back, pulled her pistol, and laid it on the seat beside her.

In the little valley below, the stone structure of the Henderson place peekabooed in and out of the shadows as the road curved. High clouds skittered across the slender crescent moon. She pulled the car over on the last rise, hesitating. What would she find down at the house?

She put the patrol car in park to give herself time to think. Overton came to Lark County to care for patients who were drug-ridden and poor. Why? He'd said he wanted a rest, but what kind of rest was that? Where was he when Jesse and Johnny Lee died? Too many coincidences and half-truths. That inscription on the cross. The picture she'd taken proved she hadn't imagined it.

Would Lansing find her concern laughable? He'd told her stories of real zombies. She'd taken them seriously and found news articles describing them on the internet.

Worrying about Overton wasn't unreasonable. Every good investigator judged a suspect's actions when first confronted with a crime. She had to tell Thad Overton about the death of Johnny Lee. Watch his eyes. Look for hesitation in his speech. A mist of perspiration or a slight shakiness.

She could do this if she steeled herself to look beyond his beauty.

She sniffed—her upper lip felt damp. She sniffed again, but her breath was too heavy with garlic to smell anything else. It would be embarrassing for Thad Overton to meet her while she wore a soy sauce mustache. She clicked on the overhead and looked in the rearview mirror. The moisture on her face was clear as water—nothing but sweat, despite the cool weather. She hoped her armpits wouldn't dampen.

After another few minutes, she turned off all the lights. Let the car coast slow and silent in the moonlight down to the old stone house.

As her car crept down the drive, she scanned the area. The workers hadn't yet cut the tree down. It still protruded through the roof, looming over the yard. The long fingers of the shadow it cast failed to hide a huge *something* at the base of the drive. Something alive, moving with each breath. Far bigger than a bear, it hunkered like a wild beast guarding its lair. Her mind swung wildly to childhood tales of The White Thing, a monster with a huge body, bigger than a bear, with giant saber-like teeth.

As the wind moved the tree, the topline of the beast rippled with muscle. It was for sure too big to be a normal animal. Its maw would have fangs long enough to make those holes in Johnny Lee.

She stopped her car. Overton's Land Rover was parked only a few feet from the hulking creature, the car pulled in hurriedly at an angle as if the driver had fled in fear. But why seek shelter inside? The building provided no protection from anything.

Perhaps Overton wasn't afraid. Perhaps it was everyone else who should be afraid.

She grabbed her gun, stepped from her car, and moved as silently as possible, staying on the overgrown edge for cover, heading down toward the dark mass. Almost at the bottom, a sudden gust of wind stirred a dust devil, ghostly in the dark, stinging her skin, and the beast rose, flying toward her like a huge bat. She clapped her hand over her mouth to mask her scream and fell on her bottom in the dirt.

It landed to her right as the gust ended. She spun around on her rear, her pistol ready. And then laughed. Her beast was a tarpaulin, poorly secured and ripped from its tie-down. The monster was nothing but a dumpster. She stood and walked to it, leaned against its rough metal side for a moment, calming herself.

Sidling along the Land Rover to stay out of sight of the building, she checked the doors. The vehicle was locked—big-city ways died hard.

The stone wall looked barren without the grape vines; the birds that had feasted on the muscadines had flown. The old door stood ajar. Sammie Rae pushed. It swung open with a deep-pitched moan. She stepped inside.

The first floor was still one massive room, the second floor missing, the roof open to the sky. The moon looked as if it were tangled in the branches of the tree. But in the massive stone fireplace, dead center in the room, logs burned, the crackle of the flames hiding the creak of Sammie Rae's feet on the ancient floor. She made her way carefully, watching for missing boards.

In front of the fireplace, partly covered by a blanket, lay two naked bodies, one male—a broad back tapering to the waist—the other more covered by the cloth, but most decidedly female. The woman's long black tresses tangled as if woven into the man's hair, which glinted gold in the firelight.

Sammie Rae froze at the sight. Though she made no sound, Darla's eyes opened, blinked, and widened. Her mouth open in a gasp of surprise, she held her hand palm up, and slipped out from under Thad Overton's arm.

He stirred and sat.

Sammie Rae turned and fled, stumbling on the loose flooring, out the door and into her car, spinning it around in the dust. In the rearview mirror she saw Overton in the moonlight, gleaming like a marble angel.

Chapter 27

HER CELL PHONE RANG and rang in its dashboard holder. The ring stopped and started up again twice more before it quit. Darla—but what would they say to each other?

The deer were gone as if they'd never been; like phantoms of her imagination, their disappearance made driving easier, with no fear she'd strike one to come through the windshield, taking her head off. Her grip on the wheel loosened.

Just before she turned onto the road to town, the goat herd crossed in front of her. She just avoided hitting a mama with an out-of-season kid. The billy ran back and forth, urging them on.

"Take your girls home," Sammie Rae said, shivering. "That baby'll die in the cold if you ain't got no shelter." But they were already out of sight behind the bushes.

It was midnight when she reached home—the witching hour. She stripped and took a hot shower, came out of the bathroom to find ten messages from Darla, all saying, "Call me." But she was too tired, too confused about what was going on. Instead, she heated some milk to sip hot chocolate in bed and drifted off in sleep.

In her dream Sammie Rae was twelve again, the starched lace collar of her too-small Sunday dress rubbing the skin on her neck. Mee-Maw at the helm of her ancient Plymouth, pulling up to the Pentecostal Church of the Lord. As they approached the red-painted doors, Mee-Maw's ancient talons hooked her skin, dragging her into the church. Cigarette-wrinkled lips, saying to beware the Devil snatching her up for being like her ma.

She awoke, rubbing her arms. Her sleep had only lasted two hours, though it felt as if half the night had gone by. She stared at the ceiling until pale rays of winter sun lit the wall above her bed. The only comfort was the memory of telling Pa, "I don't want to visit Mee-Maw anymore. She scares me."

And having him answer, "Don't listen to my mother. She's batshit crazy."

The phone rang. She sighed and rolled on her side, not sure what she'd say to Darla. But the number displayed on her phone was her father's. "Pa? You all right?" Stupid question—he was crying so hard, he choked.

"Get dressed, you gotta take me on down to Mingo. It's your Mee-Maw!"

Hadn't she just dreamed about Mee-Maw? It seemed she had, but like a wet tissue, the dream tore and dissolved until she wasn't sure. She took a gulp of the cold chocolate. "Pa, I'm in the middle of an investigation. Hazie's son! Maybe Wade could carry you down."

"Sammie Rae, don't give me no back talk." He gasped, out of breath. "She's not just your granny, she's the only ma I got."

"She sick?"

"She's took to bed, fixing to die. I gotta go and you gotta drive me. Not to mention, say your own goodbyes."

Stupefied with insufficient sleep, Sammie Rae sat for a moment, rubbing her scalp. *Drive to Mingo County. Hell no! That miserable old lady turned Christian love to meanness and fear. She was hateful.*

But she'd stepped in when Sammie Rae's mother ran away, giving her and Pa the only relief they had from each other. It had to be allowed that she'd done her best as the last female Wheedle left, not counting Sammie Rae.

Sammie Rae called Pa. "Pick you up in forty minutes. Gotta tell the office I'll be gone."

*   *   *

"What's in the thermos, Pa?" Sammie Rae asked as her father settled into her car.

He pulled at his seatbelt, caught in the door. She reached across his lap and opened the door long enough for him to fix it, then repeated her question.

"Told Wade where we was going and he brought over some liquid sympathy. Not for you, of course. You're driving. But this'll keep you from having me beside you, sniveling away 'bout my mama." He sniffed twice, like a schoolkid trying not to cry. "Mean as that old lady was, I can't picture the world without her." He untwisted the top of the battered, rusty thermos and drank deep from it. Within fifteen minutes, he was slumped over, dead asleep.

Sammie Rae wiggled her phone from her pocket, snapped it into the holder on the dash, put her earbud in, and called Al Lansing.

"Little early, isn't it?" Lansing said, yawning.

"Wanted to tell you I'll be out of town—my grandma's deathly ill."

"When are you coming back?"

"Can't say for sure but you'll have to make do without me." She smiled when he laughed in response and then said he'd miss her.

"Things are going well," he said. "We have a nurse set to roll over on local practitioners who took kickbacks from drug companies. Hopefully they'll be prosecuted under racketeering, like the fentanyl case."

Sammie Rae gave a sigh of relief. No one important to her went through medical channels. Lark had only two doctors left, anyway, and they tended to minister to the better-off. This wouldn't affect them.

But she still had the others to protect. "Al, while I'm gone will you make sure Hazie and the rest are safe? I keep shuddering, thinking of Johnny Lee's autopsy—who knows what they'd do to his ma. At least Pa's with me, so that's one less rascal you have to worry about." She passed a semi on the other side and wondered briefly if it was Darla's father. Traffic was light. It was still early. "And thinking on the Haitians, can I ask you a question about voodoo?"

"Voodoo? Sure, but why?"

"Just interested." She chewed on her lower lip for a moment. "So, are there ever any foreign bokors? White men?" Her earbud made her left ear itch, so she switched it over to the right side.

"Why are you interested?" His voice was tighter, higher than usual. He knew something he wasn't telling her. She waited.

Finally, "Voodoo is just superstition. But yes to male bokors in Haiti. But foreign men? White guys? Not so sure. So, you going to tell me why you're asking?"

"It's just there was something in Johnny Lee's root cellar. I'll text you the photos when I get to my granny's. It's only fifty-five miles, so it won't be long. Reception there is sucky, though."

"Drive safe. Stay safe. Keep in touch and get back soon." He ended the call.

Sending the photos without mentioning Overton would be all right. There didn't need to be anything about her suspicions—the ones that might make her look foolish.

"Who was that?" Pa asked, clearing what sounded to be a pound of phlegm and Red Man from the back of his throat. He opened his window and spat the brown wad out.

"Don't do that, Pa! Last time I drove you somewhere, I had to wash that side of the car with Lysol."

He cackled and squinted at her like Popeye. "Day you wash this little bucket of rust is the day our Lord comes again." Turning away, he put his window up and tapped on the glass at some enormous black-and-white hogs. "Berkshires, classy." A moment later, he began snoring again.

Her pa was no dummy. She looked at his grizzled head, leaned against the window, and wished she could ask his advice. She hadn't done that in years. All she'd done was handle his craziness. But maybe he'd have an idea of what she should say to Darla. Maybe he'd talk her through her confusion about Overton. And Lansing.

Pa had never asked why she didn't date. A mother would have. Until she was told to stay home from school unless she got a bra, as the boys were taking notice, he didn't notice her body changing. Dolly was the one who'd explained periods to her and bought her tampons. Darla was the one to sympathize with her cramps, accompanying her to the lavatory at school when they were bad and waiting outside the stall to frighten the bullying girls away.

How could she explain her desires to Pa? She'd never talked about men with him, let alone sex. He'd been the one with her in that cemetery when she was just a kid. Might make him feel bad, though, to bring up why that beautiful angel got stuck in her mind. She'd never tell what she'd been up to alone in her bed.

Pa'd been too wrapped up in himself and his loneliness to be disturbed.

Dawn was breaking when they pulled up at the house Mee-Maw'd moved to, after she refused to get along with her daughter-in-law. The shabby street of clapboard bungalows, each surrounded by chain-link fencing, each front door lit by a floodlight, was quiet but for the yard dogs that set up a ruckus at the sight of strangers. Mee-Maw's place had been fake bricked, peeling from neglect. The flower beds were full of weeds, some of the roof tiles missing.

Angie, Mee-Maw's landlady and lifelong friend, came out, wiping her hands on a dishtowel. She was nearly as old as Mee-Maw but strong and healthy as a mule. "Good thing you're here, boy!" was her greeting to Pa and, "Carry the bags in, girl," to Sammie Rae.

They walked through the main room, the walls decorated in crosses and pictures of tree-planting on Decoration Day, some from just after the Civil War. Come spring, dogwood blooms atop graves must have blanketed the whole area.

When Pa headed for the bathroom, Angie pulled Sammie Rae aside. She narrowed her tiny eyes, hooded by overhanging lids, and said, in one river of words, "Don't you let him upset her with his rowdy ways! Didn't raise her boy to be a heathen, but now they say he don't never go to church. Didn't raise him to marry a floozy, but he did anyways, and that floozy done drove your Mee-Maw from her home. She lived here in my house since before you was born. I hate to speak ill, but your grandma's weak when it comes to him."

Sammie Rae was hugged tight to her sagging bosom, to the apron starched to cardboard. The musty old-lady scent gagged her. But that was nothing compared to Mee-Maw's room. The rich odor of sickly decay mixed with Pine-Sol and urine, despite the boxes of adult diapers on the dresser and the clean commode standing ready by the bed.

Her grandmother looked like a freeze-dried rodent under the antique crazy quilt.

Pa came in, turning his hat in his hands, uncertain of what to do. In the awkward silence, Sammie Rae stepped close, took a cool, dry hand, and said, "Mee-Maw, it's me."

The old lady opened one red-rimmed eye. Her mouth moved but nothing audible came out. Sammie Rae gave a side glance to Angie, who was still at the foot of the bed, watching. Then she bent over and put her ear next to the dry lips. "Say what, Mee-Maw?"

Mee-Maw's hand squeezed hers. The tip of a pale, swollen tongue appeared but no words.

"Don't just stand there, girl," Angie hissed. "Put that there straw in her mouth and let her wet her whistle."

Sammie Rae hesitated for a moment, silently vowing that Angie might try, but no way was she going to be a replacement telling her how to live. Then she lifted the glass to Mee-Maw. The old woman took a feeble sip, and that wormlike tongue pushed the straw away. Her whisper was loud enough to hear. "You want to be good, don't you, child?"

Mee-Maw would find fault until the moment she died. Sammie Rae braced herself for a sermon, short-lived as it might be.

"I see Heaven's gates—I see them right before my eyes." She paused to cough, a pathetically weak sound, and struggled under the covers, trying to sit. "Only open for the righteous. You don't jest want to become a favorite of the Lord—you want to *stay* a favorite of the Lord." Her eyes closed again.

"Ma? Ma?" Pa cried.

But Mee-Maw only took in one huge gasping breath. They waited in the awful silence, until Angie cried out, "She done gave up the ghost."

At the wail that tore from her father's mouth, loud and wild as a panther's scream, something felt like it was ripping in Sammie Rae's chest, something hot and unexpected. She took a step toward him, but he bent over, cradling his mother to him. The loss of Mee-Maw like a hole had opened, down into the dark.

How strange to feel her eyes well with tears, to realize she *had* loved Mee-Maw. She'd always thought she hated her. Turning, Sammie Rae bumped into Angie, who was ready and waiting.

"I know what she wanted," Angie said. "For you to follow her example. Church every Sunday, no excuses, and taking him with you." Her dry eyes stared into Sammie Rae's own. "Remember, the Devil used to be God's favorite. Lucifer, the most beautiful angel. So, being as you ain't beautiful like that, falling into Hell will be easier for you."

"I'll make the arrangements."

"Already made," Angie said. "She got one of them pennies-a-day policy to cover final costs and the church is all set. Services will be this Sunday. All you need do is show up for appearance's sake."

Sammie Rae kept her expression steady—Mee-Maw was beyond appearances. Angie was a spinster with no kids of her own. Though she was mean as Mee-Maw, she wouldn't die anytime soon. But she was no reason for them to visit Mingo County again. Not now, not ever. "Let's head on back, Pa," was all she said.

Chapter 28

ON THE RIDE HOME, Pa drank steadily, pausing only to sob. "So, that's it. She's gone and I can't disappoint her no more." He wiped his eyes with the back of his hand. "Shit, girl, I'm going to miss her." He patted her knee, just as Beebe had. "My wife's gone. My ma's gone. You're all the family I got left. You won't leave me, will you? A person ain't nobody if they got no family. Can't go through life alone."

"Hmm," Sammie Rae said, giving herself a moment to gather up her courage. "Family can be tough, Pa." She sounded like one of the social workers, come to sort out a domestic problem at the jail. Mee-Maw had never taken to Sammie Rae's mother—hated her from the start. She might, as Angie said, have been driven off by her or it might have been the other way around. Before she could delve into that, Pa said, "Damn if Mee-Maw wasn't right about your ma. I should never have let that tramp drive her out of her own home. Never forgave me not standing up for her. But when a man's in love, he's blind as a bat and pig-headed as a mule."

Though it was early afternoon, the sunlight was weak, the sky cloudy, gloomy, and threatening rain. They stopped at a gas station. "I fancy a couple a' hot dogs. They got them grillers what roll the dogs around. Gets 'em nice and crispy everywhere. Bring me two with onions and mustard and that bright green relish. Bag of chips—plain, not the barbecue kind get red dust all over your fingers. A big strawberry slushie. If they ain't got strawberry, I'll take cherry."

"Yeah, Pa," Sammie Rae said, too worn out to suggest something healthy. She didn't mind bringing him the food. Waiting for him to stagger from the car to inside the store would delay them at least fifteen minutes, much of that waiting while he mulled over the candy selection. He had an awful bad sweet tooth.

She half-filled the gas tank since there wasn't much left on her credit card and made her way across the lot, past tall aluminum cans overflowing with trash.

Inside the store was a young man with a beard and pony-tail, neither too clean. He didn't look up when Sammie Rae entered. The hot dogs were in the back, grilled until they had a crisp mahogany exterior. They smelled gamey, like it wasn't the first day they'd been cooking, but she took two rolls and put a dog in each. The fixings her father liked were in open containers visited by a few drowsy flies who'd tired of the slushie drippings. At the last minute, she added hot cheese sauce, figuring the molten grease would kill any germs.

She put six dollars down for the dogs, chips, and drink. When the clerk ignored her to continue playing a game on his phone, she left, her hands full. She pushed the door open with her butt and turned to see another car, a gold Escalade at the second pump. Standing outside it was a Black man. He looked familiar. She gasped. *The Haitian hunter!*

The Haitian was staring at her pa, still in the front passenger seat. He nodded to himself as if he recognized him. He must have been at the Quonset hut with Johnny Lee when Pa and Hazie stumbled along.

Her gun was in the car, her phone in its holder. She glanced around, considered going back into the store to call for help, but that would take time. Her pa was looking straight ahead, motionless, seemingly unaware of the danger.

She held herself stiff, planning to run at the man if he moved toward her car. A *clunk!* distracted her. She glanced in its direction and saw one of the trash cans overturned with its contents strewn about. Browsing through the garbage was the billy goat, who looked up as her eyes landed on him. His brown eyes met hers with such intensity, the midday sun dimmed. His square pupils bored into her.

Sammie Rae froze. He could knock her down with ease. Would he stop if she tossed him the food?

He pawed the ground, a tell for a coming charge. She turned back and saw the Haitian start toward her little car at the same time the billy took off at a gallop. She tensed her knees, bracing for a hit, clutching the hot dogs tight despite the cheese burning her hand.

But the goat didn't hit her. He rushed past, head down, horns leading the way. Just as the man reached her car, close enough to touch the handle of Pa's door, the billy hit him directly in the groin. He was knocked on his rear, his hands between his legs, only to roll face down on the concrete, contorted in pain. The goat stood over the man, snorting, and continuing to paw the dust.

Sammie Rae moved quick and smooth as she could. When she reached her open car door, her pa turned. He was holding her pistol, lowering it when he saw her. She slid into her seat, handed over the hot dogs, started the engine, and sped away. A few twists and turns later, she looked at him, aware he knew she'd underestimated him.

"Dammit, Sammie Rae," he said, "You put that cheese crap all over!"

*   *   *

Sammie Rae insisted Pa return with her to her apartment. He couldn't go back home, not if he'd been identified.

The wooden stairs were rickety, the handrail loose. She went up step-by-step with him, cane on his right, his left hand pressing against the siding for support. Though he seemed a lot friskier since taking up with Hazie, it had been a long while since he'd conquered a flight of twelve treads.

Inside her living room, he collapsed with a loud *huff* on her saggy couch. "Not as good as my easy chair," he complained.

"It'll have to do, Pa." She hoped he wouldn't make the couch resemble his funky chair.

He chuckled. "Damn old billy seemed to have it in for that dude. Wonder why."

She wanted to tell of her time in the forest, when the hunter had killed one of the goat's does, but all she said was, "Gotta go out. I'll set you up with everything you need."

"My thermos refilled—if you ain't got the stuff, get some from Dolly. I know that's where you're going, anyway. And before you go, a box of crackers. And tobacco. An ashtray if you don't want ashes on the floor."

"Got no ashtray, Pa." She didn't want him burning the place down with him inside.

He gave her the evil eye, as he did whenever she suggested he cut down on smoking. "A saucer'll do. And I need my shotgun, so fetch it from my house. Take some of your buddies if need be. A man can't think if he's not prepared for what's coming down the pike."

No way was she getting him that shotgun, not when he'd probably blow a hole in her roof. Smoking while high on opiates was dangerous enough. Sammie Rae rifled through his bag for his pills and put them within reach. Then she went to the kitchenette to get the box of Cheez-Its and an apple that was soft on only one side. She put the apple, cut in slices, on a plate and brought everything to the living room. "I'll bring something healthy for dinner."

He looked at her with annoyance. "Dolly's good stuff is organic."

*   *   *

"Sorry about grandmother. Wade told me." Dolly put two pints of her best shine on the table for Sammie Rae's pa, though not the *myeongsul*. "Wheedle don't like Korean shine. This his favorite. When lose mother, need what you like best." When Sammie Rae didn't get up to leave, she asked, "Something worrying you?"

Sammie Rae and Darla had never, ever told on each other. Why start now? Best to find out what Dolly knew and then only add what was necessary. "Just wondering what's up. Been so busy, there wasn't time to catch up with you and Dar."

"Want *gaeran mari*?"

"Already had breakfast." That was a lie, and Sammie Rae's mouth watered at the thought of the beautiful yellow and black-swirled omelet of egg and seaweed. She looked toward the bedrooms. "Is she sleeping in?"

"Naughty girl didn't come home again last night." Dolly brought the teapot and cups to the table, along with a plate of Chips Ahoy. "Favorite cookie."

Taking one, Sammie Rae bit into it right away. Helped hold her tongue.

"Think she is with new boyfriend. Not happy with staying all night but happy he is doctor, *baeg-in*."

"Yep, he sure is White." Sammie Rae looked around the kitchen, at the familiar pans hanging on the wall, the chopping block, the pictures of herself and Darla on the fridge. Even

249

more than the sight of all those things, the smells were so familiar—the odors that said *home*.

"I'm worried, Dolly." She hastened to add, "Just a bit. Doesn't seem like Dar to move so fast."

"For long time, didn't seem like her to move at all. I want grandbaby. Boy grandbaby."

Wow, Darla might be moving fast, but Dolly's moving faster. "But we don't know that much about him." A feeling ran down Sammie Rae's back like an army of ants on the move. What did she have on him? Nothing.

Dolly squinted, her eyes simmering with suspicion. "What?"

"Just worried, is all."

"You like that Black man better because he's a cop? You want another cop in family?"

That almost made Sammie Rae laugh with frustration. Nothing was clear to her so how could she explain things to Dolly?

Dolly came around the table and put her arms around Sammie Rae. "Tell me, Second Daughter, are you jealous? Or worried Darla will not be your sister anymore?"

"No." Sammie Rae hated the way her voice had dropped into a whine, like a kid's. "I know better than that."

"Worry about her being out all night, and nobody know who is killing people? Johnny Lee and Napier kid who killed Gracie's girl?"

"She wasn't Gracie's girl anymore—she was Jesse's wife."

Dolly shot her an as-if-that-makes-a-difference look. "Those dead boys all chewed up and one ate some of the other."

Sammie Rae's jaw dropped. "Who told you that?" She had forgotten Dolly was info central. No matter who'd leaked this information, all channels led right here.

"People want shine, they talk. People have shine, they talk. I'm always there to listen." Dolly shrugged. "I worry there is a fox ghost. Johnny Lee dumb as shit but no way he's a cannibal. Have to be something very evil, very tricky, not human, so maybe fox ghost. Some people say The White Thing." She shook her head.

The White Thing? Sammie Rae had been terrified of The White Thing, back when she was little. When Pa was on night shift, her ma would leave her alone in the house, saying, "Keep the doors and windows locked. Don't even look out and no matter what you hear, don't open up. The White Thing is hunting little girls tonight." Later, she'd figured that the only white thing she'd seen would have been Ralph Beebe's butt moving up and down in the backseat of his patrol car. His pale behind, gleaming in the moonlight.

The White Thing was her ma's version of Tonton Macoute, just a way to control her child, a monstrous thing to do. Just like the Tonton soldiers had brought the monster in human form to Haiti. And now, the new Ton Tons to Lark County.

Lark County had been aswarm with monsters for centuries. Too many otherwise sane people swore that they, or their brother, or cousin, or daddy, had seen one. Too many people, eyes wide with terror, had come into the sheriff's office to tell of an encounter. Too many to just discount the stories. And Dolly was the most sensible person Sammie Rae knew. If she really believed in the supernatural, the supernatural had to be considered. But no matter how many people believed they'd seen The White Thing, if it was real, proof would exist, and none had been found. But there was plenty of proof zombies existed in Haiti and in the drug-fueled cannibal cases in America.

"I think it could be something else. Something foreign," Sammie Rae said.

Dolly slapped the table, a triumphant expression on her face. "Fox ghost!"

"Don't think so." Sammie Rae spoke with care—though nothing seemed to remain confidential, she couldn't afford to be the source so close to home. "You know there are drugs being smuggled into Lark County, right? Well, there's a gang from Haiti involved. You know, Haiti in the Caribbean. Where they have voodoo witch doctors."

"Walking Dead!" Dolly slapped the table harder, but now, not happy to be right. "Zombies, like you and Darla like to watch!"

"Like them. We have no proof the local monsters are real. But they arrested real zombies in Florida."

"Huh, Florida," Dolly said, "no wonder. Crazy place! Miami on *The First 48* all the time. These zombies ate people?"

"Their faces."

"Oooo, just like here. Okay, Sammie Rae, I'm not a stupid old lady. Don't tell story bit by bit with little spoon." She held out the ladle. "Use this. Get to part about Darla."

Sammie Rae led with, "It's just a feeling I have, but I don't have proof…" Dolly's expression made her get more to the point. "Dr. Overton was just in Haiti but left. Came here to rest, or so he says. The zombie murders started when he was in DC. He was here when Jesse Napier was killed, went back to DC, and returned here just before Johnny Lee died. He sort of lied to me, saying he wasn't coming back yet." She couldn't mention the cross in Johnny Lee's root cellar, the one warning of a White voodoo practitioner, the warning possibly pointing to Overton. No one had noted it yet and she wanted to tell Al first. To keep her job, she needed to tell Beebe, too, before the news spread through the county.

"You think he's zombie?" Dolly returned to her seat, her mouth open in a tiny *O*.

Sammie Rae shook her head. "Can't say that. But, since he lived there, he might know a lot about them. Could be there's no zombies at all."

"Drug runners from Haiti are 'round here."

"Who'd you hear that from?"

Dolly looked down at her fingernails and picked at one. "Could be Wade. Can't remember for sure. Is that doctor working with them?"

Sammie Rae shrugged.

Dolly's eyes moved side to side like she was connecting the dots to form a picture. "Those guys really dangerous, huh? My girl might get caught up in bad stuff."

"Honest, I got nothing to pin on him. Maybe it was animals ripped the bodies up." Animals might account for the wounds, but animals couldn't freeze a bit of someone and feed it cooked to someone else.

Dolly turned her teacup around and around. "Zombies and drugs. Not good, either one. Animals don't feed what they kill to people. Asking Darla straight-up sure to backfire. She likes him too much and no more stubborn girl in the world."

"You make good points. Shame you're not a sheriff."

Dolly gave a tense little grin.

Sammie Rae took a sip of tea to moisten her throat. Anxiety about discussing things with Darla had made it dry. "I'm gonna call and say I want to meet up."

Dolly took a sip. "Won't mention you drop by. Will see what I can see."

*   *   *

They met at the Dunkin' as usual. Sammie Rae was deep in a sandwich of egg, cheese, and sausage when Darla walked in, hooked her bag on a chair, and dropped into the seat. She didn't lead with an apology and plea to be forgiven, as Sammie Rae had hoped. Instead, she said, "I know why you didn't answer my calls."

Sammie Rae eyed her over the top of the croissant. The giant bite she'd taken—as soon as she'd seen Darla park—gave her time to consider a response. She held her index finger up to gain time while she chewed.

"We swore we'd never let a guy come between us," Darla said.

A guy? Which one? Sammie Rae put down her sandwich and wiped her fingers.

Darla leaned toward her, just as Overton had at dinner, and put her hand atop Sammie Rae's. "Honest, the first time just happened."

First time? Sammie Rae widened her eyes in mock innocence. "What *just happened?*"

"Jesus. Don't make this hard." Darla stared into her eyes. "We were drinking wine, talking about the building. He made a fire and that's the thing about a fire, makes you so drowsy and cozy you forget yourself. One thing led..."

"And you got so sleepy, you just fell on top of each other?" Sammie Rae bit her tongue. "What happened to you and Al Lansing? Thought you had finally found the perfect guy."

"Well..."

"I met him for dinner the night you told him you were working. After dinner, I went to your house to talk but you weren't there. Went to see what was up at the Henderson place, since I hadn't been around for a long spell. It was so late, I figured he'd be alone."

"I'm so sorry." Darla's voice was small, and raggedy. "I know you liked him."

Sammie Rae had wanted an apology, but as she looked into Darla's tight, sad face, guilt walloped her hard, like something big hitting a windshield. She rubbed her face to hide her skin's flush. She should say, *No, I'm not interested in him anymore. The way he looks, like an angel, was just part of a childhood fantasy.*

This wasn't going how she wanted it to, it was supposed to be about Darla's safety. Sammie Rae had to leave for work but, short of time or not, she wanted to find out what Darla knew about Overton. She wanted to warn her without making an accusation she couldn't prove. "Why'd you give up on Al? Was that just bullshit, all that relief at finally finding another outsider? Someone like you?" Her phone vibrated in the pocket of her jacket. She ignored it.

"I was wrong, okay? I *was* interested. He attracts attention for being different here, just like me. But it turned out we didn't really have much in common inside, where it counts." She shivered with obvious distaste. "You know I hated him being like some damn fancy-dressed peacock. And always complimenting me when I dressed up. I was just something to make him look good, the same as that flashy sports car. Plumb wore me out."

Al Lansing wasn't a peacock, more like the chameleon in the paint ad. One minute, he was down-home folksy, easygoing, the slightest bit rough around the edges, the next moment he was all official business. The car wasn't his, it was government property he'd have to give back. She wanted to defend him but, at the "*was* interested," Sammie Rae's heart had done a little skip, knocking against her breastbone. It hadn't yet settled down. She'd wondered if Darla was still torn between the two men, but now it seemed she had no interest in Lansing at all.

"Thad understands how I feel," Darla said. "He's shit-sick of people having the hots for him just because of his looks."

Blood rushed to Sammie Rae's cheeks. That felt like a deliberate jab. "And you don't? You don't like how gorgeous he is?"

"Hell, no, Sammie Rae! How can you even think that?"

"You were into Lansing because of his looks, because they'd piss off your ma. Why would it be any different with Overton?" Shit. Her tongue seemed to have a mind of its own, derailing her carefully laid-out discussion.

Darla was still discussing Overton. "It just is. I know it."

Last night had shown how far things had gone between Darla and Overton, but what had happened with her and Lansing? Darla had never slept around. Despite all the guys after her, very few had gotten lucky.

A sneaky little hope wormed its way into Sammie Rae's heart. Girlfriends didn't hook up with each other's ex-lovers, but if Darla hadn't slept with Lansing…

Stick to the topic of Darla's safety. Who screwed who doesn't matter right now! Sammie Rae took a deep breath and braced her hands on the table. "I'm afraid for you, Dar. What do we really know about Overton? Why did he leave Haiti and come here? Where did he get his money? Is he running from something?"

Darla pressed her lips together so tight, the skin around them blanched. "I trust him," she said, pushing back from the table. She stood and tugged at her shoulder bag. Her chair fell to the floor. "Sammie Rae Wheedle, I never thought it could happen, but I fear you're jealous. Maybe it's just you wishing it was you with him. Maybe I don't know what, but if you love me, think about this: he might be my only chance of being happy!" She picked up her chair and turned, then said over her shoulder, "Sorry, but if you want to know all that shit, ask him." Smiling an apology at the rest of the customers, who smiled back, she left.

Sammie Rae was too upset to finish the sandwich. She looked around the Dunkin'. Her gaze passed over the faces of several customers, but they quickly looked down. She stood, feeling a fool's smile plastered on her face. What was it Mee-Maw used to say? Oh, yeah: *Don't let your battleship mouth overload your rowboat ass.*

Sammie Rae, everybody's friend and protector, had done the unthinkable. She'd upset the town beauty.

Chapter 29

"HAVEN'T SEEN MUCH OF you lately," Charlie said when Sammie Rae walked into the office. He looked at his watch. "And look, today you're late."

"Her granny died," Ray Ben said, stepping between them. "You gotta take time off when your granny dies."

"It's okay." Sammie Rae patted Ray Ben's back. "There's different rules for jerks than for us humans." She walked to Sheriff Beebe's office and knocked.

Beebe opened the door. "Come in, come in," he said, shutting the door behind her. "Sit, sit." He pulled a chair out for her and fanned his hand over it like a carnival magician.

She dropped into the seat.

"Sorry to hear about Mee-Maw," Ralph Beebe said. "She was a nice lady. Back when your pa and me was kids and went hunting, I always brought her the fattest squirrels. She made squirrel stew with corn and beans in it." He closed his eyes and smiled. "You know those big whitey-green butter beans, remind me of the pellets detergent comes in now." He opened his eyes and looked at her. "You learn how to make that stew?"

"Nossir." The blossoming relationship between her pa and Beebe was the squirrely thing these days. "Mee-Maw was gone from here before I was old enough to cook."

"Shame, shame. But never mind." He leaned forward across the desk. "Tell me what's going on with that agent guy, the Black one you brought in here." Casually, he added, "Lansing's his name, if I recollect right."

Sammie Rae took a deep breath to give herself a moment to think. She leaned forward just as he had and dropped her voice as if they were conspiring. "I'm not supposed to say anything to anyone yet—not even you, sir—but I overheard there's a big action coming."

"Here?"

"Right here in Lark County. And our department will be front and center if I have anything to do with it. Can't say anything more yet. They didn't go into details."

A huge smile crept across Beebe's face as he rocked back and forth in his swivel chair. Then he slapped the desk as he always did when excited and said, "Keep me updated."

"I will, sir, every chance I get."

He blinked, his eyes looking damp. "You're doing me and your pa proud, Sammie Rae. You sure turned out good. Nothing like your ma."

"Thank you, sir." She bit her lower lip. She'd lusted for one man and then, in only a short time, she had gotten all hot and bothered for another. Really, how different was she from her mother?

On her way out of the office she stopped by Ray Ben, bent forward, patted his shoulder, and said, "You're my best buddy, Ray Ben."

The blush that rose from his neck, to quickly cover his face, was spectacular. The room hushed, the four other deputies and the clerk paused to stare. She went to Charlie's desk, leaned over him, puckered her lips and moaned softly, "And this is for you." He smirked until she said, "Jesus, Charlie, your breath smells like a buffalo fart."

The office erupted in laughter. She walked out with an extra swagger and a grin so wide her face almost split.

*   *   *

Sammie Rae called Al and suggested meeting in Apalachee County. She had to take her pa back to Hazie, who was still at Mamie Cousins's house. "There's an abandoned barn just across the county line. We can pull one of the cars inside and talk in comfort—doors are open so we can keep the motor running for heat. I'll text instructions and wait on the road. You can't miss it. Call if you get lost."

If the bat was rabid, it'd be dead by now.

She hummed as she drove, singing when she remembered a word. Lady Antebellum's "Need You Now."

Standing on the road by her car, waiting for him to arrive, she zipped her jacket up but still shivered. She tried leaning back on her elbows to feel more casually seductive, but the curve of the hood made her slip down until her butt almost hit her heels. Her confident, cocky swagger leaving the office had evaporated. She longed to present herself as seductive, sophisticated, without seeming too sluttish.

An SUV drove up. Sammie Rae shot upright when she saw it was a gold Escalade, stopping behind her. She felt for her gun to be ready, but when the door opened, Al Lansing got out.

"Jesus, why are you driving that?"

"Huh?" He turned to look. "Oh, borrowed it from the Haitians. Told them the Porsche attracted too much attention when I was meeting up with my contact. That's you, of course, and by the way, what a lovely hello."

His sarcasm might once have triggered a snappy response, but not now, not at the sight of the car. "Follow me." They drove both cars. She tucked her patrol car out of sight behind a small cluster of bushes, leaving room for him to back into the barn. They'd be much more comfortable in the Escalade.

Sammie Rae climbed into the passenger seat. She was separated from him only by the console.

"Tell me why the car bothered you."

"Bothered me? Freaked me out." Sammie Rae told him about driving back from Mingo County with Pa, stopping for gas and a snack. "This same gold Escalade pulled up and one of the Haitians got out, heading straight toward Pa. I was holding two hot dogs, but my gun was in the car." And then she described her miraculous rescue by the billy goat. To her surprise, Al said, "So that's why he was walking like a hooker in high heels!" and burst out laughing.

His laugh was deep and rolling. It got her going, too, part with memory of the goat's lowered horns hitting groin flesh and part with relief. He wasn't judging her. She turned to face him just as he tilted to his right, holding onto the steering wheel, and laughing so hard he was gasping for breath. Their noses bumped. He moved further right at the contact just as she moved to the left. Their lips almost met. They both pulled back in surprise.

"Sorry," Sammie Rae said, trying to turn away.

"Don't be! This is just what I've wanted." She felt the warmth of his hands on her cheeks as Lansing held her face and kissed her. His lips were pillowy, soft. She sank into them down to the firmness beneath.

At the conference, those breaths through those lips, close to her ear, had given her a squirmy, tightening, damp-panties sensation, the feeling that she'd burst if she didn't touch herself. Kissing did more than that, much more. Her lips opened with a deep intake of the night air. She felt his tongue flicker at the corners of her mouth and then slide over her teeth. Her own tongue fought back as she forced it into the warmth between his lips, into the deep drawing feeling as it was sucked in and out. That set up a squirmy, tightening feeling shooting through her body, like an electrical charge, a sensation that made her legs open as if they had minds of their own.

He moaned as she took one hand from its clasp of her face and, astonished at her own boldness, placed it between her thighs. The heel of his hand pressed against the spot where she'd once rubbed, alone in her bed. But, *oh*, it felt so much better for it to be his hand.

"We gotta move," he gasped, withdrawing his hand. "I'm too big to get around the wheel."

Despite the tightness of her breath, Sammie Rae said, "The backseat?"

"Better the hatch—cargo space's real roomy."

"Well, it *is* a Cadillac." *The hatch has carpet. Even better, because if there's blood, it'll sink out of sight!* And as Darla always said, "If you're gonna do it, unless it's your wedding night, don't ever confess you're a virgin. Scares some guys right off."

Sammie Rae opened her door and slid out.

Lansing hesitated for a moment before joining her at the rear of the vehicle. He lifted the hatch door.

Sammie Rae threw her arms around him and pressed her lips back against his. She pushed her rear onto the bed and tucked her knees up. She'd taken Darla's advice to heart.

He crawled in to put down the passenger seatbacks, turned and pulled her further in. It was then she worried there might be other bats. "Shut the door."

"Why?" He tugged down her jacket's zipper and put his lips against her neck. "Nobody's here to see. Pretty soon we'll steam up the windows."

Rabies sure could destroy a romantic atmosphere. "Please. We're in a barn."

"Oh, right, critters. City boy here." When he did what she asked, she lay back, reaching down and unbuttoning her waistband. He reached inside her jacket and ran his fingers lightly across her bra, the silky fabric slick, the lace rough against her skin. His hand was large and glowing with heat. Despite it was cold as a witch's titty, she was sweating, hoping he'd help her shrug off her jacket.

And then he pulled away, a troubled look on his face. His hands left her body. She was instantly chilled, and ashamed of her assumptions. He didn't want her.

She jerked back, desperate to pull up her jacket's zipper and arrange her clothes. "Sorry, I know I'm not Darla."

He blinked and shook his head. "What the hell you talking about? You think I don't want you? Well, you're dead wrong."

Her pants' zipper, hard enough to get down over the curve of her belly, was proving impossible to pull up while lying in the hatch. She wriggled side to side until she got her jacket closed. "Oh, am I?" she asked.

"Yeah, you are. Sure, Darla is a stunner, but that was just lust. I don't like a fickle woman who wants me mostly to piss off her mama."

"Darla's not like that."

"Anyway, we never had sex and sure never made love. Not since we, you and me, started growing close. Might have jeopardized things with you." He paused, giving her heart time to soar. "But you and me, our relationship's been professional so far. We're still working things out."

"Don't give a crap about that," she said, pulling on his arm. "You don't want to stop, do you?" Her heart was hammering against her ribs—what if he said yes? Was she embarrassing herself?

In the dim light of the moon, shining down through the open barn door and the many gaps in the roof, his eyes were liquid black, yet they seemed to burn into her. At last, he spoke. "Fuck no!"

She opened her jacket and unbuttoned her blouse. He didn't take any time appreciating her best bra, instead sliding his hands under her back, and deftly unhooking it. Her breaths, ragged and short, interrupted her as she said, "I take it that skill's in your wheelhouse, Agent Lansing."

His mouth was against the top of her right breast, so when he laughed, her flesh jiggled like blowing a raspberry on a baby's belly. She laughed, too, arching back. That slid her nipple into his mouth and those soft lips sucked in a way that brought alive the sensation of electrical wiring throughout her body, drawing her rear off the carpet. She pushed at her pants, working them down her hips.

His lips moved from one nipple to the other, his tongue wetting them as the pressure made them swell, his breathing out making them glow hot, his breathing in pulling a cold wind across them. One big, warm hand slid down, beneath the smooth nylon of her panties, to the erect little nub between the folds of her flesh, and she moaned. He hesitated at the sound she made. Had he realized she had no experience with lovemaking? Would he quit the wonderful things he was doing? She didn't want him to! She longed for him to continue.

Despite the fact he was shivering, he pulled off his jacket and sweater. His skin glistened in the faint light. She realized with a shock that she hadn't touched him, not the way he was touching her. She had to impress him with some bit of skill but what exactly should she do? Her few spells of making out in high school hadn't gone very far—should she just grab his dick through his pants? She brushed her hand against his thigh. He was wearing jeans, new ones—the material thick and stiff. Would it be better to shove her hand down inside his waistband? Was there a wrong way to handle a penis? Darla hadn't been graphic enough.

He ended her dilemma by taking her wrist and placed her hand over the fly of his jeans. Over a tube-shape that felt too hard to be flesh. Sure, in junior high, boys had pushed up against her behind and she'd felt lumps, but nothing so firm or large.

She felt along the length of him—that seemed to be the thing to do, as he groaned, and his hand tightened on her breast. When she reached the button and the tab below it that opened his zipper, she released them. His cock sprang out against her palm, the head firm, covered in velvety skin. He pushed down his pants like he was desperate to be naked.

"Wait a minute, wait a minute." He was panting, searching in his pants without finding what he wanted.

Sammie Rae missed the movement of his hands on her breasts, the pressure on her pussy. *God, I hate that word like poison.* Despite the desire making her shake, she felt in her jacket and found the old, crinkled condom wrapper stashed in the inner pocket. Darla and she had practiced putting condoms on the pestle Dolly used to pound garlic for her kimchi—good thing, as putting it on a penis was harder—at least the pestle stayed still. His sigh when she was done rewarded her for all those hours fearing Dolly's early return.

Sammie Rae ran her fingers through the curly hair on his chest and over his little nipples. Rubbing them seemed to cause the same reaction as rubbing hers had. As she played with them, Lansing rolled over onto her. She wanted him inside her but feared tensing at the pain that was supposed to come, unmasking her inexperience.

He pulled her knees up and slowly made his way inside her. It felt good at first, then she felt a tearing pain that went on longer than she had anticipated, and she sobbed aloud. He rolled off her. "Shit," he said again. "What the hell just went on?"

"Nothing," she said, wiping her eyes. "Why'd you stop?"

"Is that a joke? What kind of person do you think I am? You're crying, for God's sake."

"No, I'm not," Sammie Rae sniffled. It was lonely and cold on her side of the Escalade hatch. The comfort of arms holding her tight, the warmth of his body against hers were just out of reach, and why? Because of a moment of physical pain? She'd expected some and it had been nothing compared to this wave of abandonment. She did her best to suck her tears and snot up into her sinuses.

"Shit, here I was, falling for you, and now it feels like I was tricked into hurting you. Now my tough little sheriff, kind who can handle anything, is crying her eyes out. Turns out country girl's a virgin."

"Was," Sammie Rae said, giggling through her tears because *falling for, falling for, falling for* was sounding in her brain. No matter how much she hurt in her low belly, the joy of that was too much to ignore.

"Jesus, you're really something." He snorted and gathered her into his arms, pulling her against his chest. "Baby, you think we had to do it like this? In a hurry, in the back of a car? I would have waited for this, gone slow…"

"Oh, please shut up. You sound like the worst of my ma's romance heroes. Except for the last few seconds, it was heavenly. Can't we just lie here and maybe fall asleep?" And when they woke up, if the nagging ache was gone, maybe try some other things she'd heard about.

Within a few minutes he was snoring softly, his jacket covering them, and his arm around her. Sammie Rae was humming "Look What God Gave Her," softly to herself. Weird, the ache in her pussy was lovely. *There, I used the word again!* In school they'd discussed losing virginity as something to get over with. She was surprised to feel this was something to remember. She murmured to herself, "It's lovely because of what it means—the beginning of Al and me."

And then, without any dreaming, it was almost dawn and she had to pee so bad a headache was coming on. She smiled at him, still sleeping peacefully with his manly bladder. She crawled to the passenger-side door and opened it as quietly as she could, slipping out onto the dirt of the barn floor. She made her way in the pale light to the back corner, where she squatted and let loose. As her steaming urine hit the ground, something screeched and the sounds of a desperate struggle reached her ears. She froze, still crouched, not wanting to draw the attention of whatever it was. When her bladder was empty, she dropped to her bare knees, praying a bat wasn't dragging its rabid ass in her direction.

The light was dim, the SUV blocked light from the door, but she could just make out a small, white face, a miniature ghost's visage. It was ripping at something with fierce joy—a barn owl had silently glided down to kill a mouse. She sighed with relief—just an owl, probably the reason the bats were gone—until she realized other eyes were focused on her. One set, then another, then another, until there were six. It took a few seconds before her eyes adjusted and she could see a mound of old hay; nesting in it were the goats, chewing their cud. The billy was closest to her. He rose on his knees and let out a loud belch. The does rose at the sound, stretched their necks, and followed the billy to the barn door and the field outside. Last to go was the little late-season kid, following her dam.

The light was already brighter when Sammie Rae returned to the car. She stepped carefully—the floor was studded with round goat droppings like a mine salted with gold nuggets. The goats must have been holing up in the barn for weeks.

The herd disappeared behind the bulk of the SUV, but as she reached the car, the kid reappeared in the doorway, only to stare at Sammie Rae. She took another step to return to Lansing, raising her hand to the door's handle. The little goat let out a loud *blaaaaah!* and ran off.

Chapter 30

SAMMIE RAE DREAMED SHE was standing in the woods, in a stream polluted with mine waste, flowing green and orangey as an oil slick. Reflected in that ooze, Darla was running and screaming with blood streaming down her neck. Behind, something chased her, something hazy that couldn't quite be seen. She yelled to Sammie Rae, "Shoot, shoot!" Despite her speed, she receded further and further until her voice faded in the distance.

Sammie Rae awoke shaking. Grabbing her clothes, she slid out the passenger-side door, dressed leaning against the vehicle, and went outside the barn to take great gulps of the fresh air—now it seemed the barn reeked of goat. She paced back and forth in the tall weeds, watching the herd graze in the distance.

What she wouldn't give for a cigarette and a chat in Dolly's kitchen. When Lansing was awake, she would damn sure talk to him about Thad Overton. Her phone rang. "Are you okay?" she asked.

"Why wouldn't I be?" Darla responded. "Where the hell are you? Anyway, sorry for how it ended yesterday. I acted like a real douche, like we were still in junior high. Guess because back then, the girls whispered about me."

Junior high had been awful, the girls the lowest form of life, as far as Sammie Rae could tell. *They weren't jealous of me, though, just of Darla.* She'd always felt in Darla's shadow, invisible if her friend was near. Despite her night with Lansing, despite her feelings for him, she'd suspected Overton, given the opportunity, would choose Darla. And now she'd found out that he had.

"Anyways," Darla continued. "You're family, my sister, only one I got—I must be an idiot thinking you'd begrudge me being in love."

Sammie Rae's panties were sticky. Sex in an SUV's hatch in an abandoned barn hadn't been part of her plans. Romantic sex should involve *a bed* and *a sink right by*—she wasn't one of those trampy, behind the 7-Eleven girls. Had the condom broken? Was she still bleeding? Looking back at the Escalade, it seemed Lansing wasn't moving yet, so at least she had a touch of privacy.

Darla finished with, "And that's because you love me as much as I love you."

"But…" Sammie Rae said, wanting to make sure of where things stood, "did you or didn't you screw Al Lansing?"

"Told you that was over, but if you gotta know, never got that far. What difference would it make if we had? Can't stay with a guy just 'cause you fuck him. Has to be love."

"So, since I found you and Overton together, you've decided it's love, huh?" Sammie Rae was biding time to think, the thoughts in her mind rattling around like bb pellets in an old tuna can, trying to hook up and make sense of everything.

"Yup, been a short time, but this is it. The real deal." Darla's breath blew into her phone. "Weird thing is, when I told my ma, she wasn't as gung-ho as when she met him, despite the lily-white doctor bit. But she wouldn't say why. So, I need you to talk to her. She listens to you."

Sammie Rae was silent, considering what to say next as her thoughts raced faster. Darla didn't know what she'd said to Dolly, but sooner or later, someone would tell. No one's business was private, not in Lark County. Time to confess about the night she'd just spent, before there was more to feel guilty about. "Uh, Dar? If you're all done with Al Lansing, would you be upset if I dated him? We've been working close together, and…"

Darla's voice rose as she interrupted. "Why Sammie Rae Wheedle, you little son of a gun! I'd never have trash talked him if I knew you was getting all hot and bothered. He is pretty sexy, far as it goes, so for sure, go ahead."

Sammie Rae's mouth opened to confess but snapped shut at a sudden realization—she'd been close to committing an act of criminal stupidity. Asking permission *after* the deed had been done! Sneaky and manipulative—it would wipe out any goodwill earned by asking for Darla's blessing. "Thank you kindly, ma'am," was all she said.

"Well, good," Darla said. "May we both find our dream men. Thanks so, so much in advance for talking to my ma. Just make it soon, okay?"

Sammie Rae slid her phone back into her pocket. She hadn't said she'd talk to Dolly, or admit she already had. Chewing on a fingernail, she returned to the Escalade.

When she opened the door to climb back in, Lansing sat up, yawning and rubbing the sleep from his face. He held out his arms, saying, "Hey, come here."

Her pulse began racing at the thought of his hands on her again—what difference would another fifteen minutes or so make? But the untidiness in her pants made her hesitate. Another thing she and Darla hadn't discussed was round two without washing.

He pulled with gentle insistence until she was leaning against him. He asked, "Did a herd of goats go by a little bit ago?"

"You must have been dreaming," she said.

"Weird. I could've sworn but guess you're right. Fell back asleep for a bit. Anyway…" His hands began to explore her chest again. "Mmmm, these sure are sweet. Sugar sweet."

Her stomach growled.

His hands stopped moving. "You hungry?"

"Guess so," Sammie Rae said. Emotion always made her want to eat and now she was a tangle of feelings, mostly good, though wary. Her stomach gurgled again. She should have picked up snacks on the way. "Tudor's Biscuit is not too far."

"They have a drive-thru?"

She nodded.

"Great," he said. "You could follow and wait on the road in your car. So, we won't be seen eating an early breakfast together."

"If it's quick." Tudor's had good breakfasts. Her stomach rumbled in anticipation, but Overton and the cross in the root cellar were more pressing. "First, I need to tell you something."

"I'm real hungry again." He nibbled on her earlobe and then his tongue flicked into her ear.

She batted him away. "No, listen."

"Yes, ma'am."

"When I searched Hazie Jacob's house, where the second murder took place, there was something down in the root cellar, something I took a photo of but didn't report." She pulled out her phone and opened the photos. The rough cross was clearly visible. "Look."

His face crinkled in dismay. "'Beware the white bokor'? Shit, why didn't you tell me you found this?"

"I wanted to but didn't want to throw suspicion on an innocent man. Dr. Overton, who, by the way, Darla's now dating."

Dismay and what looked like horror crossed his face. Wasn't he over her yet, like he'd said?

"Oh, fuck, he's here?" Lansing said. He grabbed his clothes and began to dress. "Where?"

Sammie Rae's breath tightened. Lansing was increasing her worries about Thad Overton. "Henderson property, 'bout seven miles from my office, real isolated. I'll show you. Now tell me why it's *oh, fuck* that he's here?"

"No, I can't tell you. But you are going to get me there, soon as I say so."

She grabbed him by his shoulders and shook as hard as she could. "Is he involved with the zombie murders out here? What do you know about him?"

He took both her wrists and held them away from him. "Sammie Rae, you have to accept there are things I can't tell you. This is one of them." He let go of her arms. "I've got to talk to some people. Let me dress and get the fuck out of here." He opened the hatch and hopped out to put on his jeans. "Damned stiff shit!" he said, struggling with the cloth, his legs kicking as he sat on the edge of the hatch's bed.

"Are you going to try and find him?"

Umph, uhh! He stood again and zippered, pulling on his boots. "If you don't want your car here and you elsewhere, you need to go. I'm crazy for you but move it!"

"Just tell me if he's a zombie or not."

Lansing spun her around and kissed her, his eyes wide. "I hate for our time to end like this. Call you later." He slammed the hatch, went to the driver's door, and started the engine.

The Escalade zoomed from the barn, leaving Sammie Rae blinking and adjusting her pants, feeling her hands clench into fists of desperation, hoping by *end* he meant just the morning and not *them*. Then she went to her patrol car and climbed into the front, adjusting the rearview mirror to look at herself.

Right now, with her limp blonde hair straggling around her face and her sleep-deprived eyes—though a nice blue—sporting pouches, she didn't look sexy. Only her mouth was improved, her lips swollen and full.

She pulled her hair from her face and put the rubber band back on tight, started the engine, and waved out the field to the billy. The horny bastard seemed to be smirking in her direction. "All right for you, I guess," she muttered to him. "You've got a friggin' harem!"

She drove straight toward the Dunkin'. A cream-filled maple frosted seemed just about right.

As she drove, Mee-Maw's voice echoed in her mind with another of her hideous, ancient sayings, *If you waller with hogs, expect to get dirty. If you lie down with dogs, expect to get fleas.*

Actually, two sayings for the price of one. Mee-Maw's death had only increased the old lady's power to make Sammie Rae feel trampish like her ma.

*   *   *

The Dunkin' was quiet—always was after the morning rush. Only one table was occupied and that one was full of Howie. "Errrm, glad to see you, Sammie Rae." His voice rumbled in his massive chest.

"Why's that, Howie?"

"Heard a rumor goin' round, how maybe the killer's right here in Lark County. Like he maybe mesmerized some girl, snake with a mouse."

"Where'd you hear that?" Sammie Rae turned to order. "Maple Long John with custard and a coffee."

"Bring me another plain cruller," Howie's voice rumbled. "And the *Wash Post* if they got one. Maybe be some more news of the zombie deer disease. They're stumbling around the woods of Pennsylvania, starvin' to death in the midst of plenty."

Zombie deer disease? She didn't want to know if that was a real thing, not right now. The brain-itch of worry had begun. She ignored his request for the newspaper. The donuts were handed to her with her change. Before sitting across from him, she brushed blueberry donut crumbs from the table.

"Guess when you get a deer you gotta make sure none of the brain or spine's blasted, lest it pollute the meat and you get the disease. Mad cow taught us that," Howie said. "Where's my paper?"

"Tell me who told you about the killer being here."

"Lil birdy," he said, picking up the cruller. It was Howie's donut-eating time, so she'd have to wait, sipping coffee. Sammie Rae wondered if the little birdy was named Wade Goodloe.

Howie finished the cruller and pointed at her Long John. "You eatin' that?"

Her appetite was gone, so she passed her donut partway in his direction, then pulled it back, keeping her hand on its unfrosted edge. "I got to go soon," she said. "What little birdy?"

Howie raised one eyebrow, his face assuming a crafty expression. "Can't rightly remember. Forget my paper?"

Sammie Rae pushed the Long John to him, took her coffee and glanced around. A woman entered, trailed by a little girl with long auburn curls and a plague of freckles. Brandi MacDougal and her kid.

Brandi's eyes lit up when she saw Sammie Rae. "Trace," she called to the counter girl. "Go on and give Jalene what she wants. Chocolate frosted for me, thanks." Then she scurried over to Sammie Rae. "Thank the Lord I done run into you. Complained to one of the other deputies, but he did nothing. Acted like I was a fool and tried to look down my blouse."

Probably Charlie. "What all did you tell him, Brandi?" Couldn't be about her husband. He was one of the nicest, most loyal men in the county.

Brandi's voice dropped into a soft whisper. "Well, not even a week ago, when Tom was down helping his daddy put up a new shed and I was alone with Jalene, I happened to look out the back window. I'm a scaredy-cat when there's no man in the house, but I swear I saw something moving by the old outhouse."

Brandi's little girl brought a bag to the table. "Here, Mama," she said.

"Thank you, honey. Now you just go sit over there by the window and count the cars pulling up." To Sammie Rae, Brandi added, "She can count almost to a hundred," her voice louder again. Howie was looking at her steady with his pale little eyes, so much like golden raisins in his oatmeal bowl of a face. He seemed to make her nervous. She leaned close to Sammie Rae's ear. "I saw something like a big dog or a wolf just prowling around."

"White?"

Brandi shook her head. "No, ma'am. Black as sin with glowy eyes. I think that's what killed those two men. Anyways, sudden like, it just disappeared in thin air. Then I heard a noise at the front door, looked out, there it was again, faster than anything. I was scared out of my wits, worried it'd come in and eat little Jalene. So, I grabbed her up and ran to the closet in our room and hid in the clothes until Tom got home."

"Err-um," Howie's voice grated in the Dunkin's sweet air, "must've been a stray dog,"

Brandi's glance was loaded with resentment. "Nossir, weren't no ordinary dog. Too big and no normal dog just winks out like that!" She snapped her fingers.

"Din'cha used to be a Grubmann?" Howie asked.

"What difference does that make?" Sammie Rae asked.

"Grubmann's a German name. Them old Krauts filled kids' heads full of the Snarly Yow. Been telling that tale for nigh-on three hundred years."

Sammie Rae smiled at Brandi, hoping she'd not been hurt by the rudeness.

"But," Howie went on, "Snarly Yow don't come out this far west." The folds of flesh under his chin jiggled ever so slightly, as if he was pushing a laugh down deep enough to meet his donuts. And then he said, "Must've just been The White Thing, wearin' its winter coat."

"There is no White Thing," Sammie Rae said. She promised to check Brandi's property, looking for tracks and spoor. Then she left to find out exactly how her suggestions blossomed into rumors and those rumors been taken as wild, half-crocked truths. She shoved down her own worries about the supernatural. Shoved them down deep.

Chapter 31

WADE DIDN'T ANSWER HIS PHONE and when Sammie Rae pulled up at Goodloe's Garage, the sign read, CLOSED TODAY—FOR EMERGENCES CALL SOMBODY ELSE.

She phoned her pa. It wasn't surprising that Pa, multi-county, freshly minted lady-killer, answered his new cell. "Y'all playing poker again?" The odds were much greater they were conspiring to cause trouble. And right now, she was concentrating on getting the rumors controlled. "Wade there?"

"Wade? Wade Goodloe? Why, no. Why would you ask that?" Wade was probably standing right next to him, gesturing like crazy.

"Just put him on."

There was a bout of whispering and then Pa said, "It's Hazie wants to talk with you."

"No," Sammie Rae said.

Hazie's voice, gravelly and slow, answered her. "Sammie Rae, I done heared you're about to make an arrest of the monster what murdered my boy. I want to thank you."

"Who told you that, Hazie?"

"Don't make no never mind, long as it's true. It is true, ain't it?"

"You know I can't discuss police business, Hazie." She put her hand tight on the phone to muffle her voice as she murmured like she was talking to someone. Then she took her hand away. "Bye, now, Hazie. Gotta go! Tell Pa bye for me." She ended the call.

Shit fire and save the matches! What she'd told Dolly, just to get Darla to stop and think, had spread faster than she could've imagined. And Lord only knew what Dolly speculated from Sammie Rae's words. She'd really messed things up this time.

The tittle-tattle had already reached Mamie Cousins's place up in Apalachee. How? Connecting the dots pretty much made an outline of Wade Goodloe, up resupplying everyone's pills. She just needed a few crayons to finish coloring him in for sure.

And more to worry about: Did Sheriff Beebe know about the rumors? Would he link them to her somehow? Sammie Rae went home, took a quick shower with dish detergent because she was out of soap, dressed, and headed to the office, feeling fresher, though her hair was still damp.

The big room was nearly empty. Everybody was probably out on patrol or answering calls accumulated overnight. But Beebe was on the lookout for her. When she swung open the door, he bellowed, "Wheedle! Get in here!"

She dumped her jacket on a chair—she'd soon be sweating, anyway—and went to his private space.

"Shut the door behind you and sit down," he said. She obeyed.

"Didn't bring in donuts, did you?"

"No, sir, want me to go back to the Dunkin'?"

He shook his head. "Sometimes a man just needs him some sugar." His facade, never polished diamond bright, had developed a few more cracks. The Ralph Beebe who was her father's boyhood friend was shining through. "You need to tell me what that slick agent and his buddies have planned. You hear?"

Sammie Rae nodded.

"Things 'round here have gotten downright weird. Those damned, as-yet-unsolved murders have set everyone's teeth on edge. All over my county, there's sightings of monsters and aliens and goddamn undead of all sorts. Phones ringing non-stop, people calling up, screaming, *Mothman!* because someone up the road parked to canoodle with their lights left on, and taillights look like red, glowing eyes. The White Thing's prowling everywhere, stealing chickens and running off cows. Got one or two teenage rapes allegedly caused by vampires, ghosts, walking dead, crap like that. But worst of all, there's men planning to drive around at night, rifles off their racks, looking for a monster to shoot. And when you got a gun, everyone looks like a monster." He glared at her harder to make sure she was listening and said, "Bring me some coffee."

"Yessir." The abruptness of his request took her breath away, but she went for two cups, brought them back and set them on the desk.

"And the alien abductions!" He laughed, but not in a happy way. "Like aliens are interested in rectal probing fat farmwives and old insurance salesmen. Hell, even I'm too young for the Roswell crap. But this latest panic's gonna bust our budget—had to send every available man out to answer calls." He paused for a few gulps of his sweetened brew. "And the worst thing, some people are blaming Napier and Jacobs on a Haitian drug gang in Apalachee, saying those Black boys had some dealings with them. The whole thing's mixed up with Miami and New Orleans and voodoo. Mixed up with that movie star you were seen out with, too. The one now fooling around with your girl Darla. Way too much for me to keep straight." He coughed and took another sip. "I mean to uphold Lark County's heritage of anti-racism. We kept out the Klan, for the most part, at a time when them assholes were thick as ticks on a coonhound. There were Black miners on the line together with Whites fighting during the strikes. Bet you don't remember that."

"Nossir, I'm too young. Pittston was in 1990, right? I was born…"

"Can't have the boys stopping every car with coloreds looking to see if they're from Haiti. Can't afford any racist *incident* hitting the national news and making us look like backward yahoos. Need your buddy to help out right quick. Get the picture?"

"Sorry, sir?"

"I'll go slow. We got nothing on the killings. People are starting to question my leadership of this office. I need that Black DEA guy of yours to get his ass in gear and do something big like you said they was planning. Something to make me come out a hero." He banged his fist on the desk for emphasis. The coffee cups shook but stayed upright.

She jumped in her seat at the noise. "Got it. I'll see what I can do." She stood to go. "Anything else?"

To her surprise, he winked and said, "Tell your pa the old biddy ain't gonna be laying no more eggs, but I hear tell she keeps his nest warm!" His grin sent her out the door faster than she ever went.

Chapter 32

WHEN SAMMIE RAE GOT TO Dolly's house, Boozer was stretched out on the porch. Instead of greeting her with the usual mad tail thumping, the dog rose as she came up the three steps and walked toward his doghouse.

"Boozer, it's me," she called. Why was the old mutt acting so weird?

Dolly came to the door and looked at the dog's slow progress. "Boozer is sad Darla staying away." She held the door open for Sammie Rae to come in.

"Darla doesn't come home?"

Dolly was searching in the refrigerator. "Nothing to give you for snack. No cooking. Too depress." She slumped into a chair at the kitchen table. "Cannot get her to listen and now she's mad at me. She asks if you told me to worry, but I say no. Would call her daddy home but he blow a gasket."

"His truck broke down?" Sammie Rae asked.

"No, sorry, was idiom. Truck fine but if I tell him, will get super mad."

Sammie Rae took out her phone and called Darla. "Hey, I'm at your ma's," she said.

"Stay there. I'm coming as soon as I can." And she was gone.

Sammie Rae turned and smiled brightly at Dolly. "Our girl's coming home."

*　　*　　*

Darla let the door slam behind her. Her color, usually so delicate, was high, like the glow after sex. Even if the image in Sammie Rae's mind was unsettling, it made her imagine what a stunning couple she and Overton must be. Both tall, one dark, one fair—romance novel stuff if he wasn't having her for lunch!

"Ma, no, not hungry." Darla shook her head at Dolly. "But yeah, I'm still mad. How can you believe the shit that's going around?"

Dolly's eyes flickered from her daughter to Sammie Rae. Just for a micro-second, but it was enough.

"I knew it!" Darla cried. She turned to Sammie Rae. "Damn you, Sammie Rae Wheedle!" Darla's voice rose a bit higher. "What the hell you tell her?"

"Didn't tell me nothing."

Darla rolled her eyes and sighed. "Rumors are swirling all over the county and probably beyond. Rumors about Thad being involved in the murders, rumors about him being a monster, rumors that he came here to fuck up Lark County. Like it wasn't already fucked up."

Dolly's mouth opened at the first *fuck* but snapped shut. She knew better than to pull the proper mama act now.

"Arrgh!" Darla yelled from behind the two hands she'd put over her face. She leaned forward. "I'm afraid some white trash, ridge-running moron will kill him. Shoot him dead at his place." She put her hands down flat on the table. "*Someone* started the gossip. *Someone* spread it."

"We just worried," Dolly said. "Don't really know this stranger man. Murders start when he come here. Zombie murders."

"Oh, for Chrissakes. I can see you falling for that, what with all that stuff about fox ghosts, but you?" Darla turned her head.

Sammie Rae looked down.

"Just how stupid you think I am? Think I haven't taken the time to know him?"

Sammie Rae couldn't answer. There was no concrete information one way or the other. Darla might be convinced he had nothing to do with the deaths or the drug gangs, but as Sammie Rae's ma's novels had taught her, the opinion of a woman in love couldn't be trusted.

"Well, just to let you know, now we can't go into town together. Hell, he can't go into town at all—it's like stepping into that Frankenstein scene with the town folk, all pitchforks and torches. And when I go alone, the whispering starts, and everyone moves away. Work on the building's at a standstill because the guys won't come on the property. Even the ones who think this is all bullshit, all the ones who really need the money, are stopped by their wives. Or their mothers." Darla glared at her mother again. "So, fess up."

Dolly reached for her daughter's hand, but it was pulled away. "I watched *Night of Living Dead* and saw zombies rip a girl up, like Napier boy and Johnny Lee. Worse than fox ghosts. Zombies never die, just keep coming."

"But they do die," Sammie Rae said. "If you shoot them in the head."

Darla glared at Sammie Rae as if she couldn't believe what she was hearing. Then she put her head down, gasping, her shoulders shaking. When she straightened up again, she couldn't control herself for laughing so hard that she began to choke. Sammie Rae clapped her on the back.

Just when Sammie Rae was seriously concerned Darla had gone full-on hysterical, she calmed down, wiping her eyes with an apron Dolly had flung over the back of a chair.

"Well, you've gotta come with me out to the Henderson place to talk with Thad."

"Today good to visit." Dolly looked over at the stand where she stored her cleavers.

"Not you." Darla looked at her mother as if the little woman was insane. "I'll let the deputy tell you what she thinks. No sense changing the pattern."

"I can't today," Sammie Rae said. "Have to make sure Pa's okay. He's been sick."

"Right." Darla stood. "Have fun with Al Lansing," she said, looking at Sammie Rae, and slammed the door as she left.

"You with the fancy-Dan Black guy?" Dolly asked, as the echo of the slammed door faded away.

"Just for law enforcement work," Sammie Rae answered. She knew it was cowardly, but she'd had enough being put in her place, at least for one day. Using Pa as an excuse to buy time was the only thing to do. What was she facing: a zombie master, a violent drug smuggler, or just someone who'd take Darla away? Chickenshit or not, she wanted Al Lansing to have her back when she paid that visit. He didn't know how to get to the Henderson place. He was dependent on her leading him there.

* * *

Pa's shotgun was in the trunk of her car, ready to be delivered to him. She felt a little guilty bringing it to Mamie Cousins's house when she'd feared letting him have it at her apartment. As another little bribe, she had four quart-jars of

Dolly's best for the codgers to share. It was easy to imagine Mrs. Cousins having a snort or two in her kimono.

"Howdy," Wade said when he opened the door of the columned mini mansion. He was wearing that kimono, which fortunately was tightly tied shut, unlike when Mrs. Cousins had worn it.

"Y'all been playing poker again?" If so, Sammie Rae was not sure she wanted to go into the house.

"Every night," Wade answered. He looked down and blushed. "Oh, this old thing? Nah, just threw it on." He looked down at what Sammie Rae was holding and broke out a huge grin. "See you brought Samuel's gun! Come on in."

Shaking her head, Sammie Rae followed him.

Pa was on the fainting couch, snoring, obviously over-medicated, or there'd be some movement, the twitching with pain he did in his sleep.

"His back been hurting something fierce." Hazie was next to him, knitting what looked like baby booties.

"I gave him extra," Wade said, rubbing his right eyebrow with a thumbnail.

Sammie Rae patted her father's cheek. "Pa, what happened to your back?" He didn't move.

"Hurt it in bed," Wade said, walking over to Hazie's chair. "Hazie's resurrected your Pa in more ways than one."

Hazie laughed and slapped his side with a bootie. "Wade, you dirty dog! You're embarrassing me!" Her laugh was a wild, unreal cackle, like a crazed hen, until she looked at Sammie Rae. "Wipe that damn look off your face." She started knitting again, looking down at her work. "You think we're too old for all that, don'cha? Well, not one of us here is a day more than sixty-three. And don't be making no cracks about these booties. They're for Mamie's great grandbaby."

Mamie Cousins had come into the room while Hazie was talking. "You're too kind, Hazie. Not just them cute little things but saying I'm not but sixty-three."

Wade winked at her. "Good thing I like a woman with experience."

Mrs. Cousins's laugh was deep and full. She turned to Sammie Rae. "Now you come in the kitchen and eat. Made us some fried chicken. Leftovers just cooled down."

"I really got to get back," Sammie Rae said.

Hazie dropped her voice to a hoarse whisper. "Not 'til you tell about the investigation into my boy's murder. Out there." She tossed her head toward the kitchen. "Samuel needs his rest. Had a hard time, what with his ma dying. Not to beat on a dead horse, but no matter how *old* you are, your ma's your ma. Losing her made everything hurt worse." She put down her knitting and helped herd Sammie Rae into the kitchen. "Don't worry about him. Wade's keeping watch—he's the most qualified."

"Took a CPR course back in '98," Wade said.

As the swinging door to the kitchen closed, Hazie's joking disappeared and her face turned fierce. Her gnarled fingers dug into Sammie Rae's arm. "Spill the beans. We been hearing rumors, awful rumors about my baby's killer." She stopped for a breath. "Kills *me* to think Johnny Lee went through all that before he died."

Sammie Rae was trapped by Hazie and Mamie Cousins. They had her corralled between an old Hoosier cabinet and the table holding a plate of glistening fried chicken.

The door opened. Wade entered, supporting a lurching, stumbling zombie. Sammie Rae took a step back, almost knocking into Mamie. The zombie was her pa.

Wade helped Pa sit while Mamie poured him coffee. "There, baby," she said.

Baby? This house was an old folks' lovey-dovey commune. Probably having orgies every night.

Her father snapped to right quick, once the coffee had done its work. He was too used to the drugs for their effect to linger.

"Your back's out?" Sammie Rae asked. "I'm worried about you, Pa. Maybe living here's too hard on you."

He fixed her with a steady, if blurred, gaze. "Sammie Rae, you don't know nothing. I'm better off now than all those years, missing your ma."

Wade chimed in, "Funny what the love of a good woman can do. Make a man forget his troubles."

The old women smiled tenderly.

"Hazie deserves a head's up on the state of your investigation, girl." Pa eyed the chicken on the table in front of him. "Gimme some of that."

Mamie Cousins took a plate and passed some over. It looked heavenly and smelled better.

Sammie Rae had to tell them something, anything, so she could get back to Lark County with a big piece of chicken in her belly. And maybe a cup of coffee—she was really worn out. "I know what the rumors are but can't say if they're true. What I can say is, when I leave here, I'm confronting our main suspect."

"Who?" they cried, all at once.

"I can't tell you that. Want me to lose my job?"

Wade's eyes grew big, and Sammie Rae thanked the Lord that he'd needed her help so often. "Now, quiet down, everyone," he commanded. "Our girl's a law enforcement professional. She'll tell us as soon as she can. Let her get some vittles in her. Gonna be a long night."

An hour later, Sammie Rae was on her way, a fried lump settling uneasily in her stomach, and two more crispy legs in Saran Wrap on the passenger seat.

Chapter 33

AL LANSING HAD AGREED TO FOLLOW her to the Henderson place, but he refused to give her more information about Overton. He'd traded in the flashy gold Escalade for a nondescript black sedan. Sammie Rae drove her little compact and he shadowed her impatiently. At the Henderson place, Overton's Land Rover and Darla's pickup were parked next to the dumpster.

Sammie Rae wasn't taking any chances, not with Thad Overton. Her pistol was in her waistband, warm from her body heat, reassuringly easy to hold through the slit she'd made in her jacket pocket. She could shoot through the jacket to stop a mortal, but with the walking dead—if there were any—it had to be the head. No way would she let Al know, in case thinking of zombies was just plain stupid.

Darla came out the door as they parked. "Hello, Al," she said, nodding at him. "Sammie Rae. Two cars?"

"I might have to leave suddenly," Lansing replied. He craned his neck and looked from one end of the stone building to the other. "Big place. Pretty setting, real private."

"The repairs were supposed to be a lot further along by now, but, yeah, it's big. Once it's fixed up it'll be just right."

"How'd you find it?"

"Me and Sammie Rae, we used to bike out here, just to be scared, as folks said it was haunted." Darla arched one eyebrow as she looked at Sammie Rae. "That was just ignorant, childish crap. Anyway, Thad wanted a place big enough and isolated enough for addiction treatment." She sighed. "Well, come on in."

Thad Overton stood by the huge stone fireplace, his hair golden, lit by the winter sun shining through gaps in the roof. He held out his hand, saying, "Agent Lansing."

"Dr. Overton."

The two men shook hands. Neither of them seemed hostile to the other, just familiar. Their expressions were wary, but humor sparkled in Overton's eyes and Lansing was on his way to a grin.

Darla went to Overton's side and linked her arm in his, smiling up at him. Lansing moved closer to Sammie Rae. He muttered out of the side of his mouth, "Shit, they don't look real, do they?"

He had a point. Thad Overton looked like the elf prince in *Lord of the Rings,* the one Darla always called "Leg o' lamb." Darla looked like the same old gorgeous Darla. Sammie Rae whispered back, "You and Dr. Overton know each other?"

"I know he's not a zombie or a bokor." Lansing replied, sly humor in his voice. He turned to Thad, "Good to see you alive and well."

"Alive, right, Sammie Rae?" Darla said. "Never saw a movie where zombies were undead one moment and *regular old* alive humans the next." Her eyes shifted to Lansing. "But obviously, you've met Thad before. Why didn't you straighten Sammie Rae out?"

"Didn't know he was here." He moved from foot to foot with nervous energy, as if starting difficult negotiations with a suspect.

Darla lifted one eyebrow as she stared at Lansing. "Wasn't because you were mad that I stood you up?"

"No," Overton said, "it's the truth. He didn't know I was here in Lark County."

"Deputy Wheedle inadvertently let me know this morning. But I doubt I'm the only one who knows. Darla, I need your help convincing Dr. Overton to cooperate."

"Cooperate?" Darla interrupted. "What the hell does that mean?"

Overton turned to her, his expression cautious, as if concerned with how she'd take his words. "He wants me to return to the witness protection program. Dye my hair, grow a beard, become someone else somewhere else…"

"What?" Darla said. "You never told me this shit?"

And Lansing failed to mention this shit to me! While Darla was with someone who needs protection. That means someone whose presence might get her killed. Sammie Rae shot a look at Lansing, one filled with venom.

Overton held up his hands, buying time to speak. "I'm going to testify in the cooperative effort of the US and Haiti to bring down a few transnational drug cartels."

"We need you to live long enough to do just that. To put them away, here or in Haiti," Lansing said.

Overton laughed. "Layer on layer. Like Whack-a-Mole, they'll just spring up when you bang one down."

"You think it's hopeless? The government should give up?" Sammie Rae asked.

Overton explained that there was no end, they'd never get the big bosses. "… and I'd never be me again. Giving up who you are is just another way of dying. I'll be glad to appear in court, but I'll set up my own life, take what precautions I can accept, doing what I do."

"They know where you are and you know what that means," Lansing said. "They left a mention of you at a murder. We think they were trying to frame you. And don't forget, we had a deal."

"I'll do what I said." Overton's voice was tense. "I know they were setting me up, for one of the so-called zombie murders. Seems they were pretty successful at convincing the locals, since now I'm unwelcome everywhere."

"I bet the rumors flying around here helped them locate you." It was Darla's turn for a venomous look, this one aimed at Sammie Rae.

"If I hadn't had Darla…" Overton began.

Putting Darla at risk!

Darla read her mind. "I'm in this, Sammie Rae. No matter what you think."

"Where exactly do you sleep?" Lansing craned his neck to look up at the damaged roof.

"Why?" Overton asked.

"Because I'm staying right here until you leave with me."

"We only have two sleeping bags," Darla said. "We bank the fire and put them down right in front."

"Good, the two of you can share one and I'll take the other." Al was unusually jovial. "It'll be fun—my first time at camping. I'm a city boy. Hate nature. Nothing but bugs and bears and misery. Skunks!"

Overton stepped in front of Darla. "You don't have to stay. I'll make sure we're safe."

Lansing brought his hand to his mouth. *"Cough! Cough!* Sure, you will. *Cough! Cough!"*

To Sammie Rae's surprise, Overton laughed at the fake cough and the words Lansing exhaled into his fist. They knew each other even better than she'd realized.

Lansing took out his phone and scowled. "There's no service here?"

"No," Sammie Rae said. "You have to go back to the main road, almost to town."

"Another brilliant safety feature! No satellite phone?" Lansing snorted and turned to Sammie Rae. "Deputy Wheedle, will you please drive to the road and call?" When she nodded, he added, "Good, follow me outside."

He led the way to her little blue car, leaned close and said, "I was with the Haitians after you showed me the photos—they made a big deal out of the cross, laughing about the locals falling for the bokor shit. But they needed to know exactly where Overton was. They thought if they spread enough rumors, someone'd drop his hideout." He laughed. "All pissed off no one helped them. Said it was racism!"

The drug smugglers hadn't caught on to Lansing. *Or maybe they have, but he doesn't know it. They're hoping he'll lead them here.* "They figured people would be scared that zombies were prowling Lark County?" Sammie Rae laughed to show only an idiot would believe in real voodoo.

"Hell, some of the gang members are scared shitless Overton really is a bokor." He handed her his phone. "Call the last number. An agent named Mike'll answer. Tell him what's happening and where I am. He knows what to do. Now get out of here. Don't come back 'til you hear from me." He kissed her quickly. "And take your gun out of your pants. Could go off and damage something precious." He went back to Darla and Overton.

Sammie Rae pulled out onto the rough road and accelerated toward town. A moment after she turned onto the county road, three SUVs appeared from out of nowhere. They took the neglected dirt track leading to the Henderson place.

She stomped on the brake pedal, her compact sliding as it hit the graveled shoulder. She sat gasping for a second, then yanked the steering wheel, turning back the way she'd come. When she came to the unpaved road, she slowed, fearing to run up behind those vehicles. No way for her to know who was inside—two were for sure Escalades, the other a Jeep. Federal agents on surveillance could be driving them, but so could the Haitians.

She called the number. The signal was weak, staticky. Still, someone answered, "Al, that you?"

"Need help!" she yelled.

"What? Who the hell is this?"

"With Lansing. Need help!"

A pause and then, "Tracking phone, GPS. Take us about twenty to get down there." The signal was lost.

Twenty minutes could as well be a lifetime. Sammie Rae turned back up the trace. At the top of the knoll overlooking the house, she pulled over and stepped from the car, leaving the door open. Down below, the mystery vehicles were hidden from the house, shielded behind a pile of construction rubble, and surrounded by tall weeds.

The sunlight was winter thin. She shivered; the open car door was no windbreak. A flock of dun-colored mourning doves appeared, moving in the dust. Their little feet shuffled like cheap tin windup toys. Their heads jerked forward and back, watching for danger.

She had to be careful—sudden movement would set them off, wings whirring above the bare treetops, an alert to anyone watching.

The doves wandered out of sight onto the forest floor, pecking at the dirt, making their ghostly cry. Sammie Rae crept toward a better vantage point on the ridge top. The scene remained quiet and motionless. She stayed just as still, wanting to become part of the scenery. Her mouth was dry. Her chest felt as if a wall of bricks was pressing on it, cutting off her breath. She didn't look to see the time, knowing that seconds would feel slowed to a crawl and all that mattered was *now*.

A door opened in the rear car. A huge man slid out, holding what looked like a MAC-10. He slithered along the cars, approaching the side of the building. Smoke continued to waft upward from the chimney. Otherwise, there was no movement from the house.

The man moved closer, was now maybe ten yards from the house. As she watched his careful approach, Sammie Rae's pistol danced in her shaking hand—this was nothing like the gun range, shooting a paper target. But Darla was down there. Al and Overton, too. Crows called each other, flying low over the valley. The man swung his gun upward, startled by the movement, brought it back down. Ran one hand over his shaven head.

The Haitian looked back at the car he'd left. He was the hunter, the one from the gas station. She coughed in the dusty air, wished the goats would appear. A flock of doves and a couple of crows were no match for the killers below.

Lansing was armed but she had no idea if Overton had a weapon, any weapon, and Darla never carried. They needed a heads-up before the Haitian reached the building. Or before one of them looked out a window, an easy target.

Sammie Rae took a deep breath and shuffled rapidly along the drive, staying low. She stopped at a huge rock, ducked behind it, and looked down at the house. The man stepped out from behind the vehicles.

Sammie Rae aimed at the dirt in front of the Haitian's foot, sending dust and gravel pinging away from him. He skidded to a stop, looking up in her direction, and darted back to the shelter of the nearest SUV. She changed her position to see better as he crouched in the weeds. Another man left the vehicle and joined him. The first guy's arm pointed up the road toward her.

Lansing appeared from around the far side of the building—had her shot alerted him, lured him out? Had she made him believe the Haitians were creeping closer and he had no choice? He held a gun at eye level. Without turning, he waved *go back* at Overton, who had followed him, also armed. No Darla—they must've tied her to a post, or she'd be out in front.

Sammie Rae fired again, hitting the front quarter panel of the Jeep. Al looked up for a split second, now alerted that someone was on the ridge and going after the Haitians. He paused, again motioning Overton to return to the house. As soon as he turned, the Haitians let loose a burst and Lansing dropped, holding his leg. Though she felt as if her heart had stopped, Sammie Rae fired several more times to give them cover.

Overton helped him up, supporting him as they retreated to the house. A trail of blood followed. How badly was Al hit? Her impulse was to run down to him.

A shot rang out from the woods to her right. Like hers, it hit the Jeep, further back, on the rear bumper. Another shot, this one from the hill behind the house. The men half-rose in response, heads swiveling in confusion. They ducked down again.

Rapid fire traced a line close to the front of the Haitians' vehicles, shots originating close to Sammie Rae. She scanned the area—no way Lansing's men had gotten to the house yet.

A shot came from the house, hitting one of the men, who screamed and cursed, his words unintelligible. The Escalade's door opened, shut again—he was pulled inside, his cries muffled. The engines of all three vehicles started; as they began to turn the cars around, the firing from the hills increased. The shooting ended when they stopped.

Her thighs aching from the prolonged crouch, Sammie Rae looked about. No one was visible, so who was helping hold the Haitians at bay? The shots had hushed the woodland—in the quiet, she waited for someone to declare themselves. Seconds dripped by slow as water from melting ice.

The Escalade's front passenger door cracked open. A shot rang out from the house, and it slammed shut again.

"First time you fired at somethin' other than a squirrel?" a familiar voice behind her said.

She wheeled about. Pa stood next to her. Took real skill to sneak up on someone when you used a cane. "Where the hell'd you come from?" she asked in a whisper.

He lifted his chin to the left. "Wade's up on that thar ridge, with a brand-new Browning X-Bolt. New scope, too."

Where the hell had Wade gotten that?

Pa pointed to the hill behind the house. "Mamie Cousins up there. You don't even want to know what she's armed with. Not if you're takin' up with a fed. Hazie's waiting at our car. Don't want her in the action. She's my moll." He spat a string of chaw on the ground. "Saw your agent fellow was hit."

The cars below remained quiet. "How'd Mamie get up there, Pa?"

"Lotta trails you young folk don't know about. Old hunting traces. To answer your question, we followed you. Just a hunch you might say."

A car was slowly coming toward them from the county road. She lifted her pistol, but Pa pushed her arm down with his rifle. The vehicle reached them. A patrol car. Sheriff Beebe was driving, his window down. "Samuel," Beebe said, nodding at Pa.

"How do?" Pa replied. "Best back up a titch. Your ride's too easy to spot here."

Beebe obeyed.

Sammie Rae shot Pa a questioning look.

"I called him, all in the name of goodwill. We wasn't sure what was goin' down, but sure seemed like something." He shrugged. "If it turned out nothing, you'd not knowed we was ever here." He looked up at Beebe's car. "Well, maybe him."

All was quiet for a few minutes. Then the Escalade inched forward. Rapid fire from the hill burst its windshield. It stopped dead.

More vehicles approached down the road, advancing rapidly until blocked by Beebe's. The lead car skidded to a stop in a cloud of dust, the front passenger door opened, and a burly man jumped out, his vest marked FBI. He waved a Colt M4 across his body, indicating the sheriff's car should move.

Sammie Rae ran toward him, ignoring his scowl. "Deputy Wheedle, Lark County Sheriff's Department. That's Sheriff Beebe. Agent Lansing and two others are at the stone house down the hollow. Three SUVs, don't know how many inside, heavy arms. Lansing's wounded."

She looked behind her. Pa had melted back into the woods. Beebe was pulling as far off the road as he could.

The agent nodded, hopped back in his vehicle.

"Go cautiously," she called, and bit her tongue. Closing his door with a slam, the agent drove on a little further, turning sideways to obstruct the road. The other vehicles lined up behind. Men poured out running in body armor, some FBI, some DEA, a few wearing grim skull-printed masks.

The armored men moved rapidly in unison. In a low crouch, all in dark clothing, they looked like a centipede on a summer floor. She followed behind until the third man in line took a bullhorn from his belt and spoke first in English, and then Creole, ordering the Haitians to leave their vehicles and surrender.

A burst of gunfire rat-a-tat-tatted from the vehicles and the federal agents flattened in the dust. Sammie Rae fell on her behind and scooted backwards behind the trees. When the shooting stopped, she slipped further into the woods, angling downward toward the far side of the building, going as fast as the rough terrain allowed. Overton might be a doctor, but the old house wasn't a hospital and Al could die of blood loss from his wound.

The Haitians would likely stay in place, knowing they were surrounded. Odds were, they couldn't be sure how many people were armed inside the house. With the FBI pinning them down, she could reach one of the windows if not the back door. She could make sure Lansing was safe and join Overton and Darla watching for any movement outside.

The slope behind the house was raw, cold dirt mixed with jagged stones. She slid down, keeping a low profile, abrading spots on her back as her jacket rode up. The back door and many of the windows were covered with plywood. She knock-ed and softly called out, but no one answered. They were most likely all on the far side of the long house, the massive stone chimney of the fireplace dampening her voice.

Sammie Rae poked her head through a windowless frame. The huge open room was shadowed—the light pouring in through the opening in the roof was like a spotlight in the center. She peered into the shadows but saw no one. She climbed in and promptly stumbled over piled two-by-fours.

A shot just missed her head. The gunfire was followed by a scream of, "Jesus H. Christ, Sammie Rae!" Darla ran to hug her tight. "I could've killed you!"

"Good thing you're a piss-poor shot," Sammie Rae said. "Where's Lansing?"

Darla pulled her by the hand further along the back wall. Lansing lay on the ground atop a sleeping bag. It was stained with blood. She moved closer. "Al?"

"Hey," he whispered, his voice weak. His pants leg was slit up to his hip and a short length of rope, padded beneath with clothing, tourniqueted his mid-thigh. He reached out his hand. She rushed to take it.

A moment later, Thad Overton came to Lansing's side, untying the rope while applying pressure to Lansing's wound. "Need to get some blood to his foot."

"I'll do that," Sammie Rae said.

Overton shook his head. "Too much pressure could move the fracture and cause further damage, so I'll do it. Join Darla at the front window and see what's going on."

Sammie Rae waited for a second before pulling herself away, her hand lingering on Al's fingertips until the reach was too far for her arm. She headed to Darla. Outside, the Haitians' SUVs were quiet. The federal agents weren't motionless—they'd moved ballistic shields in front of them and were advancing steadily downward.

The staccato thrum of a helicopter sounded overhead. "Hope that's an air ambulance to evacuate him." Overton had joined them with his rifle. "Who was shooting before the government guys came?"

"Just some locals who knew me and Darla was in trouble." Sammie Rae didn't take her eyes from the scene outside.

Overton laughed softly. "Yeah, I heard you're everyone's best buddy."

"Hardly. But anything happen to Darla, Devil's Knob returns to total butt-ugly, everyone a troll. Not surprising the locals will do anything to prevent that."

"Oh, shut up, Sammie Rae," Darla said.

The driver's door of the front SUV, the Escalade, slid open slightly. No response—it must have been out of the agents' sight. A man slowly squeezed out of the SUV's door. "Like fish in a barrel," Darla said, firing out the window at the man. He dropped and lay writhing on the ground, screaming. "Piss-poor shot, my ass," she said.

The federal agents had used the noise of Darla's shot to move closer. The man with the bullhorn again demanded in French and English that the Haitians come out. Nothing happened for a moment, until the injured man reached up, trying to grab hold of the car door, only to fall back and remain still. After that, the SUVs emptied, the men exiting, hands up, and then dropping to lie face down in the dust. The agents, weapons pointed at their heads, swarmed them.

Chapter 34

THE AMBULANCE RIDE OVER THE ROCKY, twisty road was horrifying. The trip to the waiting helicopter seemed to take hours. Al shut his eyes tight every few minutes, as if pain was something you could avoid seeing. His face was gray under his reddish-brown skin, his lips pale blue. A moan escaped them with every bump. He had bitten down on his lower lip hard enough to bring a spot of blood.

If he'd pass out, would be easier on him. And on me.

Sammie Rae stroked his face whenever her hands were not in the medical technician's way. The man's words stuck in her mind, but she didn't dare tell Al what she'd overheard. "He's going to lose that leg."

The only hope was the driver's reply, "Maybe not, if we can get him to the trauma center in time. They got a whole team standing by and the OR's ready."

The paramedic shrugged in response.

They reached the helicopter and carried the semiconscious man to it. The transfer was swift and professional.

The helicopter flew them over Devil's Knob and on to the trauma center in Boyerstown. Sammie Rae was allowed to ride along. Once there, Al was taken straight to the operating suite, and she was directed to a waiting room.

"Mrs. Lansing?" An excessively tall doctor in scrubs, surgical mask dangling around his neck, had come to speak with her.

Sammie Rae didn't correct him. If they believed she and Al were married, that would give her the rights of family. Only if it came down to making decisions about his care would she have to come clean.

When she remained silent, he asked, "Maybe you'd rather we called you Deputy Wheedle?" He didn't wait for her to answer this time. "Before the anesthesia, Agent Lansing requested you go to a hotel and get some rest. He said you'd had a, and I quote, 'Record tough day.'" He put a hand on her shoulder and gazed down at her. It seemed he was aware of how imposing he was, as his words became friendly and reassuring. Almost humorous despite the situation. "He's quite chatty. Once we sedated him, he wouldn't stop talking." He chuckled—it sounded like something from a textbook on *managing the family's anxiety.* "We were told what you did, and we're all impressed. You're a real hero. We'll take good care of him for you, so go on, now. Transport to the hotel's been arranged. The nurse will take you to the car." He left.

Sammie Rae turned to the nurse who'd accompanied the doctor and had, by half-smiling, supported his attempts at reassurance. "No, I'm gonna stay right here and get updates."

"Honey," the nurse said, "this surgery's going to take hours, re-attaching nerves and blood vessels. We have four different teams all rotating through as needed. I'll bet you could get eight hours of rest, come back, and still wait. You need to be rested. For him."

*　　　*　　　*

On the brief ride to the hotel with a silent agent in a black sedan, Sammie Rae was sure she'd be unable to sleep, no matter how soft the mattress, how quiet the room. Once there—no check-in needed, all taken care of—she fell onto the bed. The next thing she knew, she awoke and looked at her phone. It was high morning. She'd spent nine hours in dreamless darkness.

She threw the covers off and swung her legs onto the floor. Looking down, she realized she was in the same filthy clothes, covered with dust and dry bits of leaves. And spots of Al's blood. The bathroom mirror revealed a strange, demented-appearing woman, face obscured by filth, hair disheveled and matted. A woman who could enter any junkie den and go unnoticed. She longed to shower but couldn't bear the thought of putting these clothes back on.

Shame. There were plenty of toiletries atop the sink's counter. A robe hung on the bathroom door, so white and fluffy she was afraid to touch it.

There was a knock at her door. A young lady in a front-desk suit, hotel's logo embroidered on the left lapel, handed her a plastic bag and said, "Lady in nurse's clothes brought these for you."

Inside the bag were hospital scrubs, size small, and operating-room socks with no-skid bottoms. A note read, "Still in surgery, so there's time for you to relax and get all cleaned up."

Overwhelmed, Sammie Rae sat on the edge of her bed, leaned forward, hands over her eyes, and cried. Her eyes itched and swelled, the tears pouring rivers of mud down her forearms. It was like Lark County had followed her here, in more ways than one.

The shower was as hot as she could take. Afterwards, she pulled on the scrubs and her jacket, stuffed her dirty clothes in the bag, tossed it on the bed, and headed down to the lobby, the no-skid socks lumpy in her shoes.

Unlike the pleasant woman of the night before, the tall, hefty nurse greeting her outside the surgical suite seemed determined to keep Sammie Rae on the civilian side of the divide. The nurse looked her up and down as if the scrubs were an attempt at privileges she didn't have. At first, all she said was, "You're to wait here."

Sammie Rae moved to go around her, but the nurse blocked her way. The anger flared up so sudden that her scalp felt on fire, her hair like the tip of a candle's wick. In no mood to be ordered around, ignored, or left in the dark, she balled her hands into fists. *I want to knock the snot bubbles right out of her. She's a big one, but I think I can take her.*

The nurse stood her ground, looking down at Sammie Rae.

Maybe I can't take her, and a call to security would get me kicked out of here. Instead of launching herself at the woman, she asked, "Is Agent Lansing okay? Is the surgery near done?"

"As far as I know, things are going well. One of the doctors will break soon and come speak to you. Stay here if you don't want to miss him—he'll be on a tight schedule." The nurse shifted the clipboard in her arms and walked out.

Sammie Rae went to the hot drink machine in the room, dumped four packets of sugar and three of flavored creamer in a cup of coffee and drank. Despite the rich and sweet drink, her belly continued to cramp with anxiety. Was she about to have the runs from nerves?

Just when she was about to sprint to the toilet, the doctor strode in. She scanned his face, but his expression was unreadable. His reddened eyes blinking in exhaustion, he pulled a blue paper cap from his balding scalp and said, "Agent Lansing's surgery is almost done, and then he'll be moved to the recovery room. The operation went better than we expected."

"Can I see him?"

"You'll be able to visit in about an hour. I'll have a nurse come get you."

"And his leg? The ambulance crew thought he'd lose it."

The doctor's expression didn't change. "Looks good, but only time will tell. Either way, he'll have a long recovery." Without giving her a chance to ask anything else, he wheeled about and left.

Sammie Rae went to the bathroom, then resumed pacing. She was cried out, but her hands ached from being squeezed together.

"Mrs. Lansing?" The unfriendly tall woman was back.

She forgot to lie, blurted out, "We're not married."

"You're not?" Her face cracked a smug smile. "Only family is allowed in recovery. You'll have to wait here until Mr. Lansing is in his room."

"You can't do that! I flew here with him!" Sudden teardrops blurred Sammie Rae's vision. She wiped them with the back of her right hand—better that than to try punching the woman's lights out. As the nurse left, she yelled, "That's Agent Lansing and I'm Deputy Sammie Rae Wheedle of the Lark County Sheriff's Department!"

It was the second time she'd cried in two days, and Sammie Rae Wheedle rarely cried. Of course, she cried and cried after her ma left, but only when Pa wasn't watching. And a few more times recently. And, how embarrassing, once while underneath Al.

What if that's the first thing he remembers when he opens his eyes and sees me? Maybe it was good the recovery room was off limits, give him time to wake up without her. If he woke up.

What if I never get to be with him again?

She slumped into a chair, overwhelmed by the thought of a tube in his throat moving air in and out of his lungs.

Mechanical beeping, the only indication he was alive. She mopped her eyes with her sleeves.

"Hey!" Darla peeked around the doorframe, her face devoid of makeup, her hair disheveled as if she'd taken no time before leaving Lark County. And yet she was the same astonishing beauty as always. She pulled a small cooler on wheels. Overton followed with a bulging insulated bag. "Ma couldn't stand you being here without food."

Sammie Rae leaped up and hugged her. "Oh, Dar, they won't let me in recovery to see him."

"Shit!" Darla dropped the handle of the cooler and returned the hug. "Well, thank God I left Ma home. Imagine the war she'd start, them not treating you right."

Sammie Rae wished Dolly had come. You didn't need an imaginary monster when you had that small, brick-shaped woman in your corner.

"Don't worry," Overton said. His face was calm, the very picture of a professional, just too weirdly beautiful. "Let me see what can be done." He put the bag down and left.

"Thad's going to hunt down one of the surgeons and talk doc-to-doc. If he can't find one, he'll sweet-talk the nurses." Darla's hip bumped Sammie Rae over, making room for them both on the extra-wide seat. She bent forward and opened the cooler. Inside, padded with bits of shipping foam, were jars of kimchi and of homemade booze. The bag held a thermos of spicy tofu stew, a container of kimchi fried rice, and packages of grilled meats.

Sammie Rae bent forward, holding her belly. The urgent need for the toilet had been dealt with, but her belly still felt weird. "Don't think I can eat."

Darla took a paper plate and loaded it with *bulgogi* on top of rice. She put it on Sammie Rae's lap. "Need to keep your energy up."

Sammie Rae took a bite and realized how famished she was, and how comforting Dolly's food was.

"And some of this." Darla opened a small jar of clear liquid.

Sammie Rae took a gulp. The burn caused her to choke for a moment. As soon as she could, she took another mouthful. As the warmth spread through her, the tense feeling in her chest eased. They sat silent for what seemed an eternity.

Overton returned at last. "Al's in the surgical ICU. He's stable. Very weak. He lost a lot of blood, but they were able to extubate… to take the breathing tube out of him before he left recovery. You can see him now."

Sammie Rae put her plate and the jar on the floor, rose, and followed him. Unlike her vision of intensive care—a row of curtained beds in an open space—in this one the patients were in small individual rooms arranged in a circle, so everyone could be seen from the central nurse's station. The effect was dizzying, the little rooms whirled in front of her eyes. She felt like Dumbo, confused and frightened, with pink elephants on parade. Maybe it was just the *myeongsul* she'd downed.

Lansing was lying almost flat, his eyes closed, IV lines in both arms. Clear fluid in one arm's tube, blood dripping dark, through the other.

"Shit, his leg looks like a porcupine," Sammie Rae whispered. Al's right leg was covered in plaster and had rod after rod protruding from the cast. His toes stuck out, looking vulnerable and almost indecent in their bareness. She'd never seen his feet before.

Overton put a hand on her shoulder. "They're giving him great care. All that metalwork holds the fracture bits together. They'll help start his rehab as soon as possible." He took a step away from her. "Go on in to see him."

Sammie Rae went to Lansing's bedside. "Al?" she said. He remained motionless, breathing slowly, his eyes shut even when she took his icy hand. She sat on the chair, afraid sitting on the bed would jiggle something loose, send blood squirting from its plastic bag all over the room. When she looked up and out toward the corridor, Overton was just outside the door, standing sentry. He turned as if he sensed her looking and raised one hand in a little wave. That reassurance calmed her for a moment.

When a nurse entered to check the machines' settings, Sammie Rae left. On the way back to the waiting room she asked Overton when Al would awaken.

"Probably as soon as the anesthesia wears off. The surgery, the time in surgery, were so long and his system was in so much danger from loss of blood… well, it's hard stuff for a body to deal with. And it's understandably upsetting for you, seeing someone you care about like that, even if you're used to trauma. But remember he's really strong, so I bet you'll be talking to him soon. Even in a couple of hours."

She turned to look at him, so serious and concerned with her feelings. "His leg. I know about the bone but shit, so many guys in Lark have lost legs overseas in the service. Or working in the mines. His leg's still there, that means he'll keep it, right?"

"The shot damaged blood vessels and nerves. They're hard to repair, but crucial for keeping muscle and bone alive. I'm sure the surgeons did meticulous work reconnecting all they could. Now it's just wait and see. Wish I could say for sure, but I just can't. No one can."

At least he wasn't talking down to her.

They reached the waiting area. Darla had fallen asleep, curled in the double-sized chair. Sammie Rae went to awaken her, but Overton shook his head. "She drove most of the way here." He grinned. "Insisted on it. Wanted to get to you as quickly as possible and she's got a heavier foot than I do." Darla would have slapped his hand away if he reached for the keys. She always wanted to drive—and get wherever they were going as fast as possible. "Looks like an angel, doesn't she?" he said. "The dark kind. Boss angel. Speaking of bossiness, she gave me an order to keep you from worrying."

"Don't make no never mind." Sammie Rae bit the edge of the Styrofoam cup. "Nothing's gonna stop my brain from running. I keep playing over and over, how I should've done something different. Just can't figure what that something is." A bit of the Styrofoam stuck between her front teeth. She worked it out with her tongue. "Besides, I feel dumb as a box of rocks, thinking you were…"

"Thinking I was what?" He laughed, pressing his lips together to stifle the sound as Darla stirred. She wriggled a bit and settled back down. Even began to snore softly.

"Doesn't matter what. Al vouches for you." Sammie Rae slouched back and stared at the ceiling.

"You're exhausted, too, aren't you?" he asked.

"Don't think I can sleep, though."

Overton shrugged and picked up two tattered magazines. "*Consumer Reports on Health*. Huh. Guess it's better than *Gluten Free Living*." He tossed them aside, opened his phone and began to read.

Sammie Rae awoke with a start. "Al?" she said, sitting upright, still disoriented. She turned to Overton. "What time is it?"

"You've been dozing off and on for more than an hour. Nothing new yet, which means nothing bad has happened. He just is too worn out to visit." Overton turned to face Sammie Rae.

A glance at Darla showed her still curled up on the couch.

"You didn't wake her. But she wants me to tell you my story."

"You don't have to."

"It's okay. No secret now that you know I'm supposed to testify—and by the way, if you see a few large men standing around, they're guarding me and Agent Lansing. I always would have told you whatever you wanted."

Sammie Rae, considering his words, took another bite of the cup, feeling strange, trying to see the past months the way he must have. It had been Darla approaching him at the conference, Darla arranging the visit and going to the Henderson place with them. And then Darla agreeing to spend time managing the renovations when Sammie Rae only had time to suspect him of black magic and murder. "You don't have to tell me anything."

He laughed. "Have my orders, so, where should I start? Birth? The boss lady wasn't entirely clear."

"I'd like to check on Al first, if I can."

"The nurses promised they'd come tell me if there was any change," Overton said.

Sammie Rae was certain the nurses would do just that, even the one male nurse she'd seen. "Okay, okay." She let out a long quavering breath.

"Getting to Haiti…" He looked at Darla again. She slumbered on. "I wanted to work with an underserved population, create a program that functioned. Haiti fit the bill—it's so wretchedly poor, even more in the rural areas. Even more devastated by the earthquake back in 2010. The people were hardworking, self-reliant, slow to come to the clinic and say, 'Fix it for me.' They felt responsible for their own health and tried home cures first."

Overton's story reminded her of the tales Pa and Mee-Maw told about the country folk and doctors who'd take a few eggs for payment, back during the Depression.

"The mix of superstition and fatalism made for an interesting challenge, too. In the Haitian countryside, illness is a punishment from the gods—Catholic as well as voodoo. Voodoo is like a magical thread that ties Haitians together wherever they live and ties them back to where they come from."

"Africa?" Sammie Rae asked.

"Americans have the mistaken idea that voodoo is all African and all black magic. It isn't."

A nurse came to the door. "Dr. Overton? Agent Lansing is more awake."

Sammie Rae leaped up. "Can I see him now?"

"Dr. Overton?" the nurse said, loudly this time.

Sammie Rae flipped her the bird. Discretely.

"Coming." He stood and they walked with her to Lansing's room, leaving Darla behind.

Al lay as unmoving as before, the same machines going *ping, ping, ping* with each beat of his heart. His chest rose and fell, like the heartbeat on the monitor, with a steady rhythm.

"Al?" Sammie Rae whispered.

His eyelids fluttered and his hand lifted a few inches. She grabbed it and held on. "Al?" she repeated. His fingers slipped from her grasp.

"Maybe we should return tomorrow," Overton said, gently pulling her away from the bed. "You could get a bit more sleep."

She shook her head. "I'm not leaving. Don't care if it's three a.m. when he's ready to see me. I'll be here."

Darla was awake and waiting, all the food packed away. She cocked her head in a silent question. Overton answered, "He's still too drowsy for a real visit…"

"Sammie Rae, hon, you look wiped out. Let's all go get a rest. We'll get another room, or I'll stay with you if you need me to."

Sammie Rae didn't want to be alone in the bed again, but it was Al she wanted with her. She shook her head, fished in her pocket for the hotel key card, and held it out. "Here, you two go. I'm staying. No sense paying for another room."

Overton and Darla exchanged looks and then Darla took the card.

"Just push my stuff out of the way if it's on the bed."

Darla folded her in a hug. "We're not leaving you alone."

Overton cast a longing look at Darla, who blushed and shot back a frown. It was obvious what he was thinking.

"I'll be fine." Sammie Rae wriggled her head free from Darla's bosom, where the embrace held her. She said to Overton, "Can you make them let me see him whenever and not to give me crap about not being his wife?"

He laughed. "I can give it a go."

Darla released Sammie Rae and took Overton's arm. "I really could use some sleep. We left in a hurry, and it's been a long day." The look she was giving him wasn't a sleepy one and Sammie Rae felt a flash of longing to be headed somewhere alone with a hale, healthy, and fully capable Al. And for a moment she wished she hadn't given up the room. Even being alone, thinking of him, would be better than waiting here, where a snooty nurse could walk in at any moment.

"Come on, then, Thad," Darla started for the door, saying, over her shoulder, "We'll talk to them on our way out."

Chapter 35

THE ROOM FELL INTO A PROFOUND silence when they left. The air seemed so still that Sammie Rae waved her arms to move it around and give the feeling that life continued to exist. Aside from trips to the toilet, she sat and stared at the big clock on the wall as the hands slowly moved, counting off the minutes, and then the hours. When had they made clocks so quiet?

In the wee hours of the morning, a new nurse came to take Sammie Rae to Al. So worn out that she bumped into the doorjamb entering his room, she approached his bed as softly as she could.

Al's eyes opened and his lips moved. Sammie Rae leaned close, until her ear was almost against his mouth. With strength that surprised her, he pulled her head down and kissed her cheek. When he let go, she sat on the edge of the bed. He winced as the mattress jiggled.

"Sorry!" She moved to stand but he grabbed her wrist.

"Don't be. It's worth it just to see you." His voice was grainy. "Stay with me."

She settled in next to him on his right, far from the lines in his left arm. She drew her feet up onto the cover and leaned her head on his shoulder.

The nurse returned. Before she could say anything, Lansing spoke up. "Don't make her go."

The nurse inclined her head toward the door. "He needs his rest, no matter what he says."

Sammie Rae tried to slide away, but he kept her arm tight against him.

Lansing's glare was lopsided, like a drunk's attempt at remaining in command. He said to the nurse, "If you make her leave, I'll never get off the call button. And for sure I'll get no sleep."

The nurse brought a hand up to her lips and Sammie Rae saw she was smiling. "Miss, if you promise to get up before the morning shift comes on, I'll try to disturb you as little as possible."

Lansing yawned and shut his eyes. Sammie Rae snuggled her lips against his neck.

*   *   *

"Aww. How sweet," a man's voice said.

Sammie Rae's eyes struggled to open against the sleep that crusted them. Overton stood at the foot of the bed looking down at them. Beside her, Lansing's body tensed but his eyes stayed shut as she left the bed.

A sly smile spread across Overton's face as he pressed gently on the bed and let the pressure up with a sudden movement, saying, "Morning Al!"

Lansing laughed and coughed, "Ha, ow, ha, ow! Get the fuck out of here, Thad."

"Okay, then I'll go hunt down the house doctor and see if there's anything else we should know." Overton wheeled around and left.

The clock on the wall read 7:50, just before change of shift for the nursing staff. Alone with Al, Sammie Rae pulled the chair over, sat, and took his hand again. "Sorry if I was dumb to not tell you Overton was in the county. I didn't want to embarrass myself with all that zombie stuff."

He took a big breath, blew it out, and pressed a little button taped to the bed.

"You need the nurse?"

"No. That lets me dose myself for pain. But speaking of embarrassment, no reason for it. In fact, you saved my reputation, you saved my job, and then you saved my life."

"How?"

His eyes were closed again. "Ahh, the morphine's hit. Damn leg hurts like a son of a bitch!"

"Want me to go?"

"No, just give me a minute."

It was more than a minute, but she didn't mind. *Saved my reputation, saved my job, and saved my life* sang in her mind. She wanted to hear every bit of whatever that meant.

"How are we doing?" A nurse had arrived, her wide hips brushing the IV lines, making them sway. She bustled around, checking the machines without waiting for them to answer. She woke up Lansing to feel his toes and press on the nails, seemingly satisfied by what she found. "Could you drink something?"

"I don't know." He blinked, moving his eyes as if light was confusing and new to him. The nurse twisted one more thing on the tubing and left.

"Maybe you should try," Sammie Rae said. "Tea or apple juice?"

He scratched his eyebrow. "Christ no! Morphine makes me want to puke." He turned, grabbed a little pink plastic basin from the table, and vomited into it, some missing and soiling his gown.

The nurse bustled back in. "Time he rests. We can still smell your food at the desk—no wonder he's thrown up! Don't bring anything like that here again."

Sammie Rae gasped and forced herself to stand tall as she walked out by the nurses at the desk, even when one of them said, "Damn hillbillies come in here talking mush and eating worse. Bet that's roadkill."

"Bet it's Spam and beans, their national dish!"

Another one chimed in, "And she's got that gorgeous doctor with her. Not to mention his beautiful girlfriend... think the food's hers. Chinese, maybe."

"Still think the little one's from the backwoods. Is she with that government agent? I don't understand it!"

Though they didn't seem to care, she was careful not to show she'd heard them. But when she reached the waiting room to find Darla alone, she slumped into the seat next to her. "You're here early. Did you get enough sleep?"

"Sleep? Uh, no!" Darla took a deep breath and changed her tone. "Thad said Lansing's doing okay." She put her arm around Sammie Rae's waist. "So why are you looking down at the mouth?"

"Damned nurses bitched about your ma's food. Said all kinds of shit about hillbillies. Tell me, what does Al Lansing see in me? Is it just a reaction to you dumping him? He told me no, but..."

"What the fuck is the matter with you? Is it just being plumb worn out, so tired of stuff that you're going crazy? Pisses me off! You never seem to realize how damn adorable and smart you are." She pulled Sammie Rae's head onto her shoulder. "And what else did Al say?"

"That I saved his reputation, his job, and his life. I didn't understand that. Well, I understand saving his life, maybe, but..."

"But nothing. Al was responsible for making sure Thad was safely stored away for testifying—that's why Al was at the conference. We had no idea they knew each other when we went and met them, two innocent country bumpkins that we were. It was on Al's watch that Thad disappeared. If Thad was killed, the government would have lost a key witness, and Al's career would be over. His only chance was to follow the Haitians, find out what they knew. When he finally found out, well, you got there right in the nick of time." Darla's voice changed, became enthusiastic and she did an action movie fist pump. "Sammie Rae Wheedle to the rescue!"

"Nah."

Darla's tone changed again. "Seriously, you saved all of us."

Credit Pa and the Strip-Poker Posse—it would have been a disaster if not for them! But she knew it would make trouble to admit that.

Thad returned with a paper shopping bag. "What's up?"

Darla looked in the bag and showed Sammie Rae the contents: sandwiches and a container of salad. "Fucking nurses," she whispered. "This is tasteless crap."

"Sorry," Thad said, "but I need a break from garlic, anyway."

"If you wanted that, why didn't you at least go to McDonald's?"

He sighed, sat, and pulled out the salad.

Darla let out an uncharacteristically lady-like burp and said, "Finish the story."

"Not much more to tell. Got to know the locals, set up clinics, and saw a big problem was that many local leaders and a lot of the priests were owned by the drug runners. I started to work with the central government, which was working with the American government. I had information and contacts, so I was a target for the drug dealers."

"Not that history stuff. Your story."

"Are you sure? I thought that was something just between us."

Darla took a sandwich and peeled off the crust. "No secrets from Sammie Rae. Get used to it."

"None?"

"None. Sammie Rae's one smart officer of the law. She's thinking it doesn't make sense for you to leave because testifying is risky and then run from witness protection here. Tell her about Mardochée."

Sammie Rae wanted to ask who or what Mardochée was, but clouds seemed to cross Overton's face. Clouds that made things seem obvious. "You don't have to tell me anything."

Darla held her hand up. "Hell, yeah, he does. Explains a lot, Mardochée."

"I can't start with Mardochée alone—have to start with both of you, since both of you are why I'm here. The minute I saw you, it took me back to my clinic near the Pic Macaya, back to Mardochée, back to something lost forever."

So, a woman. "This Mardochée looked like Darla?" Sammie Rae couldn't imagine two of them.

"Darla is tall like she was. Tall, long black hair. Beautiful."

"You can say *exotic*," Darla said. "Wait for a moment. I need a Coke. This white-bread supermarket sandwich is giving me an upset stomach." She headed out into the hallway.

Sammie Rae didn't believe that for a moment. Darla had left to avoid showing that she was upset. Overton had loved another woman and Darla wasn't used to sloppy seconds when it came to romance. Or being compared to any other girl.

This time, he didn't stop. "It was more the self-assured intelligence, a way of walking and taking command. Mardochée was a Creole, a native Haitian. But she wasn't exotic to me, no matter what Darla wants me to say. She was just Mardochée."

"Well, we grew up in Lark County, where Dolly was exotic. That made Dar exotic. Al only misses *exotic* by a teeny bit."

Darla came back in with a can of soda and popped the lid. "I see you two kept going without me."

"Mardochée…" Overton paused for a moment, then reached for Darla's hand. Once he took it, he examined it for a moment, palm and back. "…was from a wealthy family in a place where wealth brings far more than it ever can in the US. Her people were long linked to some of the worst of the Duvaliers' crimes."

"Al told me about Papa Doc and the Tonton."

"She wanted to make up for some of that, so she left the city to join us. We worked together and fell in love. The clinic's little valley was like paradise, if you weren't one of our addicted patients or someone trying to feed a family. Paradise if you were wealthy, like Mardochée, or American, like me. We always thought we could escape.

"There was local competition for medical care, two voodoo healers. Mardochée tried to work with them. She knew all the spiritual figures, from *Bondye* on down."

"*Bondye?*" Sammie Rae asked.

"Oh," he said, as surprised as if he had forgotten where he was. As if he was back with people who understood the word. "*Bondye,* Creole for the French *Bon Dieu,* the good Lord. "

Sammie Rae shot a glance at Darla, to see how she was taking it all in. Her eyes were closed and something about her lips seemed to indicate that she was humming to herself, though no sound came out. But her hand, clenched in Overton's, was looking bloodless.

"But unreachable or not, she believed in God. 'God *is* unreachable,' she said 'But both good and evil stalk the Earth. It's not all brain chemistry and personal choice.' She said people needed to believe in things greater than man, in a struggle to be won. Without that, life and death were purposeless.

"A local voodoo practitioner worked with us, but another one viewed the clinic as competition. The people felt that he could reach the spirits, the *loa*, better than anyone. We had no idea he was collaborating with the drug dealers.

"One day, we took off to have a picnic and wander around in the forest." His voice choked off for a moment and the green rings around his black pupils glittered like gemstones. He took a deep breath and told her how he and the girl he loved wandered the cloud forest, how they stopped to picnic on an ancient, moss-covered stone, one an earthquake had tilted from its bed, how he left her for a moment and heard her scream, how he ran to help her but was knocked out cold.

"I awoke with the world swirling around me, vision blurred and double. I couldn't stand. The sun was setting, hours had gone by. When I touched my scalp, my hand came away bloody. I yelled her name over and over. No answer. She was nowhere. Our overturned basket was on the stone, which was no longer tilted, but flat, sunk in the ground—the scuff marks of feet showed the force it had taken to move it. But where was Mardochée?

"Then I saw a ripped piece of her skirt, part stuck beneath the stone. It was as if a huge wave hit me—they must have put her there. Dropped to my knees, began to claw at the ground, trying to find a way to keep her from suffocating. It was impossible—only a thin layer of humus and then the stony earth."

He knew he needed men, many men to lift that stone and so he began to run to the village, tripping over downed logs and slipping on rot. Lost his way, slid, tumbled into brambles, but didn't notice scrapes or bruises.

His voice was steady as if it came from a machine. "She had to be saved. Everything was over, done. I was dead without her.

"I reached the village. On the main road, I called for help from men who knew me. They ran, screaming, 'The bokor is come! The bokor is come!'"

Overton stopped speaking for a moment, sat staring at the wall across like it was a movie screen playing a scene over and over. Sammie Rae looked at Darla, who, for once in her life, seemed on uncertain ground.

"I thought their terror was my appearance—filthy, covered in leaves, desperate, half-insane. I found out the truth in Port-au-Prince. Mardochée wasn't as knowledgeable about voodoo as she'd thought. The huge stone we'd chosen for our picnic had been placed to weight a zombie in her grave. When the men saw her sitting on it, they believed she was that zombie, crawled out of the earth. They were helping her by putting her back in her grave, as slavery is a fate worse than death. There had never been a chance of saving her. She was dead and part of me was too."

"Woah," Sammie Rae said. "So, they thought you were a zombie?"

Overton shook his head. "A bokor is not a zombie. A bokor is a zombie *master*, who turns people into mindless slaves. People here have got it wrong. Those who honor voodoo don't fear zombies, they fear *becoming* zombies."

*   *   *

The ladies' room was occupied. Darla and Sammie Rae were forced to wait in the hall, dancing with the need to empty their bladders. And the need to talk to each other.

Darla squinted and picked a shred of lint from an eyelash. "Thanks for leaving us alone for a while. It took so much out of Thad, going over it all again."

"You made him tell me."

"You were a giant douche, thinking he was a zombie or that other thing. Hell, thinking wasn't what you were doing. You stirred up the loonies, so you're gonna calm them down. And from now on, you best stick with The White Thing."

"Jeez, Darla, think that poor girl was buried alive?"

Darla shuddered. "I've never dared ask him and I never will. It's been three years since he left Haiti but obviously…"

"I bet that hostile witch doctor set up the attack on them."

"Maybe." There was a flush behind the closed door, then a sink running. "Probably." The door opened and a fat old woman limped out, her hair straggling from her bun. Darla smiled at her and held the door as they went in.

"First!" Sammie Rae called, dropping her pants and sitting on the toilet.

Darla went to the mirror and ran her fingers through her hair. "You know we're going back today. Are you coming with us?" She looked over at Sammie Rae.

"Turn around. I'm wiping. No, think I'll stay with Al. He wants me to go because of the award ceremony, but I'm good to watch it on TV. Beebe'll mention me…" She zipped up her pants. "… and without the 'brave little girl deputy' standing next to him, he'll get more attention."

Darla hustled over. "Thank God. Couldn't hold it any-more." She sat. "Ahhh. Yeah, that Ralphie is an attention whore."

Sammie Rae was done at the sink. She moved to let Darla wash her hands. "All that voodoo stuff was real interesting."

"There's lots more. Thad started telling me all about the *loa*, the gods and goddesses, the spirits. So complicated and weird. There's one called Kalfu, who cries black tears from his black eyes. Sounds like that sickness everybody was scared was coming over from Africa, doesn't it? Just like zombies seem like slaves, really beaten down, overworked slaves."

"Darla, you're so damn smart. Do you think people can share a memory over hundreds and hundreds of years?"

"Who the fuck knows?"

They left the ladies' room, met up with Overton, and went to the ICU so they could say goodbye to Lansing, who was watching a football game and sipping from a pink pitcher of water with a clear straw.

"You going, too?" Al reached out to touch Sammie Rae's arm.

"You said she should," Darla protested.

"That's right, I did." Maybe it was the drugs, but he sounded like a little kid grumbling about being abandoned. "Are you really leaving me?"

"Relax, I'm staying. I'll take the bus back later."

"No, you won't. I'm giving you my car. It'll be months before I can drive it, anyway. It's right here in Boyerstown. I got someone delivering it."

"Hate to break this up, but we've got to get the crews back to work fixing the roof before real winter comes. One snowstorm would bring everything to a halt," Overton said.

"Come on, Sammie Rae," Darla said. "Walk us to the car."

"Here," Sammie Rae dug in her pockets. "Take my keys—I paid the bills so the heat's on. Stay in the apartment until I get back. Or until you're okay with staying at your parents'."

"Ha! As if I'd give Ma free access to Thad. She's scarier than any of the *loa*. I know you gave her the idea, but she's the one who spread the rumors."

After they drove off, Sammie Rae returned to Lansing's room, but his bed was empty. She went down the hall to his nurse. "Excuse me, where is Agent Lansing? I know he didn't get up and walk off by himself."

"Funny. We haven't heard that one before." She rolled her eyes. "He's been taken to have his cast changed." The woman wheeled around and left, her auburn ponytail swinging side to side. Behind her back, Sammie Rae flipped her off.

The waiting room was lonely, now that Lark County had left. She called her pa. "Hey, what's up with y'all?"

"Well, gal, I was waiting on you to tell me what was up. Everywhere I go…"

Everywhere he goes? He never goes anywhere.

"… people are talking about my daughter, the hero."

"But if it wasn't for you and the others, we'd probably all be dead. Those fuckers thought a whole army surrounded them."

"No reason anybody's gotta know all that. Would only get Mamie into trouble. She supplied the real heat, none of it legal, registered, or any other liberal crap." He sucked on his teeth for a minute. "Tell the truth, was her husband's arsenal. He was some kind of crazy, sitting up all night case the Klan was coming, wanting to establish a new Africa somewhere."

"Can kind of see that, Pa."

Pa's voice was suspicious, cagey. "Your boyfriend see things that way?"

"Who said I had a boyfriend? We just worked together."

He snorted. "Think I'm some kind of backwoods stupid, huh? Anyway, Mamie said she couldn't live like that, no matter how bad West Virginia used to be. Or is. She kicked his ass out and said she'd shoot that ass off if he ever came back. She'll need to be well armed from now on, now Wade's moving in."

"What?"

"Yeah. Bet that wife of his'll come for him. 'Course, she's the kind to creep up sneaky like, with a big old skinning knife. Kind'll slice your throat or harvest your balls with one stroke and you never wake up. Wade should sleep with one eye open. Good thing Mamie got eyes in the back of her head."

"Isn't Mamie like twenty years older than him?"

"Well, lookee here at who don't want others to buck the system. Least I can't pin *racist* on you!"

Sammie Rae had a sudden flash of understanding. Pa's new status would prove useful to him, both in arguments with her and in Lark County. "What is it you want to tell me? There's something else, so just fess up."

"Well…" Pa hesitated and was probably scratching his head while he figured out the words. "I know you ain't fond of Hazie. Know you think of her as a poor substitute for your ma, who was a real looker. But Hazie done took great care of me. I was worn out, depressed all the time, raising you alone, hoping your ma would return. She never did. Now you're grown and I'm moving in with Hazie. Her house is real nice, all fixed up and clean."

How the hell had she given the impression that her ma's prettiness made a difference to her? He was right in one thing—she'd thought Hazie a poor substitute. "You moving in out of convenience?"

"'Course not, but a good woman like her, who sticks around to clean and cook, is a great comfort to a man who's been alone a long time—just bein' with her makes me spry. I take care of her, too. Think I got a bit smarter and realized love isn't just about pretty. Or about beating out Ralph Beebe for a girl." His voice did sound smug. "Should have let him have your ma all those years ago. Had her anyways for a while. But if I'd turned her loose, wouldn't have had you."

His logic was so twisty, she had to stop and ponder it a moment.

"But our house will be standing empty. No reason for you to keep paying rent. You could move in and fix it up. It's big enough for two."

"I gotta go, Pa." She ended the call. He really was something, her pa.

Still, the house *was* big enough for two. Her apartment wasn't. Not really. She tapped her phone against her front teeth. *Click, click, click.* Helped her think.

When she returned to Lansing's room, he was back in the bed, but now his cast was plastic, barber-poled brilliant pink alternating with lavender. Sammie Rae burst into laughter. "That looks so silly!"

"Yeah. My 'friends' and colleagues bribed the orthopedic surgeon. Think they're so fucking funny. But glad to see it amuses you. They're flying me to Bethesda tomorrow. I'll need a few more surgeries and then rehab. I'll be able to keep working on the case from there. So, are you coming?"

"Tomorrow?"

"Your hearing impaired?"

"Aww, don't be grumpy. That little-girly cast really is funny."

"Wasn't for the pain when they cut it open, I'd have them change it. Asked them to slap another color on top but it would be too heavy. At least it's sturdier now. Hey, shut the door. Let's see if you can swing aboard. Would make me a hell of a lot less grumpy."

"Get out of here! I wouldn't risk your leg with all those rods still poking out!"

"This plastic's pretty smooth, not like the plaster. Your skin would be safe now." He grinned. "Come here and lie down at least." He shifted his hips to the side. "They're going to get me up and walking somehow. And I only have a little while to get my strength up."

She sat on the edge of the bed—with slow care—opposite to the candy-colored cast and its imposing rods. "That hurt you?"

"Not at all. Lie here next to me, real close, so I don't have to turn to touch you."

Sammie Rae slid her legs down, avoiding the metal frame supporting his leg. He raised up enough to slide his left arm under her, turning her face to him to kiss. The kiss was long and slow, and seemed to cause a spot of warmth deep inside her. The warmth spread upward and grew more intense. She was grateful for the relief that came as he began to lift her tee. His hand was smoother than before. Slick.

"Mmm, hmm," he said. "You have the nicest titties ever." His hand withdrew.

"Hey!" She hadn't meant to protest but his hand's removal made her blush with instant indignation. She felt… what was the term? *Naked desire.* She wished she could see his face, make sure he wasn't funning on her, but her eyes had stayed closed after the kiss and refused to open.

"I'm just going to put a little more of this lotion on. Make sure nothing snags." There was a *squitt* sound and his hand was back, cooler, sliding up her rib cage and under her bra until it found her nipple.

The warmth returned, stronger, wheeling down her belly until it circled like a spinning star. Hot. How good that cool lotion would feel! She took his hand and tried to force it down between her legs, but his arm resisted her move. "Told you we'd take it slow from now on. Nothing more until you're really ready."

"Oh, God, no, don't stop," she said with a moan. As embarrassing as it was, she couldn't keep from moving her own hand down and rubbing so hard it felt like his.

Afterward, she lay gasping like a trout on the streambank, dignity as far from her as that fish's water. When she could speak, she said, "Want me to try something on you?"

"Of course I would, but I don't think the resulting move-ments would be good right yet. Give the cast a little more time to harden, babe."

"Looks like something else is hardening." She wriggled her rear into the mattress.

There was a sound in the hall, a cart rattling? Something dropping? Sammie Rae sat up and arranged her clothing. A normal-seeming conversation would cover the awkward silence.

"I'm so sorry I suspected Thad. I feel so much better about trusting him with Darla."

"Do you now?" A smile played on his lips.

"Yeah. He told me his whole story."

"Did he? It's a great yarn, isn't it?"

She would have punched him if he wasn't pinioned to the hospital bed, still sporting rods from his leg. If things were different, the way they had been. "What the hell are you hint-ing at?"

"Did he tell you about the girl in the rainforest? The huge stone?" A small, tight laugh shook his belly.

"You find that all funny?" She stared at him and suspicion overwhelmed her. "No girl?"

"Oh, there was a girl, all right. Mardochée. Like he says, she was from a prominent family linked to the Duvaliers." His voice trailed off, leading her.

"You told me about them, remember?" *This is really getting annoying.* One glance at his face revealed how much he was enjoying this conversational cat-and-mouse game. And strangely enough, so was she. It seemed to indicate that he would get back to normal. He was Agent Lansing, in control again. "My love and my sympathy for your injuries are endless, but you've got to quit screwing around and *tell* me!"

The only reply was a wider smirk.

She couldn't keep from asking, "No stone, then?"

"Stone, yes. Buried alive, yes. And I guess that's not something you want happen to anyone…"

"You think?"

He ignored her attempt at sarcasm. "So far, the superficial story's true. But the part he leaves out is that the two of them were running a scam on the pharmaceutical company his family owned. Stole pills, pretty massive quantities, and sold them to smugglers. He was busy doing good providing medical care, because he does seem to like being a healer, or maybe just being important on a real integral one-on-one level. Everything was going swimmingly. Money for the clinics and even more for them. Then Mardochée got greedy, got the bright idea of cheating the smugglers, who, by coincidence, were called the Ton Tons. Who promptly retaliated. They got to her."

"But not to him. Not yet. And that's why he agreed to testify."

"Very good! You'll make a great investigator someday, you clever little country girl!"

She mock scowled and cuffed him on the arm. "Don't be smug. But why leave the program? Why subject himself to risk?"

Al shrugged. "Arrogance? Independence? Restlessness? Inability to follow rules? Thinks he can get away with anything? Why steal from your wealthy family if they've never denied you anything?"

"Maybe that was all his girlfriend's idea. But what about Darla? Will she get tangled up in something dangerous?"

"We'll take care of the Ton Tons. And, as for him, well, I think he's learned his lesson. He's no conscienceless sociopath, just easily whipped if he believes a woman really loves him." He winked broadly. "It's a flaw of all us really good-looking guys, wondering if you want us as arm candy. And that Mardochée had him wrapped around her little finger. I don't think your buddy Darla, from my experience, will have trouble doing the same. As far as I can see, she's no crook, just someone who likes working hard, building a business. Maybe she'll keep him on the up and up."

Sammie Rae sighed. She had a lot to think about.

Al poked her in the side. "I know you'll decide to tell her what she needs to know. But you didn't answer my question before. You coming to Bethesda with me?"

Go further from Lark County? Almost all the way to Washington, where she'd never been before? At the thought, her blood rose into her head with a sudden *whoosh*. She remembered Beebe and the guys in the department. She'd scheduled no time off. If she didn't get back home, she'd lose her job.

His recovery would take months. It would make her real antsy to wait. But how could she fail him now, when he'd almost died? The thought of losing him, of losing his touch was heart-stopping. Would he forget her if she didn't go? Could she really return to being just the mascot of Lark County, everybody's friend but nobody's love?

"Ah, the meaningful pause. Is Little Country Girl about to dump me?" He waved a hand at his injured leg.

She left the bed and stood pulling her hair back with the rubber band she had stored around her wrist.

"Wait." He placed his hand over his heart. "I'm just teasing. Gallows humor you could say. Defense mechanism. Come back here."

She sat on the very edge of the mattress, out of reach.

He sighed. "Sorry. I'm teasing. I understand you're not ready to give up being Deputy Wheedle, Lark County's finest. I'd come to you if I could but meanwhile, we can talk every day and you can visit me whenever you have a few days off.

And I'm pretty sure we still need surveillance in Lark County—not giving up on my hope of getting you the job you deserve."

She stared at him for a moment. Didn't he understand? Taking care of the people she loved seemed the very best job ever. The very best life. Funny, now that she was loved, now that things were better, they were so much harder!

She was so relieved he was there, alive, looking so tempting, that she lay down again and snuggled against him, ginning up her courage. "Could we maybe have phone sex? Or, like buy webcams?"

He laughed and winced as the bed jounced with each guffaw. When he calmed, he wiped his eyes and said, "I wish this was videoed so you could watch later and see why I want you. That crafty little expression on your face was priceless. But no webcams. They can be hacked and then your fun is everyone's forever."

"You mean something like this?" She slid her hand under the cover and finger-walked his gown up his thigh. He sure was growing big, tenting his gown. One finger reached out. Big but still kind of spongy. "Sure you don't want me to try anything? After all, you're already hurting."

He pressed the morphine pump's button. "Some other time maybe."

It was disappointing—she wanted to be the one to take his mind off the pain with something better than narcotics. "I better go then."

He took her wrist and made the disappointed face of a five-year-old. "Watch Overton for me. He's a material witness. We need him."

"Can't you guys force him into protective custody? Maybe charge him for the drugs?"

"Much as I like him, the fucker's rich enough for some very expensive lawyers. And the deal was, he testifies for no charges. Court case hasn't come up yet. So, do me a favor, but be careful."

He called back as she was on her way out, his voice needy. "Come visit as soon as you can. And keep my car. Yours is a piece of shit."

Drive around in Lansing's BMW? No way—too easy to imagine what people would say, that she'd gotten stuck-up, mingling with important folks from out of county. Too big for her britches. She'd sent it back with his friend. Of course, the little red sports car would have made it harder to care what people thought.

Chapter 36

SAMMIE RAE STOOD BESIDE Sheriff Beebe on the high school's stage. The reporters and dignitaries had come from as far as DC, but Beebe wasn't focused on them but on the locals. As a real Lark County boy, his vision had always been small. The takedown of the drug smugglers and the end of the "Zombie Murders"—a catchy phrase guaranteeing great ratings for the media—meant his position as sheriff was secure.

Beebe took the mic. "Welcome, folks, it is damn fine to see you all gathered here, all my friends and neighbors. I have never been prouder to serve my county than I was these past few months. Our community went through a terrible time, what with losing two of our very finest young men, but we got through it together..."

From the stage, it was easy to see the denizens of Lark County look at each other, sarcasm shining in their eyes and their mouths twitching with the desire to say, "Fine young men? Hell, no! Good riddance to bad rubbish!" And thinking things like, *Stole my pickup! Shot my dog! Sold me bad weed!*

"… Speaking of having a time of it, those rumors that were going around, talk of monsters coming in the night, bodies defiled…"

Hazie Jacobs was sobbing, her shaking body precariously held up by Pa. And Jesse Napier's mother was crying, too, standing next to the grandbabies and the other granny, Gracie. Most of the county was in the audience, lot more people than if it was graduation day. Of course, come graduation day, there'd be a lot fewer people onstage.

"… some were even seeing The White Thing and Mothman rambling our countryside. But weren't any such thing. Were bad people, really bad people, is all." He gestured to Ray Ben, who handed him a black, evil-appearing instrument, shaped into huge tongs but with the grasping ends fanged like pre-historic jaws. Beebe held it up. "This is what they used to take those bites! This is your monster!"

The audience drew in a collective gasp and Sammie Rae's stomach acid instantly burbled in her throat—she felt like swooning in the auditorium's steamy air. She forced herself to pay attention, wondering if, in the crevices of the iron, were bits of Johnny Lee and Jesse Napier, rotting away.

"The good news, folks, is we got our sumbitches!"

Cheers dotted the audience, at first timid, like early morning birdsong, wondering if it was safe to call out, until everyone who could stand rose up and cheered loudly.

Then the governor was at the microphone, discreetly shoving Beebe out of the way and holding up a brass plaque. Sporting an election-year smile, he presented the plaque to the sheriff.

Beebe stepped to the mic to thank him. Later, everyone swore he had tears in his eyes. It would most likely be hung on the wall above his high school football trophies. Sammie Rae shook her head in wonder. *At last Ralph Beebe has something to prove he's a grown-up, not the teen boy competing for the attention of the local bad girl.*

The governor went on, "And I am proud to announce that, in addition to your esteemed sheriff, Ralph Beebe, one of Lark County's finest, Deputy Sammie Rae Wheedle, was instrumental in this action. She assisted in bringing to justice a group terrorizing the countryside all the way from our nation's capital to the western border of our great state. More than instrumental, downright heroic!" He held up another plaque, safely smaller than Beebe's own. He held on tight as she reached to take it, so the photographers' flashes caught them full-on. It made good press to have a girl cop up on that platform, sharing space with the governor. Made Lark County, its sheriff's department, and the state seem up with the times.

Darla waved to her from the front row. Overton, next to her, winked. Dolly was there, too, her hand on his forearm as if he might try to escape.

After the ceremony, she went to Dolly's house for that evening's celebration dinner. Overton had offered to take them all out for a meal, but Dolly gave a look showing exactly what she thought of the idea.

An immense outdoor grill table, with room for twelve people, jars of moonshine, and long lines of *banchan*, occupied a flat bit of land between the house and the storage shed. Darla's dad had made it in secret and transported it in his semi as a gift for his wife. Dolly stood with her chopsticks cooking the *kalbi,* the spicy pork *bulgogi,* and assorted vegetables, parceling them out to everyone. Behind her was a kettle full of chicken wings to toss in sticky sweet and spicy sauce. It seemed that, just like in the kitchen, nobody cooked in that yard but Dolly.

To take the chill from the air, the drinking started as soon as they arrived. To Sammie Rae's surprise, the shine tasted bad to her, though everyone else was knocking it back. She couldn't get any of it down. Fortunately, today the Lark County denizens could hold their booze. No one was rowdy.

Pa and Hazie, Wade and Mamie Cousins were at the table, as was Sheriff Beebe, Casey McCall, and some of the other locals working on the Henderson place as well as their wives and girlfriends.

"Didn't Sammie Rae get you the work at the Henderson place?" Pa asked Casey. "Big job when there ain't many jobs here about. And I hear tell it's done enough, and they moved back in. That true?"

Casey nodded.

"You know, my house is gonna need some fixin' up, to be ready for my daughter, the hero…"

"Pa!"

"It's taken care of, Mr. Wheedle," Casey said.

"Damn, Casey!" Darla said, "it was supposed to be a surprise!" She turned to Sammie Rae. "Thad's taking care of it. I told him we have to keep you here. The whole house will be fixed up and ready for you."

Sammie Rae looked from Darla to Overton, too surprised to speak. And too worried. Al might not like being beholden, especially while they were involved in the investigation. An agent—or his girlfriend—receiving gifts from witnesses? Didn't look good.

A deputy distributing drugs? How would that be viewed? She sighed and relaxed. It hadn't been that often and Al said it was all taken care of.

Darla should know this was all walking the fence top of propriety. Overton undoubtedly did. She was beginning to suspect his sense of humor.

She pushed her plate away. Her appetite had fled. All she wanted to do was be talking on the phone with Al, getting today's update on his progress. Find out when she should visit and when he'd be able to come to Lark County. Ask what to do about Overton's generosity. But it was late by now and she feared awakening him.

She motioned to Darla, who rose and came to her. They went back toward their badminton net to talk. "Dar, I gotta tell you something. You're not gonna like it."

Darla laughed, loud enough that the others, still at the table, turned to look. "Aw, heck, Sammie Rae. If it's about Thad and what a crock of shit his story is and what a bad boy he was, forget it." She hugged Sammie Rae and squeezed her tight.

Sammie Rae let out a relieved breath once she got free. "But are you really gonna be with a man who made his money from drugs?"

Darla cocked her head quizzically. "You did grow up here, didn't you?"

"Fair point."

"So you're sticking with Al…" Darla smiled slyly. "You do it yet?"

"Yup. In the back of a Cadillac. New carpet."

"Elegant! Just take care 'til you're sure about the two of you."

"You advised me to loosen up. And don't worry, we used a condom. I finally had a use for the one you gave me. Always carried it in my pants pocket with my keys."

Darla pressed her lips together, to prevent herself from laughing… or spewing out a curse word. "Jeez-us, I gave that to you years ago! I'm surprised it didn't crumble to bits when you opened it. My advice? Invest in new ones. I'll lend you the money."

"No need to get snotty, Dar. And I'm as sure about Al as can be." *As sure as you once were. Sure as you are about Thad now.*

Dolly had paused in her manipulation of the strips of meat and was glaring at them. Recognizing their danger, they headed back to the table.

Sammie Rae excused herself, after yawning like crazy and pleading fatigue to those drunks who insisted on toasting her. Packing for her move to Pa's house still needed to be done and she wanted a good night's rest before tackling that chore.

*   *   *

Her bedroom was chilly, what with the window she'd left open. She closed it and kept her jacket on while she pulled out the dresser drawers and flung open the closet doors. There wasn't much to pack, especially to jam into trash bags—jeans and tees, underwear, shoes. She'd unload the bags at Pa's, put his junk in them, and haul it all away.

Sitting for a moment on her bed, she looked around. The apartment wasn't much—though it had been an improvement on Pa's cabin—but it was her home, the first one she'd earned for herself. She sighed and stood, pursing her lips, letting the thought slip away.

The bathroom was next. She opened the medicine cabinet and threw out the rolled-up, crusty tubes of Proactiv from when she was breaking out a lot. She shook her box of tampons and looked inside—it was almost full. In fact, only one was missing. Odd, she'd bought the box up at the Wal-mart more than two months ago and should have had to shop for more. She dropped it into the bag going in her car. Took it back out and looked inside the little pink box again. The empty space hadn't grown.

Losing her appetite, the off-taste of alcohol, the fatigue— they'd all be easy to blame on stress. But mid-month skin breakouts had been with her for a decade, worse with stress. Why would they stop now?

Darla always said, "Keep track! Especially if you, like, do it!" but Sammie Rae had never been good at marking the calendar. There'd been no reason to.

She sat on the toilet. A soft crack sounded beneath her. The cheap plastic lid had split in two. She yelped, but loss of a toilet seat was nothing compared to the slowly dawning truth. Standing, she pawed through the cabinet again, hoping to find an old pregnancy kit Darla had left, hiding it from Dolly.

She wanted to call Darla, but by now she'd be looped on shine and in bed with Overton. The CVS up in Boyerstown was open twenty-four hours. She ran to her car and got on the way.

Once she'd made her purchase, stopping at a gas station on the way back down 119 occurred to her. All she had to do was ask for the key. She shivered at the thought of being too shaken by the test results to drive on safely. Afraid the attendant would come in the morning and find her stuck to the floor with splashed trucker pee. An hour later she carried the plastic bag into her apartment.

She tore off the wrapping, read the instructions, peed on the stick, and shut her eyes, counting slowly to one-hundred-twenty, then added twenty more to be sure. Opened her eyes and saw a colored line.

It could be wrong. Shouldn't have bought the store brand. Should have bought a backup test. Should realize the results are accurate.

Sammie Rae picked up the bucket she'd bought, grabbed the Pine-Sol, a sponge, and her mop, and headed to the kitchen. By morning, the counters and stove were shining. She'd have gotten to the cracked linoleum but had to take time out to dry heave.

*   *   *

When the sun was high enough, Sammie Rae stepped out the door. The air was crisp and clean and smelled of real pine, not chemical scent. But she was thirsty, the refrigerator was empty, and the water in the kitchen was cloudy for some reason. She couldn't bear to drink it.

When a girl's in trouble, she wants her ma. She headed for Dolly's.

Dolly jumped up when Sammie Rae came through the kitchen door. "Brave girl! So proud of you!" She hugged Sammie Rae, who pulled back.

"I'm filthy. Cleaning my place, getting ready to move out."

"Need help?"

Sammie Rae shook her head.

"Sure? Be glad to come clean. So lonely here, Darla's pa off again. Nobody to feed. Have food from last night. Or maybe omelet?"

"No, thanks, don't go to any trouble. I feel a little icky."

"From drink too much? I'll make hot ginger. Best thing." Dolly went to the range and put up the tea kettle. She sat again, reached over and stroked Sammie Rae's arm. "So glad you here. Come every day for food. Darla making own food." She screwed up her face as if that was ridiculous. "Or maybe Dr. Thad can cook." She steeped the ginger drink, added honey, put the cup on the table. "Darla say he wants to show her whole world. Whole world mostly crap I say, but she need find out herself."

Sammie Rae stirred the liquid, inhaled the rising steam. Dolly was the one person she could talk to now that Darla was superglued to Thad Overton. If she told Darla, Thad would know, and she wasn't ready for that. Dolly was a gossip but surely this would remain between the two of them, at least for a while.

Before Sammie Rae could muster up the courage to tell the real reason she was feeling sick, Dolly said, "So happy Darla is with Doctor Thad. Worried so much before him. Worried she'd have baby with that Lansing."

Sammie Rae choked on the sip of ginger tea. She coughed hard and Dolly clapped her on the back, saying, "Told you, was hard for Darla—half-Korean, half-White. Never fit in. I wouldn't want half-Black, half-Korean, half-White grandbaby."

"Dolly!"

"I know you date him, went to hospital with him. But can't be nothing serious. You live here, he live there. You a sensible girl. When you ready, pick nice Lark County boy. Maybe that Casey. He do good job on house."

Sammie Rae stirred her drink and drank it down. It did seem to be settling her stomach, but the visit had unsettled her mind. She stood and said, "Got to put more stuff away, so I better go."

"Come back later for supper. I'll make *samgyetang,* ginseng chicken soup. Build strength to clean your messy house. You don't want me to help, I'll send Darla. She stay in your apartment, time to help you!"

Sammie Rae stood waffling near the kitchen door. Darla had done enough, setting up repairs on Pa's house, nagging Overton to pay.

Sadness overwhelmed her, her secret was still firmly deep down inside.

*　　*　　*

"I'm okay, but they need to re-do the last surgery." Al said when she called, his voice low and hesitating. "Sorry, babe, to be sounding so down, but think I've had enough bad news for a while." His tone changed, as if he was forcing himself to be cheerful. "Hey, it helped to see you on TV. Very impressive. Not to mention sexiest one on the dais."

Sammie Rae was glad they weren't Skyping. Her face got blotchy when she was embarrassed or upset and now, she was both. There was no way she could tell Al over the phone about being pregnant. Couldn't lay that burden on him. She needed time to collect her thoughts. "Thanks. But what about that thing the governor held up?"

"A torture device ISIS used on women nursing babies, not in their homes but in public under those black things they wear. How the Ton Tons hooked up with getting one is a mystery. But let's not talk about unpleasant shit like that—or my damn leg. I've been dying to talk with you. That award, where are you going to put that award? It's a big deal, all those important suits giving it to you."

"Over the mantel in the living room right here in my pa's house." Nerves made her want to giggle. *Out of reach of a baby.* Her own place now, where she could hang whatever she wanted, wherever she wanted. Mee-Maw had banned anything but Jesus's sayings in her room. *You little girls look them posters of tight pants and get all het up. Touch yourselves—or worse, go with boys.*

What would Mee-Maw think of her now? Not married. Knocked-up. *Wasted my breath!* is what she'd think. *Finally turned out just like yer ma!*

"That's a great place, where everyone can admire it. But you're coming here this weekend, right? Not tomorrow. I don't want you spending another day waiting for me to come out of the OR."

"But I want to be there. Make sure you're okay."

He sighed. "We need to talk, so you should come when I'm not high as a kite. And you don't have time off work."

She didn't hear anything after *we need to talk.* "Are you breaking up with me?"

"What? I need you more than ever. Nothing's over. Nothing."

"What then?"

"I've made plans to rehab in New York at my grandmother's. I'll be with my family—aunts, uncles, cousins—so we'll have help getting around to the hospital and stuff. They'll love you as much as I do once they get to know you. Soon as

I can, I want to show you every corner of the greatest city in the world."

An educated, upper-crust family in New York ever accepting her seemed mighty unlikely. That they were Black made it even less likely. The thought of a brownstone mansion, the kind she'd seen on TV, fancy restaurants, of cocktails instead of beer, made her even more sick to her stomach than she was. "I can't go live in New York. I won't fit in there. They'll laugh at me. This here is my home." She couldn't stand still and wandered the room touching all the things that still needed doing to make the place her home.

"Nobody would ever laugh at you, Sammie Rae. New York could be your home with me. You've got to know I can't live in Lark forever. My career's too important. But I can work in the office there as long as needed."

"My career's important to me, too."

"You'd have a bigger, better career out in the real world. I want the sky to be the limit for you. Lark County's a backwater, a place to wrap up a case and leave behind. And I'm Black, in case you hadn't noticed."

"Don't make jokes. This isn't funny. People here need me. Things would be fine, for you, for us. Mamie Cousins and her community are Black, remember?"

"What about kids? I want to marry you, Sammie Rae. Settle down, have a family to come home to. Can't put being mixed race on kids, not where you live."

She couldn't breathe and wanted to vomit. She must have made a sound without noticing, as his voice changed again, was soft and soothing. "I'll see you on the weekend and we'll talk. We've got to. I'm tied to you forever."

She ended the call before her hysterical laughing began. They were tied to each other forever, more than he knew. Talking to him, talking to Dolly… How *could* they work things out? She couldn't leave and he wouldn't come. Maybe she'd never tell him about the baby—it would just be pressure to make a life he didn't want. She went to the toilet to empty her stomach. There was nothing but bile. Afterward, she took a plate of dry soda crackers and went out for some fresh air, holding a towel to her mouth, and sank onto the porch. In the cool air, she considered what it would be like living alone in the house with his child.

The wind was chilly. That was better than warm, what with the lump in her throat that had started at Dolly's and only grown. The pine tree scent seemed to clear her mind, let her think. Would people support her decision and help her out? From Pa's house, it was a drive just to get what a baby needed.

The goat herd came down the drive, the billy driving the does in front of him. They stopped and milled about, all staring with their weird goat eyes.

"Go on, get out of here," she said. "I ain't got no feed. Get on home to the Sims's place. Y'all ran loose long enough! Shoo!"

From the center of the herd came a bright brown baby doe with white markings like socks and another on the forehead. The baby that had looked back at her in the barn. The billy tried to nudge the little goat back into the herd, but it eluded him and trotted forward, up onto the porch.

As the doe shot by, Sammie Rae tried to turn her around. The goat skittered to the side, turned, screamed *Naaah!* grabbed a cracker and darted into the house, her tiny hooves tap-tap-tapping on the wooden floor. She hopped on Pa's chair, ate the cracker, leaped to the new couch, and began chewing the arm.

"Take this little troublemaker with you!" Sammie Rae yelled at the billy, who stood shifting from hoof to hoof, seeming to ponder the situation, his bearded chin quivering.

The baby reappeared in the doorway, staring out at Sammie Rae with adoration, like a new-hatched duckling stuck on the wrong critter, then she *boinged* out the door, knelt, twerked her little tail, and strutted back in the house as if she owned it. Sammie Rae sighed as the rest of the herd turned and headed to the woods, leaving her with the late-season kid. Just before they disappeared, she waved goodbye, swinging the towel, which would be easier to see in the distance.

Oh, well, maybe the Simses still have feed.

And goat's milk was good for babies.

About the Author

Rachel Callaghan, a retired physician, writes for relief from the seemingly endless renovation of a pre-Revolutionary house. She is helped by her husband, their German shepherd (a tracker in search and rescue), and a small black imp of a cat.

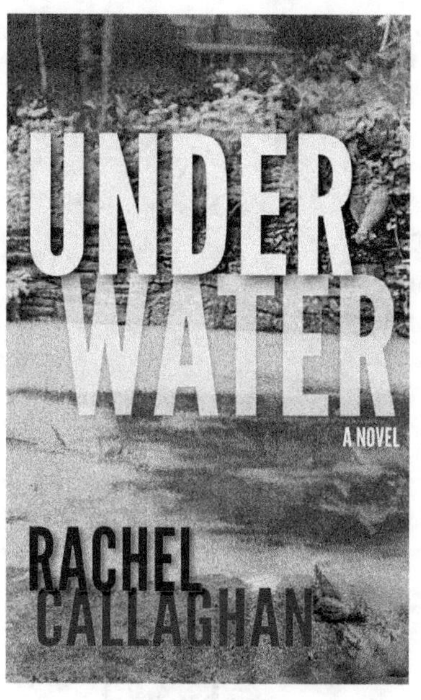

UNDER
WATER
A NOVEL
RACHEL
CALLAGHAN

For more great books from Empower Press
Visit Books.GracePointPublishing.com

If you enjoyed reading *Devil's Knob*, and purchased it through an online retailer, please return to the site and write a review to help others find the book.

9 781961 347632